SURRENDER TO
TEMPTATION

ALSO BY LAUREN JAMESON

Blush

Breathe

SURRENDER TO TEMPTATION

Lauren Jameson

A SIGNET ECLIPSE BOOK

SIGNET ECLIPSE
Published by the Penguin Group
Penguin Group (USA) LLC, 375 Hudson Street,
New York, New York 10014

USA | Canada | UK | Ireland | Australia | New Zealand | India | South Africa | China
penguin.com
A Penguin Random House Company

First published by Signet Eclipse, an imprint of New American Library,
a division of Penguin Group (USA) LLC

First Printing, April 2014

LIBRARY OF CONGRESS CATALOGING-IN-PUBLICATION DATA:
Jameson, Lauren.
Surrender to temptation/Lauren Jameson.
p. cm.
ISBN 978-0-451-46667-9 (pbk.)
I. Title.
PS3610.A464S88 2014
813'.6—dc23   2013043922

Printed in the United States of America
10 9 8 7 6 5 4 3 2 1

Set in Arno Pro
Designed by Sabrina Bowers

This one is for Deidre. I'd like to be her someday.

SURRENDER TO TEMPTATION

PART I

TEMPTED TO SUBMIT

CHAPTER ONE

All I wanted was to feel sexy.

Grimacing, I pulled the confection of openwork silk off of my shoulders and down. What had I been thinking? A girl with some curves—namely me—couldn't wear ruffles. This whole endeavor was a terrible idea.

My bangs were sticking to my forehead with sweat as I tugged the lingerie back over my head. I contemplated dropping it to the ground and stomping on it in frustration, but repressed the urge and hung it back up, nice and neat, on its plastic hanger.

That was what I always did, after all—shoved my real feelings away, smiling prettily when I wanted to scream.

Frustrated and close to tears, I eyed the last item that I'd brought with me into the dressing room at Magnifique, the fancy lingerie boutique that I'd passed by on my way to work every single day for the last year. It was also lace, but instead of being heavily ruffled and made for a woman with the build of Barbie, it was a deep indigo, made of soft silk, and sophisticated instead of cute. It would skim the body and accentuate curves.

This one had to work. It just had to. How was I ever going to convince my ever so proper boyfriend to make love to me in a position other than missionary if I couldn't find something to entice him with?

Inhaling deeply and avoiding the sight of my naked flesh in the mirror, I tugged the slip off of its hanger and over my head. It felt lovely, the material moving in a sensual glide over my skin.

With my eyes squeezed shut, I turned back toward the mirror, sucked in my tummy, and, after a lengthy internal pep talk, peeked at the reflection staring back at me.

"Oh." The woman in the mirror smiled with surprise and pleasure at the same time that I did. Smoothing a hand over the length of my now-messy blond ponytail, I scanned the image nervously, looking for the flaws that I saw every day—the swell of my stomach, the slightly too-heavy breasts, the hips that were a hint too wide.

I saw none of it. The incredibly sheer lace kissed my curves rather than clinging to them, and this made my waist, my belly, and hips all look just right. My breasts rose enticingly out of the low neckline, and the hem of the little slip hit midthigh, covering my butt yet hinting at more.

I looked . . . well, I looked hot.

It was a strange sensation.

Before I could convince myself otherwise, I stripped off the slip and put my office clothes back on. The knee-length skirt, blouse, and cardigan sweater were all solid black—bright colors made me feel fat. The monochromatic look worked just fine for the office, however—Cambridge-Neilson and Sons, the law firm where I was an administrative assistant.

The law firm where my boyfriend, Tom, was a junior partner. The slip that I was buying was in an effort to please him. *No*, I corrected myself as I brought it nervously to the front counter; it was about pleasing *me*. About looking—and feeling, I supposed—sexy enough to entice Tom into being a little more adventurous in the bedroom.

To possibly, maybe, encourage him to do some of the deliciously naughty things that I thought about nearly all of the time. Dreamt about, too.

"Your total comes to two hundred dollars and seventy cents." I'd been playing it cool until that moment, acting like I bought expensive lingerie all the time, but the sum that the tall, slender brunette salesgirl announced very nearly made me choke.

Two hundred dollars? *For that little scrap of lace?*

I couldn't afford it. I should have just let it be. Did I really want to spend that much in order to please Tom?

The salesgirl, whose nametag read *Bernadette* in swirling cursive, saw my wistful glance at the swath of midnight blue that she was wrapping in silver tissue. I forgave her the stylish boots and fresh salon haircut when she gave me a kind smile and said, "It's expensive, but we're all worth it, aren't we?"

I thought of how I looked in the slip, and then thought of someone looking at me as I wore it. Of his dark eyes taking in the way the blue set off the pale cream of my skin, of the way my nipples flushed through the soft lace.

Yes. I had to have it.

"It's fine. I'll put it on credit." Rummaging through my large leather satchel, I finally found my wallet. It caught on a cardboard envelope as I pulled it out, and the print that I had just picked up from the photography place next door slipped out and onto the counter.

Bernadette glanced over, and I saw her study it for a moment longer than necessary. "He looks familiar."

I turned to study the picture, too. It was of Tom and me, posing rather seriously at the beach. It had been a rare, unplanned moment in our courtship, on a business trip to Los Angeles, when I had begged him to pull over the car so that we could watch the sunset. Surprisingly, he had agreed. With the sun setting in a riot of glowing shades behind us, and the angle clearly showing that the picture had been taken by one of us with a cell phone camera, it should have been a romantic shot.

Instead, we looked so incredibly austere, so at odds with the sunset and the ocean, that the whole thing seemed rather silly.

Still, it was the best picture that I had of us together. I was going to frame it and keep it on my desk at work. We had been dating for over a year, after all.

"Hmm." Before I could reply, Bernadette snapped her fingers, even as she expertly nipped my credit card from my fingers and ran it through her point-of-sale machine. "Yesterday! He was in yesterday. Big spender." When she caught what I'm sure was my surprised expression, she clapped a hand over her mouth and giggled sheepishly.

"I probably shouldn't have said that. Now I've ruined whatever surprise he had for you."

"Surprise. Right." Brow furrowed, I took the candy-pink-and-cream-striped bag that she handed me, nodding my thanks before walking away.

I was quite certain that she was mistaken. I would have let it go at that, but the woman's statement niggled at my mind all the way back to work, and then as I sat at my desk, slowly pecking away at the handwritten letter that one of the lawyers needed typed up.

Never had Tom bought me expensive lingerie. He'd never bought me candy or flowers, either, for that matter. He just wasn't that type of guy and, foolishly, early on in our relationship, I had told him that grand gestures weren't important to me.

I hadn't lied—they weren't important, exactly. But some soft inner part of my heart still craved some kind of sweet gesture from time to time—something that told me I was being thought of when I wasn't there.

I was fairly certain that I wouldn't ever receive one of these gestures from Tom. Yes, Bernadette was mistaken.

But another thought formed in my mind as I worked my way through the afternoon. What if . . . what if . . .

No. Tom wouldn't do that. Tom loved me.

"Hi, Devon." One of the senior lawyers chose that moment to walk by. Though quite possibly paranoid, I was convinced that she gave me a pitying glance, barely masked by her small smile. That was what settled my mind.

Begging off early with the excuse of a headache, I hurried down to my car.

I would just go home—the home that I had not yet moved into, actually—and see Tom. Once I saw him, all of this silliness would fly out the window, I was sure.

And, I thought as I looked sideways at the Magnifique bag on my passenger's seat, maybe I could model my new slip for him.

I almost felt as if I should ring the doorbell. Tom had given me a key the previous week, after we had decided that my moving my meager belongings into his place was a sensible idea, but I hadn't yet used it. I suspected that I'd been clinging to my independence—I loved my little studio apartment, the one that I'd already given notice on, but Tom had pointed out that it wasn't nearly big enough for two people. Plus, his was closer to the office.

A shorter commute just made sense, after all, even to me. Sleeping in two separate rooms when we weren't having sex did not make sense, and never would, no matter how many times Tom told me that it would provide a better sleep for both of us. The mere thought made me grind my teeth together.

I would rather have a less than perfect night's sleep, my partner by my side, than the alternative—sleeping down the hall from each other like a couple that had been married for far too long.

I wasn't going to give in on that issue.

Sighing heavily, I again squelched the urge to knock at this place that was now supposed to be my home, and instead turned my key in the deadbolt. I had to fiddle with it, the way you do with new keys, before the lock gave way.

"Hello?" I didn't raise my voice. The apartment was dim, quiet, and though I hadn't expected his presence—he was at a lunch meeting—I almost felt relieved that he wasn't home, that I didn't have to ask the difficult question.

I could take a few minutes to orient myself. Maybe sit down and think of some ways to brighten the utilitarian bachelor apartment up, so that it felt warmer and more welcoming to me.

Before I was even out of the entryway I heard it. Faint at first, but growing steadily louder, and unmistakably coming from the direction of the bedroom.

"Oh. Ohhhh."

Confused, I cocked my head at the sound of the female voice and took a few steps down the hall. Then, when Tom's voice joined into the chorus of sex sounds, my mouth fell open, and I felt as if I'd been punched in the stomach.

Tom was indeed home. He was home, and unless I was very much mistaken, he was having sex with another woman, in the bedroom where I, his longtime girlfriend, was rarely permitted to sleep.

Bernadette had been right.

Adrenaline shot through my veins and made me feel sick. Suddenly intent on ferreting out that second piece of evidence to back up the riot of feelings that was surging through me, I scanned the apartment until I saw it, wadded up on the floor beside the couch.

A bag from Magnifique, the tissue paper ripped by eager fingers. Feeling as if I were going to throw up, I picked up the bag and shook it out.

Whatever Tom had purchased the day before was gone—

probably on the floor of his bedroom—but the receipt was still there.

Four hundred and twenty-three dollars for a bustier, garter belt, and stockings, all size extra small.

Extra small. Well, that definitely wasn't me. Tears of humiliation sprang to my eyes and clouded my throat as I stared at the area of carpet around the discarded bag. There, right out in the open, were more details that I couldn't ignore. A single, nude-colored pump, with *Prada* stitched into the sole. Two wineglasses, a film of red still coating the bottom.

That was it. I was done.

For a moment I thought that I might fling open the door to the bedroom, might confront them both and be self-righteous in my indignation.

I couldn't gather up the courage. No. I knew myself, and I knew that I was more the kind of woman to apologize for disturbing them than to rain hell on their cheating heads. I had been raised that way, to be proper and polite at all times, and it was a tough habit to shake.

In the end, with rage and unfairness and humiliation all warring through me, too many emotions to deal with, I did the only thing that I could think of.

I scribbled a note that said—very properly, of course—my good-byes, and left.

CHAPTER TWO

Three days later, I curled my toes into the sand and tried to make sense of my life.

I hadn't smelled the brine of sea air for years. I didn't have an excuse—Sacramento was only a five-hour drive from the coast, a short enough time to make the trip for something that I loved.

Well, I was here now.

Not caring about muddying the butt of my denim cutoffs, I plopped down onto the sand and hugged my knees to my chest, letting the crash of the waves fill my mind. I had to fill my mind with something, or else I'd start thinking about how incredibly off track my life had just veered, and I would start to panic.

After leaving Tom's apartment, I'd gone straight back to what was now a shell instead of my home. Possessed by the need to get as far away as possible from Tom, from work, from my *life*, I'd lugged my few boxes of possessions—mostly clothing and a few personal mementoes—down into my little blue hatchback.

I'd wanted red, but blue was much more sensible.

I'd then driven to a McDonald's parking lot and while eating a Quarter Pounder with Cheese and an extra-large order of fries—to hell with a well-balanced diet and nutrition—drafted my resignation letter on my laptop.

No way was I going back to that law firm, not when I'd have to see Tom every day. Not when I'd have to endure the pitying stares from people who surely knew what had been going on long before I had.

What a fool I had been.

Digging my fingers into the long tangles of my hair and tugging with frustration, I felt the dam break and my panic flow.

What had I done? My job hadn't been spectacular or particularly exciting, but it had been my starting point. I'd dreamt of going back to school, of becoming a lawyer myself. To do that I needed to save up the excess money from a job that paid decently and didn't involve serving old men who gave me pinches on the tushie instead of tips.

Rather than the inheritance I might have expected, my parents had left a mountain of debt when they'd died in a car crash three years ago. There was no money for law school, not unless I earned it myself.

The panic grew, snaking itself into that same oily blackness that had visited me so often in those days after my parents' accident, when I'd been treading water, just trying to make sense of both the grief and the instantaneous poverty that I hadn't been prepared for and wasn't used to.

I dug my fingers into the sand until I felt the rough granules catch under my nails.

Pull yourself together, Devon. Deliberately I drew in one last, stinging lungful of salty ocean air, inhaling until my throat stung. *You've clawed your way out before, and you will again.*

The comforting smell of the water helped—a bit, at least— but deep down the same old fears swirled.

I'd just gotten used to not identifying myself solely as Dr. Evelyn and The Honorable Rhys Reid's daughter. In truth, I had simply become the girlfriend of Tom Cambridge-Neilson, young star defense attorney.

It had been comfortable, and the loss of that hard-earned comfort was what I was grieving most of all.

Now I had to dig down, down deep, and see who Devon Reid was underneath.

I was immensely comforted by the fact that Suzanne's Diner still existed, right in the middle of what the tourists laughingly and the locals seriously called *downtown* in Cambria.

Suzanne's still had the same chicken-fried steak, mashed potatoes with gravy, and sweet buttered corn that I remembered from my youth. Now, of course, I accompanied it with rich red wine instead of orange soda, and thought that it was a vast improvement.

"Don't look now, but I think you have an admirer." The waitress was one of Suzanne's granddaughters, or at least I assumed she was, for the ringlets falling out of her messy ponytail were the same unmistakable shade of red that the owner's hair had once been. Her pale skin flushed as she gestured with a slight sideways nod, setting my fresh glass of ice water down on the table and scurrying away.

Having had one too many glasses of red wine to care about being subtle, I turned in the direction that the young waitress had gestured.

The man at the next table didn't smile when I turned and caught his eye, and despite the very nearly mocking set to his lips, I suddenly felt as though I were in the midst of the waves that I had been watching only an hour earlier—as if the heavy water that was infused with salt was pulling me under and claiming me as its own.

He was . . . dark. That was my first thought. Though his tanned skin was actually the burnished gold of tequila and his eyes were the color of rum, the tousles of hair that were nearly jet-black combined with his expression to lend him an air of power and authority, and something else that I couldn't quite put my finger on. His face was sculpted, his features arrogant and aristocratic, and I was quite certain that that face had inspired many a lusty daydream.

I was no better. As those golden eyes, surrounded by thick, dark lashes, stared so boldly into my own lighter blue ones, I felt a sexual tug like nothing I'd ever felt before. I wasn't a virgin—no, there was Tom, and my high school boyfriend, and the two somewhat disastrous one-night stands that I'd had in between.

None of those had inspired anything that felt even a fraction as seductive as the frankly intrusive examination by this man at the next table. He brought to mind every intimate fantasy I'd ever had, and I felt certain that he and that wicked-looking face were capable of inciting many more.

He lifted his wineglass and tipped it at me, then returned to his meal—some kind of healthy-looking grilled-fish-and-steamed-vegetable thing—as if he'd never seen me in the first place. I was left with flushed skin, nipples that had contracted to the point of pain, and a dull ache between my legs.

What was that? I had to sit on my hands to stop myself from reaching over and fisting them in the stranger's hair.

Instead of doing that, I focused on my plate, which, while incredibly appetizing only moments before, now held little appeal.

Scooping up a small forkful of potatoes, I pressed it into my mouth, forced myself to taste and to swallow. There were times in my life that I'd dreamt about this exact meal—my comfort food of choice—and now it was dry as dust in my mouth, tasteless and unnecessary.

I swallowed, the potatoes feeling like glue as they worked their way down my throat. When I'd succeeded in that small movement, I rewarded myself by sneaking a glance across the restaurant at the handsome stranger.

He was watching me again, and he wasn't even being discreet. Self-consciousness washed over me, followed quickly by irritation, no doubt brought on by the wine that was flowing through my veins.

"If you're going to stare, you might as well join me." My scowl was only half in earnest—the other half was hiding the tremble of my lower lip.

I needed to squash this ridiculous lust. Not only was there no way that this man—this *stranger*—was feeling the same way, but I was really in no position to be thinking about sex.

The man raised an eyebrow at my tone—unless I was very much mistaken, he was not the sort of man who was used to be being spoken to like that. He frowned slightly, as if playing my words back in his head. Then, to my astonishment, he shrugged slightly and stood, catching his own wineglass in his hand as he did.

"I think I will."

Startled by his reaction, I swallowed—hard—as he rose and made his way over. He seated himself at my table as comfortably as if he owned it, and I studied him from beneath my makeup-free lashes as I tried to compose myself.

He was dressed casually, blue jeans and a black button-down shirt, but he still didn't seem like the type of person to bum around a tiny surf town like Cambria. No, unless I was very much mistaken, he'd paid a pretty penny for the jeans, and for the shirt, as well.

I peeked under the table, no longer bothering to be subtle. Yup, I was right—his feet were clad in polished black loafers, not the flip-flops or even skater sneakers that most Californians wore on their off time.

"Do they pass inspection?" Caught in the act, I snapped my stare back to the man's face. My fascination with his footwear had brought on a small curve of his lips, and the result was so wicked, so enticing, that I picked up my wine and gulped, just to keep from drooling.

What was I doing? My life was in shambles. I was in no place to be having lustful thoughts about anyone, let alone some tall, dark, and handsome stranger. Sex would only complicate things.

"I'm Devon." Panicked when his smirk suggested that he knew where my thoughts had run, I blurted out my name. The words wanted to keep coming, and they seemed beyond my control, so I shoveled a forkful of meat between my lips and instantly wished I hadn't.

The meal that I had been so enjoying earlier in the evening now tasted like sand, scraping at the tender insides of my throat.

"Is it not to your liking?" Before I could say a word, the man had signaled my waitress, who of course came right over.

I would have done very nearly anything this man asked, too.

"Clear away the lady's plate, please. Bring a bowl of berries, if you have them, with cream." Where I would have been apologetic for sending my meal back without having finished, my dinner partner spoke as if he knew that he would be obeyed without a fuss.

Of course, he was.

"Did it occur to you that I might not have been done?" I wasn't sure that I liked having my decisions taken away from me, and I felt the start of a frown between my brows.

He cocked his wineglass in my direction and took another sip. "Was I wrong?" His tone, of course, told me that he knew he was no such thing. I wasn't about to lie, either, so instead I narrowed my eyes at him.

Grumpiness seemed to be my only defense against the attraction that was consuming me, attraction that I knew he couldn't possibly return.

"It would be nice to know the name of the man who is feeding me dessert without dinner." There. I'd surprised him again. I smirked and sat back in my chair, pleased to have scored a point in this strange game that we were playing.

"It's Zach—Zach." He seemed to cut himself off.

"Zach." I rolled the name around on my tongue, decided it suited him—mostly—though it wasn't quite as dark and intriguing as he was.

I told him so. "I was expecting something more like 'Count Vladimir the Third.'" Zach blinked, and for a moment I wasn't sure if I'd offended him or delighted him. When a full smile, a real one, broke out over his face for the first time since I'd laid eyes on him, I concluded that it was the latter.

"I find you so refreshing." He leaned in closer to me and my breath caught in my throat.

I didn't know what I was expecting—didn't even know what I was hoping for—but when he again relaxed back in his chair, I felt oddly deflated.

The silence stretched out, and while Zach seemed content with it, I squirmed.

"Where are you from?" His expression darkened at the question. I couldn't fathom what was wrong with what I had asked, but I felt the need to apologize.

"I'd much rather hear about you." I was aware of the overly smooth change of subject, but if the man wasn't going to talk, I certainly couldn't make him. I didn't much want to, either, but I'd had just enough wine, and was feeling just off balance enough emotionally that once I started to talk, I couldn't stop.

"I'm from Sacramento. Well, not originally. I was born in D.C. And I guess I don't live in Sacramento anymore." The reminder saddened me. I loved the city, had very much loved my apartment, but at the moment knew that I couldn't go back.

"I guess I'm not from anywhere, right now. My lying asshole of a boyfriend cheated on me, so I quit my job and came here, 'cause it's one of my favorite places. And I have no idea what I'm going to do next." The panic came then, washing over me in one quick wave.

Oh, no. I wasn't going to have a panic attack here. Not now. Not in front of this man.

I inhaled, then let the air out, repeating until I felt calmer. When I realized that I'd just done a relaxation breathing exercise in front of a sexy stranger, I felt like smacking myself upside the head.

Of course, I'd also just told him that I was so alluring that I couldn't keep a man, so the breathing was probably nothing.

Biting my lower lip, ashamed, I dared to sneak a peek at the man sitting across from me.

He was watching me with eyes at half-mast, and he looked so damn sexy that I actually trembled. He opened his mouth as if to speak, but whatever he was about to say was interrupted by the arrival of the dessert that I hadn't wanted, and wasn't sure I could stomach, not with my internal upheaval.

I couldn't help but notice that the scarlet color of the strawberries was enticing against the stark white of the bowl. I caught the eye of the waitress, who winked at me knowingly as she added a separate dish full of soft whipped cream.

I felt my skin flush, the same hue as the berries, with mortification. For something to do, I took a berry in my fingers, toying with it so that I didn't have to look Zach in the eyes.

He had to know how attracted to him I was feeling, I was certain of that. There wasn't a woman in the small restaurant who wasn't watching him at least out of the corner of her eye— and that included Suzanne, the owner, who had looked at least eighty when my parents had first brought me here twenty years ago.

"Let me." Zach's voice had dropped in timbre, sounding

even more alluring to my ears than it already had. Reaching across the cheerfully checkered tablecloth, he took the strawberry from my fingers.

The small patch of skin burned where his fingers brushed my hand. Inhaling sharply, I jolted, forgetting that now wasn't a good time, forgetting that I'd just met this man. His expression mirrored mine in intensity. I had no idea what had just happened, but unless I had been robbed of all of my senses, he felt it, too.

"Open your mouth." Zach swiped the berry that he had nipped from my fingers through the mound of whipped cream before pressing it against my lips. I opened my mouth, my tongue flickering out to lick up the cream.

He moaned softly. Emboldened by forces that mystified me, I took a small bite of the juicy berry, chewing slowly, licking my lips after I'd swallowed.

His eyes followed the motions of my mouth, entranced, before flickering back up to look me in the eyes.

"What is going on?" I regretted the words the moment that I'd said them—how naive was I? I knew exactly what was going on, but I didn't have the sophistication to make the next move.

Though my better judgment was screaming at me, I was praying that Zach would ask me to come with him to his hotel, to his house, to his tent, if that's where his bed was. My flesh felt swollen, full to bursting with need.

With a brief thought of the dark blue negligee that was still in its bag in my car, I told myself that I deserved one night of pleasure.

My words might as well have been a slap. Another persona entirely came over Zach, one who was calm, in complete control, and who washed away all traces of the sexual creature who'd been in his place only moments before.

"I must go. I have an early morning." He shifted on the

chair, pulling a wallet from the pocket of his snug jeans. The movement made the muscles of his arm tense, and I was entranced, as well as confused.

"Oh." That had been abrupt. I blinked, my mind sorting furiously through the last few minutes.

Had I said something wrong? Done something strange?

I didn't think so, and I had just enough wine left in me to be irritated by the sudden withdrawal of this fascinating man.

"Well, thanks for the company." My voice was heavy with sarcasm. "Always lovely to meet a new person."

Zach had been in the process of standing, and he straightened as though I'd struck him. I again got the impression that he was not at all accustomed to being questioned.

"Agreed." He peeled a bill out of the folds of a wallet that looked to be made of hand-tooled leather and placed it on the table without checking the denomination.

"Before you go, tell me something: What's a man like you doing in a tiny beach town like this?" I had nothing to lose by asking. Clearly I was not going to have all of my desires satisfied, so I wanted at least to have my curiosity quenched.

Apparently I'd asked something either very insulting or very personal, since a hint of anger flickered over his strong features. He didn't answer, just nodded in my direction before striding away to the front door.

Watching him walk away was like having a limb amputated. I tried to convince myself that the melancholy was because of the recent turn of events in my life, but I knew better.

I'd found something that I wanted desperately, something that made complete and total sense in the chaos that was my life.

It had stayed just long enough to tease me with what I could never have.

Growling with frustration, I tipped my head back and downed

the last inch of wine in my glass, wiping my mouth with the back of my hand when I'd finished. As I lowered my chin I caught the stares of two girls who were barely out of high school, if at all. They wore tight, sheer tank tops and shorts that rode up high on the thigh. Though one was a blonde and one a brunette, their faces were nearly identical, smirking with amusement at my predicament.

My face flushed. I was already embarrassed enough. And then I did what it seemed I was becoming very good at doing.

I ran.

"I own a house in Cambria. I've come here since I was a child." I gasped as the voice came out of the velvet night. Turning toward the man who had spoken, I glared, hands on hips.

"How lovely for you." Suddenly furious, and angry at myself for the burst of joy I'd initially felt at encountering him again, and for finding that the mere sight of him did strange things to my insides, I moved briskly off down the quiet street. My motel was only a block or so away.

Main Street was close enough to the water that I could hear the water lapping at the shore. The sound usually soothed me, but tonight it grated at my nerves. I'd gotten nearly all the way back to my motel when I felt a hand on my shoulder, turning me.

Then Zach's hands were fisted full of my hair, his lips a whisper away from my own. My breath caught in my throat, and my body pressed itself into his.

My entire being was drawn to his heat, to the smell of soap and musk and man.

I opened my mouth to say something, and gasped when he tugged on my hair, drawing my head back until I had no choice but to look up into his eyes.

Wetness surged through my cleft. I'd never been held this way, never been looked at with torment and desire at the same time.

I loved it.

"I am a very successful man, Devon. I've had to be ruthless to make my way." His eyes narrowed, judging my response, but I found that his harsh words only made me tremble with need.

"That ruthlessness applies to all areas of my life. I am not a nice man." His expression dared me to argue with him. I wasn't about to. He seemed like a lot of things right in that moment, but nice wasn't one of them.

"I don't care." It was naive, I knew, but I truly didn't. Part of me thrilled at his violent words, a part of me that I would never have guessed even existed.

Something flashed through his expression, gone so fast it was hard to believe that it had even been there, but I knew what I'd seen.

He liked the way that I responded to him. Liked it a lot.

"I'm not for you." I was about to speak, about to object, and instead found myself moaning when he slowly, deliberately closed his teeth over the pulse beneath the line of my jaw. He bit just hard enough to sting and, I imagined, to leave a mark, his actions those of an animal asserting dominance over his prey. As he bit, his hand found the soft mound of my breast. He pinched my nipple through the fabric of my top and bra, then pulled, then pinched again.

A short, hard burst of pleasure rocketed through me and I cried out loud, right there at the end of Main Street.

Then I was trying to stay upright on legs that were trembling ferociously. I stared up at Zach with what I knew was raw need and confusion in my gaze.

I watched as he pulled that second Zach back over himself like a cloak, the Zach who was calm and reasonable and not governed by desire. I opened my mouth to say—well, I don't know what I would have said. He cut me off before I could try to frame a sentence.

"Stay away from me."

"Excuse me. Miss Reid?" I tried to erase the scowl from my face as I turned toward the clerk who called me over to the front desk where he stood. It wasn't his fault that I had lain awake half the night with dark dreams that left me sweaty and trembling. It wasn't his fault that my early-morning walk along the beach hadn't been able to erase any of the feelings that had been stirred up the previous evening.

"Yes?" The Sand Pebble Inn was a lovely, clean motel, and I was expecting the young man to ask me to fill out a customer survey, or something of that nature.

Instead, he slid an envelope across the desk to me. DEVON was written across the white paper in masculine lettering that was surprisingly tidy.

"A gentleman left this for you while you were out for your walk." I saw his eyes flick down to the sand that caked my calves, the sandals that I carried in my left hand, but instead of feeling embarrassed, as I normally would, I grabbed for the envelope.

I only knew one person in Cambria, unless you counted Suzanne from the diner.

"Thank you." I refrained from opening the envelope until I was back in my room, where I sank down on the bed. With shaking fingers, I ripped into the paper and drew out a thick rectangle of paper.

A business card.

The card was simple, the lettering black, printed on paper of lemony cream. The words *Phyrefly Aviation* were worked into a logo with a small, sleek airplane. Below the logo were a phone number and a San Francisco address.

I turned it over, searching for Zach's name. The reverse had a handwritten message, but was otherwise blank.

IF YOU NEED A JOB, YOU WILL FIND ONE HERE.

That was it. No signature, no *nice to meet you*. No *thanks for letting me grope you last night*. Still, I knew without a doubt that it was from Zach, and even as I huffed with exasperation at the short, blunt words, I knew what I would do next.

I was going to San Francisco.

CHAPTER THREE

P hyrefly Aviation quite literally took my breath away.
In the first moment to myself that I'd had all day, I
inhaled rapidly, over and over again, trying to catch my
breath—I felt as if I had been sprinting since six o'clock that
morning.

It had been two days since I'd received that business card
in Cambria. One day since I'd arrived in San Francisco. Still
reeling from the prices of hotel rooms in the city, I had decided that a job was my first priority.

Well, truthfully, pursuing anything that might connect
me with the man who had taken possession of my mind, in-
cessantly haunting my every waking thought and my sleeping
ones, too, was more important still.

I didn't see why the two couldn't go hand in hand.

"Miss Reid." The man who entered the office where I had
been placed had to be at least six and a half feet tall, and
couldn't have weighed more than one-fifty if he'd been
drenched with a garden hose. Hair that was a forgettable shade
of brown flopped messily around his head, and he had a mus-
tache, more, I think, from forgetting to shave than by design.
"I'm Glen Stevens."

"Pleased to meet you." Standing, I held out a hand for him
to shake. It was my third interview at Phyrefly that day, and I
was exhausted. When I had torn open that envelope and
found the business card, I had expected that the company was
something along the line of a car dealership. Or maybe a re-

pair shop for small planes. Instead, at seven thirty this morning my cab had dropped me off here, in front of a massive skyscraper constructed seemingly of glass and nothing else. It dazzled my eyes, as well as my mind, and was the first hint that maybe I didn't know what I was about to get myself into.

I had taken note of the fact that I hadn't had a single panic attack since the day I'd met Zach, though, and that was something to cheer for. I hadn't needed any of the antianxiety pills that I carried in my purse, either. I'd been far too busy, my mind too full.

"I imagine it's been a long day for you already." Glen gestured for me to sit in one of the plush armchairs that sat against the far wall of his office. He was smooth, but I didn't miss the quick once-over that he gave me. I knew that I had just been assessed.

Since I had worn one of my best I-used-to-work-at-a-lawoffice outfits, a black blouse with a small ruffle around the deep collar, a black pencil skirt, and black hose, I was satisfied that I would pass the inspection.

"Well, Miss Reid, how would you like to work at Phyrefly Aviation?" Glen offered me a bottle of water from a minifridge neatly disguised as an end table. Not sure that I'd heard him correctly, I accepted the bottle, unscrewed the lid, and drank deep.

The condensation felt great on my palms, which were hot and sweaty with nerves.

"I—I mean—wow. That was fast." I blinked and laughed a bit, but I wasn't really amused. No, I was surprised, and knew somehow that Zach was behind this.

But who was he to a massive corporation—like I had discovered that Phyrefly Aviation was—to be able to land me a job like this? I knew he'd done something. The entire day had seemed like a ruse, like everyone had already known that I would be coming.

Like the job had been created just for me.

He had said he was a successful man, but what, precisely, did that mean?

Glen chuckled, and there was amusement in *his* tone, at least. Sitting back in his chair, he tossed his water bottle from one hand to another, studying me intently.

"Once Mr. St. Brenton decides that something is going to happen, it's best to just get out of the way of the steamroller that he's set in motion." The water bottle juggling was starting to annoy me—I wanted to lean over and catch the bottle in mid-air so that I could focus on what he had just said. I must have telegraphed my intent, because Glen caught the bottle, opened it, and chugged until it was empty.

"Aah." He sighed contentedly as I worried at his last sentence. Something about it was niggling at me.

"Now, your last employer was a law firm, yes?" Glen screwed the lid onto his empty bottle and leaned forward slightly. "I imagine that involved a lot of precise detail work. Perhaps some accounting."

"Yes." It wasn't a question, but I nodded anyway, pasting a wide smile on my face. I wanted this job badly, though I couldn't have explained why. "I'm proficient in Windows, Dictaphone, spreadsheet software, Excel, and PowerPoint. I'm a good proof-reader, and handled basic bookkeeping tasks. I also developed a computer program to create reports from electronic files, inventories, mailing lists, and databases, so that it didn't have to be done by hand." That last bit stung—I'd done a great job, and still, the firm had barely blinked when I'd left. No stuffy watch as a good-bye gift, which was customary—no, not even a thank-you.

This time it was Glen who blinked, his expression changing from polite to incredibly engaged. "Interesting." He spoke as if almost to himself, tapping the water bottle against the inside of his thigh. "That Zach, always knows what he's doing."

"Zach?" I felt as though a bolt of lightning had shot through my body as I heard the name. "Um . . . I mean . . . who is Zach?"

Glen cast me a look that implied that I should already know. I bit my lip and tried to look abashed, though I was really just eager for him to keep talking.

"Zachariah—Zach—St. Brenton is the founder and CEO of Phyrefly Aviation." Glen looked as though he might be reconsidering my brainpower, if I had come to an interview without at least finding out the bare minimum about the man who would be my boss. "He is both wonderful and difficult to work for."

I closed my eyes and pressed my fingers against the instantaneous throbbing in my temples. Zachariah St. Brenton. Zach. *He owned this massive corporation?* I'd suspected that he pulled some strings to get me an interview here, though I still wasn't quite sure why, but I found myself taken aback at the idea of how much power he wielded.

I flashed back, and pictured myself in my sloppy cutoffs, my face devoid of makeup, stuffing chicken-fried steak and mashed potatoes into my mouth.

I grimaced before I could stop myself. Glen took the expression for worry about the latter half of his statement, and was quick to reassure me.

"You won't actually see him very much, if at all. I'm putting you into the accounting department. Your title will be junior administrative assistant for the department, and your supervisor will be Bini Gallagher." He spoke a bit more, telling me about my salary, the benefits, company policy, and more.

I didn't hear a word of it once he'd stopped talking about Zach. I had begun to think of that last night in Cambria, of the man who had fed me strawberries, who had kissed me to within an inch of my life, had made me crave wicked things and then left with a warning. The mere mention of the man made me soft and warm everywhere, and I was supposed to not worry because I probably wouldn't actually see him very much, "if at all"?

Just knowing that he was somewhere in the same building made my mouth water and my thighs clench. I wanted him, and I was certain that he wanted me . . . or at least, that he had.

What game was he playing, bringing me into his employ? He'd warned me to stay away from him.

"Do we have a deal?" Glen had stood, which is what finally caught my attention. Leaving the water bottle, I stood, too, wiping my palms on my skirt to get rid of the dampness.

I shook his hand, but wasn't entirely sure of the question. *Shit.* I settled for smiling at him, and though his return smile was a bit confused, he did repeat the question.

"Well, you can start right away, if you'd like. That is, if you say yes. You accept the position here at Phyrefly?"

"Yes." Did I ever.

The Santa Rosa was a small bar much like thousands of other bars across the country. California paraphernalia decorated the walls—vintage postcards, autographed surfboards, old ads for orange juice and citrus fruits. Though I hadn't been given much say in the matter, I felt myself relax just the tiniest bit for the first time in days as I was handed a beer and ushered to the table where many of my new coworkers were seated.

That relaxation fled quickly as I put down my bottle after a sip to find all eyes on me.

I felt the familiar sensation of panic rising, thickening my throat until I couldn't breathe. I needed one of my pills, but could hardly grope for it in my purse without rumors flying about the new girl's drug habit.

"Who wants to order some appies? On me?" Glen, the man who gave me my final interview, gave me a very subtle pat on the back, a reassuring touch, as he slid some of the laminated menus from our end of the table down toward the others. "You guys figure out what we should all share."

This, of course, meant that everyone broke into loud discussion, bickering back and forth about liking black olives but not green ones, and whether artichokes were disgusting or not. I smiled gratefully at Glen and again lifted my beer.

"Thank you." I murmured just loudly enough for the man to hear. The panic receded as the attention on me faded.

I didn't like being the center of attention. I wasn't used to it, having always spent my time in the shadow of my parents and then Tom.

Glen nodded, his expression somewhat paternal, even though he couldn't have been more than ten years older than I was. He leaned in close, casually, and I followed his lead.

"I'm afraid you're going to be in for it for a while, Devon." My brow furrowed as I pondered his meaning, and as I looked down the table, I saw that even with Glen's distraction, a few of my new coworkers—Anna, the girl from the front desk behind security, Tony, the senior admin assistant in my department, and a few that I didn't know, were all sneaking curious glances my way.

I met Glen's eyes, which were somber. "I don't understand."

"Listen up. I approved of your hire because you have a solid résumé, and you are more than adequately qualified for the job. Truth is, I would have hired you if you'd walked in off the street." I cocked my head, a stone sinking into the depths of my stomach.

"But I did walk in off the street," I whispered, and knew that my feelings from earlier had just been validated. It had been a little too easy, from start to finish, a little too simple to become a fully employed member at what I now understood was one of the biggest corporations in the country.

Glen shook his head. "The day Mr. St. Brenton came back

from his home in Cambria this week, he told me that if a Miss Devon Reid were to stop by the building, call, or make contact in any way, I was to find her a decent position. I objected at first." It felt like a blow to hear that from my only supporter, but he continued before I could say anything. "He said that I would find you more than qualified for many of the positions here. Regardless, it was not negotiable. I did some research before you showed up, so I was satisfied about the kind of person you are."

My cheeks flushed with mortification. Glen thought that I had slept with Zach—with Mr. St. Brenton—and that this was my payment.

"I shouldn't take the job. I'll quit. Oh God." Rising to go, hoping to leave without too much attention, Glen tugged on my sleeve until I forced to again sit.

"I meant it when I said I would have hired you anyway." His eyebrow rose, and made his long face look even longer. I searched it for signs of deception and found none.

"Why did you research me? How did you know I'd come?"

Glen smiled then, a smile that was a little bit amused and a little bit bittersweet. "I've yet to meet a woman who can walk away from Zachariah St. Brenton."

I wasn't sure what to say to that. Glen moved down the table, joined in the discussion about the appetizers. No one else had spoken to me, and my beer was nearly gone, so I made my way to the bar to order another, just to have something to do. Not to mention that the beer was working nearly as well as a pill at keeping my anxiety at bay.

"Not many women drink plain beer." Feeling the warmth of another body to my left, I turned to find Tony, the senior admin assistant in accounting. He was holding an empty martini glass, which he held up for me to see. "Not many men do, either. They make a killer martini here."

"I'll keep that in mind for next time." My smile was a genuine one, because someone from work was actually talking to me, instead of looking at me like I was an exotic bug.

"Can I buy you one now?"

I hesitated, my emotions battling it out in my gut. I should probably play nice with my new coworkers, if I wanted them to stop seeing me as a freak. But hard liquor had an odd, often not very desirable effect on my behavior. Plus, Tony, while good-looking in a Latin lover kind of way, was standing a bit too close to me for my liking, and while I didn't want to assume, I got the impression that he was flirting with me.

I compromised. "Maybe not a martini, but another beer would be nice."

The look in Tony's eyes was appraising and admiring. "A girl with conviction. I think I'm in love."

"I sincerely hope not." I felt the heat slam into me at the same time that Tony's expression changed. It was him. It was Zach. Standing next to us.

Tony forgotten, I whirled, my eyes narrowing, questions on the tip of my tongue.

But Zach wasn't done with Tony. "Relationships between coworkers in the same department are against company policy. But you're aware of that, right, Mr. Figuero?"

I didn't even turn to see what Tony's expression was. It might have been rude, but I didn't care. At any rate, he stammered something and left, and I was alone with the man who had been haunting my every thought for days.

"Hello, Miss Reid." His face was very nearly expressionless as he looked me over, but I thought I could discern a hint of . . . was that lust? Need?

He had to be feeling it, *had* to, because having him so near to me had made me molten inside. Lord, but he looked good. Gone were the jeans and button-down from the restaurant, replaced by a black suit, charcoal shirt, and slick purple tie.

"Hello." My voice was breathy. He looked good enough to eat, and I very nearly told him so, but bit my tongue just in time.

"May I buy you that beer?" His words were phrased as a question, but the tone I heard told me that he would, in fact, be ordering me a drink. It was bossy, but somehow I liked it better than Tony's tactic.

"Yes." I knew that I would say yes to quite a lot of things if he suggested them to me right then. I could smell the heat emanating from his skin, those same scents from Cambria, overlaid with a hint of the sexiest cologne that I'd ever smelled.

"Two bottles of the Stone Imperial please, Angie." Though Zach looked at the bartender briefly to make sure that she heard him, he seemed not to notice—truly not to—when she uncapped the bottles and handed them over, accidentally on purpose grazing his hand.

"Anytime, Mr. St. Brenton." She cast him the patented *come fuck me* look that some girls seem to master in middle school, then sent a little bonus smirk my way.

Zach didn't appear to even hear her, instead handing me my beer and placing his hand at the small of my back, guiding me to a small table with two chairs, set against a back wall.

"How come you didn't have to pay for those? And aren't we going to sit with everyone else?" He chuckled a bit as he pulled out my chair for me. The action caused my heart to skip with delicious anticipation.

"I'm not interested in spending time with everyone else."

Oh man. Which meant . . . that meant that he was interested in spending time with *me*?

I could feel my legs begin to tremble under the table, and I smoothed my palms down the length of my thighs in an attempt to steady them.

As if trying to put me at ease, Zach changed the subject.

"Did you know that Cambria was originally called Santa

Rosa?" I was so mesmerized by the way his full lips looked that it took a moment for his words to sink in. The Santa Rosa Bar. Cambria. Not paying for his drinks. The bartender knowing his name.

When things lined up, I reared back in my chair, an accusatory stare on my face.

"You own this place!" My reaction seemed to puzzle him, but I carefully set my beer bottle back onto the table and looked at him with alarm.

"What's the matter?" He leaned in again, concern on his face, but I slid back, keeping some distance between us.

"Don't. I can't think when you're near me." I chose that moment to look over Zach's shoulder and across the bar to the big table where my coworkers sat. They all, to a man—even Glen— were watching Zach and me, not bothering to hide their interest. Some merely looked fascinated, but some—most of them female—had expressions ranging from shock to disgust to hatred. These last few were also whispering and pointing and not seeming to care who saw.

They thought I was a whore. They thought that I was Zach's mistress, or call girl, or hooker, for heaven's sake, and that he was trying to pass me off as gainfully employed within his company.

I felt sick. The worst part of all was that, if he had allowed it, they would all be absolutely right.

"I have to go." I couldn't look at him, couldn't say anything else. I made my way to the entrance and out as quickly as I could.

Tears threatened to fall as I walked—nearly ran—down the street. I'd walked to work that morning, thinking that the motel where I was staying was closer to the office building than it was.

My throat felt thick with unshed tears, but more than hysterics, I felt sick with mortification.

I'd never been anything but the good girl, the prim and proper princess, and I simply didn't know how to handle this.

The days that I had spent in Cambria had reawakened my addiction to the sound of the ocean, and so with a split-second decision I veered off course and turned in the direction of Aquatic Park.

Halfway there, a dark, fancy town car pulled up beside me. It followed me for a few steps as I began to walk faster and then faster still.

What kind of city had I moved to?

While my heart was in my throat, the door opened, and someone grasping my elbows in strong hands lifted me clear off of my feet.

"Don't you ever do that again." I didn't give him the satisfaction of my struggling, instead staring at him with defiance that I didn't feel, my body tensed at his touch. I was mad, oh yes indeed, but something about him still made me feel . . . safe. The panic was beaten completely into submission in his presence, and it was a strange, yet welcome, sensation.

"Put me down." I emphasized each word, my eyes shooting daggers. He did not look pleased, and held me just long enough to make his point. The second that my heels touched concrete, I pushed off, stomping now, determined not to let this overbearing ape of a man ruin my evening walk on the beach.

Even if he was an awfully sexy ape of a man.

He was right with me, a shadow that I couldn't detach.

"You can't go for a walk alone at night in the city." He had a valid point, but right at that moment I didn't care.

"Watch me." The words had barely left my lips when he picked me up and threw me over his shoulder. He actually did, as if he were a caveman and I was the woman he had just hit over the head with a rock.

I shrieked with indignation and kicked at his torso. The

street was deserted except for a male couple holding hands as they walked their tiny dog. They watched avidly, clearly entertained, but didn't offer assistance.

What the *hell* kind of city was this?

"Put me down." I tried emphasizing all of my words again, slow and loud. Zach didn't appear to notice, his hands tightening where they pressed against my flesh, flat against my back, and splayed over the globe of my behind.

"Put me down!"

"Happy to." Back at the fancy black town car, he slid me down his body slowly, deliberately, making sure that I felt every bit of him.

That happened to include a massive, rock-hard erection. He was *aroused* by this?

A strangled sound of frustration bubbled up from my throat as I shoved away from him. He was *such* a bastard.

Never mind that having just been pressed up so tightly against him had made me wet.

Zach cocked his head as he took in my stance, my hands fisted on my hips, my teeth grinding together.

"You're angry with me." One corner of his mouth turned up in the beginning of a smile. "Nobody gets angry with me. Especially not women."

"That's what you think!" Beyond frustrated now, in every meaning of the word, I placed my hands on his chest and tried to push him away. Instead of giving me space, he caught my wrists in his fingers, a strong grip that I couldn't break out of.

We stared at each other for a long moment, me still grinding my teeth together, and him looking at me as I were the most wonderfully fascinating thing that he'd ever seen. And then, before I could catch my breath, his mouth was on mine and I was pressed back against the car. The cool, unyielding metal I could feel through the back of my blouse was a strange contrast to the undulating heat searing my breasts, my torso, my belly.

I felt as if I were being branded, and I didn't mind at all. When his tongue traced the seam of my lips, demanding entrance, I parted my lips and let him sweep his tongue inside. My hands slid up to clench onto the solid muscles of his upper arms, and his hands fisted in my hair, tugging as they had the last time.

We broke away, panting, when the clear, sharp sound of a wolf whistle sliced through the night. Turning as one, we looked across the street to where the two young men walking their dog were grinning at us. One gave us a thumbs-up.

We both laughed a bit, breathless, and it should have broken the tension.

It didn't.

"Get in." Without waiting for an answer, Zach picked me up and placed me gently on the long bench seat in the back of the car. He followed, hitting the button that raised the privacy panel between us and the driver.

"Just drive." He said this at the last possible moment, and then we were alone. While I, given my way, would have instigated a discussion about what this meant, how it couldn't possibly be a good idea, and how I really didn't want to be involved with a coworker again, Zach seemed to prefer a more direct approach.

Pulling me onto his lap to straddle him, he eased my pencil skirt up to my hips, forcing my legs wide.

"What are you—" Cutting off my protest with a kiss, he fisted the neck of my blouse and yanked, hard enough to send buttons flying. My simple black bra was revealed, and he pulled it down, the straps stretching to the limit before my breasts bounced up from the cups, now sitting on the fabric like a plate of something tasty for him to devour.

"Fuck," Zach muttered as he watched them jiggle, the movement caused by the motion of the car. He stared long and hard before lunging close to nuzzle his face into my cleavage. "They're just as I imagined."

As he'd imagined? He'd been imagining them? The thought disappeared when he sucked one of the tight nipples into his mouth, suckling so hard that I felt a tug all the way to my cunt.

"Aah!" I squirmed, my hips rocking against his. His response was to begin rolling my other nipple between the fingers of his right hand.

Both of my hands were on his chest, trying to create some distance, some space so I could breathe.

I didn't want to breathe. I didn't want this to stop, ever.

"Undo my pants."

Suddenly embarrassed, I buried my face into Zach's neck and shook my head. I didn't think that I could undress him—I wasn't brave enough.

Tom had always just undressed himself. And while it certainly wasn't fair to compare the two men—not fair to Tom, at least—my sexual experience was limited enough that I couldn't seem to help it.

As the flush of my cheeks burned into his neck, Zach removed his touch from my breasts, and I groaned at the loss of pleasure.

"Devon." His voice was stern enough to make me rock back and look at him in the face. "I give you permission to undo my pants. Unbuckle my belt, undo the fly, and pull out my cock. If I didn't want you, and you alone, to do this, I wouldn't tell you to."

It seemed like his words should be strange, but they were the impetus that I needed. I did as I was told, and as I did, he pulled a small foil packet from his pocket. Tearing it open with his teeth, he pulled out the ring of latex, waiting for me to finish my task.

When I finally pulled his cock from the soft material of his dress pants, I felt desire stab through me in a way that it never had, not with Tom, certainly not with anyone else.

I wanted that cock. I wanted to touch it, to lick it, to bury it inside of me.

I wanted it to be mine.

Mixed with that potent desire was a heavy dose of shyness. Wrapping my fist around the thick shaft was all that I had the nerve to do. A strangled cry slipped from Zach's lips, and in a series of quick motions he had sheathed his length in latex, angled my hips toward him, shoved the crotch of my panties to one side, and seated himself inside of me.

He was not gentle. He was also not small, the length and girth making my eyes widen in appreciation and surprise. It hurt, taking all of him in, but mixed with that hurt was a delirious amount of pleasure, and the sound that escaped from my throat was very nearly a scream.

"I should have warned you." Zach nipped at my neck and, without giving me even a moment to adjust to the sensation of him inside me, filling, began to thrust up in hard, rough strokes. "I don't do gentle. Ever."

"I think I like it." Even more than the fact that I was drowning in waves of pleasure, I wasn't feeling much like the meek, mild Devon who would have been shocked to be handled so roughly.

Zach growled, liking my words. Fisting his hands into the length of my hair, which looked nearly white in the stripes of light from the streetlamps as we passed them by, he tugged hard. The sting only added to the deliciousness of the moment, and soon I found myself meeting him thrust for thrust, my fingers curling into his shoulders until I was sure my nails would draw blood.

"Fuck. Fuck!" I had never been one to use profanity, but as

the pleasure gathered and stretched like a string being pulled tighter and tighter, there seemed to be no other word. "Fuck!" Zach pressed his thumb against my clit as I climbed, the look on his face wicked as the devil, and an orgasm slammed into me like I'd been struck by lightning. Unable to control any part of myself, I screamed, thrusting down as hard as I could, greedily asking for everything he could give me.

"Devon!" His own words were a shout as he released, the sensation of my climax bringing him over. In me to the hilt, he groaned, long and loud, as he emptied himself inside of me.

We stayed that way for a long moment, curled into each other. Once my mind began to function again, and unsure of the protocol in the situation, I shifted and looked down into his face.

It was unreadable. The walls were up, fully up, and all entrances were locked tight.

"I . . ." There wasn't anything that I could think of to say. Slowly I peeled myself off of him, though I wanted nothing more than to stay curled on his lap, pressed again him.

He let me go without comment, and it hurt.

Sliding down on the bench so that we were no longer touching, I tucked my breasts back into my bra, smoothed down my skirt, buttoned the two fastenings that hadn't been ripped off. I shifted uncomfortably, aware that my panties were soaked through and had been stretched so much that they would likely have to be tossed into the trash.

Zach wrapped the condom in a tissue and cleaned himself off with another before redoing his pants. He didn't look at me, so I stopped looking at him.

He must have signaled the driver somehow, because within minutes—minutes that stretched long with discomfort—we were in front of the hotel where I was staying.

How he knew that, I didn't know, and was certainly not about to ask.

"Um. Well. Good-bye." Emotions were rioting through me, and I wanted to scream, to cry, to throw something. I wanted that pleasure back. The driver opened the door for me, and I scrambled out awkwardly.

"Devon." My heart jumping, I bent and looked back into the car. Zach was looking straight at me, and he looked ferocious. "You are a temptation."

"Thank you?" I had no idea what to say. I wished for, longed for, a sweet kiss good night, a brush of the hands, *something* . . . but then, he had warned me, he didn't do gentle.

I was several steps away, my heels clicking on the pavement with a much more decisive manner than I felt, when he again said my name. I turned, and saw that same fierce man watching me.

"Devon. You have no idea what you started."

CHAPTER FOUR

"Miss Devon Reid." The words that sliced through the frenetic air of the big room that housed my small desk at Phyrefly Aviation would have been unmistakable, even if they hadn't been saying my full name. The sounds were female, forced sharply through a well-stuffed nasal cavity.

That distinctive voice, combined with the quirk of addressing a person by her full name, belonged to Bini Gallagher, the administrative manager at Phyrefly—my supervisor.

"Yes, Mrs. Gallagher?" Though she addressed everyone by their full name, there would be hell to pay if one of us *girls*— and that included my male coworker Tony—dared to use her first name in any context. I smiled brightly, trying to maintain the expression even when the other woman pushed her tortoiseshell spectacles down her nose and peered over them at me with disdain. I tried—as a rule—to be nice to the older woman, because her negativity had struck me as stemming from a deep personal unhappiness.

Besides, I was happy for the distraction. It had been an entire week since I'd seen Zach. A whole week of silence following one of the most intense experiences of my life.

I thought that I might go mad.

That lack of contact had been good for the work side of things, however. With no more sightings of the two of us together—no grist for the rumor mill—people seemed to have moved past the drama quite quickly, and on to the next entertaining thing.

All of this was reason for a big smile, indeed.

My smile, no matter how genuine, didn't crack Bini's fa-
çade, and I let it slip. I didn't have the energy to pretend to be
cheery today, not when I'd been up half the night, again, thinking about—obsessing over—Zachariah St. Brenton.

You have no idea what you started. "Starting" would imply
that whatever was between us wasn't over.

Then where the hell *was* he?

Mrs. Gallagher sniffed when she saw that she didn't have
my full attention. With a loud huff of coffee-scented breath, she
slapped a small parcel, plainly wrapped in brown paper, onto
my desk.

I tucked a stray wisp of hair from my ponytail behind my
ear and blinked at the unmarked package. When I looked up at
the woman with a questioning expression, she huffed again,
and I felt as if, somehow, I should have known what the package
contained.

"This was just delivered. It came with instructions. You,
and only you, are to deliver this upstairs to Mr. St. Brenton.
Make sure that you are the one to deliver it into his hands."

I barely registered the aggrieved expression on Mrs. Gallagher's face—why was I being sent into the sacred den of he who
ruled the building when she had seniority, after all? But my heart
had leapt into my chest when I'd heard the man's name, and anticipation followed, making my skin prickle with gooseflesh.

I stared at it, willing the brown paper to unwrap before my
eyes and give me some hint, some clue, about what I was to face
upstairs. All I got was a pencil rapped sharply on the glossy surface of my desk, very near my knuckles.

"Get going, then, Miss Devon Reid. Unless you think you're
too good to play delivery girl." With murmured words to the
negative I stood, took the parcel in hand and scurried toward
the elevators.

I could feel the older woman's stare following me, poking at the chicken wings of my shoulder blades. When I turned back briefly after pressing the elevator button, I was surprised to see that the expression the other woman wore was no longer one of annoyance, but worry.

Why would she be worried about my delivering this package? I was the one who was about to face the unknown.

Why, oh why did that word make something dark and needy twist itself tightly inside me with anticipation?

I quickly forgot about Mrs. Gallagher as the elevator climbed from the third floor of the building, up and up, sliding toward its goal of floor twenty-six. I caught sight of myself in the mirrored walls, and I wasn't thrilled with what I saw.

My black skirt and sweater were tidy, but plain. My hair was in a ponytail, loose ends flying out every which way, and soft bruises under my eyes caused by several sleepless nights were clearly visible through the thin layer of makeup that didn't hide much in fluorescent lighting.

It didn't matter what I looked like, in my heart I knew this. But as I thought of the feeling of Zach inside of me, of his mouth on my breasts, I shivered, my nipples tightening, and I wished—hard—that I had worn something else. Something prettier.

Something sexier.

The woman who sat at a desk as big as a lake, directly in front of the elevator doors that opened in front of me, was clearly younger than me—quite a feat, since I was only twenty-four—and had smooth, icy blond hair and an equally slick smile.

She beamed that smile my way, but I didn't feel welcome. She didn't speak, just waited, and I knew that I had been out-bitched in a major way.

"I'm here to deliver this to Mr. St. Brenton." I raised my chin up a bit and tried to forget that that morning I had noticed a tiny hole in the seam of my skirt. It was at my hip, covered by my sweater, but I was so uncertain in that moment that I was sure the perfect-looking creature knew.

She smiled some more, and I held up the box. She reached for it, and I pulled it tight against my belly.

"I'll pass that along to Zach—Mr. St. Brenton, as soon as he's free." I knew that the name slip wasn't an accident. The woman was challenging me, and I couldn't imagine why.

"I need to deliver it to him myself." I tried to keep my words steady, though I was hugely intimidated. But facing off with this paper-doll princess was, I was quite certain, shades better than what would befall me if I dared to disobey the order that I somehow knew had come directly from the man whom I hadn't seen in a week.

I didn't know him well, but I knew that he didn't take kindly to being challenged.

"Oh, you're so cute." The woman smiled again, but there wasn't any humor in her voice. "But really, you can leave it with me."

I clung to the package as if it were a life preserver, feeling as though I was being tested. I opened my mouth, to say what I wasn't sure, but the words were forever swallowed down when the voice that echoed in my dreams crashed over me like a warm wave.

"Thank you, Philippa, but I did indeed give Miss Reid orders to deliver that package straight into my hands." Philippa turned the sweetness in her smile up in wattage, all aimed at the beautiful man who had opened the heavy wooden doors of his office, but she had been swept from my mind with one look at Zachariah.

"Miss Reid." He was waiting, his eyes blue as the innermost flickering of a fire. I moved toward him hesitantly, and when he placed his hand at the small of my back to usher me the rest of the way into his office, adrenaline surged through my veins and made my legs tremble.

I froze just inside the door, which he swung shut behind us. I had a sweeping impression of a room that was huge, with a desk and chair, two sofas, and various small tables scattered around. The walls were sheer, huge panes of glass. That was all the detail that I noted, however.

All of my senses were trained on the man who was still behind me, not touching me but invading my space nonetheless.

"You have obeyed this order to the letter, Miss Reid. I am impressed." I felt warmth suffuse my neck—his breath—and then it was gone, leaving behind a flush that swept over my skin.

"I'm good at following orders." This was the truth. All of my life, I had done as I was told.

"I don't believe that is entirely truthful, Miss Reid. In fact, you are in big trouble." I wanted to lean back, to touch him, just to feel the contact, but his voice was ominous, and I knew that he wouldn't allow it.

"What . . . what have I done?" I tried to stand still, straight, and fisted my hands so tightly that my nails bit into my skin. Excitement and anticipation made me tremble. I felt him come closer, come up behind me. His breath hit my ear as he spoke, and it sent a delicious shiver down my spine.

"I told you to stay away from me. You did not. And now look where we are." With an intimate nudge, he insinuated his knee between my own, urging me forward.

"Walk to my desk, Miss Reid, and then open the parcel." The timbre of his voice dropped, and it scraped over the words huskily.

He sounded aroused. I hesitated, wondering, and his voice nudged at me.

"Go."

Again I did as I was told, walking to the desk in a straight line, wobbling a bit in my heels. My fingers took a quick impression of the smooth, hard surface before they moved to the flaps of folded paper on the box.

What on earth was in this box?

Why did I care?

I tried to remove the paper neatly, but I was shaking with nerves, and it ripped. The box was brown, too, simple and made of thin cardboard.

I cast a quick, hesitant look back over my shoulder. I was startled to find that Zach had come up behind me, following just close enough to keep my nerves on edge.

"Open it." I didn't hesitate—by now my muscles were tight with curiosity and anticipation. The cardboard crumpled a bit as I pulled back the lid hastily, and I heard a low chuckle.

"Oh." Whatever I might have dreamt of finding in this box, I didn't think it was . . . well, whatever this was. It looked almost like something a person might use to dust, except that it was made of leather and was far too pretty for such a menial chore. Yes, this leather was beautiful, long ribbons of bittersweet chocolate cascading from a palm-sized handle. The strips of leather crisscrossed over and around that same handle, and my fingers itched to touch.

I traced one of those curious fingers over the handle, still not sure what I was looking at, though I was quite certain that it was of vital importance to the man behind me. I heard his sharp intake of breath as my touch caressed the object, and then his hand was over mine, molding my palm to the handle, my skin pale white, his tawny from the sun.

He let me hold the object for a long moment, then pried it from my hands. Rounding the desk, he placed the object on the flat surface, then sat in the large chair, his palms flat on the grainy surface.

"Take off your sweater." My mouth fell open and he grinned at me, but it wasn't necessarily a nice smile. His lips curved with desire, with need, and even with a hint of cruelty, but I was too stunned to be afraid.

"I beg your pardon?" We were in his office, for goodness' sake. I tried to make my words haughty, to draw some dignity around me like a cloak, but I knew that it was useless, and from the grin that he shot my way, he knew it, too. "That is so inappropriate."

He leaned forward, catching me in that gaze of his.

"I want you to take your blouse off, Miss Reid, because I want to look at you. I think that you want me to look at you." I couldn't speak. I couldn't even swallow. I was mad at him for the week-long silence, but that did nothing to tamp down my desire.

"I—" What was I supposed to say to that?

"Tell me the truth." Could he read my mind? "If you don't want to let me look at you, then you have my sincere apologies. But if you forget about what you think is appropriate—what you think you want—I suspect that your desires are very much in line with my own. You want to submit to me."

He watched intently as my mouth opened, then closed again soundlessly. His eyes tracked the movement of my tongue as it traced my lips.

I couldn't deny the wetness, the heat that had surged between my legs.

I was at war with myself, and he knew it. He murmured, low in his throat, soothing the tangle of my nerves.

"What do you want, Devon? What do you truly want?" The sound of his voice saying my first name was intimate, and was ultimately my undoing.

Slowly, so very slowly, I reached up for the top button on my sweater. My fingers felt thick, clumsy, but I managed to work the button through its hole.

Zach made a small sound of approval, his eyes gleaming with wicked intent.

One fastening fell free, and then another. Then my sweater was open and, before I could lose my nerve, off. I was standing in my shell pink cotton bra, my skirt and hose and heels, my arms crossed over my midriff self-consciously.

Before I could blink, Zach had the strange object in his hand and had flicked it toward me. I saw the strips of leather fly, and then felt a sharp sting on the plumpness of one breast, then the other.

Holy hell. That pretty leather thing was a whip.

He flicked twice more, and this time the sting landed on each of my nipples. I cried out and jerked back, hugging my arms around me protectively.

"Stop it!" I stared at him agog, my eyes wide and shocked. "What the hell do you think you're doing?"

He held the object out toward me, his expression serious and honest.

"Take it away if you want to, Devon." I eyed the thing warily, but didn't move from where I stood a few steps back from the desk. "This is a martinet. It is used for pleasure. Pleasure that I would like to give to you."

"Don't you mean 'pain'?" My words were nasty, as I meant them to be. He had thrown me off my game, thrust me out of my safe little bubble that I'd built over the last week, and I didn't think I much liked it. "My pain, your pleasure?"

I did notice that, despite the fact that I had just been marked by a flogger, my habitual panic had yet to make an appearance.

"Think, Devon." I glowered at him, not fooled by his soothing tone. "Did that really hurt? I don't think it did."

Damn it, he was right. It stung, a bit like a paper cut, and it had startled the hell out of me. But it didn't really hurt—not unless I counted the ache that was now burning between my thighs.

Cautiously, his eyes never leaving mine, Zachariah again placed a hand on the object—the *martinet*. Clutching it firmly in hand, he rounded the desk, moving until he was again behind me. He tucked the handle between my breasts and placed his hands on my shoulders, sliding them down my arms to trace the stripes of my ribs and then to smooth over the skin of my back. One smooth movement and my bra was unclasped, falling in front of me. He caught the martinet that he had tucked into my cleavage with one hand and with the other spun me, twisting my bra at the same time so that my wrists were bound together in the pale pink fabric.

"Lean back." He whispered the words. I felt as if I had been drugged, because I didn't entertain any option, besides doing what he said, even though the rational part of my brain screamed that complying was insane. The cool surface of the desk pressed against my back, pulling at my skin as I squirmed with anticipation.

"Close your eyes." I shifted restlessly, my hips swaying awkwardly. I had never felt so needy, so on the edge.

The edge of what, I didn't know.

I tensed, waiting for sharp bite of the martinet. Craving it, if I were being honest.

Instead I felt the soft kiss of the cool leather dancing over my abdomen. I gasped at the sensation, so very different from what I had expected, but nonetheless pleasurable.

"This is how my mouth will feel when I get you naked and kiss you all over." The picture sprang into my mind all too clearly, of myself bare and laid out on his desk, waiting for the touch of his mouth. I whimpered, just the slightest bit, and was hushed with the kiss of the leather over my lips.

"Spread your legs." I did it before I even thought about it, the fabric of my skirt riding up, exposing the edges of my stockings, the flush of my panties, and the inches of skin in between.

The leather traced over my bare ribs, the valley between my breasts, my hard, tight nipples. I began to pant, more excited than I'd ever been in my life.

"Hold on to the desk." I did, swallowing hard, wondering what would happen next.

Instead of the flogger, I felt Zach's fingers toy with the crotch of my panties. I moaned lightly and leaned into the touch, but he didn't linger.

Deftly, he pulled the fabric aside, and I felt slick pressure at my entrance. Instinctively opening to it, I was startled to feel something heavy and round being inserted in my most intimate of places, followed quickly by its twin.

I tried to clench my thighs together at the strange sensation, but Zach was there to block the movement.

"What . . ." I straightened up a bit to ask Zach what he had just done, and as I moved, the balls shifted. They created pressure in delicious, private places, and an unfamiliar ache bloomed through my belly.

"If you are to take this journey with me, then you must learn to trust me." I was too distracted by the heavy sensation of the balls rolling around to ask him what he meant. "These are ben-wa balls. You will keep them inside of you until I say otherwise." I shifted experimentally, and the balls moved, forcing sensations that were rich and impossible to ignore to flood through me.

"Bend over the desk again." Oh, Lord. Bent over, the balls pressed heavily on the flesh above my clit. I wanted to rock back and forth, to build that delicious pressure so that it could be relieved, but a palm pressed to the curve of my back warned me against it.

Focused on the new sensations inside my cleft, I wasn't expecting the hiss of the flogger when it came, the bloom of pain between my thighs. One kiss of the leather on each smooth expanse of leg, then several short, quick flicks right in my center.

I cried out, fingers scrabbling for purchase on the slick surface of the desk. He hit harder than he had the first time, and the blows hurt, hurt quite a bit, actually, landing as they were on my most sensitive flesh. But combined with that pain was a sense of pleasure, one that was dark and rich and seductive.

As my body jerked, the balls rocked inside of me. It was almost unbearable, that pleasure which melted so effortlessly into the sting of the whip.

The pleasure built, wave upon wave that finally reached the shore in a tidal crash of pleasure. I cried out again as the sensations washed over me, riding the darkness until I'd wrung every last bit of it out and I could see again.

Stunned, I slowly rolled over, propped myself up on my elbows and looked up at the man in front of me. His eyes were glowing like those of a cat, and they were full of an emotion that I couldn't read.

I didn't know him very well, after all, no matter what he'd just done to my body.

Something in his stare, though, was too personal, too raw, for anyone to see. In fact, I didn't think that he meant for me to catch him that way, for as soon as he saw that I had come back down to earth, his eyes shuttered and his face tensed up. I watched as he closed his emotions back off from the rest of the world, again becoming the controlled, charismatic young billionaire who held the interest of the world.

So even all of his money couldn't protect him from the demons that haunted him, that haunted us all.

Feeling exposed, though I supposed it was useless to at that point, I tugged my bra from my wrists and stuffed it in my pocket. I didn't feel as though there was time to fuss with putting it back on. I wrestled my blouse back over my arms, my shoulders, and closed it hastily, not bothering to double-check if it had been buttoned straight.

I had no idea what had just happened, but I didn't intend to think about it there. Zach was frozen in place, his eyes unreadable as they assessed me.

Pushing away from the desk, I hastily made my way toward the door, the balls rocking as I moved, making me moan. It was all just too much—too intense. I didn't know what to do with it. I would rather have faced Philippa the paper-doll princess while mussed and braless than have continued to try to breathe in a room that suddenly had no air.

"Miss Reid." My hand was on the door before he spoke. I turned slowly, not letting go of the knob.

The sexy man who just seduced me had changed. The tortured one who made me come had disappeared. In their place was the cool, controlled CEO, complete with arrogant posture and the hint of a smirk on his lips.

"Be in the first-floor lobby at half past six this evening. We need to have a discussion." His words were serious and very nearly foreboding.

"Do not remove those ben-wa balls this afternoon."

I shifted, aware all over again of the gentle rocking of the balls inside of me. Though I'd just had a huge orgasm, I felt the need beginning again. I tried to imagine going through the afternoon with them inside of me, of working at my desk while they weighed down on my clit. The thought made my cheeks flush and my lips part.

"I have exposed you to some of the pleasure of my . . . lifestyle, Devon. But I haven't yet exposed you to the pain." I couldn't move, not without those balls sending jolts of need through my veins.

"I need to know if you are open to both." My eyes were wide. Pain? More than the martinet? Feeling as though I were in the presence of a predatory animal, I watched, cautious, as

Zach strode across the room to me, tilted my chin up for a soft, short kiss.

"Go back to work now. I will meet you in the lobby at six thirty." Somewhat dazed, drugged by the sensations in my blood, I nodded and turned to leave the room. Right before I exited the door, he whispered one last thing in my ear.

"And whatever you do, don't come."

PART II

TEMPTED TO REBEL

CHAPTER FIVE

By six twenty that evening, I was sitting in the vast, sleek lobby of the Phyrefly building waiting to meet Zach. My hands were bound so tightly together in my lap that my knuckles had turned white. My face was warm, and my trembling legs were crossed at the thigh, my every muscle clenched.

The slick silver ben-wa balls that Zach had secured inside of me earlier that day sat heavily in my pelvis. I tried to hold entirely still, for even the smallest of movements—any movement—set them rocking against my womb, and overwhelmed me with the sensation.

The vast building seemed to be empty, everyone else having gone for the day. I knew, though, that Zach was still around somewhere. I could feel the tension that being in his vicinity brought to me, vibrating in the air like a tangible substance.

I looked up at the sleek security monitor, wondering if he was watching, if he could see me. At the same time I saw myself, a small, curvy blonde dressed severely in black, picked out in slightly distorted black and white. The woman on that monitor seemed to be waiting for something—searching for something—and I blinked at my own image, startled by the thought.

What was I doing here? Was I really throwing myself at one man so soon after being burned by another? Could I really find myself while in the arms of someone else?

The sound of the chrome elevator sliding into place on the

first floor had my heart clenching in the suddenly tight confines of my chest. My palms became slick with sweat, and I unclasped them and nervously wiped the moisture off on my skirt.

"You're early. I'm pleased." And then there he was, Zachariah St. Brenton, the charismatic billionaire, striding across the ultramodern lobby toward me. He was dressed in another expensive-looking black suit that made him look all the more mouthwatering. I began to tremble as those crystal blue eyes fastened on me, warm with hunger.

My head told me that I wouldn't—couldn't—find myself by pursuing a man. Everything else in my being screamed at me to take what I wanted, for once in my life.

"Come." Zach held a hand out for me, and I took it without question, just as I was sure he expected me to. I found that I didn't want to think, didn't want to analyze my actions, my feelings and my thoughts.

I just wanted to live—and nothing had ever made me feel more vibrant or alive than this man.

"Oh!" The heavy balls rocked as I stood, causing twinges of need all throughout my abdomen, and my knees buckled. Zach's muscular arm caught me around my waist, holding me steady.

"Maybe I asked too much of you."

I looked up sharply, certain that he was criticizing me. I was crushed, because for reasons that I didn't quite understand, I wanted to please him.

Instead, the lines etched deeply into his forehead told me that his mind was filled with nothing but concern for me. I was surprised and touched, and it made me want to please him all the more.

"No." Zach looked at me sharply as I spoke, the beginnings of a frown crinkling the corners of his lips. He struck me again as the kind of man who was not accustomed to being told *no*.

"Very well." Those opalescent eyes studied me for a long moment, trying to unearth my secrets, it seemed, before Zach guided me to the parking garage entrance, where I had parked that very morning. He seemed to be trying to understand me, to figure me out, which puzzled me.

After all, I wasn't very interesting.

"Where are we going?" The balls continued to rock inside of me, moving with every step that I took. My breath was coming in short pants as pressure built in the muscles between my thighs.

Zach led me past the now-deserted booth where the parking attendant habitually sat, and through a door that I hadn't noticed before. It led to a smaller, more finely finished garage, detached from the main employee area.

It held half a dozen expensive-looking vehicles. Well, I didn't know anything about cars—anything at all, other than ideally, when I put the key into the ignition, they would start. Still, I knew without a doubt that all of these vehicles were well out of my price range. The shine of the chrome, their sleek lines— they screamed expensive.

I realized in a rush that they must all belong to him.

"We'll be going to the Seacliff house tonight, Charles." I jumped, a jolt of adrenaline shooting through my veins, when a man dressed all in black, whom I hadn't noticed at all, rose from the folding chair on which he had been sitting to greet Zach.

"Very well, Mr. St. Brenton." He nodded crisply, but I felt his eyes linger on me—not in a sexual way at all, but with curiosity. I found myself looking back, in short little glances, at the man who looked like he had only recently joined the senior citizens club—not that he would be joining the backgammon league anytime soon. He was tall, muscular, and stood with a rigidity that spoke of military training.

Suspicion was etched into the lines on his face. I swallowed, feeling the need to prove myself, though how, I didn't have a clue.

"Charles, this is Miss Reid." Zach splayed his hand on my lower back, and I felt the heat of his body seeping through the thin cotton of my blouse. I shivered, which caused the balls to rock back and forth, and I couldn't help it any longer.

A small moan escaped my lips, a needy plea. I had never been more aroused in my life.

Zach looked down sharply at my sigh, and I noticed his body tensing in response to my desire. He nodded crisply at Charles, who climbed into the driver's seat of the car.

I was puzzling over why a man like Zach, who clearly liked to be in control, wouldn't drive his own fancy car, when he quickly took my hands, spun me so that I faced the rear of the vehicle, and placed my palms flat on its slick surface.

I choked back a cry as the balls swung wildly inside of me, pressing on my entrance, slicking my tight channel with arousal.

"What are you doing?" My whisper nearly caught in my throat when Zach crouched behind me, clasping long fingers around each of my ankles. He ran his hands up the insides of my legs.

"Zach!" The crevice between my legs flooded with wetness as he gently but firmly continued his caress up to the tender skin at the insides of my thighs, reaching beneath my flirty skirt. My face flushed crimson, my breath panted out, and I looked quickly to the front of the car.

Charles was seated in the driver's seat, facing forward. I could see his stern, focused expression in the rearview mirror. He appeared to be at attention, and at the same time he didn't appear to be at all interested in what his employer was doing.

Maybe Zach had women in his locked parking garage all the time. I didn't know, and at that moment, as his thumbs grazed the place where my bikini panties met my skin, I didn't care.

"Relax." The word was a murmur against the back of my leg. This late in the day, he had the barest hint of shadow on his jaw, and he rubbed it back and forth over the tender skin behind my knee.

It made me tremble. I knew that it was stupid, since Charles didn't seem to be looking, but I tried to school my flushed cheeks and parted lips into a mask of indifference.

I struggled to cover my cry with a cough when one of Zach's hands pulled the elastic of my panties to one side. The other nudged at the swollen lips of my labia, teasing for a moment before entering. My fingers clawed helplessly at the cool surface of the vehicle as Zach extracted first one ball and then the other from my slick channel.

Pressing a kiss to my right buttock, he pulled my panties back into place and lowered my skirt. I gaped at him, aroused beyond anything I'd ever felt and also confused, as he spun me back around and ran a single finger down my cheek.

"It was wrong of me to ask you to wear these all day." Casually, he withdrew a cloth handkerchief—did people actually carry those anymore?—and wrapped the two ben-wa balls in them. The little metals globes glinted in the light, winking mischievously at me before they were tucked into the pocket of Zach's pants.

"Come."

He was going to leave me like this now? No. No way. I had been aroused to the point of pain all day, and my skin felt too tight. It wasn't fair.

It was cruel.

"What was the point of all of that?" When I was finally able to coax my voice into speaking, I was fully irritated, if breathless. No matter how much Zach turned me on, I didn't want to be pulled along by anyone else's will.

A flicker of consternation appeared on Zach's finely honed features, but it was gone in a breath. It was replaced by *that* look—the one that said that he wanted me, here and now.

I swallowed thickly as desire pooled within me and scattered my thoughts.

"Delayed gratification can bring you to heights of pleasure that you have never dared imagine, Miss Reid." Pressing his hand in the indentation between my shoulder blades, he rubbed lightly with his index and middle fingers. "Now. Into the car."

I planted my feet, trying to glare up at him, even though my body was screaming at me to do as he said. But I felt the need to take some sort of stand, to ascertain that I was not a shrinking violet.

I was just beginning to realize that I had been exactly that for nearly all of my life. It was time to change.

"Tell me where we're going. Then I'll think about getting in the car." I quivered with nerves when Zach's expression darkened. I saw his fingers curl, his nails biting into his palms.

"We are going to my house." The pressure of the fingers on my back increased, and I was startled enough by his words that I moved with it, bending to climb into the car. It was the same one that I had been in before, the sleek insides similar to a limousine, and I pressed my hands to my skirt to keep from flashing him a glimpse of my simple panties.

When I had seated myself, I looked back to find Zach grinning at me widely, even though the lust and the danger were still on his face.

"What?" I couldn't possibly have embarrassed myself in the last sixty seconds, could I? "What's so funny?"

Zach slid into the car behind me, much more gracefully than I had. I thought that he might sit beside me, might touch me—he had just had his fingers in between my legs, after all. But instead he settled himself on the soft leather bench seat directly across from me . . . the one where we had coupled so feverishly on my first day in his employ.

With him sitting straight across from me, I couldn't help but look directly at him, right into his gorgeous face. He loosened his tie, one patterned with green and gray today, then ran his fingers through his hair.

I imagined doing both of those things for him myself, and my mouth went dry.

"Why . . . why are we going to your house?" I wasn't an idiot—I knew very well where this was heading. However, the man and his mercurial mood changes had me feeling just uncertain enough that I wanted it in words.

Leaning forward, Zach pressed one single finger against my lips. I smelled copper and heat, and realized that the scent had come from me. I flushed all over, and that tense coil of need tightened even more.

"We are going to spend the night there."

I nervously tried to keep up a conversation as the car twisted its way along winding roads that were a slender black ribbon of asphalt bordering the ocean. Zach appeared to be entertained by my monologue, though he couldn't possibly have listened to even a fraction of it.

Still, his entire attention was focused on me. Combined with the slightly lessened but still very present ache from the ben-wa balls, I was ready to climb the walls.

Or him.

"This car is beautiful." I didn't actually care much about cars, but the combination of the low-slung vehicle, its black leather seats, and the view from the coast road made me itch to go for a fast drive with the sunroof open. "It must be amazing to drive this road in this car."

Zach didn't speak, but something in his silence changed. Turning my attention from the window to the big, beautiful man who was seated across from me, I understood immediately that I had said something wrong.

The face that had been so open and engaged only moments earlier was shuttered, and something flickered through the depths of those incredibly blue eyes.

"I don't drive." As if a steel rod had snapped into place in his spine, Zach sat upright. After a long pause, he drew his phone from his pocket.

"You'll have to excuse me for a few minutes. I have some e-mails that I need to send." The words were innocuous enough, but they provided him with a shield, an excuse to separate himself from me for the remainder of the drive.

Mortified, I clasped my hands around my suddenly trembling knees, staring down at them as the car glided onward, up a hill that was dotted with houses that looked increasingly more expensive the farther up we went. What had I said that caused Zach to shut down so absolutely?

I swallowed, hard, daring a glance up at the man through my eyelashes. He was scrolling through something on his iPhone, ostensibly reading it. His large frame was angled toward me, though, and he was stiff with tension. I knew that he was as overly aware of my presence in the car as I was of his.

Biting my lip, I let my stare travel down his body. I blinked when I saw the outline of his cock, pressing against the thin fabric of his pants.

I thought I had upset him, perhaps even angered him. But he was aroused?

Oh, he was so confusing.

I stayed silent, even as the car began to slow, and as Zach looked up from his phone. Sliding it back into his pocket, he looked at me with an unreadable expression on his face.

The car coasted to a stop. Peering out the window, I saw a massive garage door yawning open, and then we glided inside, pulling into line with another half dozen pricey-looking vehicles. I heard the sounds of the driver's-side door opening then closing, and then Charles opened the door to the area where we were seated. He helped me out first, and as I righted myself and smoothed down my skirt, again trying ridiculously hard to keep my underwear to myself, I heard Zach thank the man in a low voice.

"That will be all, Charles." I looked up to find the chauffeur peering at me with his curiosity more apparent than it had been earlier. He nodded at Zach, then at me.

"Good night, Miss Reid. Mr. St. Brenton."

And then I was alone with Zach. His expression still yielded no explanation for the sudden switch in his mood in the car, and I didn't like being in the dark.

Where once I would have just kept my mouth shut, I now felt compelled to question him. Perhaps some of Zach's brusque, confident demeanor was rubbing off on me.

"Why does Charles look at me that way?" Zach didn't pretend that he didn't know what I was talking about. Instead he sighed, ruffled a hand through his hair, and shoved his fingers down deep in his pockets.

"I've never brought a woman here before." I wanted to be suspicious—Zachariah St. Brenton had surely dated scores of women—but the simplicity of his words told me that he spoke the truth.

"Why?" I'd come this far, after all. Why not poke the sleeping bear a bit more?

He raised an eyebrow at me, and the hint of a wicked smile played over the corners of his lips.

"I've never wanted to." His eyes roamed over me, daring me to ask him another question. I felt the fire that had been banked by his mood change suddenly roar back to life.

"And you always do just what you want to?" I spoke before thinking, but I was still irritated with him, and at the same time envious. *What would it be like to live like that,* I wondered, *doing only as you wished, all the time?*

"Always." My question had been meant to provoke, but as Zach suddenly stepped toward me, I realized that I had pushed him in an unexpected way.

His eyes had darkened, and he looked like he was capable of devouring me. And even though all I had wanted for days now was to feel his hands on me, when he looked at me the way he was, I felt slightly—very slightly—afraid.

He closed his hand around the back of my neck and dipped his head. I closed my eyes, waiting for the kiss. Instead of the brush of his lips on my own, I felt the warmth of his breath as he whispered.

"Will you still stay the night?" My eyes flew open. His face was a study in seriousness, and I realized that the answer to this—my consent—was incredibly important to him.

Weighing my options, I let both the good angel and the bad berate me. Staying the night at some remote fortress of a mansion with an enigmatic stranger was not the brightest idea I'd ever had, and I was more than willing to admit it.

I also knew that if I said *no,* if Zach asked Charles to drive me home right then, I would regret it for the rest of my life.

"Yes."

Zach exhaled loudly at my simple word, and I realized that he had been holding his breath. Before I could contemplate what I had agreed to, he clasped his hands at my waist and lifted me.

"Zach!" I let out a very undignified squeal as my bottom made contact with the hood of his car. The metal beneath me was warm in parts, since we had just driven in it, and bitingly cool in others. The contrast seeped through the thin material of my skirt, teasing my skin with its warring effects.

"Lift your skirt." My mouth fell open at the order, but I did as I was told, remembering the feeling of his hands on my inner thighs. His stare fell on my parted lips, and with a growl he descended on them, his tongue immediately demanding entrance, then sweeping inside my mouth to claim.

"Oh." A breathy moan escaped my lips. One of his hands tangled in my hair, and the other slid down to my waist, then up and under the back of my blouse. My hips arched upward instinctively, and he nipped at my lips, sharply.

"I hadn't intended to do this just yet." With a final pinch of his teeth on my mouth, he drew back, breathing heavily, his gaze wandering up and down my body. "When I'm around you, I can't seem to help myself. It's a serious problem."

With his stare locked tightly with my own, Zach stood straight and undid his belt. Not bothering to pull the strip of leather from the loops of cloth, he undid the snap and then the zipper of his pants.

Heat flooded through me, a slow, wicked burn, when I saw that he wore nothing beneath them.

"Use your fingers. Hold your panties to one side." A shudder racked my body.

I had never been spoken to in this manner, never been treated like I was incredibly desirable.

I loved it.

I began to tremble when, opening my legs and drawing my knees up, I did as he asked, hooking a finger in the elastic of my panties and drawing them to one side. There was something thrilling about being fully clothed, yet exposing this most intimate part of my body.

Zach looked his fill at the neatly trimmed blond curls that I knew had been revealed.

"Shit." He muttered an oath at the sight, and then pulled a small foil packet from his pocket. Grasping the base of his cock with one large hand, he ripped into the foil with his teeth, shaking out the ring of latex before smoothing it down the length of his cock.

The sight of his long fingers on the engorged shaft had saliva pooling in my mouth. I wanted to demand that he come to me, right then—to order him to fill me, to fuck me hard.

I did none of that, instead watching wide-eyed as the magnificent creature approached me with a wild look in his eyes.

"I don't know what it is about you, Miss Reid." Releasing his cock, he slid one hand up and under the front of my blouse, finding and squeezing a nipple that was erect to the point of pain. I gasped, and as I did he took two fingers from his other hand and quickly slipped them inside of my slick heat, crooking them back toward himself in a quick succession of motion.

Those fingers brushed against something inside of me, something that was exquisitely sensitive. I cried out, then clapped a hand over my mouth.

"I want you to beg." Pulling his fingers back out, Zach positioned his cock at the entrance to my pussy. I wanted to slow down, to savor these amazing sensations, and at the same time I wanted him to fill me up so that I stopped feeling so damn empty.

"No." I shook my head and uttered the word in a whisper. As I did I looked over Zach's shoulder and caught sight of a bank of security cameras and a monitor not unlike the one in the lobby of Phyrefly.

"Oh." My body clenched, and I tried to close my legs. Was someone watching this? Charles? A maid? A butler?

Zach seemed like the type who just might have one of each.

He followed my stare, looking over his shoulders. When he turned back, his expression held just the slightest edge of delicious taunting.

"Do you like the idea that someone might watch us?" With a

very controlled motion of his hips, he pushed just the very tip of his cock inside of me. I arched my hips and cried out, wanting more, but he grabbed either side of my waist and held me still.

"Don't move until I tell you to." At that I uttered a soft whimper, my patience long gone.

He had teased me, tortured me, all day long. I wanted my reward for being good.

He waited for me to still. Impatient, my eyes flicked back to the monitor. I wasn't sure I would have liked someone right there in the garage watching us, but the idea that someone— anyone—could be watching a monitor like the one I could see made my pussy become even more slick.

"Look at you." I tried to turn back, to look at Zach, but he caught my chin in his fingers and forced me to look at the monitor. He turned his head, watching it, too, and we both saw our television images do the same.

"Look at that woman up there. She's the sexiest woman I've ever seen." I didn't for a moment believe that, but looking at the image—the length of my blond hair splayed over the sleek black surface of the car's hood, my legs wrapped around Zach—I felt wanton. I felt desirable.

I felt sexy.

"Please." I gave in. I just wanted him inside of me. Rocking my hips forward again, I groaned when he pulled back, the tip of his rock-hard cock slipping out from between the moist heat of my lower lips.

"Please what?" Placing one hand on my chest, flat between my breasts, he pushed lightly until I lay back on the car, my legs loosely wrapped around his hips. The metal was hard and un-yielding against my skin, and I stared with longing at the thick erection that Zach fisted, rubbing his hand up and down lightly.

"Please, Zach." Propping myself up on my elbows, I gave in to what he wanted . . . to whatever he wanted. "I . . . I want . . ."

Spit it out, Reid. The words stuck in my throat. I had no experience in talking dirty. But something told me that Zach wouldn't give even an inch—he wouldn't reward me until I'd told him what I wanted in plain terms.

"Please . . . please fuck me." I ducked my head, embarrassed.

All hints of discomfiture were shattered when Zach grabbed one of my hips in his hand and thrust inside of me in a long, hard plunge.

I gasped, crying out. My voice echoed off the plain plaster walls of the garage as he pulled nearly all the way back out and then seated himself inside of me again. There was nothing gentle in his actions, nothing kind. He was a predator who had cornered his prey.

I had never been so aroused.

"Move." I had started to arch my hips to meet him, then had stilled when I remembered his admonishment to do so. "Move however you want to, Devon."

His rough stroking had aroused me beyond thought. Throwing caution to the wind, I sat up, wrapped my arms around his chest and my legs around his waist, and met his thrusts with my own.

"Fuck." He growled when I scraped my nails down his back, through his jacket and shirt, frustrated that I couldn't find flesh. "Fuck!" His movements came faster and even harder, pounding into me with fury. I fisted my hands in his suit jacket, feeling the pressure within me finally, gloriously rising, bringing me close to the edge.

It wasn't enough. I wanted more. I wanted him to brand me with his body, to let me know that I was woman enough to make Zachariah St. Brenton lose control.

"Harder." I barely recognized my own voice, gone guttural with need. "Don't hold back."

Something wild flashed in Zach's eyes, and then, molding his hands to my ass, he lifted me right off of the car as he thrust in, so deeply that it hurt, but the hurt was so good. My ass slammed back down on the car as he pulled back, and then he lifted me up again.

"More!" Arching my body, throwing my head back, I let him pound into me again and again. I bit my lip until I tasted blood, desperate for release.

"Fuck!" My world shattered into a million brilliant pieces when he forced one hand between our straining bodies and rubbed his thumb over my clit. I shuddered against him, clinging to him with arms and legs, and felt him seat himself deeply inside of me and let go himself. He shouted as he came, his heat warming me from inside.

It was several long minutes before either of us so much as moved. When Zach finally stood, my front felt cold, protesting the removal of the heat from the solid body that had pressed me back into the car.

Despite the fact that my limbs were like jelly, I felt wariness steal over me when I noted that Zach wouldn't meet my eyes as he pulled a still-semi-erect cock from between my legs. Pulling the condom off, he tied a knot in the end and tossed it toward a trashcan that sat beneath the glaringly white security monitor.

As he stepped back, fastening his pants, I started to feel exposed—a ridiculous feeling, really, given what we had just done.

Regardless, I straightened my shirt, ran a hand over my tangled hair. As I smoothed my skirt over my hips, I noted that the elastic of my panties was stretched all to hell, and that they were soaked through.

Swallowing, I slid off the hood of the car. Well, what had I expected, coming here to have sex with my boss? That was exactly what had happened, and now I supposed that he was going to call Charles to drive me home.

Instead he offered me his hand formally, his expression guarded. Hesitantly I took it, flushing when I thought of how that hand had just touched me.

"Let's go have a drink," he offered, to my surprise.

CHAPTER SIX

was far too apprehensive to look at our surroundings in detail as I followed Zach into an elevator, up several floors, and then down a dim hallway. From the quick peeks that I made from my downcast eyes, I noted sleek, masculine decor, done by someone who had a flair for modern style and no taste for warmth. There were none of the touches that made a house a home—no flowers, no half-melted candles, no framed photos of family or friends anywhere that I could see.

I supposed I could have missed those touches, since I was so distracted. His lightning-quick mood swing hung in the air like a rain cloud pregnant with thunder. Our footsteps echoed off the walls and the ceiling, and though I had no idea what Charles or any of Zach's other staff did in their spare time, I had the impression that we were entirely alone in the house.

I tried to hold back the great lump in my throat as I followed Zach into a cavernously large room that opened off of the hallway. It, too, was dim, until he picked up a remote and, with a few punches of his fingers, brought a fireplace that was big enough to stand in roaring to life.

"Wow." I knew that it made me sound naive, but I found that I couldn't help it. I had been brought up in a household that had never wanted for anything, but as the harvest moon–tinged light of the fire lit up the room to life, I knew that I was seriously out of my league.

Zach either ignored me or didn't hear me, crossing the intricately tiled onyx and alabaster floor to a heavy wooden hutch that stood against a wall of smoky glass. To give myself something to do and to ease my nerves, I wandered across the room, letting my fingers trail over the butter-soft leather of a massive couch, the cashmere weave of an artfully placed throw, the slick glaze of an emerald vase that was likely worth more than my car. The flames cast everything into shadow, making it all look much more mysterious than it likely was, but it served as a reminder that I didn't know the first thing about the man who was now sloshing liquid of some sort into a glass.

Deliberately positioning myself so that my back was to him, I found myself facing a window that took up an entire wall. I had to step close to the icy sheet to see outside, since an indigo twilight had fallen, but when my eyes adjusted I let out a gasp.

The house itself jutted right out over the ocean. When I looked down, I saw jagged teeth carved from obsidian rock and the whipped-cream froth of the water as it thrashed against the cliff. My mouth fell open at the spectacular sight, which was both breathtaking and terrifying.

"It's why I built the house here." Zach's voice was quiet as he came to stand beside me. He pressed a short, heavy glass into my hand, and I noticed that he avoided touching my fingers with his own.

Just being near him was enough to set my nerves humming with anticipation, even as my mind frantically tried to keep up with his moods. The man was ridiculously confusing, and I was frustrated with myself for being so intrigued.

The silence stretched out as Zach sipped at his drink. I held mine up to eye level, taking note of the thick golden liquid pooled in the glass before sniffing at it. The fumes were potent, and I felt as if I had taken a sip without actually doing so.

My nerves stretched tight along with the silence. Helplessness began to poke its little fingers into my mind—why was I even here? It was torture.

No. Gritting my teeth, I reminded myself that I was no longer a doormat. I wanted to know why I was here, and I was damn well going to find out.

"What is this, Zach?" He looked at me sharply as I spoke, the flames of the fire reflected in his eyes. It made him look powerful and unearthly, like an angel who had fallen. It made my mouth dry, and so I hastily sipped at my drink, coughing when the alcohol fumes of what I recognized as cognac hit the back of my throat.

If he was amused by my gaffe, he didn't show it. Instead he kept his eyes fixed on me, and I shifted beneath the fierce stare.

"Devon, this isn't going to work."

I swallowed thickly, trying to ignore the fact that his words hit me as if someone had punched me in the stomach. It shouldn't have hurt so much—I barely knew the man.

I didn't know what to say, and so I bit my tongue and gulped again at my drink. The potent substance burned my tongue and my cheeks as it slid down my throat. Fortified with liquid courage, I lifted my eyes to his and held his gaze.

To my surprise, he seemed discomfited by my direct focus. He rolled his own glass between his palms, and we both watched the cognac splash against the slick sides.

"I asked you here tonight to discuss an . . . arrangement." That mask that he seemed to always have just under the surface slipped out, and he regarded me coolly. "An arrangement that's somewhat unorthodox."

"Unorthodox?" I had no delusions that he had been planning to ask me to wear his ring and go steady, but an arrangement sounded a bit more businesslike than what I had expected.

"It doesn't matter now. I won't ask you to make this commitment. It's not for you." I frowned, my forehead creasing with agitation.

"How do you know it's not for me if you don't ask?" My

words were quiet, but firm. I wanted to make my own decisions.

Exasperation washed over his face, and he raked a hand through that beautiful blue-black hair.

"Devon, you are nothing like the women that I usually bring into my life. What I wanted to ask of you . . . I would only be asking for selfish reasons." His expression dared me to argue with him. "I shouldn't have touched you at all. In fact, I didn't mean to."

"Then why did you?" Though I whispered, my voice sounded loud in the silence of the room.

"You tempt me." The way he looked at me as he said those words made me shift restlessly, my thighs rubbing together. "But no matter how much I want you, I have nothing to offer you."

"What have you offered to other women, then?" Anger was coiling in my belly. "Don't tell me you're chaste, because there's not a hope in hell that someone who looks like you do is perpetually single."

The ghost of a smile whispered over Zach's lips. "True enough. I have offered them pleasure. But it is a pleasure that someone as sweet as you won't understand."

Suddenly I felt enraged at his dismissal. Why them and not me? I knew that he wanted me, even now, after our explosive encounter in the garage—in the dim light of the room I could see the outline of his cock, erect again and pressing against the cloth of his trousers.

"And why won't you offer me the same thing?" Was I not wild enough? Not experienced enough? No matter how much bravado I tried to clutch to me like a hug, my ever-present insecurities reared their ugly heads.

Why was I not good enough?

"You don't fully understand what I'm saying." He looked as

if he were daring me to run, the corners of his lips curling up with a hint of mockery. "I don't care for vanilla sex."

Though I was taken aback by his words, I arched an eyebrow at his proclamation, trying to steady the rapid tattoo of my heart. I was feeling all kinds of things, some of which I didn't have names for, but I wasn't going to let him pull my strings as if I were his puppet.

I was through with going along with what others wanted, simply to keep the peace. I wanted—I craved—the ability to make a statement, to carve out my existence, just like the rocks outside had been worn smooth by the constant crash of the waves against them.

"You enjoyed vanilla sex just fine fifteen minutes ago." If the atmosphere in the room hadn't been so heated, I would have laughed as Zach's mouth dropped open, just the slightest bit, at my words.

I was quite certain that the other women he had brought into his life didn't make a habit of challenging him.

"Vanilla sex doesn't fulfill my need for control." Nerves skittered over my skin, and at the same time arousal wound its way through me in a sensual dance. "If you knew what I wanted to do to you, you would run screaming into the night."

"Show me." My tongue moved independently of the rest of me, and I spoke before I could think. "Show me what you want."

I held my breath, staring at Zach defiantly. I watched as he changed before my eyes. He seemed to become even larger in stature, more rigid and unyielding. His face was dark with lust, but also held a hint of cruelty.

The tiny part of my brain that was still capable of rational thought told me to run.

It was overruled by the rest of me, which found the dangerous man in front of me both exciting and arousing.

"You do not give me orders." Even his voice had changed, layered now with unyielding steel.

I inhaled sharply, wondering if I dared to reply. The hand holding my now-empty glass of cognac trembled, and I licked my lips.

"Then give me one." Tension was so thick in the room I could practically taste it, but it was a tension that was hot and sweet and seductive. "Tell me what you want me to do."

I wanted to do whatever he told me to do. I couldn't have said why, but I recognized it all the same.

Zach regarded me for a long moment, and under his stare I felt naked. Finally he nodded, and I was relieved, as if I had passed a test of some sort.

"At the end of this hall is a bedroom." Zach gestured with the hand not holding his glass, back toward the hallway from which we had entered this room. As he spoke, his eyes never left my own.

"Go into that bedroom. Comb your hair with the brush that you will find on the dresser, and then tie it back in a ponytail." My fingers strayed to the tangles of my hair, the ones that had come loose during our tryst in the garage. "When your hair is tidy, remove all of your clothing, except for your panties."

My nipples contracted to hard, tight points that rubbed against the fabric of my bra. My breath began to come faster. I knew I should rebel at the orders that he was throwing at me, but instead I found myself growing wet, soaking the thin cotton of my panties all over again.

"I will come to you in precisely ten minutes. When I enter that room, you will be kneeling on the floor at the foot of the bed." I nearly moaned—how was he making something that should have been unbearably bossy sound so delicious?

I wasn't given time to speak.

"Do not disappoint me."

Never before had ten minutes seemed to pass so slowly.

As I had been ordered, I had combed my hair, then pulled it back in the sleek ponytail that I wore most days. With trembling fingers I had unbuttoned my blouse, then unzipped my skirt.

Now I sat on my heels on the floor, naked but for the panties that had had quite an abusive day. The damp cotton pulled at my moist skin, and the slight chill in the room had gooseflesh prickling the skin of my arms.

I had never felt more nervous, or more exposed. Not knowing what to expect only aggravated the sensations.

Finally, *finally* the door that I had closed behind me opened. My body clenched, and I looked up with wide eyes as Zach entered the room.

"Lower your gaze to the floor." His words were harsh, but I heard the lust that was layered beneath them. I hesitated before obeying—I didn't want to look at the floor.

I wanted to look at him.

Sometime in the last ten minutes, he had shed his tie and his dress shirt. His chest was gloriously naked, and I was not happy that I wasn't permitted to look at it.

He had kept it covered during all of our encounters, and the quick glimpse that I'd had had shown me tawny skin pulled tight over rope after rope of hard muscle and dusted with soft whorls of dark hair.

"Keep your eyes on the floor." I stared at his ridiculously sexy bare feet as he came fully into the room. I heard the clink of ice against glass, and then the sharp click of glass against wood as he set a drink on the dresser, and then opened a drawer.

"You were ready when I came in. I am pleased." I watched his feet as he walked to me, then lost sight of them as he moved behind me.

Zach placed his hands on my shoulders, brushing the skin there lightly with his thumbs. Then something soft and silky was placed over my eyes, blocking my vision entirely, and I cried out, startled.

"Shh." Brushing the long wisps of my bangs back with one hand, he smoothed the silk over my temples. "You don't have to do anything that you don't want to do. You just say the word, and I'll stop."

I stayed tense as he snugged the silk to my head, tying a knot at the base of my neck, below my ponytail. When his hands wandered down to stroke the column of my neck and to dance over my naked shoulders, I relaxed, just the tiniest bit.

"What's the word?" I laughed weakly, trembling under his touch. His fingers stilled for a moment, and he murmured low in his throat, as if I had pleased him somehow.

"What would you like the word to be?" His fingers resumed their movement, sliding down my shoulders, my upper arms, then moving forward slightly to stroke the flesh at the sides of my breasts. "You choose a word, and it will be your safe word. Anytime I push you too far, you use that word and I will stop immediately, no questions asked."

Anytime he pushed me too hard. What could he possibly push me to do that I would need a safe word for?

Before I could overthink it, I clenched my fists, feeling my nails bite into the skin of my palms.

"Dark." My voice was hoarse and sounded like it belonged to someone else. "My word is 'dark.'"

Zach's hands cupped my breasts, weighing them. His thumbs stroked lightly over my distended nipples, and a jolt went through me, straight to my pussy.

"'Dark' it is." The soft strokes melted into a harder caress, with slightly more masculine force behind it. He rolled my flesh between his thumb and forefinger, and each movement seemed attached to a string that tugged at something deep inside of me. "Tell me why you chose this word."

I gasped as he tugged lightly at my nipples, wetness surging between my thighs in response. It was a long moment, and yet another tug, before I could find the words to answer.

"Because the first time I saw you, that was what I thought." I arched my back, pressing my breasts more fully into his hands. "I thought that everything about you was dark."

Zach's hands stilled, and then he removed them entirely. A chill hit my flesh at the loss of heat, and I swallowed a groan as I heard him stand.

I sensed him circle me once, slowly, and I felt his eyes on me, drinking in the sight of my naked flesh. I strained to see beneath the edges of the blindfold, but he had secured it so that my world was nothing but black.

He moved to stand in front of me. I held my breath.

The rasp of a zipper unlocking its metal teeth broke the silence in the room.

"Have you ever had a cock in your mouth, Devon?"

I should have been shocked at the brash question, but instead found myself shifting, rubbing my thighs together, feeling the pressure on my clit.

"Y-yes." The memories of the times that I had made me want to wrinkle my nose—not a single one of them had been pleasant for me.

Zach stepped closer and placed his palm flat on the back of my head. He pulled my cheek to the jut of his now-naked hip-bone, and I inhaled deeply, wanting to nuzzle into the flesh that smelled so deliciously of him.

"You are going to take my cock into your mouth, Devon." I

opened my mouth before he finished speaking, eager to please, and he chuckled.

"Not just yet." The muscles above his hip stretched tight as he leaned over. Seconds later I heard the clink of ice against glass again.

"Open your mouth." Eyes wide under the blindfold, I parted my lips. He pressed the glass against them, then tilted it so that the liquid—cognac again—flowed into my mouth.

"Don't swallow." I shuddered as the fumes hit the back of my throat, then gagged a bit with discomfort as a small wedge of ice lodged itself against the tender skin at the inside of my cheek. I felt the insides of my nose sting and my eyes begin to water as the potent alcohol pressed against my tongue.

"Now." Cupping my chin with his hand, he tilted my chin up, guiding me where he wanted me to go.

I felt the slick tip of his cock slide between my lips, and the slightest hint of salt mixed with the taste of the liquor.

"Ungh." I panicked momentarily, not sure that I could breathe. The fingers at the back of my head moved in a circle, caressing my hair soothingly. I felt myself relax into the touch.

"Now swallow." Zach pushed a fraction farther into my mouth as I inhaled deeply through my nose, then swallowed around his cock. The cognac burned my throat, and the ice stayed lodged between my cheek and his shaft, strange sensations all, but hearing his breath rasp in and then out had satisfaction flooding through me.

Zach was still inside of me for a long moment. Not sure of what he wanted me to do, I tentatively flicked my tongue over the head of his shaft, licking at the salt that I found there.

He hissed and pulled back until only the very tip was between my lips.

"Stay still." Both of his hands were fisted in my hair now,

and when he tugged at the length of my ponytail I found myself thrilling to the sharp sting.

"I'm going to fuck your mouth, Devon. I want you to stay just as you are while I do." His breathing was coming harder, and I loved that I was the one who had pulled the reaction from him. Feeling daring, I slipped my tongue out between my lips, sliding it down his shaft, dislodging the sliver of ice that remained.

He growled, tugging at my hair again in warning. I stilled, though inwardly I smiled.

"You won't be able to speak. If it becomes too much for you, I want you to give me the peace sign." He slid back and forth experimentally, just the tiniest bit, and I pressed my lips more tightly around him.

"Try to open your throat. I want you to take all of me." I wasn't sure what he meant until he pressed forward with his hips, sliding his shaft slowly into my mouth and beyond. I felt the head of his cock nudging at the back of my throat, and I tensed, gagging, again feeling that strange sensation of not being able to breathe.

He stilled, giving me a moment to adjust. After a long moment, I found that I didn't mind my mouth being filled with him in this way. To let him know that I was okay, I pressed my lips around the base of his shaft, tugging slightly.

"Stop that." He didn't sound displeased. Slowly, he pulled back out, and then I found myself shifting all of my focus to keeping my mouth and throat opened wide as he began to fuck me as promised.

He moved in and out, varying the depth and the firmness of his thrusts. I moaned around him, wanting to do more than be simply a receptacle, but every time I flicked my tongue over his flesh he pulled my hair, reminding me to do only as he said.

I narrowed my eyes at his order. I heard his breath come faster, but he didn't otherwise answer my unspoken plea for permission to please him.

Surely he wasn't going to complain if I went against his orders and did more with my mouth than open it?

Swallowing around the girth of his cock, I wrapped my lips more tightly around his shaft. Tracing my tongue along the ridge that bordered the head of his erection, I began to suck hard, hollowing my cheeks with every pull of my mouth.

"Devon!" My name was a gasp; I could hear both protest and hunger in his tone. "No . . . no!"

His movements at odds with his words, he thrust his hips forward into the hot, wet cavern of my mouth, then again, groaning.

Euphoria rushed through me as I realized how much satisfaction my mouth was giving him. Emboldened, I ran my teeth delicately under the head of his erection.

"Fuck!" With what seemed to be a supreme effort, Zach placed a hand on either side of my face, holding me still as he pulled back. His shaft left my mouth with a wet popping sound. Before I could even close my mouth Zach had lifted me by my elbows, pulling me to my feet.

Gently he slid a finger between the silk of the blindfold and my skin, tugging the fabric off of my head.

I blinked as my eyes were uncovered, the dim light seeming far brighter than it was.

When he caught my chin in his hand and forced me to look up, I could sense the force of his blue-eyed glower.

"I told you to stop." His voice was rough and firm.

What had I done? I had pleased him with my mouth—he couldn't deny that. And yet I felt as if I were in deep trouble somehow.

The sensation was a strange one to combine with the craving that I still felt for him.

"Do you know what happens when you disobey me?" Zach leaned in until his lips were a whisper from my own. I tilted my chin up farther, waiting for his kiss.

It didn't come. Instead strong arms were wrapped tightly around my waist. Zach sat on the bed, pulling me so that I sprawled over his lap. I let out an undignified squeak as he shifted back on the king-sized mattress, pulling me with him until my breasts pressed into the soft black cotton duvet on one side of his lap, and my knees on the other.

No. My breath caught in my throat as even my fairly chaste mind realized what he had positioned me for.

"Oh!" My cheeks flushed scarlet, and I wiggled in his lap, fully aware that I wore nothing but a pair of damp, sheer cotton panties.

Surely he didn't plan to . . . normal people didn't . . .

"I am going to spank you, Devon." He said it. He actually said it. My mouth fell open, and I squirmed on his lap.

He chuckled, the sound dark and sensual, and ran a hand over the mounds of my ass.

"This is what will happen to you when you disobey me in any way. Do you understand?" His hand on my ass stilled, and he seemed to be waiting for an answer.

I had so many thoughts running through my head, and yet nothing to say.

An undeniable thrill had coursed through me when he had told me what he was about to do, one that made my nipples tingle and my clit pulse with need. And yet . . .

"Remember, Devon, I'll stop whenever you tell me to." I opened my mouth to do just that, but the words wouldn't come.

Did I actually want to stop?

Zach continued, his hands again smoothing over the skin of my behind, stroking soothingly, as if he were gentling a skittish animal.

"I've asked you once before to forget about what you think you should say. Move past that, and think about what you truly want, right at this moment."

I sucked air in through clenched teeth. I knew my answer without having to think on it . . . Zach was entirely correct when he said that I was protesting because it was what I thought I *should* do.

I inhaled deeply and squeezed my eyes shut. I willed my body to relax in his lap, surrendering myself to his touch.

"You please me very much, Devon." His fingers strayed lower, tracing the crevice of my ass. Pinching the material of my panties in his fingers, he tugged at the cloth, creating a sudden and delicious pressure against my clit.

"Will it hurt?" I buried my face in my arms and the crisp cotton of the duvet as I spoke. Though I had admitted what I wanted, I still felt mortified.

"It will." Zach's voice held no trace of sympathy as I thought that it might. "But as you discovered in my office this afternoon, pain is often the gateway to much, much pleasure."

Without warning, his hand slapped down over the right cheek of my ass. My entire body jolted, tensing at the sting as I cried out loud.

The soothing circles of his touch returned, and I smelled the musk of wetness that flooded to my pussy even as I tried to regain control of my thoughts.

"If you want to say 'no,' do it now." Zach shifted underneath me, and I felt the impossibly hard ridge of his erection press into the soft flesh of my belly. I pressed down against it, and he warned me to stop with a sharp tap of his fingers, right over the juncture of my thighs.

"I thought that I could use my safe word?" My voice was breathless. I tried to hold still.

Dammit, I *wanted* that sharp sting on my ass.

Zach paused, and I could feel the darkness that descended upon him from time to time thickening the air around us. Finally he spoke, and he was as serious as I had ever heard him.

"You may use the safe word, and I will stop." Something in his tone told me that what he was saying was of great importance to him. "But I need you to understand that you can trust me. The entire point of all of this is for you to trust me. I will push you past your limits, and I will take you to places within yourself that you never knew existed. But to do that, *you must trust me.*"

I understood. If I used my safe words, this—whatever *this* was—was over.

I was terrified.

I wanted him anyway.

I found that my throat had dried up so that I couldn't speak. Instead I arched my back, raising my ass higher in surrender.

Zach's sharp intake of breath sounded loudly in the thick air of the room.

"I am going to give you twelve blows, six to each cheek." His voice was tense with excitement. I sucked in more air than my lungs could hold, nerves skittering over my skin.

Twelve blows? Surely that was excessive?

"One." Before I could argue or plead, the first blow landed on my right cheek, the sound of his open palm striking my flesh a crack as loud as thunder.

"Aah!" The skin where he had struck burned. I shifted awkwardly, uncomfortably aware of the discomfort.

"Two." His open hand landed on my other cheek. I cried out again as heat suffused my skin.

Three. Four. Nine. Ten. I counted each cry that I made as the blows fell, my skin burning hotter with every one. I thought that twelve would never come.

"Twelve!" I began to shake as he finished, not from an overdose of pain but from the onslaught of emotions that had overtaken me. I was embarrassed, and excited, and angry, and above all aroused. From above me I could hear Zach's breath, which was coming fast and heavy. I could feel his cock beneath me, and the unmistakable rigidity of his erection.

"Your ass is so pretty and pink right now." Inexplicably, my spirits lifted at Zach's praise. I had pleased him, and that in turn pleased me.

I began to squirm again, knowing that his eyes traveled over the blushing skin of my behind. The blows had reverberated through me, and I was wetter than I had ever been, desperate for his touch.

"Do you know why you needed to be spanked, Devon?" Catching my panties in his fingers again, Zach pulled lightly. I gasped as the material pressed tightly over my clit, which by that point was engorged and sensitive.

"Yes . . . no." He pulled again, this time sliding the material up and back. I gasped as it dragged along my clit, the crack of my ass, and then was pulled back the other way.

"Zach . . . please." I pressed against the mind-numbing sensation. When I moved greedily he stilled, and I could feel his stern disapproval.

"You're going to have to learn to trust me, Devon."

A sob caught in my throat. I had never been so overwhelmed, so full of need.

Only once I was again still did Zach resume his actions, tugging my panties this way and that, stimulating my clit and spreading the sensation all the way through to my other, forbidden entrance.

"I spanked you because you disobeyed me. You need to realize that when I give you an order, I have a reason." With one hand he continued to tug at the cloth of my panties, teasing my clit. The other nuzzled through the damp curls beneath the cotton and deftly parted my folds.

His finger slipped inside of me, sampling my heat. I choked on my moan as he began to move inside of me with that finger in the way I wished he would with his cock.

"You . . . seemed . . . to like it . . . at the time." I was panting, my body beginning to clench in anticipation of a delicious release that I had only ever experienced with him. As soon as I spoke, his fingers stilled.

"You have a smart mouth, my little minx." He withdrew his fingers completely.

I could have cried. I was beyond frustrated.

"I told you to hold still because I wanted to take care of your pleasure first." His voice was a quiet admonition, and his words made my heartbeat skip.

He sounded so matter-of-fact, his words so simple, that I felt foolish for my earlier actions.

"You must trust that when I give you a command, there is a reason behind it." One finger teased back underneath the elastic of my panties. Though I understood his words, and heard the importance in them, in that moment I would have done anything, said anything, to feel his touch.

"Now, do you agree to these terms, or shall I get the paddle so that we can discuss it some more?"

I squeaked again. Even though I heard the wry humor in his voice, I wasn't entirely sure that he was joking.

"I agree." My voice was soft, and as I spoke the words aloud, I felt my muscles go lax. It felt surprisingly good, this conscious decision to cede control to Zach, who so clearly wanted it.

Needed it.

"Devon." My name was whispered like a prayer. Clasping me around my breasts and behind my knees, Zach lifted me from his lap. Cradling me in his arms—arms that I couldn't help but notice were rippling with muscles as he carried me— he placed me back down on the bed on all fours.

"Don't move." The fabric beneath me was cool to the touch. I burrowed my cheek against its softness, suddenly shy and with no clue what to do next.

I felt the tickle of one finger, tracing down the length of my spine and into the cleft between my buttocks. A delicate, teasing touch smoothed over the heated skin of my ass. A finger ran underneath the elastic along either side of my bikini underwear.

Snap. One hard tug and the elastics snapped. I reared up, but Zach's hand on the small of my back pushed me gently back down.

"Hold still. *Feel*." With one hand on my belly, one on my back, Zach began to glide the fabric back and forth through my cleft. Without the elastic attaching the sides he could move it more freely, targeting every sweet spot between my legs, which he did without mercy.

The fabric caught, tugged, pulled at my sensitive flesh. My breath began to come faster, my heart beat to speed up. A flush of arousal settled over my entire body, and my hips began to rock in time with the movement.

"Come for me, Devon." I shivered all over, feeling something dark and needy coil low in my belly. Zach continued to manipulate my flesh with the taut fabric of the panties that he had torn right off of my body, and I pressed back against the pressure.

"Oh. Oh, I . . ." My words caught in my throat when the cloth pressed against the edge of my clit. The sharp, quick tug from Zach's deft touch made me cry out loud, and then the pressure that had coiled was springing free, flooding my body with bliss.

"Fuck." Dropping the panties, Zach's hands slid over my hips and up, cupping my breasts where my torso hung over the bed as I shivered. Clasping the nipples in his fingers, he pinched, adding another shock wave to my release. "You have the most beautiful fucking breasts, Devon. Everything about you is beautiful."

"What?" I couldn't think, wasn't sure that I had heard him properly. With another pinch to the erect peaks of my breasts, Zach moved back, climbing off the bed. I groaned, the edge taken off my hunger, but not even close to satiated.

I heard the rip of a condom wrapper, and then the drawn-out hiss of his breath as he rolled the latex over his length. I squeezed my eyes shut and pictured his talented fingers sliding down the length of his own cock, and felt my pussy clench in response.

"I want to be inside you." Standing behind me, Zach clasped my hips in his hands and drew me back until my ass was snug against his pelvis. I pressed back, savoring the sensation of his cooler skin against the fire of my bottom.

"I want you inside of me." Pressing my breasts against the bed, my palms flat on either side of my shoulders, I raised my ass up to give him easier access. "Please, Zach. Now."

"Look at that pretty cunt." Without warning, he bent and swiped a tongue through my wet folds. I moaned, wriggling to position myself closer.

"I want to bury my face between your thighs, little minx. I want to savor the taste of you." His breathing was ragged as he stood. Parting the cheeks of my ass with his hands, his cock slid through the division of my ass; then he positioned himself at the slick entrance to my pussy.

"I'm too eager to be inside of you to take my time right now. But soon I'll fuck you with my mouth, with my tongue." I had never been spoken to like this, never been treated as if my body was something that could so delight another person.

I thrilled to it.

I loved it.

"Brace yourself." I had a moment to remember that he wasn't gentle, and then he was balls deep inside of me, his length and girth stretching me to the point of pain.

"Fuck!" I had cursed more since meeting Zach than I ever had in my life. There was no other word to describe the sensation of being filled so deeply.

"Devon." My name was spoken gutturally, and I reveled in it. I fisted my fingers in the bedding as Zach pulled nearly all the way out of me, and then slammed back in, demanding that I take him entirely.

"You're so fucking tight."

I groaned and pushed back against him. He was right—I was tight, and he was large, larger than I could comfortably fit inside of me. I found that the edge of pain that sliced through me as he seated himself again and again, demanding that I open to him, was surprisingly delicious.

"More." My vision blurred, and my world narrowed until all I was aware of was the sensation of his body, riding inside of mine. "I want more."

"Devon." This time my name was an oath, and I again felt that I had done something to please him. He began to move faster, slamming himself into me again and again, the heavy weight of his testicles colliding with the still-heated skin of my ass with every thrust.

"I'm going to come." He moved faster, harder. My pussy was burning, clenching—I wanted more.

"Yes!" I wanted it all. Need pulled my skin tight.

"Get on your knees."

I obeyed without thought. Zach clasped me around the waist, one arm banded over my belly, holding me tightly to him, my back to his front. His other hand slid over my hips, between my legs. Slowly, still thrusting inside of me, he worked one finger along the edge of his cock, working it inside of me, making my pussy burn.

"Oh. Oh!" I was full, so full—full of him. Widening my legs to take as much as I could, I bent at the waist, bracing my palms on the mattress. Zach still held me around the waist, but now he worked his finger in and out with the thrusts of his cock, his knuckle rubbing against my clit with every plunge.

Though I had already come, the sensations assaulted me, and I ricocheted off the edge of release yet again, crying out loud and not caring who heard.

As my impossibly full pussy spasmed around him, Zach seated himself inside of me, as deeply as he could go. I tried to push my legs even farther apart, giving him access to my very core as his body was racked with pleasure and his heat warmed me inside.

"Devon." He buried his face in my hair, and his voice was very nearly desperate. "Perfect."

Even through the aftershocks of my climax, I felt myself tremble at his words.

I had never felt perfect. Not even close.

His orgasm finally receding, Zach stilled, holding me tightly against him. I savored the sensation, the heat, until I felt his release, combined with my own, begin to trickle down the insides of my thighs.

"Lie down." Gently he pulled out of me, and I winced, though it wasn't the discomfort I minded as much as the feeling of emptiness. I did as he told me, curling into the fetal position, my head on a pillow. I watched through heavy eyes as he moved into what looked to be a bathroom, holding the used condom to his cock.

I couldn't help but lick my lips at my first view of his naked, hard, perfectly muscled ass.

His bare feet made soft noises as he padded about on the tile. The toilet flushed—he had disposed of the condom. The faucet turned on, and then he returned, moving toward the bed where I was curled, with a white cloth in his hand.

"Lie back." Suddenly shy again, I rolled onto my back, knowing that he would be content with nothing else. Still, I felt exposed—vulnerable, even.

It was a strange time for me to feel that way, after what I had just let the man do to my body.

Zach pressed the cloth to my cheek. It was warm and wet. He massaged it over my cheeks, my lips, and the heat helped to ease the ache in my jaw from having him thrust so hard inside of my mouth. "You did so very well."

I didn't know what I had done, besides give him access to my body, but nonetheless the praise buoyed me up, as did the near-reverent expression on his face as he massaged the cloth down over my torso.

When he reached the skin of my labia and began to clean me I hissed, sore from his attentions.

"Hold still." He pressed more firmly, and the sting dissipated as the warm cloth soothed my abused flesh.

The skin that he had dampened cooled in the air when he returned the cloth to the bathroom. I sat up, clutching my knees to my chest in an attempt to ward off the chill.

Zach sat on the edge of the bed when he returned, staring down at me. Those cerulean eyes of his seemed to hold so many intense emotions, but I couldn't read a single one of them.

What did we do now? I had no experience in this sort of thing. Tom and I had dated for months before we'd been intimate, and an adult sleepover was expected by that point in our relationship.

Zach had asked me to spend the night.

But we'd also argued.

I was the first woman that he had brought to this house.

"Is it . . . may I . . . should I stay?" It was ridiculous to be so awkward with someone who had just played my flesh like a virtuoso, but I felt that I couldn't just assume, no matter how we desired each other.

It reminded me that no matter how well this man now knew my body, he was still a virtual stranger to me.

"Yes." He paused before speaking any further. I watched as he pulled back the duvet and the flat sheet of the immaculately made bed and slid beneath the covers, somewhat discomfited by the awkwardness he displayed.

This was Zachariah St. Brenton, the control-freak billionaire. He was supposed to know what to do, all the time.

He held up the covers, gesturing for me to clamber beneath them. I balked for a moment—it was so strange to be in bed nude. I slept in baggy T-shirts and flannel pajama bottoms, as a rule.

Well, we were both uncomfortable then.

I settled back on the pillow. I was hyperaware of Zach beside me, both of us staring at the ceiling, not touching.

This was ridiculous. He had just been inside of me.

Going with my gut, I curled onto my side, shuffling over until my head rested on his shoulder. He stiffened for a moment with surprise, then wrapped one arm around me, seeming to relax into the embrace.

In the now-dark room, I smiled. I inhaled deeply, enjoying the scent of myself on his skin.

"Good night, Devon." I thought back over my day briefly, wondering if I would wake up and find that it had all been a dream.

At that moment, I didn't care. I snuggled in, drawing warmth from his embrace.

CHAPTER SEVEN

couldn't sleep.

When I had first rolled into his arms, Zach had been stiff and as uncertain as I was. I knew he wasn't in the habit of asking the women he entertained to sleep in his bed with him. The tension soon melted from the arms that held me, though, and it was mere minutes before he sighed into the strands of my hair and fell into sleep.

It was hours later now, and sleep still eluded me. It made me unaccountably happy to be nestled in his arms as he breathed evenly beside me, but I just wasn't used to being skin to skin with someone as I tried to sleep. Tom had rarely been happy with the prospect of my staying over, and I hadn't been brave enough to press the issue. Now I found that even though it was Zach's bed that I was in, I was jealous of my own personal space.

Besides, I was too hot, pressed right up against him as I was, and I had to pee.

Rolling onto my back, I looked at the iridescent blue numbers of the clock mounted on the wall across the room. At first I thought that the clock was mocking me, but I blinked several times to clear the sleep from my eyes and found that the number didn't change.

It was four thirteen in the morning. I groaned as I realized that I had to work that day. A frisson of uncertainty snaked through me when I realized that I still had to shower and get ready for work . . . and I had to go home first to do it. I could call a cab, I supposed . . . except that I wasn't entirely sure of where I was.

It was a really good thing that so far Zach didn't seem to be an axe murderer, because I kept making ill-advised decisions around him.

Sighing, I shifted slowly, trying to extricate myself from Zach's embrace. He rolled over and moaned when I slipped out of his arms. I was tempted to smooth the furrows from his forehead with my hand. They were at war with the otherwise peaceful expression on his face.

The enigmatic billionaire seemed much more vulnerable in sleep . . . much more human. It was strange to be a witness to it.

My bladder again called, and I shuffled off to the bathroom. I took care of my personal business before standing and taking a good look around the room with tired eyes.

My stomach did a slow roll as I surveyed a bathroom more opulent than anything I could ever have dreamt up. I had known Zach was rich, had heard the term 'billionaire' applied to him, but . . . wow.

It was slightly amusing that it had taken a bathroom for me to fully understand how wealthy the man who had been inside of me only hours earlier was.

Uneasy and in awe, I circled the room. The floor was made of tiled river rock trapped in a clear, thick varnish. Warmth seeped from the surface into my chilled toes as I wiggled them. The floor seemed to heat beneath me as I walked, cooling where I had already been, and I assumed that it was controlled by some kind of motion sensor or weight detector.

I had never even heard of such a thing, and I had grown up in a family that was well-off. The realization had me staring down at the beautiful floor, at the pale white of my skin against it.

My life was so incredibly different from Zach's. I didn't know what, exactly, there was between us, but whatever the term, I knew in that moment that it couldn't last. Our lives were so different.

I was way out of my league.

Feeling slightly sick, I shook my head to rid myself of the depressing thought. Since I was up, I decided to take a shower—I would bathe, then dress in the clothes that I'd worn the day before. Well, minus my now-shredded bikini panties. By then perhaps I could find Charles, and be driven back to my hotel room to change.

Even if Zach had been taken out of the equation entirely, I really liked my new job. I liked the city of San Francisco. I was fairly certain that I wanted to stay, wanted to find a home here, and to do that I had to be ready to work, even if the big boss himself would know I hadn't exactly spent a restful evening alone.

The innermost part of me didn't want to leave. I wanted to bathe my sore muscles in hot water, and then return to Zach's bed and the protection of his arms.

But I knew I was already feeling more gushy emotions than was wise. A man who could afford a house like this, who owned a corporation like Phyrefly, wasn't going to have any feelings for me anywhere outside of the bedroom.

I began to shiver, despite the heat from the tiles at my feet. Padding across the floor to the shower, I slid open the clear glass door and stepped inside the walls that could have comfortably enclosed a horse, or maybe even two.

Wow. I turned in a slow circle, surveying the shower that was bigger than my hotel room. The very air itself seemed to echo off the cavernous space.

I tilted my head up, and saw not one, but four, showerheads that were bigger than dinner plates. I thought of the measly spray from the rusted head back in my hotel room, and my sore body clenched in anticipation of the rainfall of warm water. It might have been shallow, but I thoroughly appreciated Zach's wealth, or at least his taste in bathrooms, as I bent to turn the shower on.

The only thing that would make it better would be if he were to join me.

Though the idea made my pussy clench, I thought better about waking him up and inviting him to a shower for two. His mood swings were varied enough that, tender as he had been the night before, I wasn't certain which side of Zach revealed his true nature.

Scowling now, I reached for the knobs of the shower only to discover that there weren't any. Confused, I looked up and down and found nothing but a control panel of buttons.

They weren't labeled. I picked one at random and jabbed at it. I jumped when, a moment later, a glass-covered fireplace roared to life at the back of the stall.

My mouth fell fully open as I stared. The man had a *fireplace* in his shower. Well and truly unnerved, I hit the fireplace button again, quieting the flames, before scurrying out of the stall altogether.

My sore body protested.

"Dammit." I furrowed my brow at the shower, then turned toward the bathtub. It was the size of a small lap swimming pool, and appeared to be carved out of some kind of silvery gray rock. There were steps leading down into it.

Apart from the size and extravagance of it, though, it seemed to be nothing more than a bathtub. I was fairly confident that I wasn't going to be unnerved by a fireplace in its depths.

Perching on the edge of the tub, I turned the hot faucet all the way, and the cold a half turn. The cool stone nipped at my buttocks as I waited for the tub to fill, my knees clenched to my chest.

When I looked up from the swirling, crystal water I was confronted with the same visual that had blown me away the night before. The bathroom jutted out over the ocean, giving me the impression that I would be bathing in the blue-gray water of the sea.

I stared out the wall of glass as I sank into the tub, my eyes wide with wonder.

The heat felt wonderful, though I hissed when the tender flesh between my legs was submerged. Zach hadn't been gentle, and though I'd loved it, I was incredibly sore this morning.

Memories of how he had handled my body made me flush all over. Despite the warmth of the water, I shivered.

No matter what the rational part of my brain told me, no matter that we'd been together only hours ago, I wanted him with a ferocity that I hadn't known I was capable of.

I couldn't do this again. Shouldn't do it again. Wincing as the thought pained me, I reached for the bottle of body wash that sat on the edge of the tub, and began to hastily wash myself.

The soap smelled like Zach.

Scrubbing it through the long strands of my hair, I leaned back to rinse it away. Even stretched out lengthwise in the bath, it was so big that I couldn't touch the sides. I floated for a moment, enjoying the way the warm water buoyed me up when my thoughts wanted to weigh me down.

Sitting up, I slicked my dripping hair from my face. At first I thought the sound was just my sense of hearing readjusting after my ears had been submerged in the bath.

"No! No!" The words sounded almost strangled, like they were wrenched from someone's chest.

I straightened, my body suddenly tense. My senses weren't playing tricks on me . . . what I heard was Zach, in the throes of what sounded like a terrible nightmare.

"Slower . . . go slower . . ."

My heart ached as I clambered out of the tub, water sluicing off my naked flesh in streams. I had had nightmares myself for a long time after my parents' death. I still did once in a while. I knew how very real they could seem, even after waking.

The sounds from the other room quieted, and I was relieved. Still, I groped for a towel. I'd decided to just go check on him before I got dressed.

Though I didn't know him well, I knew that Zach wouldn't thank me for catching him at such a vulnerable moment, no matter what it was that he was dreaming about. But I also knew that being alone when horrific images were playing in your mind like a movie could make a person sick.

I heard a rustle, the sound of a body shifting over bedsprings, and then the padding of feet over carpet. He was awake.

My concern swung from wanting to make sure that he was okay to trepidation.

I'd never had a morning after quite like this one.

The heavy wooden door opened, and Zach burst into the room. He was still fully naked, and I could see that every muscle in his big body was tensed as if anticipating a blow.

One look at him told me that he wasn't fully awake yet—his eyes were open, but they searched the room as if he had never seen it before. I stood, mouth agape, uncertainty playing over my features as his stare roamed the room, finally settling on me. I felt as though that stare sliced right through me, a hot knife through soft butter, as he glowered at my naked, shivering self.

"Are you okay?" He blinked, clearly trying to focus on me through the haze of sleep that still fogged his consciousness. Though he had seen every part of me the night before, I felt so exposed, wishing that I had had the time to pull a soft bath sheet to me, to hide my nakedness.

Zach's eyes narrowed as I watched him, wide-eyed, and he looked furious. I didn't know what I had done to provoke him, if anything—I couldn't tell if the nightmare was still clinging to him, like a sticky spider's web—couldn't tell if this was his reality, or if he was still caught in the dream.

Crossing the room in three long strides, he caught me by the shoulders and shook me. As his fingers dug into my shoulder blades, the fury was still apparent on his face, but it was mixed with the slightest hint of confusion. My heart melted, even as nerves skittered through my veins.

A clammy chill settled over me when he finally spoke, his voice still husky from sleep.

"What the fuck are you doing here?"

PART III

TEMPTED TO OBEY

CHAPTER EIGHT

"Are you awake now?" I sat on the edge of Zach's massive bed, my fingers fisted in the cool fabric of his sheets. The way they were tangled over the massive mattress spoke volumes about the nightmare that still clung to him with dark tendrils.

Though my entire being shied away from the thought, I recognized the blackness that hung around him like a shroud. It took me right back to those awful first months after I had lost my parents. Zach's grief, though he refused to share it with me, opened the wound back up like the slice of a scalding knife.

That, though, was the entire reason I had forced myself to stay, to move past the sensation of his fingers digging into my arms, of the fear I had felt when he had looked into my eyes and not recognized me.

I understood. I suspected that many of the people who surrounded him didn't . . . and that was if they even bothered to look closely enough.

"I'm awake now." Zach's eyes, though now free of the fog of sleep, were shadowed with the ghost of something painful. He stood facing me, naked and completely unself-conscious about it. Those eyes were unreadable as they raked over my face.

Though I was wrapped in a soft towel that covered me from shoulders to knees, my damp hair and the rivulets of water that clung to my skin made me shiver. I felt exposed under the intensity of his stare, even though I was covered and Zach was not.

I was entirely out of my element. For years now I had become accustomed to burying every emotion that I had, not having the strength to deal with them. Because of that, I was rusty at handling the onslaught of sensations that this man was continually sending my way.

"Devon." Bending at the waist, he tangled his hands in my hair, tugging just hard enough to awaken the nerves that ran over my scalp. I hissed at the seconds of pain I felt, then found my protest swallowed when Zach took my mouth with his own.

"Zach!" My head swam as he kissed me with a fervor that said he would die if he didn't have me right then and right there. For a moment I held still, frozen in place, still disconcerted by the morning but not wanting to reject him.

The way his lips slanted over my own, the slight pain from the tugs on my hair, broke through my uncertainty, shattering it like a pane of glass. Responding to the heated need that was emanating from him in storm-sized waves, I dug my fingers into his broad shoulders and pulled him closer, opening my mouth eagerly for his tongue.

A sound of approval rumbled through his throat. Removing one hand from my hair, he parted my knees and slid his hand up the insides of my thighs, which were naked beneath the plush towel. He moved swiftly to the heat of my pussy, which was already wet with want.

He slid one finger inside of me without warning, and I cried out against his lips. My mind went blissfully blank as my hips moved, trying to get closer to him.

When he abruptly broke the kiss and moved away, I shivered at the cool touch of the air where the raging inferno of his body had been. I watched, the air in the room thick with silence as Zach padded across the plush carpeting to his dresser. His entire body, in all of its muscular glory, was exposed to my gaze, and I drank in the sight.

Opening and shutting the top drawer, Zach pulled an object from its depths. When he turned and the long coil of braided leather fell from his hand to the floor, my stomach clenched.

"Zach . . ." I was not in the mood for play. Though he had apologized, albeit stiffly, for grabbing my arms, and though I truly believed that he had been asleep still and hadn't recognized me, the intimacy of the night before was gone.

I didn't think that he would hurt me—in my very core, I believed this. But the darkness that shrouded him as he moved to stand directly in front of me sent shivers dancing over my skin.

I opened my mouth to say something, and was startled into silence when Zach put the whip into my hands. The leather of the handle was cool against the clammy skin of my palm.

I tilted my head and peered up at him with wide eyes.

"I want you to whip me." I heard the dominance that he had shown me a taste of the night before, but it was twined with a thread of grief so deep that he seemed to choke on it. When my eyes met his, I saw that agony threatening to overwhelm the big, beautiful creature in front of me.

Under my searching gaze, Zach's face became shuttered. He replaced anguish with arrogance and authority.

"I told you to whip me." His voice was like a whip itself, lashing against my bare skin.

I swallowed hard. Part of me was drawn to what he represented in that moment, pain and dark clouds bound up together with pleasure. I wasn't sure that I liked being drawn to the darkness, especially not right then.

Everything in me wanted to please this man . . . but I didn't feel that a whipping would ultimately bring him pleasure.

"Devon." Dominant Zach faltered for a moment, allowing

me a glimpse into his nightmares. What I saw there—pain and agony swimming up from the dark depths of his eyes—made pity roll through my gut.

He was asking me to help alleviate his pain, though I didn't quite understand how whipping him would do so.

Still, how could I possibly say no to this man, when he had already brought so much to my life?

Biting my lip until the taste of blood spread out over my tongue, I wrestled with the decision in my head, though I ultimately knew what I was going to do. At my core, I wanted to obey and please him. Was even excited by the idea.

I just wished I had assurance that striking him would bring him peace.

Cringing inwardly, I lifted my head and held out the whip. "You'll have to show me how."

His breath rasped out of his lungs in a harsh burst, and I realized that, dominant or not, he was as uncertain about this as I was.

Uncertain, but still aroused. As he reached out for me, helped me off the bed, his cock hardened swiftly. The hot silk of it brushed my hip through the gap in my towel, and as conflicted as I was in that moment, everything in me tightened with desire at his touch.

"Like this." Pulling me against him, my back to his front, he helped me position the handle of the whip in my hand and covered my fingers with his own. "The power comes from your body, not your arm or your wrist."

Lifting our twined arms, he brought them down swiftly, and I felt the ripples through the muscles of his torso. The braided leather of the long, serpentine whip carved through air that was thick with tension, its harsh crack muffled only somewhat by the soft carpet that it bit into.

Air left my lungs in a heated rush; my nipples tightened,

and moisture slicked my inner thighs. I was still so uncertain, but at the same time I saw with startling clarity the relationship between pleasure and pain. Wielding the whip felt powerful, decadent. Dangerous.

What would it feel like to stripe skin with the scarlet kiss of the leather? Or to feel that touch, myself?

Every person that I knew in my old life would have been appalled by how much I was drawn to the idea. I battled with the shame, myself. I knew that my participation was mostly for Zach, but I couldn't sort out in my brain what was drawing me in otherwise, like a moth to brilliant flame.

Trying to clear my mind, I breathed in, then out. With wide eyes I twisted and looked up at Zach. The pain was still there in his eyes, but so was hunger—hunger for me.

"Again." He rasped the word out hoarsely, lifting my arm with his, swinging them together. It cracked against the floor again, and then again.

My breathing became faster, and I pressed back against him, craving his heat. After three practice lashes, Zach tenderly untangled his fingers from my own and stepped back, leaving the whip trailing from my hand.

With one finger he traced a warm path from the nape of my neck and down to where my skin met the edge of the plush towel. Inserting a finger between the cloth and my back, he tugged gently and the towel tumbled to the floor around my ankles.

He continued to trace the path down, his finger sliding over the contours of my body, all the way into the cleft that divided my buttocks. My mouth was dry, and my tight grip around the handle of the whip became damp with sweat.

"You're ready." I inhaled sharply when his finger moved swiftly down the entire length of my cleft until it pressed against the engorged nub of my clit. My hips pressed against his touch instinctively.

He moved in front of me, and I shivered at the loss of his heat against my back. Striding to the large wooden chest of drawers from which he had removed the whip, he placed his palms flat on its varnished surface and bent at the waist, allowing me full access to feast upon the hard planes of his shoulder blades and back, narrow waist, the lean hips and taut ass.

Although the erotic encounter had aroused me, I didn't want to mar his burnished skin, and hesitated to lift the whip.

"Devon. Now." Even when he was bent in supplication, his voice was layered with dominance, and I itched to obey. "You won't hurt me."

I would hurt him, though, and that was what he was counting on. I blinked, my vision clearing as my hand faltered before I lifted the whip even halfway.

He was asking me to do this because he wanted to be punished, punished for whatever demons had danced through his dreams.

I couldn't, not when he was clearly unwilling to share those demons with me. This was not how I longed to help him.

More so, I wouldn't. Though I had only begun to know myself, I knew that I couldn't be a party to this.

"No, Zach." I extended the hand holding the whip. It was a beautiful instrument, long and sleek, the color of warm brandy. It enticed me, it aroused me, but the thought of using it on Zach made me sick.

Turning slowly, Zach scowled at my outstretched hand.

"Are you defying my order?" I might have quaked, had I not seen those shadows still playing over his face. He hid them well, but they were there, barely discernible to the naked eye.

"This order doesn't have anything to do with me or with sex, Zach." Pain clutched at my own heart as I spoke. His eyes narrowed, he took the whip from me, his body stiff with anger.

It was over. I knew that he wouldn't tolerate the disobedience, or, perhaps more accurately, the fact that I had seen a glimpse of his vulnerability. I didn't have a chance.

It shouldn't have hurt so very badly after being with him such a short time, but it did.

"You don't know a thing about me, little girl." The words were meant to be cruel—and they struck home. Emotionally I was reeling from the blow, but I lifted my chin and looked at him straight on.

I wasn't going to make it easy.

"I need to get ready for work." The tension of the moment was broken, but only on the surface. Zach moved toward the bathroom, his movements casual and arrogant. "There is a spare room next to this one. Your things are in there." He closed the bathroom door, shutting me out.

The king of his castle, dismissing his cheap whore.

I wanted to cry. Even knowing that this wasn't about me, not really, I felt sick.

Well, what had I expected? I barely knew the man, and he didn't know me any better. It had been foolish of me to expect his confidences.

No matter how right it felt when we were together. I stared down at the whip in my hand, the gorgeous swath of leather, then threw it onto the bed as if it were burning my palm.

I never wanted to see the thing again.

From the bathroom I heard the sound of the shower turn on. Shaking and unnerved, I surveyed the room for my clothes. They were nowhere to be found—that had been what he'd meant when he'd said my things were in the next room.

Fine. I'd walk down the hall in my towel, no matter how uncomfortable that made me. I didn't have another choice, after all. I stooped and picked it up off the floor, wrapping the towel around me again and cinching it tightly across my breasts.

I drew comfort from its soft warmth, though it didn't do much to ease my chill.

I shrieked when I opened the door to the bedroom and found Charles on the other side, his hand poised to knock. I clutched the towel to my breasts, waiting for the older man to turn away in embarrassment, as I did.

He didn't. He looked me in the face without a trace of the mortification that I was feeling. His scrutiny made my skin flush the color of red wine.

"Good morning, Miss Reid. If you'll follow me, I will take you to your room." *My* room? Surely that had been a slip of the tongue. I frowned as Charles turned away from me, his manner the same as it would have been if I were fully clothed.

He seemed awfully good at this. Perhaps he was used to leading half-naked women around Zach's mansion. The thought had a scowl furrowing my brow.

"This way please, Miss Reid." Charles opened a door that lay halfway down the wide hallway. The first signs of pale morning light were beginning to filter through the vaulted skylights, and when I looked down, I saw that the skin of my legs was very white in the watery light.

"Thank you ... um, Charles." Clutching my towel ever more tightly to my chest, I slipped past the man and into a bedroom that wasn't nearly as massive as the master one, but was still much larger than my hotel room. A pile of neatly folded clothing lay on the large iron bed that was draped in an expensive-looking charcoal satin quilt.

Swallowing my modesty, I turned back to the stern man who still stood in the arched doorway.

"Charles, if you could give me a minute to dress, do you think you could please take me back to my hotel?" I winced as I spoke—the fact that I was still living in a hotel sounded so tawdry. I needed to remedy that, and soon.

That is, if I stayed in San Francisco. I was paid well at Phyre-fly, but after fucking my boss, was my job secure?

I thought I saw a flicker of pity flash over the man's nor-mally stoic face, and then he shook his head slowly. He stood so rigidly that not a single other part of his body shifted when he moved his head.

"I'm sorry, Miss Reid. Mr. St. Brenton has left orders for you to dress and eat, and then you are to travel with him to the of-fice." My mouth fell open slightly.

He had left orders, had he? When, and how? Had he called from the bathroom, after insinuating that he wanted nothing more to do with me?

Did he really dare to expect me to listen to him, after how he had just treated me?

"Thank you, Charles." I tried to suppress the sparks of anger that ignited my voice—it wasn't this man's fault, after all. No, my current anger was directed solely at the thickheaded man who was showering in the ostentatious barn of a bathroom.

"I'll get dressed. I don't usually eat breakfast, so I hope you haven't gone to much trouble. I don't think I'll be making an ex-ception today." I saw the corners of Charles's mouth quiver, and drew my eyebrows together in irritation. I thought that he might be about to chastise me, but then I realized that he seemed amused—yes, very slightly amused.

Well, then. Perhaps people didn't often make a habit of challenging Zachariah St. Brenton's orders.

Thinking back to the visual of him leaning against his dresser, commanding even as he offered himself up, I realized that a strong, proud man had relinquished his power to me. And I had shoved it back at him, knowing that I didn't have it in me to cause him pain.

I had nothing left to lose.

"After I dress I'll go wait at the door to the garage." Well, I would if I could find it. Regardless, I wasn't going to suffer through an awkward meal, whether Zach was present or not. I couldn't picture sitting next to the man who had placed a whip in my hand, neither of us speaking, as we ate pancakes and scrambled eggs.

"Very well, Miss Reid." The amusement had been banked by the time Charles left the room and shut the door behind him. Finally alone, I closed my eyes for a long moment and pressed my fingers to my throbbing temples.

Even if Charles wouldn't go against Zach's orders and drive me back to the hotel, I was sure that I could have convinced him to at least call me a cab. He struck me as the type of man who would be a sucker for a damsel in distress, and I was feeling very distressed, indeed.

But there was one thought that held me back from calling out to him. If I had Charles call me a cab, then this—whatever "this" was between Zach and me—was truly over.

It was cowardly, but I wasn't sure that I was ready to face that. Pain ripped through my heart when I thought of how coldly Zach had left me alone in his room. He might have already made the decision for me.

I sighed shakily. This intense spectrum of emotion was exhausting. Letting the towel drop to the floor, I reached for the clothes that were folded so neatly. I frowned when I realized that they weren't mine.

Instead of the floaty ebony skirt and matching blouse that I had been wearing the day before, I found a pair of sleek black dress pants, an incredibly soft cardigan, and matching shell. The pants looked expensive, and the sweater set was pure, luxurious cashmere.

Squeezing my eyes shut against the migraine that suddenly threatened, I tried to process the fact that there were shoes as well—black pumps with a high, sexy heel.

He hadn't forgotten the underwear, either, ever so thoughtfully providing a pair of sheer bikini panties and a matching lace-edged bra, also colored in my favorite raven black.

Zach had been with me since we'd entered his house last night, so he had sent someone—probably Charles—to buy me new clothes. While it was thoughtful, it was also horrifically embarrassing.

Someone else had selected my underwear. This just wasn't something that I was prepared for. The thought of stoic Charles, with his bulging muscles and buzz cut, sifting through a rack of ladies' panties, had me swallowing back a laugh that was tinged with hysteria.

Ridiculous. This was all just insane. How on earth had I found myself here?

I thought of barging back into the master bedroom, of demanding to know where my own clothes were—my affordable, sensible clothes.

I . . . couldn't do it. No matter how bad the scene in Zach's bedroom had been, the fact that he had thought to save me from the morning-after walk of shame was a sweet gesture. I couldn't find it in myself to throw it back in his face, no matter how angry I was with him.

And as I swallowed my pride and dressed in the clothes, I had to note that they fit me better than my own had, almost as if they had been made for me, or had at least been tailored to my specifications. They were also a much finer quality than anything I could afford. I tried to ignore the designer name stitched into the sole of the pump, because if I let myself think about it, I'd choke on the amount that they must have cost.

The clothing was all black, something else that didn't escape my notice.

Someone was paying attention.

I found an array of cosmetics in the en suite bathroom, everything from deodorant to mascara to perfume. Everything was still in its packaging.

They were all the brands that I used, even the toothbrush, an exact duplicate of the one on my hotel room counter, bright pink color and all.

A gnawing sensation made its presence known in the pit of my stomach as I slapped on a minimal amount of makeup, just enough to help diminish the dark circles in the thin, ghostly skin under my eyes. I pulled my damp, bedraggled hair back into a ponytail, tucking the wisps that wouldn't be tamed behind my ears. I couldn't reconcile the man who would take the time to find out what kind of lip balm I preferred with the specter who had handed me a whip. And neither of those images would merge at all with the dominating creature who had enthralled me since the moment I laid eyes on him.

Who, exactly, was Zachariah St. Brenton? There was nothing in this spare room to tell me—nothing personal at all. And though I could see more of the house in the early-morning light, nothing new was bared to my eyes as I cautiously left the bedroom I had been in and retraced the route to the garage.

"Can't you do a single thing that you're told?"

I whirled, startled at the forceful voice, and pressed my back flat against the cool plaster of the wall. Zach stalked toward me, irritation painting his features with shadow.

He was dressed for work, his black suit fitting so perfectly to his amazing body that I was very nearly jealous of the fine cloth. His tie was dark red today, and my fingers itched to undo it as my mouth watered.

No man should look so damn good. It wasn't fair to those of us who were supposed to function around him.

"I would do as I was told if it made any sense to do so." As much as a raw need clawed at me at the very sight of him, I hadn't forgotten what had transpired between us. Anger sliced at me like razor blades. It was irritating that he looked just perfect, while I was emotionally wrung out, pale and exhausted. "It wasn't fair for you to ask that of me, Zach."

He halted in midglower, surprise and—was I imagining it?—uncertainty flickering over his face. Feelings that I didn't quite understand made me tremble as I watched him struggle to get himself under control.

I knew that he wasn't as flawless as most of the world saw him, though to me his shadows made him all the more intriguing. Was I the only one who saw more than the good looks and the money?

Zach moved quickly. Before I could breathe again, I was caged where I stood, my back to the wall, a strong arm on either side of my head. Surrounded by him this way, I could smell soap and cologne and that scent that I had become so intimately familiar with the night before—that essence that was uniquely *him*.

I raised my head, hoping desperately that he would brand my lips with his own, and cursing myself for wanting it all the same.

The kiss didn't come. Instead he looked down at me, that intense stare scorching me wherever it touched.

"Zach . . ." The word was a whisper as it left my lips. As if I had burned him, he jolted back, putting space between us in more ways than one.

I dropped my stare and swallowed thickly, wishing I could somehow ease whatever it was that tormented him. If whipping him would do it, then I'd lash his skin in a moment; but I just couldn't see how raining blows down on his skin would exorcise the pain he was so clearly trying to tamp down.

If only he understood that.

"Are we leaving now?" I needed to break the silence that felt as if it might choke me with every breath.

Zach pulled his arrogance around him like a cloak, dismissing me as if he hadn't been a whisper away from claiming me only moments ago.

"Charles will drive you to the office now." Despite the expression on his face that told me he didn't care how I got to work, one way or the other, I knew that a man who had ordered someone to buy me lacy underwear cared. It was so incredibly frustrating, the way he chose to show it. "I will follow later. If we arrive together it will cause unnecessary gossip."

I nodded, partially relieved, half-disappointed, and full of fatigue.

"And I trust that you will be extremely discreet at Phyrefly." His raven-dark eyes bored into my own, and I knew that this was one order I would not disobey. "Gossip isn't going to hurt the man who signs the paychecks. But it could be very damaging to someone new, someone with a lot of potential. I won't have that."

Though his face still seemed carved from stone, Zach's words showed me that alluring and compelling side of him again. I very nearly groaned with frustration.

How could I show him that I saw it, and that I was drawn to it?

"Thank you for the clothes." Slowly I raised a hand to the scooped neckline of my shell. My fingers caught at the wool, relishing the softness.

Zach's gaze followed the path of my fingers, and then moved farther down. A slight heat colored his skin, and when I dared to glance down, I saw that his cock had risen and was tenting the front of his suit pants.

He was thinking of the underwear that he had ordered to be purchased for me; I could see it on his face. Since he had been with me, he didn't know what it looked like, and the thought had gotten him hard.

My pulse increased, my heart fluttering against my rib cage

as heat descended over me. No matter what had happened, I wanted him.

He wanted me.

He said nothing in response, instead nodding and turning to walk away.

It had been a week.

I sat at my desk, unable to concentrate, for the umpteenth time. I was falling behind in my work, and my supervisor, Mrs. Gallagher, had been hounding me all day about a report that was to be turned in that afternoon. Each day it had gotten worse. I wasn't sleeping. I wasn't eating.

I sipped at a cup of sweet strawberry hibiscus tea that I didn't particularly want, but I soaked in the heat of the ceramic mug against the chilled skin of my hands, and tried to focus.

"But it could be very damaging to someone new, someone with a lot of potential. I won't have that." Zach's last words to me had told me that he felt something for me—something more than the lust that raged between us whenever we were in the same room. Despite every lecture that I had given myself in the last week, I had hoped for . . . something from him. Some gesture, or communication between us.

Instead it was as if we had never met. No phone calls, no texts—I hadn't even seen him inside the Phyrefly building. I wanted to take the elevator to the top floor, to storm past Philippa the paper-doll princess, to confront Zach and ask him what the hell was going on.

My fling with him was supposed to be different from every other relationship that I had had. I was supposed to leave it feeling stronger, more secure in myself. Instead the weeklong silence had left me feeling even worse than I had right after I'd discovered Tom's infidelity.

Though I had been with Tom for much longer, the intensity of my feelings for him were a pale shade of what I already felt for Zach.

It was equally tempting to put down my tea, to walk out of the Phyrefly building and to never come back. To go back to the familiarity of Sacramento—though not to Tom—or to someplace entirely new, where no one knew me or had any expectations of my behavior.

Yet, deep down, I didn't want to run anymore. I liked this job. I liked this city.

And more than any of that, I knew that there was more to be explored between Zach and me, even if he was too stubborn to admit it.

I scowled as I set my mug down on my desk hard enough that Tony looked over from his own workstation, which was beside mine.

"Everything all right?" He had been nothing but impeccably polite to me since Zach had warned him away, but I had still caught him checking out my ass when he thought I wasn't looking. I didn't really mind—it was nice to be found attractive, and Tony was a good-looking man. But his ogling didn't do any more for me than raise my spirits for a moment or two.

The mere thought of Zach looking at me in any way at all, even with that terrifying glower of his, made my temperature rise.

As if my thoughts had become real, I looked up across the busy accounting office, and met the stare of the man himself. My lips parted involuntarily with shock, and my pulse felt like a flock of birds had taken flight in my veins.

There was heat in his stare, and he looked me over thoroughly as I gaped at him.

Then, as if our gazes hadn't connected intimately, he turned back to the group of suit-clad men and women that he was ushering into the conference room.

My vision was shaded with crimson. I had never before felt fury like I did in that moment. I was on my feet and halfway across the room before I even realized what I was doing. I vaguely heard Tony call my name; I didn't care.

Zach had no right to treat me this way. No right to use me the way that he had.

I wasn't going to be anyone's doormat, no, not ever again.

I had very nearly marched into the conference room behind the group when I thought of what Zach would do if I embarrassed him in front of his staff. I could picture the thunderclouds on his face, the fury radiating from his frame.

Above all else, I wanted to please this man, and so my steps halted. It also crossed my mind that I wanted to keep my job.

Inhaling deeply, I turned and marched back to my desk. More than one head turned my way with curiosity, and though my face flamed, I ignored them all and seated myself at my desk again.

I could feel Tony's eyes, watching me warily. I pretended to be scrolling through a report on my computer, when in reality I was watching the words whirl by in a stream of black on white.

To make my hands stop trembling, I lifted my mug, sipped at the sweet tea. The heat warmed my insides very slightly, and I calmed, but only a bit.

For my own peace of mind, I had to speak with Zach. I almost wished that I had found the strength to continue into the conference room, because I was finding it hard now to pull out the strength to confront him.

"Do you have a minute, Devon?" Tony's face was a study in wariness when I looked over at his desk. Though I wanted to snarl, deep down I knew that it wasn't him I was angry at.

Forcing my lips into a semblance of a smile, I raised my eyebrows questioningly.

"I wondered if you could take a look at the first-quarter report for Spartacus Records." The record company was a big client of Phyrefly, purchasing their private jets solely from us. "I've input something wrong somewhere, and I've gone over it three times, but I just can't find it."

Numbers. Spreadsheets. I could do this. Within minutes Tony had sent the file to my computer and I was poring over it with enough concentration that my anger ratcheted down a notch.

"Here!" Excited when my eyes locked in on the error, I gestured Tony over, pointing to the place on the screen. "It's right here, in Column D."

"How the hell did you find that so fast?" The look that Tony gave me was filled with admiration, and I wasn't so upset that I missed his up-and-down stare. "This spreadsheet is pages long."

"Oh." Flushing at the praise, I pointed to the total at the bottom of the column. "Well, when two columns should balance and don't, an easy check is to subtract one total from the other. If the difference is 1, 10, 100, 9 or 99, then you've probably made an error in addition. In this case you typed an O instead of a zero, and it threw the math off."

"You're amazing." Tony leaned in slightly, the interest on his face easy to read. I swallowed forcibly, wishing with all of my might that it were Tony, or someone like him, whom I was attracted to.

Life would be much, much easier if I were.

As if on cue, I felt that tingling sensation on my skin, the one I got when Zach was near. I looked up and across the room to find him standing just outside the conference room door, speaking with a member of the team that he had been meeting with.

His eyes were fixed on Tony and me with our heads together, and he did not look impressed.

A tremor ran through me. He would be alone in a moment. This was my chance.

I had to do it before I lost my nerve.

"Tony, could you excuse me for just a moment?" I smiled at the man with as much sincerity as I could muster. It wasn't his fault that I was fixated on someone whose mood swings gave me whiplash.

"Sure." Tony's stare followed mine as I stood and smoothed my skirt. He frowned, his brows furrowing together. "Devon, I know no one can hold a candle to the amazing St. Brenton, but I can guarantee that I'd treat you better."

I smiled at Tony, and the smile held more than a bit of regret. I couldn't bear the idea of hurting his feelings, so I opted to skirt around the truth of the matter, which was that after Zach, I wasn't sure I would ever be attracted to anyone else.

"Too bad coworkers in the same department can't date." Tony snorted through his nose, seeing through my bullshit. But as he made his way back to his desk he made sure to rub a hand over my shoulder with a grin.

"Give him hell, Devon."

Tony's words gave me strength. It looked like Zach was close to wrapping things up, so I sucked in a deep breath and hurried back across the room.

He saw me coming, and his eyes narrowed in warning. I felt my fury begin to boil again, rapidly reaching the boiling point.

"Mr. St. Brenton." I spoke right on the heels of his conversation's end, knowing that I needed a witness to get him to cooperate. "I need to speak with you for a quick moment, if you don't mind."

I kept my voice polite, but the man who had been meeting with Zach looked at me with curiosity, telling me that my anger wasn't quite as well hidden as I thought.

"I'll leave you to it." The man nodded at us both before leaving. Zach moved to go with him, and I hissed.

"I don't want to make a scene, Zach, but we need to talk. Five minutes. You owe me that."

Zach's face showed no emotion as he studied me, his stare hot and steady.

"Very well." Relief washed through me as he stalked into the conference room, leaving me to follow.

The uppermost layer of my hot wrath evaporated into chills as I found myself suddenly alone with Zach, for the first time in a week. I began to tremble with nerves and anticipation, a heady combination when mixed with abject rage.

I was aware of the curious stares of those outside the conference room, my coworkers trying to watch what was going on without actually seeming like that was what they were doing.

I tried not to show any of my feelings on my face, which was difficult, since I was shivering.

"You can't treat me this way." Zach watched me as I spoke, his face impassive. I wanted to cry with frustration. "If what we had was just a fling, then fine. But you should have the courtesy to tell me that we're through, instead of leaving me hanging. It's cruel."

Anger rippled over Zach's face, but I couldn't tell if it was directed at me or not. He picked up a remote and pressed a series of buttons that caused the windowed walls of the conference room to become opaque, and excitement licked through me.

"I won't be just another of your hangers-on, waiting for any scrap of attention that you toss my way." In the last week I had made the mistake of searching the Internet for information on him, clues to his past. What I had found instead were reams of gossip on the billionaire mogul's personal life, namely the women with whom his name had been linked.

There were so many—some famous, some not, all gorgeous— that I had felt physically ill.

"Come here." Zach's voice was hot and struck straight to my core. My head told me that to obey would be the stupidest thing I had ever done; my body couldn't have cared less.

I had to struggle to hold myself in place, but I had something that I needed to say before I let him touch me again.

"Are we done, or are we trying to figure out what this is?" It was so hard to hold my voice steady. "I'm not asking you to make a major commitment. But if we're going to explore this, then I need to know that . . . that that's what you want."

If he laid those hands on my skin, and then left me again, I wasn't sure how I would recover. I would—I could—but I didn't want to have to go there if we weren't on the same page.

How could he possibly want me—how had he ever wanted me—after all of those beautiful, smart, accomplished women in his past?

"Devon. Come here." Cautiously I moved across the large conference room to where he stood, so large and arrogant and *male*. I could feel the sultry heat of his body, drawing me in, and it warmed me to the marrow of my bones.

Be careful, Devon. More so than any person I had ever known, this man was dangerous.

I stood in front of him, my fingers twisting nervously in the starched fabric of my black button-up blouse. When he grabbed me by the arms and turned me around, pressing my back to the hard length of his front, I gasped, heat pooling instantly between my legs.

I cursed how much he could make me feel with only the slightest of touches.

Fisting a hand in the length of my ponytail, he tugged my head back, twisting until I looked him in the eyes. The licorice-dark depths of his eyes sparked with the same fire that I felt.

"While we are together, no other man touches you." The words were hot against my ear, and he followed them with a sharp nip of warning on the tender lobe. My throat felt dry, but he pulled my hair again, urging me to answer.

"No one but you." I whispered. He growled, the sound low and deep.

"Take off your panties." I inhaled sharply and looked sidelong at the frosted wall that separated us from those milling around outside the conference room. Though when the temporary opaqueness was activated, the wall was impenetrable to the eye—and I had been on the other side during enough meetings to know that it worked—yet I felt incredibly exposed.

The door wasn't even locked.

"You wanted this, Devon." With his free hand Zach reached around me to cup my throat, squeezing gently. The gesture reminded me of our night together a week earlier.

I had to trust him, and he me, or this was over before it had even begun.

"Will you help me with my skirt?" I felt excitement whip through his frame, which was pressed so tightly against me. His erection dug into the flesh of my lower back as I bent forward, and I thrilled to the knowledge that I had such an effect on him.

Lowering both of his hands to my hips, he squeezed the flesh there once before gathering the fabric of my A-line skirt in his fingers, lifting my skirt bit by bit.

When I could feel the cool air of the room kiss the skin of my upper thighs, I hooked my fingers in the lace strips that ran over each of my hips. I tugged at the scrap of fabric until it fell to the floor, skimming my legs on the way down.

"Step out." I did as he said, my knees trembling. "Now pick them up." He pulled my ass into his pelvis and urged me to bend at the waist. I felt the rigid length of his erection pressing into the heat of my center as I bent and caught the small garment in trembling fingers. I pushed back against him, a sudden wild image of him opening his fly and shoving his cock into my naked heat then and there burning its imprint into my mind.

I felt every inch of his hard flesh as I stood back up.

"Give them to me." I forced myself to look up, to look into his eyes as he took them from me. They were composed entirely of bits of black lace, and were part of the outfit that had been provided for me at his house a week ago.

They were a far cry from the simple, tasteful cotton that I usually wore. The flicker in his eyes told me he knew that, knew that these were the ones he had given me.

Cupping my jaw in one large hand, he traced a finger over the planes of my face. My mouth was swollen with need.

"Does it excite you, knowing that someone could walk in on us at any minute?" His words caused a tremor to run through me. I licked my tongue over my parched lips. It sounded so dirty, so very unlike something that I would like, but I couldn't deny it.

"Everything about you excites me." My voice was soft. Pleasure painted Zach's features at my words, just for a moment, before his habitual control returned.

Releasing me, he stepped back, putting a definite amount of space between us. Lifting my panties to his face, he held them to his nose and inhaled, looking as though he were sampling the bouquet of a fine wine.

I gaped with shock. Had he really just sniffed my underwear? My eyes widened as he went one step further, tucking the bits of lace into the pocket of his pants. They were so small that it didn't look as though there was anything there.

"Go back to work, Devon." Before I could do anything rash, like throw myself at him, he pressed the buttons on the remote and unfrosted the windows to the conference room. Nervously I ran a hand over my disheveled ponytail, then fussed with my clothes before forcing my hands into fists that fell still at my side. Perspiration slicked my skin, clinging at the long wisps of my bangs.

Without having to look, I knew that the eyes of everyone outside the room had swung toward us, on display as we were. I suspected that most people in the cavernous accounting office beyond were watching, too.

I hadn't been employed there for very long, but I had already come to understand that the employees of Phyrefly Aviation regarded anything to do with their enigmatic CEO with fascination.

We hadn't been alone in there long enough for anything untoward to have happened. But I knew, and Zach knew, that my underpants were now in his pocket. And I knew that I had turned him on.

"I want those back." Pasting a smile on my face, I narrowed my eyes to let him know I was serious. "They were a gift."

Finally, *finally*, that smile of his that I loved so much made an appearance. He laughed out loud, and I glowered further, even though I was thrilled to have pulled the sound out of him.

"You'll get them back." To the people in the hallway, Zach was merely sharing a joke with an employee. I, however, was standing close enough that I could see the dangerous glint in his eyes.

"I intend to deliver them personally."

CHAPTER NINE

Though I'd now had contact with Zach, my afternoon was proving to be just as unproductive as my morning. I was hyperconscious of my bare skin pressed against the soft fabric of my skirt. More than embarrassment, I found that sitting at my desk, naked beneath my skirt, was terribly exciting. Every time I shifted and my thighs pressed together, I could feel the sensitivity of my arousal.

What was Zach doing with my panties? Did he have them out on his desk? In his hand? Or were they still in his pocket? I delighted in having a secret that only the two of us knew.

Frustrated beyond reason, I stood and made my way to Mrs. Gallagher's desk. Though it was an adult work environment, and though I was perfectly entitled to leave for a short break, I still felt as though I needed to ask the woman's permission. She made me feel as if I were back in grade school. It was a discomfiting sensation.

"I'm going to run downstairs for some coffee, Mrs. Gallagher. Would you like anything?" The woman tucked a strand of rich copper hair behind her ear and slid her tortoiseshell reading glasses down to the tip of her nose so that she could focus on me where I stood, at the edge of her office.

It struck me then that she was an attractive woman, though she hid it well with her condescension and irritating manner.

"I do not drink caffeinated beverages after ten in the morning, Miss Devon Reid." She slid her glasses up on her nose and looked back at her computer screen, and I knew that I had been dismissed. "And if you had a decent night's sleep, rather than cavorting till all hours of the morning, you wouldn't need to, either."

I felt the warmth of a blush spread over my cheeks. It had been a week since I'd been up late doing anything exciting, but the memory of that night had disrupted my sleep ever since. Her tone also rankled, though from what I saw she was just as abrupt with everyone.

When I reached the bank of elevators I felt the prickles on the back of my neck that told me someone's eyes were on me. I turned back and found Mrs. Gallagher watching me, her features furrowed with concern.

Though she made a show of looking away and ignoring me from that moment on, it wasn't the first time I had caught her examining me with concern. Given how at odds it seemed with her typical behavior toward me, I couldn't even begin to guess what it was about me that worried her.

I was too tired to begin to figure it out.

The lobby was quiet. I passed through the security sensors that guarded the entrance to the employees-only section of the building and followed the scent of roasted arabica beans.

I had just joined the end of the long line—the Phyrefly building stood thirty-two floors tall, and though coffee was available on every floor, Higher Grounds allowed us a chance to stretch our legs and socialize for a moment, so it was very popular. Anticipating the jolt of caffeine that might help me to get through the rest of the day, and contemplating a sugary doughnut to go with it, I became dimly aware of a commotion back out in the lobby.

"Employees only beyond this point." The deep grumble belonged to one of the security guards who manned the entry into the depths of the gigantic building. There were rumblings from the two other men who worked with him—big, intimi-dating-looking men—but above all the ruckus sounded a voice that was very familiar to me.

"My girlfriend works here, and I'll visit her if I damn well want to!" The tone of voice was thin and arrogant and full of ag-itation. It also sounded familiar.

No. Surely not.

I turned slowly, hoping that I was imagining it.

I wasn't. Caught in the beefy arms of Ron, the one security guard who actually smiled at me occasionally, was my ex-boyfriend, Tom.

Tom, the cheating bastard.

I watched, strangely nonplussed, as Ron finally let him go. Tom straightened like a bird whose feathers had been mussed, shaking as if he could remove the imprints of Ron's hands like droplets of water. His version of casual clothes consisted of neatly pressed khakis and a starched button-down shirt in navy and white checks. They were now wrinkled, and a tuft of hair stood straight up from the rest of the neatly combed golden strands that covered his head.

I wasn't happy to see him. Neither did I feel an overwhelm-ing urge to storm up to him and slap him across the face.

Mostly I wanted to hide. I didn't want to deal with him or any of the feelings that his appearance dredged up when my mind was already so full of Zach.

"Shit." I hissed as I spoke, and the man in front of me in line cast an uneasy glance at me before inching forward, placing distance between us. My mind raced as I grimaced. I had to be an adult. Though Tom had been fully in the wrong, I hadn't been acting like an adult when I ran away, and I had to make that right.

Inhaling deeply, squaring my shoulders, I exited Higher Grounds and crossed the lobby to where my ex still sputtered.

"Tom." My voice was even. He looked up, saw me, and gave one last shudder, presumably trying to remove the sensation of being manhandled from his skin.

"What the hell kind of company are you working for, Devon?" Now that he had straightened himself out—except for that tuft of hair, which I certainly wasn't going to tell him about—I watched Tom fall back on his usual arrogance and swagger.

That swagger wasn't something that sat well on my ex. Though it probably wasn't fair to compare the two, when I thought of Zach and the high-handedness that was ingrained right into his every act, I found myself growing warm.

"The security is here to keep employees safe, Tom." He looked a bit surprised that I hadn't immediately agreed with him. Part of me felt the urge to slip right back into my old ways—to acquiesce, to placate.

I couldn't do that. Forcing myself to hold my chin high, I looked my ex right in the face, noting the puzzlement that ran over his features when he took in my demeanor.

"They don't have the right to rough up innocent people." Tom brushed a hand fussily over his shoulder, smoothing away dust that I certainly couldn't see. I stifled a roll of my eyes. Catching Ron's eye over Tom's shoulder, I had to bite my cheek to keep from smiling when the man cast me an incredulous, "do you actually know this idiot?" look.

I *had* known this idiot, once upon a time. And though I didn't know where things stood with Zach, I now certainly knew better than to settle for someone like Tom.

I couldn't blame him for my insecurities—they were my own issues, though Tom certainly hadn't helped matters any. Never mind his cheating, he had never made me feel anything as intensely as Zach did, and the thought of going through life without experiencing sensation like that made me shudder.

"Tom, if you tried to get past the gates, then you weren't innocent and you know it." I heard the sharp edge in my voice, and instead of trying to hide it, I found myself embracing it. Seeing Tom dredged up all kinds of old devastations, ones that I had come so far in working through in the past few weeks, and I found that I didn't appreciate it at all.

"How did you find me?" I hadn't told anyone where I was going—I hadn't known, myself—until I'd gotten here.

Tom pursed his lips, studying me as if trying to discover what was different, before he spoke. "I linked our cell phones several months ago. All I had to do to find you was to log into the program. You've been spending work hours here every day for the past couple of weeks. It was easy enough."

My mouth fell open at the audacity of his response—there were so many things in it that I didn't agree with. Zach had discovered my clothing sizes and cosmetic preferences, and the resources he had to have accessed in order to obtain such information blew my mind. Still, he made no secret of the influence his wealth bestowed on him or his controlling nature. I fully intended to have it out with him over his invasion of privacy. However, while Zach's actions had only irritated me, I found this cell phone stalking of Tom's to just be creepy. It also made me angry. I had thought that I was truly alone when I was in Cambria, and had found comfort in the fact that no one in the world knew where I was. To find out that had been a sham was deeply upsetting.

"Why on earth would you have linked our phones?" Per his own dictate, our finances were separate—it wasn't like we shared a phone bill, or even a grocery app.

The barest hint of guilt crossed Tom's face, and I understood in a flash. Though I didn't have romantic feelings toward my ex at all anymore, his betrayal still had the ability to cut me to the core.

"You wanted to know where I was all the time so that you wouldn't get caught." It wasn't a question. The bastard. The lying, *cheating* bastard.

I had had enough. Punching as much disdain as I possibly could into my sneer, I turned on my heels and walked away, heading toward those security gates that Ron and company had refused to let Tom through.

I, however, was an employee of Phyrefly Aviation. And I intended to use those gates to get the hell away from Tom.

"Devon, wait. Please!" I slowed, gritting my teeth as I did. "Can't we at least go for a coffee, to talk?"

He made it sound so reasonable, like I at least owed him that much. And maybe I did. I found myself spinning back around and striding toward him, though my every step felt as though I were slogging through mud.

"Make it quick, Tom. I have to get back to work." Without waiting to see if he was following or not, I reentered Higher Grounds.

I still wanted my coffee, dammit. I was going to need it to get through this clusterfuck of a day.

I watched as Tom stared out the window of the coffee shop, his mouth agape at the couple who had just walked by. Two women held hands, one a tall, attractive blonde dressed in a neatly cut business suit, the other a petite girl with her hair dyed bright blue, the dye job accented by the rings that pierced the skin of her ears, nose and eyebrows.

"What the hell kind of city is this to live in, Devon?" He turned to face me with no surprise, but plenty of disdain, and I bristled. I loved the vibrancy of San Francisco, loved that everyone in the city seemed comfortable in their own skin.

Though the city wasn't that far from Sacramento geographically, it was worlds apart in every other way.

I wasn't quite in the San Francisco mindset yet, but I was working on it.

"Tom, hurry up. Please." The longer I sat there with those calculating eyes of his assessing me, the closer I came to reverting to meek, compliant Devon, the one that even Tom, the most vanilla man I had ever met, had become bored with.

I felt as if I were stranded in the choppy waves outside of Zach's house, trying to keep my head above water.

"When are you going to drop this nonsense and come home, Devon?" Settling back in his chair, Tom sipped at his coffee with a casual air.

I placed my own coffee on the table and stared at him, knowing that incredulity must be written all over my features. I continued to stare, waiting for him to explain further.

He seemed annoyed when I didn't answer right away.

"Tom, I left you a note. I told you I was leaving. Given the situation in your apartment when I left the note, I think you're fully aware of *why* I left." I watched as Tom became visibly irritated, setting down his coffee cup hard enough that the steaming liquid splashed out of the small opening in the lid.

"You can't possibly be serious, Devon." There was that disdain again, and anger began to simmer in my core. "I let you have some time away, since you clearly needed to . . . deal with the situation. I even convinced the other partners to hold your job for you. But they—we—are expecting you back."

Time to deal with the situation? Was he serious? I barked out a laugh, and then another. I felt like I should be furious, but it became clear to me in one crystalline moment that this man wasn't worth so extreme an emotion.

"We'll get married, Devon. Next year we'll buy a house.

That's our plan." Tom looked incredibly puzzled that I wasn't falling into his arms. I shook my head in disbelief.

"Tom, you are delusional." Sitting forward in my chair, I looked him over thoroughly. He was good-looking, in a bland way, but what I now saw in his personality made him seem thin and weedy to my eyes.

Even if I hadn't met Zach, hadn't had my eyes opened to the vitality of a real man, I couldn't picture myself married to this poor excuse for a human for the rest of my life.

"Maybe I shouldn't have left the way I did. But you cheated on me. Cheated on me, Tom! You fucked someone else." Tom reared back at my profanity, a word I probably wouldn't have used weeks earlier.

I didn't care. I was on a roll.

"I deserve more than that, Tom." I couldn't quite put a name to the emotion that I was feeling as I pushed my chair back from the table. "And I don't want to see you again."

"Devon." Tom caught me by the wrist before I could leave. I looked down at his hand clasped around my wrist, its touch slightly clammy against my dry skin.

I felt nothing. No heat, no despair.

Just nothing.

"Get your fucking hand off of her." The growl from behind me could have come from a wild animal. I yanked my arm free of Tom's grasp and spun, adrenaline slicing through my veins like a knife, my heart in my throat.

Zach towered over nearly everyone else in the small coffee shop, taking up more than his fair share of space in that way that he did. Though he was still dressed in his fancy suit, the green tie that he wore that day as tidy as always, his stance and his expression spoke of danger as he glowered at Tom.

Here, I thought, was everything that I had been searching for. Here was everything that Tom and I hadn't been.

Though I at least knew Tom well enough to see the anxiety travel through him, he retreated into the uptight persona that he had perfected. Not bothering to stand, he still tried to look down his nose at Zach.

"Who are you? More of the hired muscle?" To my surprise Zach laughed then, but it wasn't a pleasant sound. Even as his lips curled upward, he looked capable of murder.

I was appalled to find myself thrilling to the barely restrained violence in him. Whatever was running through his mind, it fed some need deep in my soul. I wasn't proud that I found I liked being able to evoke such a visceral reaction from him.

"That wasn't a joke." Clearly—finally—feeling threatened, Tom stood. Next to Zach he looked almost like a child, weak and immature.

"I didn't think it was." Zach held out his hand for me. Instead of grabbing my arm like Tom had done, he gave me the choice to put my hand in his. Though I was stunned at the intensity of his reaction to the strange situation I had found myself in, I didn't have to think for even a fraction of a second.

I took his hand, and allowed myself to be drawn to his side.

Tom smiled nastily, and I shuddered. I had almost moved in with this man—if I hadn't walked into that apartment right when I had, I likely would have married him.

"I see how things are." My ex had the nerve to size up Zach as if they were equals. I bit my tongue, though I wanted to tell him that they weren't even playing in the same game.

Tom was television in black and white. Zach was high-definition, big screen, surround sound.

"Watch how you talk to her." Zach's voice was quiet, and I was sure that I alone heard the threatening undercurrents running through it. I reached out, placed a hand on his biceps and squeezed in warning.

This didn't need to become violent.

Tom ignored Zach, and I bit my lip, afraid of what was to come.

"You have some nerve, walking away because I was with someone else when you've been doing the exact same." Tom's eyes flicked from Zach to me and back again, as if trying to understand how the two of us could possibly be together.

If I had had any lingering feelings for the man, they would have died then and there. How could I—why *would* I—be with a man who didn't believe that I was worthy of the world?

Tom moved to grab me again—for a lawyer, he was not very bright. Zach grabbed his hand in midair, his massive palm swallowing Tom's smaller one as he squeezed slowly.

"It takes a lot to make me lose control, Mr. Cambridge-Neilson." I watched, dumbfounded, as he slowly increased the pressure that he had on the other man's hand. I was somehow not surprised that Zach knew my former boyfriend's name. Tom howled like he was being beaten. The others in the cafe were silent, watching the spectacle as intently as if they were part of it. "But I find myself dangerously close right at this moment. Now, listen carefully. You do not touch Devon. You do not speak to her. No calls, no text messages. Nothing. In fact, don't even come into this city if she is in it."

Ron and another of the guards came up behind Zach, but they stayed back, waiting for their boss to give them the signal. Tom took in their approach, had to know that he was beaten.

He just wouldn't back down.

"You're messing with the wrong person, pal." How had I never noticed how nasal his voice was? Trying to yank his hand from Zach's grip, he grew red in the face as Zach held on just a moment too long, proving that he was the one in control. "I'm a lawyer. I'm going to sue you for laying hands on me."

Tom didn't even look at me. His campaign to get me to return home had ended, overtaken with thoughts of himself and his own fragile ego.

"You're going to be sorry." Tom stalked forward, assuming, it seemed, that Zach would move out of his way. He didn't, and Tom had to skulk around Zach inelegantly. "Does your boss know that you treat people this way on his property?"

Turning with an almost lazy air, Zach finally nodded at Ron. The two security guards immediately flanked Tom, who squawked, and began to hustle him out of the coffee shop.

"Who the hell do you think you are?" Zach didn't bother to reply, instead watching as Tom was escorted to the front doors of Phyrefly. Just before ejecting him from the building, I saw Ron shake his head, and heard his comment.

"That's Zachariah St. Brenton, numb nuts. He owns this company, this building, and half of the freaking country. Ever heard of him?"

My last view of Tom was one that I would remember, as he stared with wide eyes and an open mouth, silent for the first time since I had met him. As he left, I felt lighter, as if he was taking some of my baggage with him.

That lightness vanished as I slowly became aware again of my surroundings. I looked around and found that Higher Grounds was still silent, everyone to a man staring agog at the spectacle that was Zach and me.

Zach looked down at me, and I read barely banked fury on his face.

"Come with me." The words were bitten out from between clenched teeth.

"Now."

CHAPTER TEN

The elevators at Phyrefly were designed to hold twenty people at a time, comfortably.

As I followed Zach into the sleek interior, however, it felt very small. Too small to hold the two of us, especially if all of our issues were going to come along for the ride.

The silence was heavy, and I felt like I was going to choke if I had to breathe this weighted air in for even a moment longer.

"You didn't get your coffee." I blurted this out as I stood beside Zach, my arms crossed tightly over my chest. The inches between us seemed like miles. Were we never going to figure out how to manage this thing between us?

He looked at me as if I were speaking in tongues.

"I didn't come for a coffee, Devon." The emphasis that he put on the word *coffee* went a long way to giving me an insight into his thoughts.

He had come for me.

But how had he known that I was with Tom?

"How—" I stopped before the words left my lips. Phyrefly Aviation was ripe with security cameras.

I may not have known Zach very well, but I did know that he was far too controlling not to have access to those cameras 24/7.

I wasn't sure if I should feel flattered or angry that he had been watching me without my knowledge.

I looked up to find his eyes trained on me, his expression daring me to make an issue of it.

"I keep a very tight hold on what I consider mine, Devon." His words tipped me over that last edge into anger.

All of my life, I had had very precise expectations placed on me, and I had always felt that I had fallen just a bit short. I had thought that Zach might be different, for he seemed to like me just the way I was. And yet here we were, my billionaire lover furious at me for breaking rules that I hadn't even known were in place.

"I'm not your property, Zach." I shivered with both lust and fury when he stepped closer to me, his pupils dilating until his eyes were pools of black. "All I did was have coffee with an ex. Now, because of that meeting, I have some closure."

"You're too good for that asshole." Reaching out, he pressed his hand over the place where my heart had begun to beat triple time.

My eyes widened, and I arched into his touch, closing my eyes, savoring the sensations that besieged me.

He pulled his hand away as if I had burnt his fingers, settling that mask of distance over his features again.

"Anyone is too good for him, actually. I can't believe he's ever had a girlfriend."

My heart sank at the casual words.

For a moment . . . for just a moment, I had felt special. As if Zach was angry at Tom because Tom had once had me.

His words made me wonder all over again if I meant anything to him at all—or if all he wanted was the comfort he found between my thighs.

"Don't think you can control me like you do everyone else." I muttered the words below my breath, certain that he wasn't even listening.

I gasped when I was pushed against the wall of the elevator with just enough force to get my attention. Zach's hand cupped my throat, just under my jaw, and pressed gently.

"No, I can't control you, Devon." His powerful touch was calculated with just enough force to make me work harder to have to draw in a deep breath. "But I can impose consequences when I don't care for your behavior."

I should have shoved at him, told him to get away, broken things off then and there. I was getting tired of his hot-and-cold behavior toward me. Instead I found slickness pooling between my legs, my clit heating with anticipation.

In that moment I discovered that I trusted him implicitly—with my body, at least. And I couldn't resist the surge of passion that ran through me as I saw how he looked at me, touched me with such strong desire.

A siren sounded as Zach removed the heated touch from my throat and slammed his palm against the red emergency button on the panel. The elevator ground to a halt, and, after he retrieved a key card from his pocket and waved it in front of the sensor, the siren halted, the air ringing in its aftermath.

I barely had time to register that he had halted the elevator between floors and seemingly locked it in place. When Zach spun me to face the wall of the elevator, I nearly lost my balance. I pressed my cheek against the cool chrome of the wall, the flush of my skin warming the metal.

My hands were pulled gently but firmly behind my back as Zach whispered my name seductively in my ear. Something soft and lacy was wrapped tightly around my wrists, binding them together at the small of my back.

"Your skin looks lovely against black lace." Zach's voice was rough, silk over gravel, as he whirled me around yet again. I leaned back against the wall, my arched back thrusting my breasts and their erect nipples forward, an offering for him.

Black lace. Oh, Lord.

He had tied me up with my own panties.

"Does this turn you on?" His voice was matter-of-fact, as though he already knew the answer. And as I pulled at my bonds, examined the anxiety that being tied gave me, I saw that he was right.

My anger at him had nothing to do with the way in which he was touching me now—in fact, the uncertainty and anxiousness brought about by his physical demands made me want him with an abandon that I hadn't been aware I possessed.

I trusted that he wasn't going to push me further than I wanted to go, physically.

Emotionally . . . well, I was still figuring that one out.

My pulse exploded when Zach—big, gorgeous Zachariah St. Brenton—dropped to his knees in front of me. Hooking his fingers into the cloth of my skirt, he impatiently tugged it up until it was bunched around my waist. His hands cupped the backs of my knees, then slowly slid up until my buttocks were grasped, and he kneaded with firm fingers.

"Open your legs." I wanted to obey. Heaven knew it was to my benefit to do so. But I found myself so overwhelmed with sensation that I couldn't move, frozen in place against the wall.

"Consequences, Devon." Then those strong hands slid forward, over my hips and between my thighs, shoving my legs apart with a roughness that I knew would leave a bruise.

I thrilled to the edge of violence in his handling of me. I was wet, my skin hot, my body trembling.

"I'm going to have your pussy." With his thumbs he delved between the lips of my labia, opening me to the world. I shivered when the cool air hit my clit.

Zach lowered his head, blowing heated air over my tender flesh. I cried out, my hips bucking forward, and earned a sharp smack on my hip for my impatience.

"This isn't for your benefit." I couldn't imagine how it could be for the benefit of anyone else when he closed his lips over the extended bud of my clit. A wail escaped me when, without warning, he closed his lips and his teeth over the sensitive nub and began to work me with the skill of a confident lover.

Though he was clearly upset with me, I thought I saw the ghost of a smile whisper over his lips at my heated reaction to his touch.

I struggled against the fabric that held my arms behind me. I wanted to fist my hands in the wealth of his dark hair, wanted to pull his face even closer. Not being able to touch the gorgeous creature who was tonguing my pussy was torture.

The thumbs that had been holding me open slipped inside me, just enough to stretch the tender flesh and make me buck my hips forward. I felt release circling like a hungry shark, so close to its prey.

Zach took me to the very edge, right to the moment before my flesh began to spasm with pleasure, and slid his thumbs out of my slick heat in the same moment in which he removed his lips from my clit.

"No!" Frantic, I stepped away from the wall and pressed myself against him shamelessly. I wanted—needed—his heat, his fire. I almost sobbed, my legs shaking, when he pushed me away, again turning me so that I faced the wall.

Fisting one hand in my ponytail, he tugged until I leaned back against his chest. I resisted, furious at what he had just done.

"You have to understand." Releasing my hair, he pressed his palm to the flat of my back, pushing me into the hard wall. I could feel the chill through the thin material of my blouse and my bra, and squeezed my eyes shut in defense against whatever was to come next.

I heard the sound of his belt buckle, then the harsh rasp of a zipper being lowered, rending the air in two. The naked length of his erect cock nestled against my buttocks as the swish of leather through cloth told me that he was removing his belt.

"Three blows." He paused, waiting for my reaction.

"No." My heart pounded, but I couldn't quite tell if it was in fear or desire. "No. I don't want that."

"Are you using your safe word, Devon?" My breath hitched in and out roughly as my mind whirled.

"No." I forced the word out. I was scared, but at the same time I wanted this, though I still didn't know why. "No, I'm not."

I screamed in a mix of desire and frustration when the leather of the belt hit the flesh of my right cheek. The sharp sting spread outward from the site of the blow like heat radiating from the sun. Tears sprang from my eyes as I fisted my hands and struggled against my bonds.

He was holding back. I knew he was holding back, because the first lash, and the next when it came on my left cheek, didn't hurt nearly as much as the spanking he had administered to me the week earlier. Still, I felt more raw, closer to a breaking point when that third blow came glancing over the flesh between my legs.

"You're a fucking bastard." The skin of my ass was on fire, and the flesh beneath felt swollen. And still I was aroused to the point of pain, aching for the feeling of his cock inside of me.

"You know your safe word, Devon." Craning my neck, I saw him kneel behind me again. With those strong hands he positioned my legs tightly together before the leather of the belt was looped just above my knees. He threaded the length through the buckle and cinched it snugly.

I felt myself begin to shake uncontrollably. Yes, I knew my safe word. I also knew that I wasn't going to say it. If I used it, I would never see him again.

I couldn't stand the thought. There was a flame inside of me, one that he had ignited, one that craved the feelings that he was pulling from my very core.

Whatever he chose to give me, it was what I wanted.

I closed my eyes. Behind me Zach stood up. I felt his grip at my hips, pulling me so that I was bent at the waist, hands still bound, thighs tied together, ass naked and presented to him.

I felt the head of his cock slide between the cheeks of my ass. As soon as he found my entrance he shoved inside of me, pushing until his balls swung heavily, tapping the sensitive skin of my labia.

Bound as I was, I had no choice but to bend farther. His fingers digging relentlessly into my hips, he pulled back and drove deep again, fucking into me with an animal ferocity.

I loved it. He satisfied a need deep inside of me that even I didn't understand.

My legs were bound so tightly together that the friction was nearly unbearable. My ass was still on fire from the blows, the skin burning every time the jut of his hip bones slammed forward into the delicate flesh.

Though I could flex my fingers, I couldn't otherwise move. I was helpless, completely vulnerable to him.

It was the best thing I had ever felt in my life.

He moved faster, his pelvis slapping against the mounds of my buttocks. This time when I felt pleasure spiraling low and deep in my belly, I fought to stave it off.

I didn't want to come yet. Not until he was done with me.

As if sensing my thoughts, Zach seated himself to the hilt one final time and then, with a strangled groan, pulled his cock free of the tight channel of my flesh. I whimpered as he smacked my ass with the flat of his palm.

"It would be so easy to come inside of you right now." Grasping my ass cheeks in both hands, he caressed my flesh.

"Deep inside of your pussy. Or, even better, inside your hot little ass. You'd like that, wouldn't you, my little minx?" Those hands smoothed over my cheeks, opening me so that he could look his fill.

Excitement bloomed deep inside of me at his crude comments, even as nerves flared. Was that to be my punishment—was he going to push himself inside of my ass, inside the tight heat that had never before been breached?

I was turned on and terrified in a thrilling way. Could I do it?

"I think you like that idea." One finger traced over the stripe of my spine. Then he closed his grip over my bound wrists, tugging until I turned awkwardly. Before he could forbid me not to, I eagerly looked him over, my eyes drinking their fill of the man who was slowly, steadily driving me wild.

His hair was messy, standing in sexy black spikes as if he had run his fingers through it. His tie had been loosened and was askew. His skin was flushed, the sexy hue of arousal painted over his features.

Best of all, his suit pants were hanging loosely on his lean hips. I could now see that he wore nothing beneath them—there was nothing keeping me from the thick, incredibly hard length that jutted forward from its nest of dark curls.

"On your knees." My eyes widened, and I bent, trying to do as I was commanded. With my legs bound, it was a nearly impossible task. Zach clasped me on either side of my rib cage, biceps beneath his dress shirt rippling as he lifted me off my feet and dropped me on my knees in front of him.

"I didn't like seeing his hand on you." The wild look in Zach's eyes pulled my own dormant grief from the depths of my soul. I wanted so badly to heal this beautiful, damaged man.

If only he would let me.

"Zach . . ." I squeezed my thighs together, trying to assuage the deep ache that had bloomed from his caresses. I was scared that he would never give me release, that he would keep me here, bound and at his mercy, forever.

"I don't like how he makes you feel." Lacing his fingers behind my head, Zach brought me toward him.

I thought I sensed a new warmth in his demeanor toward me, and then I remembered my earlier disappointment in thinking he cared for me.

I was suddenly so, so tired. I was a train wreck of emotions. I wanted to be done with games.

"Trust me, Devon." His touch gentling the tiniest bit, Zach pulled my head forward until the head of his cock brushed my lips.

Clamping my lips between my teeth, I shuddered in a breath and looked up at him. What I saw on his face halted my anger in midstride.

Gone was any anger, any arrogance from his gorgeous features. In their place were wonderment, encouragement, and even pride.

I felt my mind empty of everything except sensation as he pushed forward between my lips.

I did nothing more than to purse my lips around his thick length as he thrust into my mouth again and again. The head of his cock rammed against the back of my throat, and I gagged, but still kept my mouth clamped around him.

If this was what he wanted, then this was what he would get. I would try to learn about pleasure without emotional attachment.

I felt a trickle of salt stinging the back of my throat, heard him hiss in a breath as his thrusts came faster and faster. I opened my mouth wider, strained to take him deeper, pressed my body against his legs.

I gave him everything.

With a hoarse shout he pulled free of my mouth with a wet popping noise. Grasping his cock in one hand, he fisted the shaft up and down once, twice; and then he was coming, hot, salty streams of ejaculate that he caught in the handkerchief he always carried.

"Mine." His voice was harsh, coarse with need. "You are mine."

I nodded and licked the salt off my lips with my tongue. Eyes closed again, I lifted my head and let him shake the final few drops of his orgasm onto my tongue, which I tucked back into my mouth before demurely swallowing.

I stayed kneeling, my knees numb, feeling as though a great well inside of me had been filled. I kept my eyes on the floor as self-awareness gradually came back to me.

Above me, Zach was breathing heavily, his hands still tangled in my hair.

"Jesus." The word was a whisper. I heard him search in his pocket, then felt him clasp my chin in his hand. "Devon, look at me."

I looked up, but I had nothing to say. I wasn't angry, I wasn't embarrassed. I just didn't know how much longer I could play his games.

"Come here." Hauling me to my feet, Zach wiped my face with the tail of his shirt. He wiped away most of my makeup with it, but I didn't care.

I was strung tight, and yet peacefully empty. It was incredibly strange.

"Devon." Zach growled when I refused to look him in the eye. Lowering his head to mine, he claimed my mouth with his own. Forcing his tongue past my lips, he claimed me with his kiss, branding me. He had to have tasted his own release on my skin, but he didn't seem to care.

His lips moved to the curve of my neck, and as they did he

slipped his hand between my legs. I cried out softly when his skilled fingers found my clit. He manipulated the engorged nub skillfully and I came apart beneath his touch, screaming as the pressure inside of me finally exploded.

He held me to him until my shudders quieted, then smoothed my skirt back over my hips. My tears ran freely then, purging my flesh of all of the nasty emotions that I had been clutching at so tightly—my devastation and the sense of inferiority from seeing Tom again, the anger at Zach, even the guilt over not living up to what my parents had expected me to be.

Embarrassed, I shrugged my face into my shoulder to dry my tears as Zach undid his belt from my legs, my panties from my wrists. After a long moment he tucked them back into his pocket.

They were far too stretched out to wear.

I was silent as I massaged sensation back into my wrists, assessing the situation as Zach pulled out his cell phone. We were in the elevator at Phyrefly. Surely by now someone had noticed that it was stuck between floors. That someone was going to know exactly what had transpired as soon as we started moving again and I had to step off onto my work floor, my clothes wrinkled, my hair a snarled mess, and my makeup smeared across my face. Tears had left salt tracks down my cheeks, and I smelled of sex and of Zach.

"Mrs. Gallagher. This is Mr. St. Brenton. I have sent Miss Reid on a personal errand for me. She won't be returning this afternoon." There was that thoughtfulness again, shown in his understanding that I couldn't face my colleagues right then—and possibly ever again.

"Philippa. Are there any meetings waiting on me? No? All right, then. Please head down to the Starbucks on the corner and get me a venti dark roast, black. Yes, you." As he ended his call, Zach ran his key card in front of the elevator sensor again and then slammed a fist into the button for the top floor—his floor.

"Zach, I can't take any more today." My voice was tired. The day had been an emotional roller coaster.

I wanted to go to bed. And when I got there, I wanted to sleep. I needed time to think about how I was feeling.

How could he inspire such passion in me, how could he make me want to do these dirty things, when he hadn't told me straight out that he felt as strongly as I did?

"I'm taking you to my office so that you can clean up." His voice was steady, but was underlaid with something that I couldn't quite identify. "I have a shower, and something that you can change into. Then I'll have Charles take you home."

I almost corrected him, reminding him that I didn't currently have a home, since the hotel where I was staying certainly didn't count. But what did it matter, really?

I needed some space. I was seriously freaked-out.

The elevator doors opened onto an empty reception area on Zach's floor. I was thankful that he had had the foresight to send Philippa the paper-doll princess on an errand, and I smirked a bit to myself at the thought of just how disgruntled it must have made her.

"The bathroom is through there. There are towels, soap, a robe—use whatever you need." For the first time since I had met him, Zach sounded off of his game. Avoiding eye contact, I hurried into the bathroom, shutting and locking the door behind me.

"Christ." I whispered out loud to myself and breathed in deeply, bracing my arms on the counter and leaning over the sink. "What the hell was that?"

My head cleared minutely now that I was in a separate room. Zach was so charismatic, his personality so imposing, that I couldn't help but attune myself to him entirely when he was with me. Though I was acutely aware of him in the next room, I gulped at my aloneness, trying to slow my thundering pulse and calm my skittering nerves.

You are in way over your head, Devon. Slowly I looked up, looked at myself in the mirror. I barely recognized the woman in the mirror. Oh, the wide blue eyes were the same, and so was the blond hair. Same face, same body.

But Zach had revealed a part of myself that I hadn't known existed. Somehow I knew that he wouldn't hurt me. I trusted him—and I had from the very start. What scared me was how much I had liked it. The kink, the edge of violence, the obsessive need, *that* was what made me terrified.

I was craving more, even as my flesh was still tender from his touch. And what I craved wasn't restricted to the physical—no, those rare glimpses into the vulnerable Zach, the one that I suspected no one else saw, those were more addicting than the pleasure he pulled from my body.

Squeezing my eyes tightly together, I talked myself out of banging my head into the wall repeatedly in frustration. Instead I turned on the shower—unlike the one in his bedroom at his mansion, this one had a normal faucet. As I stepped beneath spray that was as hot as I could handle, I tried to get a grip.

He had warned me—he wasn't interested in a typical relationship. And I knew that I would accept whatever proposal he threw my way, because now having had a taste, I was desperate for more.

But could I do it without losing myself along the way?

I schooled my face into a smile as I stepped out of the office bathroom. My hair was slightly damp from the mist of the shower, but I had combed it and pulled it back into a tidy ponytail. Zach hadn't had any makeup in his drawers—which I couldn't deny pleased me, because that meant that he didn't often have women in his office shower—but I had at least washed the remaining smudges of makeup from my face.

Though my skirt was still fairly presentable, my blouse was a disaster. It was missing two buttons, and had wrinkled horribly. One of Zach's dress shirts had hung on the back of the bathroom door, and after a long hesitation I had shrugged out of my shirt and into his.

Though I regretted it as soon as I had, I didn't have a choice. He must have worn the shirt and not had it laundered since, because his unmistakable scent—the one that he had branded me with—rose from the fibers of the garment as I tucked it into my skirt.

Well, I wouldn't be able to return to my department dressed like this. But I was at least presentable enough to go home.

Nerves rioted through my belly as I crossed the office to stand in front of Zach's desk. He was at the window that comprised the entire wall of his office, and though his face was expressionless, his body had tensed as soon as I had opened the door to the bathroom.

"Zach." What I was about to do terrified me, but I felt compelled to regardless. He might have considered it a "misplaced sense of give and take," as he had called it the night we met, but that was just how I functioned.

As much as it scared me, he had given me an emotional release that afternoon that I knew had taken me one giant step forward on my personal journey.

I owed him one.

He didn't respond to my soft query—he may not have even heard me. I repeated his name, a little bit louder. He turned, an eyebrow raised, and when he fully faced me I almost ran out the door.

The arrogant billionaire who ran a massive corporation had displaced the emotional, vulnerable lover completely.

"I—I know you don't want anything serious." His lips thinned, and I stuttered, struggling to get the words out. "But you gave me something today, something big and scary and . . . well, big. I owe you."

I inhaled deeply and forced myself to expel the next words on a rush.

"I will whip you. That is, if you still want me to."

Pain and pleasure streaked over his face, then fury. I stood with my hands balled so tightly into fists that my nails cut through the skin. I watched as the enigmatic billionaire fought through his emotions and finally emerged on the other side as the calm, controlled man who was king of his own empire.

"I'm not interested."

I blinked, certain that I had heard him wrong. The man who had just fucked me seven ways to Sunday in the office elevator was more than interested; he was in as deep as I was.

But the words stung, and a trickle of insecurity worked its way through me.

"If you want to forget it, that's fine." My eyes scanned his face anxiously. What was going on?

"You presume too much, Miss Reid." Pulling his chair away from his desk, Zach sank into it with controlled precision. He stared up at me with cool disinterest painting his features, and sickness rolled over me in a wave.

"What am I presuming, exactly?" Ice frosted my veins as I looked at the stranger across from me, the stranger whose taste was still in my mouth.

"Presuming that I want anything more from you at all, Miss Reid." Casually he reached over to his computer monitor and flicked it on, seeming ready to dismiss me and start work. "I have had you now—had you more than once, so kudos to you for holding my interest. But I'm done with you. There is a world of beautiful women out there to fuck."

Pain blossomed within me, in a surge of bright red and tasting coppery like blood. I was smarter than this—I knew that this was just an act. He had to be as scared as I was, but he was being a coward about it, pushing me away instead of clinging tightly like I wanted to.

"You fucking bastard." I stared at him, my body stiff with pain. Why was he doing this? Why now, once I had become addicted to him and in need of my next hit?

"No one has ever claimed any different. Now, if you please, I have a lot of work to catch up on. I hadn't planned on taking such a long break this afternoon." I stared as he deliberately turned toward his computer, seemingly ready to get back to work.

As he did, I caught the smallest of flickers in his eyes. It was there and gone in a flash, but it told me what I needed to know.

He wasn't as unaffected as he was pretending to be. But the mere fact that he was acting like this when we were both in over our heads was more than I could take.

Slapping my hands on his desk, I leaned over, getting so close to his face that he had no choice but to look at me.

There was that flicker again, right in those licorice eyes, pushed away mechanically. I saw the slight shift in his body, the minuscule amount that he allowed himself to angle toward me.

He opened his mouth, presumably to say something else cruel. I didn't think, I simply acted, pulling my hand back before letting it fly.

I slapped him across the left cheek so hard that my palm stung. To his credit he barely moved, certainly didn't flinch as he assessed me with those cool eyes.

"Fuck you, Zach. Fuck you." I straightened, daring him to say something, to do something, anything.

He blinked, then looked back down at his computer.

Turning on my heel, clutching the loose folds of his shirt to my chest, I left, slamming his office door behind me.

PART IV

TEMPTED TO ENTICE

CHAPTER ELEVEN

Zach had done it again.

I knew that it was slightly irrational, since I was the one who had stormed out of his office, but I had hoped that he would show up at my tiny new apartment, or come by my desk in the accounting office, or even send me a text message. Something to tell me that he was sorry, that it had all been a mistake, and that he wanted to let me in—truly let me in—to his life.

As the days passed by, five and a half of them, to be precise, I came to understand that an overture from Zach just wasn't going to happen. The billionaire was nothing if not stubborn and set in his incredibly eccentric ways.

Crushed as I was, I knew that I needed to pick up the shattered pieces and try to start living my life again. The problem with that plan was that life without Zach in it seemed fuzzy and dull, lacking something important.

That missing element was Zach. But as long as he ran hot and cold, with those mercurial mood swings giving me whiplash, I didn't see that I had a choice.

I remembered the very first time we had met, in the small restaurant in Cambria. He had done it even then, coming on to me only to walk away.

It was exhausting.

Listlessly, I tapped away on my computer late in the afternoon of the sixth day. On day five, in a moment of personal crisis, I had stopped into a small clothing store on my way

home from work after a sexy, crimson wraparound blouse in
the window had caught my eye. That blouse was now wrapped
around my own ample curves, and I felt uncomfortable and
conspicuous in the unabashedly sexy top. I missed my habitual,
severe black.

I had noticed Tony eyeing me from the corner of my sight
line all day. I couldn't be mad, since the cleavage spilling from
my shirt invited attention that I didn't particularly want.

Well, that wasn't entirely true. I wanted it, but the one man
I wanted it from wasn't prepared to give it to me.

The clock told me that it was four thirty. Only another half
an hour, and then I could escape the office building, where everything reminded me of Zach.

Right. I could escape the office, only to go home and think
about him endlessly, reminders or not.

Get a grip, Devon. Grinding my teeth so hard that I could
hear the noise of the friction, I chugged a sip of the ice-cold coffee that had been sitting on my desk since that morning and
turned back to my computer with what I hoped was renewed
focus. When I wasn't miserable and mooning over Zachariah
St. Brenton, I actually really liked my job, and I didn't want to
lose it, not now that I had signed a lease on a place of my own. It
was a tiny studio apartment, and the monthly rent was double
what I had paid in Sacramento.

But it was not a cheap motel room. No, it was all mine.

As I set my coffee cup down, I caught the eye of Mrs. Gallagher. When I had walked in that morning she had taken one
look at my red blouse, sighed heavily, and walked away. Since
then, I had caught her staring at me with that concerned look
etched in thick lines between her eyes—by now I knew that I
wasn't imagining it. She had even been very nearly pleasant in
our interactions.

Her strange attitude hadn't helped the sense that my life

was off balance. Even now, as she pursed her lips in my direction, I wanted to scream. Though there was no way that she could know just how far my relationship with Zach had gone, she clearly suspected and disapproved, even as she felt pity toward me.

I didn't want anyone feeling pity for me. If I couldn't be in a relationship with Zach, pale as things seemed in the aftermath of our intense chemistry, I needed to move on with my life. And I didn't want to lose sight of what I had gained since moving to San Francisco.

I looked at the clock. Twenty minutes. Just a small fraction of my workday, but at the moment they felt like an eternity.

I gave up on work. It just wasn't going to happen. Instead I opened my e-mail browser and, after rubbing my temples with tense fingers, I set out to do what I had been trying to do for days.

I needed to get some sense of closure. I needed to have my say. Though, after our final encounter, I wasn't sure if he would actually read my e-mail or not, but at least I would have tried.

From: Reid, Devon [d.reid.accounting@phyrefly.com]
Sent: Friday, 4:53 PM
To: St. Brenton, Zachariah [z.stb.ceo@phyrefly.com]
Subject: Closure

Zach,

I'll keep this brief . . . I don't know if you will even read it or not. If you are reading, then I want you to know that I'm sorry. I didn't meet with Tom to upset you. I certainly didn't invite him here, but since he showed up I thought it was a good opportunity to tell him the things that I didn't when I left. This was something that I needed to do for myself.

I'm also sorry that I can't be who you need me to be. I know you think that I should be afraid of you, but I'm truly not. I am afraid of how I feel when you push me away, though, and since

you won't let me in, then there doesn't seem to be much hope. I
know that this isn't easy for you, either, and I know that that
kind of trust takes time. I wish . . . I don't actually know what I
wish anymore.

    Thank you for everything you have done for me. You helped
me uncover parts of myself that I didn't even know existed. I
have to find the strength now to continue that journey on my
own.

    I wish you all the best, Zach. I'd say that I'd like us to be
friends, but I think it would be too painful for me to be around
you at all and not be able to be with you, so I will stop at that.

Devon

I swallowed past the thick lump in my throat as I hesitated,
then clicked the Send icon on my screen before I could lose my
nerve. My nose prickled and my eyes were damp—it really felt
like it was over now.

The rational part of me knew that it wasn't normal, feeling
this upset over a man that I had known for less than a month. I
tried to tell myself that my behavior was obsessive and not a little bit crazy.

It didn't matter. I was devastated.

Looking at the clock yet again, I saw that it was after five.
Most of my colleagues had rushed out the door minutes earlier,
eager to shed their suit jackets and hit Friday night happy hour
at the bar across the street.

I was going to go home, have a good cry, and then get back
to trying to pull myself back together.

"Good night, Miss Devon Reid." Startled, I stopped in my
tracks momentarily when Mrs. Gallagher's voice cut through
my thoughts. I peered into her office, perplexed, and hoped that
my eyes weren't overly red from unshed tears.

"Good night, Mrs. Gallagher." The woman never bid a hello
or a farewell to any of her employees, and though her expres-

sion was stern as I clutched my worn leather purse to my chest, I was thoroughly unnerved by the gesture.

"I hope you're feeling better by Monday morning." The woman lowered her reading glasses to the tip of her nose and peered at me over the top of them. "This cold that's going around is brutal. If you're not well by then, take Monday off. But I will expect you back in shape first thing Tuesday morning."

Mrs. Gallagher shoved her glasses back up her nose and looked down at her work, effectively dismissing me. I blinked at her in surprise before hurrying away to the bank of elevators.

The woman was astute, and knew damn well that I didn't have a cold. The kind gesture of a long weekend to pull my act together was unexpected and incredibly strange.

Her underlying message, however, had been perfectly clear: Get over him and get your life back together.

It was exactly the kick in the pants that I needed, though I suspected she wouldn't appreciate it if I told her that, for the persona that she demonstrated in the office was not of the warm and fuzzy variety. Sniffling, I straightened my spine, inhaled deeply, and tried to get myself together.

My life wasn't entirely occupied by Zachariah St. Brenton. I could be happy without him.

Maybe if I told myself that enough times, it would be true.

The elevator pinged and then opened, and I did my best to shove all thoughts of myself bound on its floor during my last encounter with Zach from my mind. Making sure to keep my chin up, I stepped in and turned to press the button for the lobby.

I choked on my own breath when I saw Zach standing by the control panel, appearing calm and in control. He looked at me and nodded, stepping back to make space for me.

After a long, flustered moment in which my self-control

was shattered, I nodded in return, then faced the elevator door and tried to calm my racing heart.

This was to be expected. He was my boss. It was a big building, but we were bound to see each other from time to time. If I wanted to stay at this job, it was something that I would have to accept.

The silence was like a weight on my shoulders as we descended through the building. My mind tormented me with images of our last elevator ride together, and I couldn't help but wonder if he thought of it, too. As I chased the mental image of him binding my hands with my own lace underwear, I looked up to see his reflection in the polished chrome of the door, and I scowled to myself. It wasn't fair that he should look so mouth-watering when I felt—and looked—so ragged. His suit was charcoal today, and beneath it was a pale gray shirt with subtle stripes. He had removed his tie and unbuttoned the top button, and despite all of the lectures to myself, I found that I wanted nothing more than to place my lips against the enticing triangle of skin that that one small button revealed.

The elevator had almost reached the lobby, and I was congratulating myself on being strong, when he spoke.

"You said that you're not afraid of me. Is that true?" Startled, I turned to look at him sharply. He was still staring straight ahead, his expression a mask of control.

"Of course it is." Unsure of the situation, I twisted the strap of my purse in fingers that were trembling. "Whatever else you make me feel, fear isn't any part of it."

Zach nodded, then subsided into silence. It wasn't until the elevator hit the ground floor and the doors slid open that he pressed his hand to my elbow and drew me to his side.

A burst of fireworks exploded inside of me, starting at the small patch of skin where his fingers rested and sparking outward. My breath caught in my throat as I looked up at him, uncertainty and an undeniable need all twisted up together.

"I would like you to come somewhere with me." Holding out his hand, he caught the elevator doors before they were able to close. My heart pounding a staccato rhythm in my chest, I stepped out of the confined space, then turned to face him, my expression serious.

"Why?" By this point I had nothing to lose by asking. "Why now?"

Zach's eyes clouded, but I continued to stare directly into them, relentless. I needed him to give me something, anything, before I could step into the insanity that was our relationship again.

He seemed to be on the verge of refusing, and my heart sank. I reminded myself that Zachariah St. Brenton was not a man who was accustomed to explaining himself.

Then he spoke, and his words were guarded. It was almost as if he wanted to make sure that he said the right thing, and I felt a trill of hope swelling where it had no business to.

"I'm not ready to give you the things that you really need. I might never be. But I find that I can't stay away from you." His brutal honesty broke my heart in two before seaming it back up again. He was trying, trying so hard, and how could I refuse that?

"What do you think I need that you can't provide?" I measured my words carefully. "Because I'm an adult, Zach, and I'm walking into this with my eyes open. I want you. I want all of you."

Without warning, he tugged me into his arms, fisted his hands in my hair, and kissed me until I was breathless. My world narrowed until it was entirely focused on him. *This* was what I had been missing for six days. The force of his desire for me had kept me awake at night longing to touch him again. When Zach released me, I stumbled back, then pressed my fingers to my lips that were now swollen from his kiss.

"I'm a selfish bastard, and I want you. I can't share my past with you, because I can't even deal with it myself. But if you trust me, I can take you into my life as it is now."

The expression on his face was unabashedly sensual, and I saw that the front of his dress pants had tented during our kiss. I was hot, twitchy all over, and wanted nothing more than to lose myself in him.

Eyes wide, I nodded quickly before I could lose my nerve.

"Devon, be sure." He drew me to him again roughly, pressing his hardening cock into the soft swell of my belly. I trembled against him.

"Be sure that you're ready to go deeper."

The ride in Zach's car, with Charles at the wheel, passed in a bright blur. The only things I was entirely conscious of were the sensation of my hand clasped tightly in Zach's, and the heat of his thigh as it pressed intimately against my own.

We pulled up in front of a brick building. Small and dark, it had a slightly gothic look to the exterior, and it took a moment before I located a sign painted the color of chocolate.

"*Lush*?" I turned to Zach, suddenly self-conscious. "I'm not dressed for a club, Zach."

His eyes burned a path over the skin that my low-cut red blouse had left bare, and I shifted uncomfortably, my body overly warm, as if he had touched me.

"You always look lovely." He took my hand and helped me from the car as Charles opened the door. "And this isn't a typical club."

I raised my eyebrows in question, but he didn't respond, just placed his hand at the small of my back and led me to the door of the building.

"St. Brenton." The man holding some kind of digital device

at the door scrolled down the screen, his eyes widening when he found what he was looking for. I wondered if there was a note beside Zach's name that said something like "temperamental billionaire: treat with utmost caution."

Before I could ponder it further, we were passed off to a woman, some sort of hostess, I thought. She was a statuesque beauty with jet-black hair that fell in a sleek sheet to her ass, and the low-cut back of her dress rode nearly as low. Though her manner was utterly professional, I couldn't miss the up-and-down stare that she directed at Zach, nor the blatant hunger in her gaze as she did so.

He seemed oblivious, but he was an intelligent man. He had to be fully aware of it. I just didn't know how he felt about the attention that he received everywhere he went.

Insecurity plagued me, though I reminded myself over and over that he was there with me. I didn't comment on my thoughts, either, because I didn't think that he would take them well.

The gorgeous woman led us into a theater. It was a venue unlike anything I had ever seen before. I gaped as we were led to a private balcony, one of fifteen that I could count, all arranged in two neat semicircles before a small stage.

Each balcony was like a private dining room, though the walls extended only waist high to allow a view of the stage. Each contained a small table draped in a heavy black cloth, and on top of the table was a lush arrangement of deep, wine-colored roses, an array of fat white candles, and a silver bucket holding a pale green bottle.

As we sat, Zach gestured to the bottle. "This is the Stella d'Or that I requested?"

The woman nodded, her mouth pouting wetly. I was more than a little bit impressed with the brand of wine—Stella d'Or was high-end, and I had never tried it. I gulped as I thought of the cost, but was distracted when Zach sat on the curved leather loveseat that was pulled up to the table in lieu of regular chairs.

I wasn't sure what was about to happen, but anticipation hung in the air like a heavy velvet curtain. As Miss Come-Hither-Stare popped the cork on what turned out to be a beautiful Bordeaux the color of berries and poured Zach and me each a glass, I watched others being shown in to the theater and seated in their own balconies.

All were couples, with the exception of one group of three, who nonetheless seemed to all be together in a way that my mind couldn't quite comprehend. Clothing ran the gamut from a tuxedo and evening gown to a tiny red lace teddy and matching satin shortie robe.

"Zach, what is this place?" Though he shook his head to tell me that he wasn't going to tell, a small smile played over the corners of his lips—a small, wicked smile.

I took a large sip of my expensive wine, trying to wet my suddenly dry throat.

"That will be all, Marguerite. Thank you." Zach turned his attention entirely toward me, and I could see that our hostess didn't care for being dismissed. A small frown marred her features, and she stepped in closer to Zach, as if trying to insinuate herself between us.

A jade green streak of jealousy flashed before my eyes, and before I could think it through, I leaned in close and placed my hand flat on his chest, right over his heart. I looked up at the woman with wide eyes, as if startled to find that she was still there.

"Yes?" My voice was sweet, but even I could hear the venom underneath. I was surprised at myself. I'd never been the jealous type.

The woman whom Zach had called Marguerite scowled at the placement of my hand on Zach's chest.

"If you require anything else, all you have to do is press the buzzer." She gestured to a small device that sat on our table. "Anything that you require . . . anything at all . . . and I will come to serve you."

I blinked up at her, certain that I had misunderstood the double meaning layering her words. She smirked back at me, and I saw red.

"All that we require is to be left alone." Zach's words had me focusing my full attention on him, and I barely noticed the hostess leaving, because pleasant strands of sexual desire were humming merrily over my skin.

Once we were alone he pulled me onto his lap, arranging my legs so that I was straddling him. I gasped and looked around as my face flushed carmine.

No one seemed to be paying much attention to us, and if they were, they weren't overly shocked at our behavior. I, however, squirmed as Zach palmed my breast, squeezing the flesh gently and nibbling at my ear.

"I think I like it when you get jealous." My breath caught in my throat as heat from his touch spread throughout my skin and down to my core. Though his hands slid down to catch me at my waist, he didn't hold me in place, so I slid off of his lap and onto my own bottom.

"What the hell was that?" Though no one else seemed to care, I was mortified. "We're in public!"

Zach didn't seem the least bit ruffled, and I felt compelled to play the good angel.

"What if there was a photographer here? They could have gotten a really dreadful picture right now!" I closed my eyes, not able to even imagine what would happen to my life at work if a picture of me straddling the CEO made the rounds at the office.

Zach seemed nonplussed. "Cameras aren't allowed in here.

They're very strict about it, and you'll soon see why." He snaked an arm around my waist and pulled me close, though he kept his touch chaste—if any touch from him could be considered so. "And if a picture was taken that I didn't want made public, I'm fortunate enough to have enough money to bury it."

He spoke as if having that much money was just a mundane fact of life, and I supposed that for him it was. It made my head hurt.

I buried my nose in my glass of wine to change the subject.

"Do you like it?" Though he had a glass of his own, Zach took mine once I had finished sipping. The casual intimacy of the gesture made me hope for things that I knew I shouldn't.

My pulse stuttered when, instead of tasting wine from my glass, he leaned in and pressed a heated kiss to my yielding lips, sampling the wine from my tongue.

"Mmm." I trembled as he caught me with that hot stare as he eased back. "It tastes much better this way."

"It—it's wonderful." My throat was dry with need as I agreed. I wasn't by any means a connoisseur, but I knew that the wine was richly layered and that its flavors mingled seductively on my tongue. "You didn't have to go to such trouble, though."

Zach shrugged and handed me back my glass. "Stella d'Or is owned by a friend of mine. I like to support his business, but I would purchase it even if it wasn't his. It's exceptional wine."

At that moment the lights in the house began to dim. Before the theater went black, Zach turned to me, and traces of the levity that he had displayed over the past few minutes were gone.

"I said that I wanted to share a part of my world with you," he began, and my mind immediately ran in a million different directions. "I brought you here tonight to open your mind to possibilities. I hope that you're going to enjoy what we're about to see. That said, if you're uncomfortable and want to leave, just tell me and we'll go." There was no dominance in his tone, and he wasn't ordering me.

It made me want to enjoy whatever it was that we were about to see, though his words made me nervous. I thought of a thousand possibilities as we waited for the lights to come back up—was it a risqué play? A little-known singer songwriter that Zach was a fan of? Was he strangely into opera?

The lights came up all at once, illuminating two figures on a stark stage. My heart stuttered in my chest, and I clutched at Zach as I realized what we were about to see.

We were at a live sex show.

"Zach!" I felt as though I should be horrified, but I wasn't . . . at all.

The sight of the couple on stage, both of them completely naked, aroused me beyond belief.

"Devon, do you remember what I once told you? Forget about what you think you should feel, and just immerse yourself in the experience." I fidgeted in my seat, unable to keep my eyes on the couple for more than a few seconds at a time.

I already knew what I really felt, and it was raw and dirty and not what was expected of a good girl.

I wrestled with myself, mortally uncomfortable. When Zach caught my chin in his hand and turned my face to look at him, I looked down, feeling ashamed.

"Devon." With the hand not holding my chin, he tucked a wisp of my ponytail behind my ear. When I dared to look up at him, I found no pretense in his expression or demeanor.

"There's nothing wrong with wanting what you want. What *I* want is to share something with you that I think will bring us both pleasure. The choice is simple. If you want to stay, we will. If you don't, we'll leave. Just tell me."

There was no judgment in his tone, no coercion, though I figured that if he had brought me here, he wanted to stay, wanted to experience this with me. And even if I hadn't wanted to please him, which I did, I found that a big part of me wanted to stay.

It felt deviant, and it felt wrong. It was so different from anything I'd experienced before. But, as Zach had pointed out, there was nothing wrong with wanting what I wanted. So I licked my lips with the tip of my tongue to moisten them, and, staring down at my hands, whispered, "I want to stay."

I felt a shudder pass through Zach's body, and an answering heat in my own. I found it strangely reassuring.

No matter the difficulties that we faced in the strange and intense relationship that we shared, there was something primal in each of us that responded to the other. It was indefinable and thrilling, and in that moment, comforting.

Zach was teaching me there was nothing wrong with being who I was—and the person I was discovering I was would sit back and enjoy a live sex show.

On the stage, the couple kissed softly. Though they were both fully nude, it was not what I expected. It was sweet. It was romantic.

I cast a sidelong glance at Zach. He was watching calmly, and I took my cue from him.

The woman threaded her hands through the man's hair. He ran his palms over her back and down, caressing the cheeks of her ass. She moaned, the sound echoing loudly throughout the theater.

The man dropped suddenly to his knees in front of her, and she placed her hands on his shoulders. Her lips were glistening from his kisses. With a sure touch he parted her thighs, then her labia, opening her to his mouth like a flower to the sun.

My mouth fell open as the man bent and placed a wet, openmouthed kiss on the woman's cunt. She smiled with pleasure, arching her hips into his face, and heat suffused me.

I shifted in my seat, uncomfortable and at the same time fixated on the scene in front of me. I found that I could not look away.

Watching the man lick and suck and bring the woman to climax was one of the most erotic things that I had ever seen. Neither was the type of person that I expected to see on this stage—both appeared to be in their midforties, and while attractive, were clearly not models. The woman had a soft curve to her belly that told me she had borne children, and the hair between the man's legs was streaked with iron gray.

Still, something in their caresses drew me in, held me captive. As the woman's shudders subsided, and she dropped to her own knees while urging the man to his feet, I realized what it was.

"Are they a real couple?" The sureness in the caresses that were being played out in front of us, the familiarity between them, spoke of years of togetherness. Still, I was shocked at the idea of two people, whose wedding rings were visible now that I looked for them, choosing to pleasure each other in a venue that was designed for others to watch.

Zach looked down at me, and though I could see the same arousal that I felt on his features, he gave me his full attention.

"Most of the people who perform here are." Reaching out, he ran his thumb over the swell of my lower lip. Aroused beyond belief, I caught it in my teeth, then soothed the nip with a swipe of my tongue.

He growled before pulling his hand away.

"Why would someone want to do that?" A thought hit me, and I grabbed at Zach's leg with tense fingers. "When you said you wanted to show me a part of your life . . . is this what you meant? You want to be on that stage?"

My stomach dropped. Watching the scene before me, where the woman now wrapped full, pink lips around her husband's erect cock, was surprisingly yet incredibly arousing.

But the idea of standing on that stage getting fucked, even if it was Zach doing the fucking, left me cold.

Zach scowled at my question. Leaning forward, he placed a hand on my knee, the heat of his palm warming skin that was bared beneath the hem of my skirt.

"Nobody gets to see you come but me." With one swift movement he slid his hand higher, finding and toying with the elastic of my panties. I squirmed with excitement, all the while trying to maintain an expression of nonchalance, though clearly no one in this environment would care.

Zach slid his finger beneath the cloth of my underwear. My body bowed as he found the entrance to my pussy and slid one finger into the wet, waiting heat. Anyone around us who chose to look into our balcony would know exactly what we were up to from the expression on my face, even though the half walls provided a modicum of privacy.

No, I didn't want to be on that stage, but having Zach's hand between my legs in public held a definite thrill.

"Nobody gets to experience any part of this cunt but me," Zach continued, his words hot and stern. I nodded my agreement and pressed my weight down on his finger. He chuckled and withdrew all but the very tip, and I groaned with frustration.

"Watch the show, Devon." I tried to keep still, but it was next to impossible, with the intrusion between my lower lips.

On the stage, the woman began to move faster, sucking her husband's cock with enthusiasm. Zach began to move his finger in time with the thrusts, fucking my pussy with his hand as the woman fucked her husband's cock with her mouth.

I could feel myself growing wetter with every glide of Zach's finger inside of me. I moaned and shifted restlessly; it wasn't enough, I wanted more.

The man on stage shouted and thrust once, hard, into his wife's mouth. Semen dribbled out from between her lips as he came down her throat. I watched, mesmerized, and at the same time Zach withdrew his finger from my heat and pinched my clit once, hard.

He pulled me toward him and swallowed my cry with his kiss as I shuddered into his palm.

"Zach." My voice was thready and weak, my attention completely focused on him. "I want to go. I want to go someplace and be with you."

His expression darkened at my words. Bravely, I reached forward and cupped his groin in my palm. He was hard, and I squeezed gently, hoping to urge him to agree with me.

"One more." Lifting the hand that had been between my legs to his lips, he licked the finger that had ridden inside of me as I watched openmouthed.

"Later, I'm going to spread you open and have as much of you as I want." I swallowed a whimper at the heat that snaked through me, brought on by the mental image of Zach's tousled head between my thighs. "But I want you to watch one more. Then I'll take you home and fuck you."

"Christ." I muttered the word to myself as I dragged my attention back to the stage. What I wanted to do was to unzip Zach's pants, to free his cock, and climb astride him then and there.

At the same time I realized the feelings he could bring out in me were so intense that they scared me a little. But they felt so right—*he* felt so right with me—as if I was discovering who the real Devon truly was the more time I spent with him.

Taking Zach's advice, I leaned against him and focused on the new scene unfolding below us. I didn't want to analyze, didn't want to think. I wanted to let sensation take me as far as I could go.

When two men walked onto the stage, I caught my lower lip in my teeth. Was this going to be a ménage scene? Was a woman joining them, and they would take turns with her?

Anticipation had the muscles of my belly clenching tightly. I squirmed in my seat, and Zach took my hand and placed it flat on the top of his thigh. I traced patterns over the hard muscles with my fingers, and imagined doing it with my tongue.

The two men on stage were both large and in incredible shape. The rippled muscles that were displayed in the naked chests and arms above their faded denim told me that they were both involved in some sort of physical labor. One was blond and looked like he would be at home riding the waves. The other had hair buzzed short and a tattoo of undulating red flames that wrapped around his tanned skin from his back to his torso.

Both men were attractive enough to have me clenching my thighs together in defense against the heat. But when they turned to each other, and the one drew the other in for a hot, openmouthed kiss I became unglued.

"Zach." The passion was unfolding onstage between this couple far more quickly than it had with the first pair. The man with the buzz cut was tugging at the zipper of the blond's jeans even as he caught the other man's lower lip between his teeth and tugged. The blond cupped the other's ass in his hands and squeezed the hard planes over and over again. "Zach, are you okay with this?"

"I'm more than okay with it." One glance told me that Zach was as aroused as I was, riveted to the action on stage as the blond man's pants hit the floor. The man with the buzz cut drew a small tube from his pocket. After unscrewing the lid he squirted a thick amount of clear liquid onto his hands and the blond man's bare ass.

"Holy shit." I was ready to climb the walls. I had never fantasized about two men having sex before, had never even considered that it might be a turn-on. But watching as it played out before my eyes, and knowing that Zach was finding it as arousing as I was, made need crawl beneath my skin.

I couldn't believe that Zach was as into it as I was. He had never displayed any bisexual tendencies, at least not to me, but I could hear his heavy breathing as he watched the male couple beginning to make love.

Turning, he caught my questioning gaze and smiled, the expression wicked.

"I'm not interested in sex with a man, Devon." I relaxed a bit, though I hadn't realized that I was tense. It was stressful enough knowing that Zach could have any beautiful woman he wanted. If he were open to both sexes, I just might lose my mind.

Zach placed his arm over my shoulder and covered one of my breasts with his large hand. Sliding his hand inside the low neckline of my blouse, he began to toy with my nipple, and I felt an answering tug all the way to my womb.

"Just because I don't want to have sex with a man doesn't mean that I don't find watching this arousing as hell." Even as I pushed into the hand caressing my breast, I looked over and met his eyes. He was looking at me as if waiting for me to be upset or disgusted. I couldn't imagine feeling either emotion, not at that moment. "Ever heard of Alfred Kinsey and his scale?"

I shook my head.

"Kinsey created a scale where a true heterosexual was located at one end, and a true homosexual at the other. Everything in between was numbered, in degrees of sexual preference." His eyes flashed as he made sure that I was listening. "Even if a person identifies with one end or the other, Kinsey found that most people are located somewhere in the grayer areas in between. So though I am only interested in having sex with women, I am turned on by watching two men together. Why should I ignore that pleasure, just to force myself to the far end of the scale?"

My mouth was open by the time he had finished speaking. He was so incredibly sexy, so in control of his sexuality. There was so much I admired about this powerful, passionate man. The kinks in his personality fascinated me, drew me in.

Apparently done talking, he pulled at my nipple, and I moaned. The man on stage ran a thick finger through the crevice that divided his partner's ass. I cried out, a bit louder.

I needed an outlet. As I watched the two men on stage, I reached over with both hands and unfastened Zach's belt.

"Devon!" His voice was shocked, and I smiled into the darkness. I liked being able to shock him.

After struggling a moment with the button and zipper of his slacks, I freed his cock from the confines of the fabric. I wrapped my fingers around the silk and steel of Zach's erection, enjoying the hiss of his breath as I slid my thumb over the weeping slit at the top.

"Devon." His voice was far less stern now, and he thrust up into my hand. A strange sensation washed through me as he leaned back against the leather of the seat and thrust up into my hand again, surrendering to me, for the moment at least.

I felt powerful. It was such a small thing, but Zach giving me leave to take charge made me feel in control of my own life.

I relished the sensation, and wanted to give something back.

I sighed with longing as I ran my fist up and down the length of Zach's cock. My entire being was full, full of need, and my skin felt too tight.

I wondered if I would ever get enough of this man.

"Devon, stop." Zach's voice was hoarse, and he placed his hand over my own, slowing my movements. I tightened my fingers and watched the thrusting on the stage below increase in tempo. "I want to be inside you when I come."

"Please, Zach." The soft cloth of my bra abraded my nipples as I shifted restlessly, my hand still wrapped around Zach. "I need this. I need you."

I felt him shudder, and then he nodded, arching into my grip once more. I stroked him hard and deep, imagined that I was taking him inside of my body. On the stage, the man who was thrusting inside of the other one slowly pulled himself free, then pumped his own length with vigor as he rested a hand on the clenched muscles of the other man's ass. Within moments he came, his orgasm spattering across the back and buttocks of his lover, who moaned and arched into it.

I ran my thumb down the length of Zach's cock again, to the tip, and heard him groan, low and deep. Seconds later liquid heat filled my palm, salt scenting the air. I continued my strokes as he shuddered, arching into my touch. He came long and hard, and as on edge as I was myself, I smiled with satisfaction at being able to bring him so much pleasure.

Once he had stilled beneath my hand, Zach inhaled a long, broken breath. He turned his head, and I found myself pinned beneath the bright stare of those golden eyes.

He glared. I grinned. I couldn't help myself.

"You're going to pay for that, Devon." My smile faded as a black thrill shuddered throughout my body. Zach had told me that he was going to take me deeper, and I had played right into his hands.

Rather than feeling fear, I was full of delicious anticipation. I relished the powerful sense of desire he brought to life within me, and the sense of the unknown about what he would show me next.

"Can we go now?" I could hear the eagerness in my whisper. Though the two men on the stage below had switched positions and were caressing each other with renewed passion, I had lost all interest in the scenario.

All I wanted was Zach, and whatever he wanted to bring me.

In response he smiled, and in the curve of his lips were both danger and promise.

CHAPTER TWELVE

I stared at Zach with incredulity. Having just arrived at his house in Seacliff, he had led me directly into the kitchen and informed me, "You need to eat something."

I was still shaking with need and anticipation of sex. Food was not what I had in mind.

"I'm not hungry." I tried to reach for him, to wrap my arms around his waist, and was stung when he pulled away.

Zach saw my hurt expression and huffed out a breath, raking a hand through his hair. He looked irritated, which didn't help to soothe me at all. Biting my lip, I studied the vast expanse of veined marble counter, the sleek chrome appliances, the overhanging copper pots and pans that, if I had to guess, I would say had never been used. I was forced to again focus on Zach when pulling me into his arms, he pressed a quick kiss to my forehead, then released me. "I'm not used to having to explain myself, Devon."

Not entirely placated, I narrowed my eyes and moved out of his reach. I felt as if ice water had just been poured over the live wires of my nerves, and I didn't much care for the sensation.

He followed me with his stare, assessing my mood. I was on edge, and met his appraising glance with one of my own.

He sighed, then slid a glass of water down the marble counter toward me. I took it after a long pause, and had to admit to myself that the icy liquid felt incredible on my raw throat.

"You agreed that tonight I would take you deeper into my world. Well, we've only just begun." I coughed as a too-large gulp of water forced its way down my throat.

We had only just begun? I had expected that as soon as we got here we would satisfy the lust that had been riding me for the last week, but Zach's words made it sound as though I was about to be led to a land from which there was no return.

Perhaps there wasn't. I knew that I had only experienced a taste of his dominance, and I was ready to admit I craved more.

"What does that have to do with my eating?" Truly, I was so worked up that I didn't think I could possibly swallow a mouthful. I didn't understand why he was pressing the issue. "I'm really not hungry, Zach."

Frustration painted his features and I watched, fascinated, as he worked to smooth it away.

"When you put yourself in my hands, I am responsible for your welfare." I could hear in his tone that he really didn't care for having to explain himself. Though there were so many levels on which I truly wanted to please him, in this situation I found that I liked provoking him.

I suspected that, in the end, his frustration would lead to my pleasure.

"Zach." I wanted to move on to that pleasure right now. The stolen touches in the theater had only whetted my appetite. I wanted an entire night in which I could touch him, could look at his magnificent body, could feel his skilled hands on my own. "Please."

"I need you to eat something, Devon." Turning from the fridge, he slid a bowl of raspberries down the counter to me. They reminded me of the night that we had met, and my cheeks flushed.

His voice was tight, and the look on his face told me that he wouldn't give on this matter.

"I need to know that you are going to have the strength for what I have planned for you. Now eat."

My initial reaction was to refuse, just on principle.

"Devon." Exasperation thick in his voice, he raked his hands through his hair again, then tugged at it. "I shouldn't have to explain. Just do it."

I didn't appreciate being spoken to like a parent might to an errant child. Looking down at the bowl pointedly, I crossed my arms tightly over my chest.

"I want to know why." I held my breath, nerves slicing through me with jagged edges. I might have just pushed him too far, and I knew it.

He had said that he wasn't ready to share. From what I had seen, he might not ever be ready. But I couldn't just obey him blindly. There were things I needed to know.

Things like, what did he have planned that would be so strenuous that I needed food in my belly?

Nerves danced over my skin with even greater force than before, and I eyed him with uncertainty.

He scowled. I refused to break eye contact.

Finally, begrudgingly, he spoke. "A few years ago there was a woman I was involved with. I had always been careful before her, and nothing bad had ever happened. I relaxed some of my rules with her. She wound up in the hospital, and never forgave me."

A small sound snuck past my lips. What had he and this woman from the past been doing that she ended up in the hospital, no matter what his rules were? I opened my mouth to ask the question, and to demand to know if he had something similar planned for me, but he shook his head before the words could leave my lips.

"I'm not telling you what I have planned for you. And I'm not talking about anything else from my past." A quick glance

at him told me that he was entirely serious. Just those few simple sentences seemed to have drawn great amounts of energy
from him, and I started to understand then what it cost him to
visit those demons from his past.

With that in mind, I pulled a plump, juicy red berry to my
lips and took a bite, holding his gaze the entire time.

"You're learning." A relieved and self-satisfied smile curled
Zach's lips, and in response I threw a raspberry at him, deliberately trying to lighten the mood. He was only too willing to
move on, and he caught it in his mouth, drawing a giggle out of
me.

Things between us felt so light, so blessedly normal, that I
couldn't believe it had only been hours earlier that I had been
convinced we were done.

I bit into another berry. Zach's stare followed the movements of my lips, my tongue, as I chewed and swallowed.

"Did you enjoy what we saw tonight?" Walking—no, he
stalked—across the kitchen toward me, he pulled my fingers
from the bowl of berries and fed the next one to me himself. I
made sure that my tongue swept across the pads of his fingers
as I accepted the fruit, nodding as I chewed and swallowed.

"You are amazing, Devon." I shook my head when he lifted
another piece of red fruit. With him standing so close, I could
smell that essence that was so uniquely him, and I had tightened all over with need.

I didn't want any more food. Not one more bite. I wanted
him.

Shoving the bowl to the side with barely restrained excitement, Zach bent at the knees and swept me off of my feet, quite
literally. My arms curled around his neck with barely restrained
glee as his arms tucked beneath my knees and my butt.

He may have meant it as a display of power, but it made my
heart stumble in my chest. I tried to swallow down the feelings

that blossomed under his tender touch, knowing that he wasn't in any place to reciprocate them, and only just succeeded in hiding them.

At the moment, I would take any part of this man that I could get. And if it meant hiding away the fact that I was starting to care for him, really, truly care for him, then that was what I would do.

Kicking open the door to his bedroom, he strode across the carpet before depositing me gently on his meticulously made bed. I thought of how he had awakened, tangled in nightmares, in that same bed, and felt a frisson of uncertainty.

No matter how I felt about him, at the core I knew next to nothing about him. Whatever was about to happen, I was placing a large amount of trust in him.

I looked up to find him watching me with a shuttered expression.

"You can still decide, Devon. Yes or no." His face revealed nothing. "But once we begin, you need to trust me. That trust is the basis of this entire relationship. You will have your safe word, but you have to have faith that I am not going to push you past what I know you can handle."

This was it, the decisive moment that would decide the path of our future. I could say no, could turn around and walk back into my calm, normal life.

The life that had felt like it belonged to someone else. The life that couldn't hold a candle to what I had experienced since I met Zach.

"Yes." It was all that I needed to say. Before my eyes I watched Zach channel the dominant aspect of himself. He seemed to grow taller, stronger, more arrogant, and yet at the same time I felt myself relaxing into his presence.

No harm would come to me around this man. He would protect me with his own life. I was sure of it.

He stared at me, unblinking. I held his gaze and found it intensely uncomfortable—it agitated my soul. I found that what I wanted to do was sink to my knees on the floor at his feet, but the little voice in my head that hadn't completely surrendered argued against that notion. As a compromise I folded my hands in my lap, and stared down at the place where my fingers became tightly entwined.

"Very good." His voice was benevolent, a king speaking to his subject. He went further, leaning forward and catching my chin with his finger, tilting my face up and giving me permission to look him in the eye.

"Devon, I am going to go retrieve some objects that I wish to use with you. When I return, you will have shed all of your clothing except for your panties. You will be sitting on the bed exactly as you are now, your hands folded in your lap, your eyes down." Without pausing to see if I had heard or understood, Zach left the room. I blinked after him, my heart racing, then hurried to do as he had said.

My fingers trembled as I undid the waist ties of my scarlet blouse. Not having the patience to fold it neatly, I still caught it before it fell to the floor and draped it over Zach's massive wooden dresser. My skirt followed, and then my bra.

By the time I sat back down on the cool sheets, clad in nothing but the thin cotton of my plain white bikini panties, I was shaking with nerves.

Everything that Zach had introduced me to so far, I had thrilled to. I knew, however, from his earlier indications, that he was about to take me deep, far deeper than my mind could currently contemplate.

I tried to slow my breaths, which were huffing from my chest. My fingers, which were laced together in my lap as he had commanded, were icy cold and slick with sweat.

I started to look up when I heard Zach return to the room,

but caught myself halfway, certain that that would earn me a reprimand. I stayed still, tracking his movements in my mind's eye as he moved around the room this way and that, finally returning to stand before me.

"Undress me." His voice was coarse, almost cruel in its intonation. I looked up, into his face, and he hissed in warning, but not until I saw and recognized that he had become a completely different person. No, that wasn't entirely correct. The Zach that I knew was still there, but in this situation, he was also . . . something more.

I had experienced enough with Zach to know what he was capable of, even when he wasn't fully channeling his dominant side. And wondering what was to come now made me instantly wet.

"Start with my shirt." I stood and lifted my fingers to the top button of his dress shirt. He had removed his tie himself at some point, and I was thankful, because I wasn't sure that my trembling fingers could have dealt with a Windsor knot.

The small buttons running down the front of the shirt were enough trouble. I fumbled, slipping several times and having to retry. He said nothing, his patience infinite, despite the lack of grace to my movements, and finally the shirt hung open, revealing the glorious, tawny expanse of his chest.

I ran a palm over one of his pectoral muscles, and a fierce noise issued from his throat.

"I have not given you permission to touch me, slave." I reared back at the title. *Slave?* I wasn't sure I was into that at all. Glaring at him, I took my hand away, daring him to say it again.

"Only when you accept how sexually submissive you truly are, Devon, are you going to find what you're looking for." Irritation began to burn in my fingertips, traveling up my arms and out to the rest of my body.

Much as I didn't know him, he didn't know me, either.

I stepped back, hesitating. I knew that I could end this at any time. I had my safe word.

Zach watched me calmly, his face unyielding. I pinched my lips together and told myself to get over it.

Did it really matter what he called me? It didn't change the fact that I wanted him, wanted him badly.

"Good girl." Zach spoke as the tension left my shoulders, my decision made. I thrilled to his praise, happy to have pleased him.

"Remove my shirt from my body. Then my pants." Tentatively I resumed my work, unbuttoning the cuffs of linen that bound his wrists and peeling the fabric from his torso. His skin, naked and glowing in the fading light revealed by the great panes of glass in the walls and ceiling, made me sigh and long to touch.

"Zach." I dug my nails into my palms to keep from reaching out for him. He glared down at me, his brow furrowed, and I knew that I had done something wrong.

"While we are in this bedroom, you will call me 'master,' or 'sir.' Do you understand?" I stared at him, my mouth parted in surprise.

Was he serious? What did it matter what I called him? But each time his dominant instructions brought me up short, I realized anew that it didn't do anything to lessen the desperate want I felt toward him.

In response to my hesitancy, Zach reached out and gave a quick slap to my left hip, hard enough to sting. I jolted, shying out of his reach, but he followed, staying too close for me to relax.

"I asked if you understood me. Answer." He wasn't joking. There was no hint of levity on his face at all.

I stuttered twice as I tried to reply.

"Yes . . . sir. I understand." *Sir* I could swallow. I wasn't about to call him *master*.

Wary now, I reached out for his waistband, half expecting to be scolded for that, too. But he had given me permission to remove his pants, and so he said nothing as I unbuckled and removed his belt, then unzipped his trousers and sent them tumbling to the floor.

"Pick them up." Bending at the waist, I retrieved the garment, folding it neatly and placing it on the dresser with my own clothing. I coiled the belt on top of it, shuddering with a mixture of pleasure and wariness as I remembered his use of it on me days earlier.

"Come here." Nervously, I crossed back to where Zach still stood. He was now gloriously naked, completely bare before my eyes, but I wasn't allowed to lift my eyes from the floor.

When I reached him he turned me, sliding his hands over my shoulders and down my rib cage, brushing the sensitive sides of my breasts as he stroked his way back up my body.

Trailing his fingers delicately over the nape of my neck, he wrapped his hand around my long ponytail. As he tugged gently, I could feel him tying the length in a knot, ensuring that the abundance of hair was completely out of the way.

"Now, let's discuss your punishment." I gasped as he drew me back against him sharply, using his hands to press my hips back against him. His cock, which was erect if not completely hard, nestled in the crevice between my buttocks, and I fought the urge to grind myself back against him.

"My punishment?" I was truly puzzled. I was trying to follow his orders, I really was.

"Though some of your recent activities leave much to be desired, there is only one thing that you are to be punished for tonight." His lips brushed over my ear and I shivered involuntarily, even as my gut clenched at his words.

This was not something that I was going to like. I was somehow certain of it. Still, the brush of his fingers, following the trail of warm breath along my neck, told me that I would like anything he told me to.

"What have I done?" A sharp pinch on the nerve that lay in the tender spot where my neck met my shoulder reminded me that he hadn't given me permission to speak. Grinding my teeth together with frustration, I quieted, though I didn't want to.

"Your former lover placed his hands on you." Shock whipped through me and I tried to turn, to confront him over the unfairness of his comment. His hands had come to rest on my waist, holding me still, and I was forced to speak while looking away from him.

"That is not at all fair. I didn't invite Tom to San Francisco. And I certainly didn't ask him to touch me!" Surely Zach wasn't serious. He couldn't be.

He squeezed my waist, his touch firm.

"You placed yourself in a situation in which he was able to lay his hands on you." I jolted forward, twisting this time until I did break free from Zach's touch. As if he had been expecting it, he said nothing, simply eyeing me contemplatively.

"We went for coffee, Zach. Coffee. And I managed to get some closure. So what's the problem?" I found that I was angry, truly angry now. Somehow, I had thought that these games that Zach and I were playing would be based upon honesty, and this seemed like a ruse.

I was humbled by his next words. "You didn't consider how it would make me feel, seeing you with another man." I opened my mouth to retort, then closed it quietly when I realized that I had nothing to say.

By telling me this, by punishing me for this, he was opening a part of himself up. He had just told me that I had the power to hurt him. And that seeing me with another man, someone I used to date, had hurt him.

It made me want to please him all the more.

Still . . . "Haven't you already punished me for this?" I thought of the pain wrought by the supple leather of his belt, and something red and slick rolled over in my gut.

Zach shook his head slowly, and I caught the glint in his eye that told me that he was thoroughly enjoying this.

"A quick fuck in an elevator is not proper punishment for how you made me feel, Devon." Gesturing across the room with his right arm, he motioned for me to look. Turning, I saw a large wooden post positioned by the glass wall, so that if someone leaned against it, they could peer out at the raging waves of the sea at the same time.

Coiled on the floor at the base of the post was the whip that I had held in my hand before. I felt my heart skip a beat, then resume its pounding, double time.

I knew, without a doubt, that the whip was not about to be used on me.

"You said that you would whip me, if I still wanted you to." The expression in Zach's eyes was flat as he looked at me. The need for him to be punished ran deeper than I had ever imagined.

I tried to hide it, because he wouldn't have appreciated it at all, but sympathy washed over me in a wave. What was it that clawed at his soul? What made him crave such punishment? "Zach." Before, his request to be whipped had seemed to be a knee-jerk reaction, something to help scrub away the residue of his nightmare. Now, I could see how deep he truly craved it. I could also see that it wasn't fully about him.

He knew that I was uncomfortable with this. Therefore this was the punishment for my flagrant disregard of his feelings. I wished I could explain to him that I hadn't been intentionally careless with what he felt.

Rather, I hadn't had any clue that I was capable of making him feel anything at all.

Humbled, my head reeling, I crossed the room and picked up the whip. My fingers were cold, numb, and they felt clumsy as I wrapped them around the thick length of the handle.

I couldn't speak. But I could give this to him. Starting to tremble with the knowledge of what I was about to do, I looked up at the beautiful, complex man before me and nodded once, sharply.

"Good girl." He wasn't as joyous as he might have been, having won this battle. As he crossed the room to the post, and I saw the stiffness in the lines of his frame, I began to see how deep the connection between his need for pleasure and pain and his nightmares ran.

"Do you remember how to do this?" He twisted, looked back at me before positioning himself at the post. I let my mind run back to the sensation of his hand over mine, swinging through the air, the tail of the whip cracking as it landed on the floor.

I shuddered, and not with pleasure, before forcing myself to nod.

"I remember." What I was about to do, I did entirely for Zach.

I watched numbly as he positioned himself against the tall wooden post. Lifting his arms above his head, he pressed a cheek against the smooth, pale width and widened the stance of his legs.

"You are going to give me five blows." His voice told me that there would be no arguing. "And I will know if you are holding back."

I watched as he closed his eyes. He was completely on display as he leaned against the post, the twilight shadows casting interesting art on the glory of his body. I found myself pondering the dichotomy of a being so perfect on the outside, and so twisted and scarred within.

"Devon!" It sounded as though he spoke through gritted teeth. I cringed, then lifted the hand holding the whip.

I would do this quickly, and get it over with.

Every muscle in my body was tense. But despite myself, I could sense his need for what I was about to do to him. With my hand lifted in the air, I froze, not sure if I would be able to follow through.

Then I looked at the man standing in front of me. I had asked him to open himself up. Though this was not at all what I had imagined, I had gotten my wish.

Squeezing my eyes shut, I sent the whip flying.

I knew before it landed that I had missed, the tip hitting the floor inches to the right of Zach's foot.

He said nothing, no chastisement, no further encouragement. I watched his reflection in the glass. He waited, his eyes closed, his expression blank.

Pure sensation crashed over me as I watched him standing there. Feelings that I hadn't wanted clenched around my heart with needy fingers and squeezed tightly.

In that moment I would have done anything for him. And so I lifted the whip again, and this time brought it home.

The moment the fifth lash had been administered, I collapsed on the floor, my knees no longer able to support me. Though my throat felt besieged with emotions, my eyes remained dry as I watched the man in front of me unfurl from his position at the post, his back striped liberally with red, and one small cut of crimson where the lash had dug too deep.

"I'm sorry." My heart pounded, the blood that rushed through my ears sounding like the hooves of a horse in full gallop. "I am so sorry. Please. Please forgive me." I began to tremble, icy cold spreading over my skin.

Zach knelt on the floor next to me, and began to rain tender kisses over my face, my shoulders, my neck.

"You darling girl, don't be sorry." He seemed lighter than he had since I had met him, as if the blows of the whips had chased away some of the demons that haunted him. "You have helped me so much. You've done so well. It is time for your reward."

I sniffled, determined not to cry. I watched with wide eyes as he stood and then helped me to my feet.

Heat began to rain down over the chill that permeated my body when he danced his eyes over me, looking his fill at my naked flesh. His cock rose as he stared intensely at the damp heat between my legs, which was still partially hidden by the thin white cotton of my panties.

"Take those off." He was again in full control. I felt as if a piece of myself that I used to know had been bulldozed to the ground, and I didn't have the strength to argue or to question.

Hooking my fingers in the elastic at my hips, I pulled the cotton down until it dropped to the floor. Unabashed, Zach drank in the view of my naked pussy with greedy eyes.

"Sit on the end of the bed." As I moved to obey, he brought a large bag over to me. Reaching inside, he removed two objects, one of which I recognized, one that I didn't.

He handed me the one that was unfamiliar. It was composed of four connected beads that were graduated in size with a ring at one end. I couldn't imagine what it was for.

"You liked watching the two men fuck at the club, didn't you?" As he spoke, he unscrewed the lid from the object that I did recognize—a tube of lubricant.

Heat spread over my skin as he drizzled a stream of thick, clear gel over the string of beads that I held in my hands.

"You know I did." What had turned me on even more was

that the entirely masculine Zach had been just as into the scene as I was.

"Anal play feels good for both men and women." Closing the tube of lubricant, Zach reached over and rubbed it into my fingers. My entire body tightened with excitement.

"You've given me pain tonight, and now I want to share in the pleasure." He turned away from me, my eyes level with his trim waist, and I could feel my clitoris pulsing with the heat of extreme arousal.

This was not something I could ever have imagined, but I was so, so into it.

"What . . . what do I do?" I felt again that he was allowing me to be empowered, even though he was the one telling me what to do.

I had never before in my life felt so in control, and I relished the sensation.

"Rub some of the lubricant over me." I did as he said, placing my slick hands on his flesh, massaging the liquid in.

Fully aware of the ultimate goal, I held my breath and trailed one finger up to the entrance of his ass. When I pressed against the pucker of his anus, the tip of my finger breached his flesh, pulling tightly at me.

He hissed in a breath, then moaned long and slow.

"Now take the beads." I removed my finger from his heat, shuddering with need. "Hold them by the ring, then press the smallest bead right where your finger just was."

I did as I was told, my every nerve on fire. I placed the smallest bead against his anus, then pushed, slowly.

Zach let out a strangled moan and pushed back against me. The first bead slid inside his flesh.

Perspiration dotted my brow, and yet I felt myself grow wetter between my thighs.

"Now the next one." It was harder to get the bigger bead in, for his flesh fought the intrusion. Finally all four beads were buried tightly inside his body, the ring snugged against the hard planes of his ass.

Zach turned then, and I saw that his cock was engorged to what had to be the point of pain. Fisting his hands in my hair, he brought me just close enough to reach out and flick my tongue over the semen that had pooled at the tip of his shaft.

"One day soon I'm going to fuck your ass with my cock." I whimpered, then closed my mouth over the tip of his cock. He allowed me just a taste before positioning me back on the bed and flipping me so that I lay on my stomach.

One finger stroked down the trail of my spine, skirting my ass and delving into the slickness of my pussy. Using my own wetness to ease his path, he pressed his finger against my anus and pressed until he breached the firm ring of muscle.

I cried out, pressing my face into the cool, crisp covers of the bed. With just the tip of his finger he fucked forward and back, just teasing me with a sample of what he must have been feeling at that very moment.

"You've been so very patient, Devon." Pulling his finger from me, I felt him reach for the bag that had held the anal beads and the lubricant. What he removed this time sounded metallic, and I lifted my head, trying to see.

"Be patient just a little bit more, little minx." Pulling at my hips until my pelvis and legs hung off the bed, he placed his hands between my thighs and shoved them far apart.

"I want your legs as wide open as they can get." I felt him kneel behind me on the carpet. "I'm going to be deeper inside of you than anyone has ever been." He placed one hand on my inner thigh. With the other he shoved a finger right into my waiting cunt, moving back and forth several times in quick succession.

My hips bucked against him, my movements hindered by the bar.

"I'm going to fuck you until you are sore. Tomorrow, every time that you move, you'll think of my cock, deep inside of your cunt."

"Zach." I shifted restlessly. I wanted—no, needed—his touch.

"I'm not done yet." Only then did he let me see what he had pulled from the bag. It looked like nothing so much as a thin silver clothespin. Its twin joined it, and I eyed them warily, fairly certain that I wouldn't like what was about to happen.

"That's going to hurt." My arms were still free, and I covered my breasts with my hands. An arch look from Zach had me dropping them again, albeit reluctantly.

"I promised that I wouldn't take you further than you could go." Before I could say another word, he began to roll one of my already-erect nipples in his hand, pulling and pinching until it was a hard point. I arched into his hand involuntarily, and with experienced fingers he had the nipple clamp in place on the tip of my breast.

"Ouch!" I shook, hoping that it would fall off. He took advantage of my distraction to clamp my second breast. I inhaled sharply as a painful sensation burned its way over both globes of my heavy breasts, spreading to my collarbone, my rib cage, and making it hard to breathe.

"Once more." I was lifted yet again and twisted, my front again pressed into the bed, my ass presented fully. The pain from the clamps on my nipples eased a bit when I rested them on my bed, but I could feel blood rushing to the spot where the metal pinched into my skin, and found that the tips were becoming quite numb. It was an incredibly strange mix of sensations.

"Now." Zach pulled one final object from his magic bag of tricks. He held it out so that I could see, and when my eyes took in the pale wood of what was unmistakably a paddle, one side polished to a shine, the other covered with some sort of fur, I shook my head vehemently.

"No way." I just wanted him to fuck me already—was that really too much to ask? I'd whipped him, I had clamps on my nipples, and he had told me that I wasn't permitted to close my legs. I didn't think I could handle anything else.

Zach stilled, and his face when he looked down at me was deadly serious.

"Do you truly mean 'no,' Devon?" His eyes searched my face for the truth. "Are you safe-wording on me?"

I opened my mouth, then closed it. If I used my safe word, then this—this entire strange, sensory, emotional journey— was completely over.

No. I wasn't going to end things now.

Inhaling deeply as I thought of that paddle smacking against the bare skin of my ass, I buried my face in the covers, waiting for him to do as he would.

"We'll only do ten blows tonight. You've been through a lot." I choked on my own saliva at his pronouncement. *Only* ten blows?

Shit.

"Count for me, Devon." This was the only warning I had, and then the hard side of the wooden paddle was smacking against the flesh of my right ass cheek. I cried out as fire spread across my skin.

"One." I sucked in air as I waited for the second blow. My ass burned against the cool air.

"Two!" This was hit against the other side of my butt. It burned just as much.

Three, four. Nine, ten. I screamed out the last number, the paddle on my already-burning flesh just too much for me to handle. Tears leaked out the sides of my eyes as I clutched my fingers into the sheets, gasping as I tried to catch my breath.

Behind me I could hear that Zach's breath was labored, as well. I knew that if I turned around, I would find him as hard as he had ever been, ready to plunge himself into my waiting heat.

First, something soft pressed against the heated skin of my rear. I winced and shied away from the touch until I realized that he was rubbing the fur side of the paddle over my abraded skin.

Though strange at first, I finally arched into the sensation, which was cool and refreshing and oh so soft.

Then the paddle went away. I heard it hit the ground and braced myself, knowing what was coming.

It was still a shock when Zach grabbed my waist, pressed my scorched behind to his pelvis, and seated himself inside my pussy in one rough thrust. I couldn't hold back any longer and screamed as I felt myself filled to the edge of discomfort.

He wasn't gentle, and he was big. He held me open with the hard muscles of his thighs. I couldn't close my legs against the onslaught of sensation, and as such had to take his entire length and girth into my body, which fought against the intrusion.

"Aah!" He was so incredibly big, and I had nowhere to move to alleviate the sensation. As he began to thrust, his strokes deep and fast and rough, the pain tore an intense excitement from my very core, and I felt myself beginning to shudder around him.

"Not yet." Sliding his hands between my torso and the bed as I began to tense in anticipation of climax, Zach's fingers found the tips of my breasts and, in one quick movement, tugged the clamps off.

"Fuck!" Blood rushed back into the numb tips, making them so incredibly sensitive that the sheets dragging back and forth over them sent me over the edge. I screamed long and loud as my climax shattered my world, my body racked with the pleasure that Zach had introduced me to.

"No more." He drew his erection from my drenched heat and rolled me onto my back. Stepping in between my splayed legs, he pressed back inside of my pussy and at the same time, bent and sucked a still-burning nipple into his warm, wet mouth.

I felt myself beginning to climb again. As he suckled my breast, he began to roll my clit between sure fingers.

The pleasure slammed back through me, and it rolled on and on. Dimly, as if from a distance, I heard Zach shout at me to remove his beads.

As if pushing through a fog of pleasure, I reached behind him and fumbled for the ring. Tugging as hard as I could while my own pleasure continued to crash over me, I felt the first bead give way, then the second, then the final two at once.

He pulled his cock out of my heat as I ripped the beads from his body. He shouted, his voice hoarse, and then I felt semen splatter wetly across my skin, scalding the tender flesh of my stomach.

I closed my eyes, wanting to savor every nuance of sensation. When I opened them again briefly, I saw Zach standing over me. Those incredible eyes of his regarded me with satisfaction, not a little bit of pride, and something else that I couldn't quite put my finger on.

I smiled up at him sleepily, then closed my eyes again, wanting to hold on to the bliss that was drifting throughout me.

For the first time in a long time, I felt at peace.

The first rays of morning light were washing over the bed when we finally settled down to sleep. I basked in the lemon yellow sunshine as I lay beside Zach on the bed.

I was wearing one of his T-shirts. He was wearing nothing. The covers had disappeared off of the bed and onto the floor sometime in the night, and so I snuggled into his side for warmth in the chilled early air.

I couldn't remember a time when I had felt happier, really truly happy, not like I was just pretending.

After Zach had tenderly rubbed an ointment made of arnica and crisp-smelling tea tree into my tender bottom, he took me into his massive bathtub and washed off the traces of our passion with warm water and kisses. After an hour of soapy groping, we had fallen into his bed and made love again.

My little minx. He had whispered the words into my ear as he soaped my skin, and I couldn't help but wonder if he realized what he had said. Either way, the tender endearment made my heart flutter and my insides melt.

Even without paddles, anal beads, or nipple clamps, he took to me to places that I had never even dreamed existed.

I was exhausted, but it was wonderful. It seemed like it was too good to be true when Zach spoke.

"Let's go to Cambria." I propped myself up on an elbow so that I could look down at his face. He seemed to be serious, and I felt my heart clench in my chest.

"Why?" My feelings had intensified during the night, to the point that I would go anywhere he asked me to.

Though I knew that I shouldn't, I couldn't squelch the hope that maybe, just maybe, he had feelings for me, too. Feelings that went beyond sex and his compulsion to dominate me.

I watched Zach shift uneasily under my scrutiny, and bit my teeth into my tongue. He had been so carefree, so easy during the long night. I didn't want to remove all of that amazing progress by saying the wrong thing.

"I love Cambria. You love Cambria." Rolling slightly, he pillowed his head on his hands. "A whole weekend in which I get to pleasure you however I want to, in a place we both love. Sounds like a good idea to me."

My fingers itched to trace over the scarlet line on his back, the contusions where the whip had cut through his perfect skin. I knew that if I did, it would remind him of all of the shadows that had led him to demand that I rain those blows down on him.

Once again, I bit my tongue. I just wanted to enjoy the pleasure of his company, this easy togetherness, while it lasted, and I didn't think that that was too much to ask.

"Sounds like a good idea to me, too." Unable to resist, I feathered my fingers through the silk of his hair, inhaling the scent that rose from the touch.

As I eased myself back down beside him on the bed, he burrowed into the mattress, trying to get comfortable enough to sleep. Before he nodded off, he raised his head, something to tell me before he forgot.

"We'll sleep as long as we want. Then Charles can drive us out." Content, he lay back down, leaving me frozen and unhappy.

"Um, Zach. Can't . . . can't we just go ourselves? Just the two of us?" I had found that I liked Charles, I truly did. But he in no way factored in to the picture I had of Zach and me away from the city, a chance to work past that shell that he held around himself so tightly.

Beside me, I felt Zach stiffen. Though he didn't move, all vestiges of sleep were gone from his voice when he spoke.

"Charles has to come, Devon. I don't drive. We've talked about this." He rolled more fully onto his side, indicating that the conversation was now over.

The idyllic peace that I had felt was gone, burnt away in that one quick moment. Agitation filled me up, anger that he had such ridiculous rules about his life—rules that were affecting me, too—but that he couldn't, wouldn't offer me an explanation. Or even compromise the slightest bit.

"I can drive, Zach. Then it will be just the two of us." To me this sounded entirely logical—in fact, it made far more sense than having someone who was not a part of this relationship drive us all the way out there, only to spend his time waiting until we decided to go back again.

"No." He still didn't sit up, and I felt like thumping him over the head with a pillow. The issue wasn't closed until we both agreed, and I didn't agree.

"Zach, this doesn't make sense. I can drive. I have a valid license. Please." My voice became softer. I wasn't going to beg, but I found that I wanted this time away with him quite desperately. "I want to be alone with you."

Finally Zach sat up, and when he twisted on the mattress to face me I felt as though cold water was slowly trickling down my body. His face was set in a cruel sneer, and his eyes looked like black ice.

"This isn't a relationship where we give and take and talk things through, Devon." Standing, he looked down at me with a ruthless expression, and I suddenly felt silly to be wrapped in his oversized gray gym shirt, like a high school teen with her boyfriend's letter jacket.

"What is it, then? Why don't you tell me, exactly?" I stood, too, determined to meet him on equal ground. I could already feel my heart breaking yet again. The look on his face never led to anything good for us.

"I've told you all along that there are parts of my life that I won't share. I live my life the way that I do for reasons that are my business and no one else's. It's how it is, and you can take it or leave it." The expression on his face told me that he didn't particularly care which option I chose.

At one point, I had been convinced that I meant something to him, something more than sex, even if he had no idea how to handle a traditional relationship.

But we had gone down this road so many times already in the brief time that we had been in each other's lives. It began to dawn on me that I was being a fool, and I couldn't even blame him for stringing me along.

He had told me what he did and didn't want, had been completely honest the entire time. I had chosen not to listen, to read into things, to build dream castles where nothing at all could stand.

Damn if I would let him see how much he had affected me. I was stronger now than I had ever been, and if nothing else, Zachariah St. Brenton had shown me that I was worthy of a lot of things.

I deserved someone who wanted me the way that I wanted him.

I stood there in his T-shirt as the man I wanted so desperately walked away, shutting himself in the bathroom, shutting me out as he had done so many times before.

Yes, I deserved someone who would give me everything I wanted. The problem there was that all I desired was Zachariah St. Brenton.

PART V

TEMPTED TO REVEAL

CHAPTER THIRTEEN

My hands shook as I contemplated lifting my coffee cup for a drink. After a night without even a minute of sleep, it seemed like more work than I could manage. I had been here, in the office, for an hour already, hoping for the distraction that my workload might give me.

Instead, everything in the entire building seemed to whisper Zach's name, tormenting me like a thousand tiny needles pricking my tender skin.

I squirmed in my seat at the thought, my bottom sore and hot after last night with Zach despite the tea tree ointment he had administered and the warm bath we had soaked in together. As the discomfort washed over me, so did anger.

We were over. After all I had been through with him, it was absolutely, positively, one hundred percent over.

I had tried, dammit. I had opened myself up to things that had shocked me to my core, just to please him. I had let him tie me up, had let him paddle like an impertinent child.

In the end, it hadn't mattered. He couldn't give me what I needed. I had hoped for more than he said he could give, and look how that had turned out for me. And try as I might, his rejection—again—forced those little fingers of self-doubt to play over my neck in a discomforting sensation.

Get a grip, Devon. Scowling, I shoved my coffee, now ice-cold, to the corner of my desk and pulled my keyboard closer. As eight o'clock neared, I welcomed the distraction of my co-workers as they began to trickle in.

Diversion was good. I would welcome anything that could help me forget Zachariah St. Brenton.

"Morning, Devon." Tony smiled at me as he placed two cups on his desk, then shrugged out of his jacket. He studied my face intently, and didn't bother hiding his displeasure at the shadows that he saw beneath my eyes.

"I got this for you." He crossed to my desk with one of the disposable cups, setting it down near my elbow.

I blinked with surprise and not a little pleasure. Sometimes my coworkers would bring coffee or muffins for one another, but no one had yet included me in the tradition. I hadn't been there long enough to make friends, and I had the additional black mark of extra attention from the CEO, which hadn't sat well with many of the women.

A genuine smile crossed my lips as I curled my hands around the cup, savoring its warmth.

"Thank you, Tony. Can I give you some money for it?" He scowled at the question, making a shooing gesture with his hands.

"Absolutely not. You can get the next one." The surge of acceptance, combined with my shaky emotions over Zach, made me suddenly tear up.

Tony looked alarmed.

"Hey, what's wrong?" Sliding behind me, he placed his hands on my shoulders and rubbed gently. "I won't bring you coffee anymore, I swear."

I barked out a laugh through my dry throat. I wasn't quite sure how I felt about his touch on my shoulders. He had offered it out of comfort, and that was nice, but I had caught his interested stare too many times to think that the caress was strictly platonic.

"Um." I was trying to formulate a polite way to extract myself from Tony's handling when I felt those fingers dig into my muscles.

"Ow." I jerked away from the bite of his nails on my skin, distancing myself from his touch at the same time. "What was that for?"

I shoved an errant lock of hair behind my ear as I looked up, and my own fingers clenched involuntarily. I sucked in my breath, steeling myself.

Where had he come from? Zach stalked—there was no other word to describe his movements—across the crowded accounting office toward us. His thunderous expression told me that he was not pleased at what he saw, and the manner in which he approached reminded me of a jungle cat—smooth, graceful, and deadly.

"Mr. Figuero." Zach fastened that terrifying stare directly onto Tony, not looking at me, not even a glance. "Must I remind you of the policy on dating within one's own department yet again?"

"No, sir." Tony's words were tense as he stepped farther away from me. As he marched to his own desk, not daring to look back at me, my spine stiffened in outrage.

I couldn't believe Zach's audacity, interfering here like a jealous husband. He could cite interdepartmental dating policies all he wanted, but we all knew that he was marking his territory.

After his behavior last night, he had no right. We were through.

Standing, I opened my mouth to tell him just that. I only hoped that I could get it out before the angry tears began to choke my words.

"Please come with me." He spoke before I could, persuasively, effectively disabling my anger with that one sentence. I narrowed my eyes at him with suspicion.

"Go where?" Zach had put me through enough of an emotional typhoon. I needed him to spell out his intentions more clearly.

He sighed, raking a hand through his hair in the way that I loved. I did my best to squelch the desire that snaked through me at the gesture.

"Come with me for a second." Thoroughly irritated, I followed him into an empty office. Shutting the door behind us, he looked me right in the eyes.

"Let's go to Cambria, Devon. Now." My mouth fell open at the words.

I cocked my head with confusion. "What's changed?"

"We can talk about this on the way." He rocked back on his heels, clearly impatient for us to be on our way.

I planted my hands on the empty desk. Through the glass of the window I could see that the department outside the private office had all but come to a standstill, everyone gaping at the enigmatic billionaire.

I knew that it was a good sign that he was willing to come to me at work. I was still angry enough not to want to make it easy for him.

"Tell me what has changed now, or I'm not going anywhere." I quaked as an expression of dominance flashed over his face, and I wondered if he would haul me over his knee and spank me for disobedience then and there.

Instead, I watched as he visibly struggled to rein in his need for control. Inhaling deeply, then letting the breath out, he ignored the spectators and fastened all of his attention on me.

"I want to tell you everything that you want to know, Devon." His words were hardly more than a whisper, but I was so focused on him that they were loud and clear to me. "I simply am not ready."

Disappointment was a cold rain, chilling me to the bone. I shook my head slowly, then turned away.

"Then there's no point in your being here, Zach." My heart

felt like it was being squeezed by a giant, invisible fist. I began to tremble, but I vowed that I wasn't going to break down.

If Zach had shown me anything, it was that I was stronger than that.

Inhaling deeply, I left the private office. Conversation in the department outside hushed for a moment as I rejoined my co-workers, then restarted when I refused to make eye contact with anyone.

"Devon."

I ordered myself not to turn around, but in his voice I heard the anguish that I had only seen from him in the aftermath of his nightmare.

"You can drive." Cursing myself, I looked back at him. He dangled a key fob from his fingers.

I thought I could see on his face a new vulnerability, a hint that he had dropped some of his defenses. And at that sight, I wanted nothing more than to wrap my arms around him and never let go. I couldn't believe that he had chosen to approach me and take me aside in front of everyone. Gossip would spread the story to every set of ears by the end of the day.

In the end, that was what pushed me that last inch. It couldn't have been easy for him to come here, to do this. In his own infuriating way, he was trying.

That meant I could try, too.

"I have work." I had already made up my mind, but still felt the need to go through the motions.

"You have an in with the boss." His voice was wry, and I did my best to swallow a smile. When he saw that I was wavering, Zach continued.

"I've already informed Mrs. Gallagher." A look across the room revealed the woman sitting in her desk, watching us as everyone else did.

She didn't look pleased, and in fact, she looked worried for me.

Rubbing my temples with my fingers, I closed the distance between Zach and me, lowering my voice.

"I don't have an overnight bag packed." It was my last line of defense and, as I'd expected, he broke through it with ease.

"I have one for you."

"Awfully sure of yourself, aren't you?" I supposed I should be angry that Zach had assumed I would fall into line, but I couldn't muster up any sense of outrage. I liked that he made decisions, and that I didn't have to. It made me feel cared for. Still, I worked up a token sneer.

"I'm never sure of myself with you." Zach's face was somber as he regarded me, and I felt my heart trip in my chest. "Definitely hopeful, though."

I tried to keep my expression neutral as I studied Zach's face. Though I couldn't understand the cost of his pushing himself out of his safety zone, I knew that it was not something he often did.

But he had because I had asked him to. More than anything else, this told me that there was more between us than sex.

"All right." My voice was so soft that I could barely hear it myself. Though I wanted, more than anything, to go with Zach, and for everything to be all right between us, I hoped that I wasn't opening myself up for more emotional distress.

The weeks since I had met Zach had been full of extreme highs and devastating lows. Right now, my emotions were creeping back up, and I wanted them to stay there.

"Let me get my purse." As I stooped to pull the leather satchel from under my desk, I caught Tony's eye. His lips were pinched tightly together, his expression disapproving. I looked away, but as I did I realized that nearly everyone in the office was staring at the spectacle that Zach and I had just provided.

Faced with the onslaught of curiosity, jealousy, and disapproval, I wavered. My hands, which were clutching my purse tightly, broke into a nervous sweat.

I could just imagine what everyone was thinking.

"Devon. Let's go." Zach moved to the back of my desk where I still stood, frozen in place. Tilting my head high with one finger placed under my chin, he draped the strap of my purse over my shoulder, then placed his hand at the small of my back, urging me forward.

Any resistance that I had felt over succumbing to his request melted as he shared his strength with me. Under his fierce look around at the onlookers, the office came back to life, people doing their best to at least pretend that they weren't watching us, though I knew the truth.

Though I knew that the speculation would increase tenfold when I returned from this little trip, for the moment, I could handle it. I could handle going after what I wanted. And the only reason that I could do so was Zach.

Though I knew it wasn't smart, I couldn't help it. As Zach ushered me across the lobby to the elevator, I realized how deeply I could love this man.

Zach was unlocking the door to his private garage when I caught sight of my own car in the staff lot. My mind flashed to the bag that was still crushed underneath the passenger's seat.

"Wait just a second." I scurried across the cement to my car while Zach stared after me, bemused. I knelt gingerly on the uneven surface as I tried to extract the bag, which had been smushed to the point of no return.

Good thing it's not breakable. I grinned triumphantly as the bag gave way, tearing open. Carefully I pulled the swatch of midnight blue silk out from its hiding place, folding it gingerly and tucking it into my purse.

I had purchased it for myself, after all, not for Tom. And the thought of Zach's face when I wore it caused heat to wash over my skin.

"What were you doing?" Zach raised his eyebrows when I grinned at him and sailed through the door that he held open, my spirits high.

"Never you mind." When he narrowed his eyes, I could tell that he was thinking of ordering me to tell him.

I stared right back, and finally he nodded.

"Very well, little minx, keep your secrets. I'll enjoy punishing you for it later." I jolted at the surge of sexual heat held in Zach's words, nerves and anticipation assaulting me at once.

"Well." I eyed the sleek black vehicle, both nervous and excited to drive such a car. "Let's go?" The fob in my hand was far more high-tech than the simple key for my own sedan.

Zach didn't reply. Turning, I found him standing ramrod straight, his hands in tight fists at his sides, his jaw tense.

"Zach." My heart melted, even though our argument from the night before rang in my head. I knew now, though, that he wasn't trying deliberately to withhold the cause of his pain.

Whatever it was, I suspected it would pain his soul to relive it.

"Hey." Crossing to him, I placed a hand on his upper arm and rubbed. He blinked down at the gesture, his brow furrowing as if he couldn't quite conceive of being comforted. "We don't have to do this."

Stubbornness darkened his features, and I sighed to myself. Zach didn't do compromise very well, and he had apparently used up his store of it with me already.

"We're going." His movements still stiff, he opened the driver's-side door and waited until I slid in. After he had walked around the car and gotten in himself, I opened my mouth to ask him a question about adjusting the seats before deliberately biting my tongue.

He didn't drive the car. He would have no idea. There was no point in reminding him of his unease.

"Give me a minute." I squinted at the dashboard. The car had a lot of fancy features—an incredibly complex-looking stereo, an ionizer, and something that looked like a small television. But apart from the fact that the car started with the press of a button rather than a key in the ignition, everything else was normal, if prettied up.

It had been a while since I had driven a manual vehicle, and I prayed to myself that I wouldn't do anything awkward while I got back into the feel of it. I didn't think that Zach was the kind of man who would appreciate showing weaknesses, like his anxiety at even being in this car with a new driver.

"How do I open the garage door?" I pressed the button and the car rumbled to life. My foot on the brake, I shifted the car into first. Beside me Zach tensed, but after a deep breath forced his muscles to relax.

"It's a motion sensor. Just start going." I eased off the brake, and once the vehicle had started moving, the garage door opened in front of us. The pale lemon color of midmorning light made me blink.

I watched Zach from the corner of my eye as I maneuvered the sleek vehicle out of the garage and onto the street. His jaw clenched when I shifted from first to second too quickly and the car jerked forward, jolting us back in our seats.

"I'm sorry." Though this was what I had wanted, to take this trip, just the two of us, I felt my nerves begin to fray as the pressure between us grew.

I didn't want to abuse the precious trust that Zach had given me. I'd drive like a little old lady from Florida the entire way, if that was what it took to encourage him through this gigantic step.

"Don't apologize. You haven't done anything wrong." Zach

leaned back in his seat, turning to stare out the passenger's-side window rather than straight ahead. Though he seemed to be the picture of nonchalance, there was still an underlying tension in the way he held himself, one I could detect only because of the vast amount of time I had spent studying his body.

Those muscles relaxed a bit as we made it down Market Street and through the busy downtown core without incident. I thought about turning some music on, but was stymied by the dash that looked like it could launch a space shuttle. Zach seemed content with the silence, and I would do whatever it took to keep the peace during this trip.

Turning the signal light to indicate that I was exiting onto the 101, I heard a growl from beside me. Taking my eyes off the road for a moment, I found that Zach had gone rigid in his seat and was shaking his head.

"Not the 101. No." His voice was fully channeled from his dominant side, but I heard the ice that coated it. "Take Highway 1. You have to take Highway 1."

He reached over from his seat and curled his fingers around the wheel. Fear shot through me in a searing bolt.

"Zach! Stop it!" I stomped on the brake without thinking to shift down, and the car shuddered.

My heart rate slowed a hint when he pulled his hand back and I realized that he hadn't done any more than touch the wheel.

"I'm sorry. I'm so sorry." His eyes were wide and not a bit wild when I dared look his way. I shivered, at a loss.

"It's . . . it's okay. Just . . . maybe close your eyes. We'll take the coast. You just can't do that again, all right? You scared me." Bleakly Zach nodded, then deliberately reclined his seat and shut his eyes. I drove on, forgoing the exit that would take us to the 101, a much shorter drive than the one along Highway 1.

It wasn't long before hints of the ocean began to glimmer

on my right, like shards of blue jewels welcoming the sun as it moved across the sky. I couldn't appreciate the wonder of the water as I normally did, however, preoccupied as I was with Zach.

"Shit." I muttered the word under my breath as I glanced over and saw that, though he had positioned himself for sleep, the rigidity of his body wasn't letting it happen.

What happened to you, poor baby? He had made it clear that I couldn't ask. Not knowing and still trying to accommodate the issue, however, was a challenge akin to creating a work of art without the benefit of eyesight.

The man took overwhelming control over everything in his life, and something in me thrilled to it. I found myself at loose ends in this situation, in which our roles had somehow become reversed.

The silence became less dense as the minutes passed, then a half hour, an hour. The smooth movement of the sports car had lulled Zach to sleep finally, his breathing light and shallow beside me. I felt myself relax as well, the boulders of my shoulder muscles softening as the pressure to put Zach at ease ceased.

Five hours into the drive, I dared to press some of the buttons on the panel in search of music. I managed to bring up a satellite station, and, with the volume low, grinned when I recognized the tenor rasp of Steve Perry and Journey.

"When the lights go down, in the city." I grinned and sang along softly, feeling the last bit of my tension drain away and elation take its place.

Zach had done this for me. We were going for a weekend alone in my favorite place in the world.

For the next few days, we had nothing to do but focus on each other. The thought of just how he might focus on me made me shiver with delight.

"So you said, you're lonely." In the rearview mirror I saw a massive semitruck coming up behind the car rather quicker than I was comfortable with. Frowning, I signaled and changed lanes, grumbling a bit at the impatient driver.

Adrenaline hit hot and fast when the solid length of the truck, now even with the tiny sports car, began to drift into our lane.

"Fuck!" Slamming on the brakes and downshifting hard, I laid on the horn with my elbow. Zach jolted awake beside me with a shout, and I felt his arm fling across my chest, a gesture designed to protect as I wrestled the car to the shoulder of the highway and forced the car into park.

Ahead of us, the truck jolted back into its own lane as if the driver had drifted off and the sound of the horn had woken him up. The pair of us sat there for a long moment, panting as we gathered our composure.

"Holy shit." I turned to face Zach with wide eyes. "I am so sorry. So sorry. He came out of nowhere. That's so not what you needed. I—"

Zach grabbed my face in his hands and pulled me to him for a rough, hot kiss. I moaned beneath his assault, trying to move closer to his seat and seething with frustration when I found myself held in place by the seat belt.

My lips felt swollen when he pulled back. Those dark eyes of his scanned my face rapidly, searching for something.

"Find a safer place to pull over." The tension in his voice was like ice.

Guilt and nerves made my movements jerky as I slowly pulled back into traffic. From the corner of my eye I could see that Zach was gripping the sides of his seat, his knuckles white as snow. His face was set in a pained grimace.

My heart sank. Changing lanes, I spotted a rest stop not far ahead. My own hands shaking, I pulled over into it, out of the direct flow of traffic.

When I turned off the ignition, Zach released the long, shuddering breath that he had been holding.

I furrowed my brow, confused, then distracted when he reached over and unfastened my seat belt.

"Zach, it's okay. Maybe we should call Charles to come get us." After the near miss, I would be fine with anything that eased Zach's anguish.

Instead, he barked out a laugh and hauled me from my seat and onto his lap.

"I promised you a weekend alone." Before I could reply, my lips were teased apart by his tongue as Zach thoroughly sampled my mouth.

The tart burst of desire that I felt when his lips pressed to mine flowed into my blood, whooshed through my veins, made my hands tingle and my stomach burn.

My heart began to pound as a realization washed over me.

This beautiful creature, this man, had chosen *me*. Me, even if just for right now.

It was a powerful reckoning, a benediction.

Zach laced his fingers through mine, capturing first one hand and then two, crushing them between the soft flesh of my breasts and the hard planes of his chest.

I was lost. As I was crushed tightly to him, my mind briefly took me to the first moment I had seen Zach, and how much I wanted him right from that instant. Then all thought was drowned, swallowed whole in a vaporous quicksand of something more intense than simple lust. It sweetened the air in that tiny, enclosed space, drugging me and, I think, him with its perfume.

My breath whooshed out of my lungs when his mouth moved from my own to whisper a kiss over the curve of my neck, sending shivers running down my spine.

A passing semitruck honked loudly. Neither of us jumped

or jerked away. But it was a reminder of where we were and what we were doing.

My attention was caught on the hand he'd clutched in his, where his palm was surprisingly rough for someone who wielded such authority and strength in the boardroom. Thick pads of skin scraped my own smaller, softer fingers as they explored, traced, and memorized my curves.

Though we had been together countless times now, I still couldn't quite believe I was here. It felt like the very best of dreams.

"I want you now." Zach teased as he playfully pulled me closer. "Here, where anyone could see us."

I made a face that betrayed my nervousness, a face that was quickly kissed away.

Then he groaned, and a surge of triumph shot through me.

I pressed hard against him, twining myself tightly around the ropy muscles of his chest. I gasped when, with a movement so smooth I didn't even know how it had happened, I found myself straddling his lap, pressed tightly to him, face buried in his neck.

"Sorry." His voice was muffled against the heated, sensitive flesh of my collarbone as he tasted, the rough expanse of his tongue ratcheting up my excitement with each stroke. "Not much room to maneuver in here."

Adjusting myself, I reached down with my left hand, groped blindly for the lever that would recline the seat. I found it, yanked, and the jolt of the seat as it fell backward pressed the soft center of my heat against a hardness that I couldn't imagine I'd caused.

For one long, ragged minute we stared at each other, the tawny gold of his eyes swallowing my cobalt blue. I imagined that the gold of his gaze was reflected back to him in my own.

We came together like lovers separated for years, the heat

between us burning away any remaining awkwardness. I was spellbound, pulled under by the sexy rasp of breath, the intimate friction of rubbing cloth, as our small cries were swallowed by the other in the steamy confines of the car.

The pale light, the passing traffic, everything but the two of us seemed a million miles away. I lost my inhibitions along a stretch of highway along the Pacific coast. We were ensconced in our own little world, the only people left.

My soul sang under his caress.

His hand traced up the soft skin of my inner thigh unhampered, the cloth of my skirt having ridden up around the curve of my hips. I made a series of small, sharp cries when the tip of a finger traced the edge of my underwear, half on cloth, half on skin, and my hands raced down the muscled swath of his chest to clutch at his waist.

His hand moved mine to the buckle of his black pants. I drew in a breath as my fingers met the taut expanse of stomach.

I wanted more than I'd ever wanted in my life.

My hands shook as, instead of moving down, I moved up, fumbling as I coaxed the buttons of his shirt out of their holes.

It wasn't enough. When I slid a hand down his chest tentatively, he growled, fierce and animalistic, and rolled me until I was on my back. My shirt was tugged up midroll, the cotton catching on my sweat-dampened skin and pulling painfully. The expression of near reverence that he gave me at the sight of my breasts, plainly offered up in a simple black bra, erased the sting.

"I will never get tired of these." Lunging, he buried his face where my flesh spilled out of the spandex-and-wire constraints. I bucked beneath the touch, tugging his shirt the rest of the way down his arms, and then, with a surge of renewed bravery, reaching for the buckle of his belt.

My knuckle grazed the hard ridge of flesh, and he inadvertently bit into me. I choked back a noise that was halfway to a scream and lost my grip. Soothing the sting with his tongue, he worked his hands between us and undid the fastenings with the quickness of familiarity. Without thinking about what I was doing, I tugged until his ankles were bound by cloth, and began to explore.

"Devon." My name fell from his lips on a soft moan as I closed a triumphant fist around him. Hands shaking with visible need, Zach shoved up the cups of my bra without releasing the clasp, then cupped, pinched, and pulled. The pleasure and pain rushed over me in shades of deep pink and crimson.

I worked my bra the rest of the way over my head. "Exquisite." He said as my breasts fell free. Their tips were so sensitized that one flick of his tongue over a tight peak tore that half scream from my throat again.

The scream cast me a lifeline in the tsunami of hormones and lust and intensity, waking me up from my sensual daze. I pinched his biceps to get his attention, even as I wound my legs as tightly as they would go around his waist, the weeping tip of his erection leaving a sticky trail across my inner thigh and nudging at the seam of cotton that covered my heat.

"Zach." In return, he exhaled my name into my own mouth, his fingers dancing down my stomach. I pinched him again, this time at the waist. "Zach."

Sex-hazed eyes blinked, cleared the tiniest bit.

"I don't want to have sex here." His brow furrowed. I should, perhaps, have been worried about him being angry, but I wasn't. I knew he wouldn't hurt me.

Still, the creases along his brow deepened, then cleared as he nipped at my earlobe and gathered hold of himself. "All right. Let's move the car a few feet." He grinned, and my womb clenched.

I loved it when he was playful.

"No." Again my mouth was saying one thing, my grinding hips another. "No. Someone might see."

There was a moment in which we both held still, frozen with the thin, icy sheen of uncertainty. He backed away, just a bit, and I was surprised at the ease with which he gave up.

He was a dominant man, one who always got what he wanted. So far I had found that what he wanted, I wanted too.

Swallowing my nerves, I banded my arms tightly around him, raked my nails roughly down the firm lines of his back. He grunted in pain, his eyes darkening again with want.

Biting my lip, I slid down in the seat while urging him up. The first taste of him on my tongue was like the stinging bite of a shot of vodka. Surprising at first, but addictive. Mouthwatering, powerful.

When he began to shudder, his hips bucking, he eased out of my mouth and moved to slide down my body, which was as sticky with sweat as his. With a strength I'd only guessed at, he reached between my legs and tore at the scrap of cloth that barred his entry. The sound of fabric ripping sliced through the thick air and changed the pace of our desire for each other.

Cupping my breasts together with my hands, I offered myself up to him and moved to close the small distance between us. His fingers triumphantly feasted on the wetness between my legs, and the intense sensation made me buck, wild and rough.

Our eyes met again, and the roughness grew in intensity.

The low heel of my sandal dug into his calf, where a couple of drops of blood swelled and scented the air with copper and salt. He peppered my neck, my shoulders, my breasts with bites, sharp stings that urged extra slickness to coat his fingers.

He came first, the hot, steaming seed spurting onto my breasts, my collarbone, and flecking my lips. I licked the taste away, breathing hard, startled by my own release when those rough fingers found a spot previously unexplored, and pinched.

We lay there in the confined space, a tangled mass of arms and legs and clothing, glued together after our exertions with sweat and semen.

He had found a way to appease me and to get his way also, damn him. The fact that he had outmaneuvered me was an incredible turn-on. I loved that not only was he amazing to look at, but his brain never stopped. And he found ways to urge me past my fears and inhibitions.

When he tugged my hair, forced me to meet his gaze, I nearly cried, as girls are wont to do in the face of such extreme emotions.

"You're beautiful." In that moment I believed that he was telling what he found to be the truth. "You're beautiful."

My heart soared as I pressed my forehead to his and tried to regain my breath. We were both sticky with sweat. Outside the car, passing vehicles whirled by in brightly colored blurs.

"Good Lord." My eyes widened when I realized what had just happened. Zach had just made me come on the side of the highway. Anyone could have seen us. Hell, a trooper could have stopped to investigate why we were pulled over and been treated to an eyeful of my bare breasts instead.

I felt like a sixteen-year-old caught fooling around with her boyfriend.

"Zach!" My hands fluttered to cover my breasts as I pulled away from him. They came away damp with his release, and a distressed mewl left my lips.

To my utter surprise, Zach threw his head back and laughed—a full, deep laugh that came straight from his gut. The sound was so infectious that after a moment I giggled, too.

"No one saw, Devon." Shifting in his seat, he pulled his pants up and removed his handkerchief from his pocket in one smooth movement. I reached for it, but he shook his head, a gleam in his eye.

"Let me." I opened my mouth to protest, then sighed with pleasure as he began to clean the salt from my skin.

"Mmm." I settled into the touch, savoring the feeling of his hands on my skin.

A car passing by us honked long and loud, breaking into the moment. Grabbing for my shirt and bra, I scrambled back into the driver's seat, mortified and still incredibly turned on.

"Oh, my little minx." Zach laughed again at the indignation on my face when I tugged my shirt back over my neck, planning to maneuver myself into my bra from under its comforting cover.

"I'm glad you're entertained." I sniffed, then caught my breath when I caught the gleam in his eyes. "No. Not again. Not here. Damn it, Zach, you can't be ready again yet!"

The laughter dying down to a predatory smile, Zach leaned in closer, then closer still. I held my breath, waiting for the kiss.

"Here is a lesson, little one. Submissives don't get to say no to their doms." He plucked my bra from my fingers, running his free hand up under the shirt that was twisted around me, palming a breast in his warm hand.

"You must be punished for breaking this rule. No bra for you." I moaned as he rolled my nipple between his forefinger and thumb. I had just climaxed in the intense, earth-shattering way that only Zach could pull out of me, but his caress on my still tender flesh made heat pool deep in my belly all over again.

When he removed his hand and pulled my shirt down over my torso, I glared, not happy at the loss of sensation.

"Subs don't get to stare down their doms, either." His eyes narrowed in warning. I narrowed mine right back, partly because he was irritating me, and partly because I thrilled to the idea of his style of punishment.

"We haven't been together for a long enough stretch to determine whether or not I'm your submissive." I snapped the words as I threaded my arms through my sleeves, then restarted the car. I was feeling thoroughly off balance.

Zach was silent for a long moment, as I waited for a break in traffic, then slipped the car back onto the road. When I dared to sneak a peek at him, he seemed lost in thought and, surprisingly, not focused on the cars on the road around us.

"Is that what you want, Devon?" I caught a breath at the serious tone in his voice. "It's not uncommon to have a contract outlining limits in this kind of relationship."

"A contract?" I was taken aback and not a little hurt by his choice of words. Whether deliberate or not, I felt the connection that we had just shared shrink, being shoved neatly into a box labeled *unconventional BDSM relationship*. "I . . . what . . ."

My words tapered off as my mind reeled. I felt that pressing need to please him, and yet I found the notion of a contract decidedly unromantic.

Maybe that was the whole idea. Maybe the contract would bring the focus back to the sex, easing the appearance of the lovey-dovey feelings that had recently begun to flutter around in my chest.

"Whatever you want." I tried to grab hold of some of the joy that I had felt earlier, and instead was left feeling flat and unfulfilled.

"No." Zach's voice was stern. "This has to be your decision."

I ignored the order in his tone. "I choose whatever works best for you." I was being stubborn and I knew it, but I wasn't going to put myself out there, demanding that he tear up any such contract that existed because our relationship couldn't be defined on paper.

"All right, then." He paused for a long moment before he spoke, and when he did his voice held the smoothness that it did when he was at work. "I'll have my lawyer draft one."

I felt my mouth begin to fall open at the notion that a lawyer would draw up such a contract. But then, what had I expected? I was sleeping with Zachariah St. Brenton, eccentric billionaire playboy, the dominant who was into kinky sex.

"You're wearing all black again." Zach broke the uncomfortable silence. His observation lifted my spirits the tiniest bit.

"I am." I didn't look down to see what I had on—all of my clothes, save the revealing red blouse that had now been shoved to the back of the closet, were so very similar that it really didn't matter.

"Why do you do that?" He seemed genuinely curious. I opened my mouth to tell him that dark clothes helped to camouflage the fullness of my hips and butt, the softness of my belly, all things that I disliked about my figure. The black kept the attention focused on my mind, which was, in my opinion, far more appealing than any of my physical assets.

The simple clothing also kept the spotlight off of me, letting me fade into the background, a place that I found infinitely more comfortable.

A place that I hadn't been allowed to hover in since I met Zach. His attention was like a laser, cutting through the darkness and illuminating whatever he focused on.

I still couldn't quite understand why he was focused on me.

Yet, as I opened my mouth to tell Zach all of these things, I quickly recalled his refusal to share his issues with me. I remembered the contract, and how it shoved the focus of our relationship off of our hearts and back into the bedroom.

"I'm sorry, but I'm not comfortable discussing that." My voice was flat, even a little bit cold. I thought that my words would make Zach mad, would make him demand that I tell him under threat of a spanking or some such thing.

Instead, when I cast a sidelong glance his way, I found his face completely calm and expressionless. Indifferent, even, as if he had only asked to be polite and couldn't be bothered to listen to the answer, anyway.

"I understand." Leaning forward, he punched some buttons on the big screen and brought up the map screen of a GPS. The system announced that it was downloading the latest traffic news, then informed us that we would be at our destination in just under an hour.

"It hasn't been that bad of a drive." An hour earlier I would have found immense pleasure in Zach's words, would have felt joy that he finally trusted me enough to let me have the wheel without panicking.

Now it felt as though he was just making conversation.

"I'm looking forward to this weekend." I heard the sensual promise in his voice and couldn't help but respond. There wasn't a woman alive who would be left cold when that face, those lips, those eyes spoke of decadent pleasure.

"Me, too." I swallowed hard, clinging to the tendrils of joy that were dissipating far too quickly for my liking.

Yes, I responded to the pleasure he could bring to my body. I couldn't deny that.

When Zach had given me the keys to the car, I hoped that it was symbolic of a new step forward in our relationship. I had had faith that his willingness to trust me with his safety in the car meant that we were becoming more intimate emotionally.

Instead, he had just reaffirmed that he was in this solely for the sex. And if I was truthful with myself, I didn't think that was enough to keep me happy.

CHAPTER FOURTEEN

felt my spirits lift as we drove into Cambria—suddenly every tense minute of the long drive had been worth it. Rolling down my window, I inhaled the salt-infused sea air deep into my lungs as Zach directed me to his house.

I caught him laughing at the blissful expression on my face, and I didn't care. San Francisco, Phyrefly, all of the problems in our relationship—they all seemed so far away.

Being back in the place where we met was not only romantic, it was refreshing. I felt my worries start to drift away on the cool ocean breeze that was tickling at my skin.

"This is it." Zach's instructions had led us to the outskirts of the village and up a winding path to a rocky cliff. I had been expecting a duplicate of his house in San Francisco—something large, high-tech, and modern.

The spacious but cozy bungalow surprised me in the best possible way.

"It's lovely!" Hurriedly, I exited the car, my feet carrying me halfway up the charming pebbled path before I realized that Zach might not appreciate my just rushing into his home.

I turned, biting my lip, and found him right behind me, a leather duffel bag slung over one of his broad shoulders.

"It's somewhat different from the house that you've seen." While he looked pleased with my reaction to the house, he also seemed a bit uncertain. "It doesn't have nearly as many bells and whistles."

"Of course it doesn't." If he thought I was going to be disappointed, he had another thing coming. Thinking of the confusing panel of buttons in his massive glass shower, I shuddered a bit and grinned up into his face. "That's why we're here, isn't it? To get away from all of that?"

Zach studied my face intently, as if searching for some hidden meaning. I let him look, sensing that it was important to him that I was telling the truth.

"I've never brought anyone here before." He stuffed his hands into the pockets of his jeans and rocked back on his heels. "It's not exactly what people expect of me."

He stared at me until the full meaning behind his words dawned on me.

"No one?" I blinked, suddenly shaky. "What about Charles?"

"He drives me here, then stays at a motel until I'm ready to go." Pulling a small copper key from his pocket, he flipped it into the air and then caught it with an air of nonchalance that I could tell was slightly forced. "This is the only place where I can truly let go of everything else in my life. I've never had any desire to bring anyone here before."

My mouth fell open a bit. I forced it closed. Though I wanted to fling myself into his arms, I didn't want to frighten him with an overly intense reaction.

Instead, I smiled up into his dark eyes and held out a hand for him. "What do you normally do when you first get here?"

He looked slightly wary at my easy response. I smiled innocently in return and finally, he took my offered hand.

I savored the touch of his cooler palm against my warm one.

"I put my bag in the bedroom, strip, and go ride a few waves." When he pointed to the stairs that had been carved out of rock, which spiraled to the craggy beach below, I drew in a startled breath.

He had called my bluff. I would follow his lead, but the idea of surfing was not something that appealed to me in the least.

"Of course, you could just stay up here. Wait for me with a cold beer. Naked." Heat flashed through his eyes, and his smile became that sensual curve of the lips that I had become so intimately familiar with.

I had no doubt that if I didn't join him in the water, he would make me do exactly that.

"I don't have a swimsuit." I followed him to the door, noting that he was carrying only one duffel bag. "Someone didn't give me a chance to pack one."

Zach slid the key into the dead bolt of the door, then turned to give me a wicked smile that was full of promise.

"You can swim naked, too."

"Just need to finish waxing the board. Then we'll go in and you'll be a lot warmer." The top of his wetsuit hung around his waist, exposing his gorgeous golden torso to my stare. His hard muscles rippled as he rubbed the wax into the board, and saliva pooled in my mouth.

"Oh boy." I tugged uncomfortably at the wetsuit that Zach had provided for me. In it I felt as though I couldn't quite breathe properly.

I wasn't convinced that it would keep me warm in the water. I could feel the surf splashing around my toes, and it was icy as snow.

"I'm pretty sure it's going to be colder in there, actually." I eyed the waves that were rolling in. Nothing too big, but their pale blue shade looked frigid.

Despite his threat, Zach wouldn't let me surf naked, saying that it would be irresponsible of him to give me hypothermia. Providing me with the brand-new wetsuit and a neon yellow scrap of fabric that Paris Hilton might consider an adequate bathing suit, he had insisted that I would love the sport.

I hadn't been able to focus on a convincing protest. Seeing things meant for me mixed in that bag with his clothing and toiletries had done something funny to my insides.

"Generally a person would practice on dry land before taking the board into the water." Zach's eyes twinkled at me as he spoke. He looked more free than I had ever seen him. "We're heading straight for the water."

"Why?" My nerves made me indignant.

"Let's call this an exercise in trust. Now, let's give this a try." Zach grinned as he gestured me over to the freshly waxed longboard. I grimaced.

"Did you just frown at me?" His voice was layered with only a hint of the dominance that he used in the bedroom, yet it still caught my attention and I widened my eyes.

"No." I fidgeted, eyeing the waves. This wasn't going to go well, I could tell.

"Devon." Standing, Zach wrapped his arms around me from behind and squeezed once, gently, before letting go. The embrace—and the boost of confidence I took from his touch—warmed me as no wetsuit could.

"What's got you so nervous about this?"

I couldn't even bother trying to hide my expression. I knew that he would make me tell him, but as I formulated the words in my head, I realized how incredibly silly it would sound to say them out loud.

"I'm—I'm not the kind of person who will be good at this." I blurted it when he raised an eyebrow to let me know that he was waiting. "Surfing is for people who are . . . carefree. Athletic. In control."

A meticulous planner who hated the gym and used minutiae to try to exert control over her daily life, I was none of these things.

"What a bunch of bullshit." I huffed out an exasperated breath at his words. I had expected the attentive Zach who made me feel better about myself, not the man who was glaring at me with irritation.

"It's not bullshit. That's how I see it." I furrowed my brow and glared, holding on to my preconceived notions as tightly as I could.

"I shouldn't have to spell this out for you anymore, Devon." I saw that I had seriously irritated him as he picked up the long-board and balanced it vertically on the damp sand. "But since you have such a blindness about yourself and a lack of self-worth, I'll do it one more time."

Lack of self-worth? I sputtered as I tried to think of something to say to refute it. In the end it didn't matter, because he wouldn't let me reply.

"Well, you're not exactly carefree, but I think what you're meaning is someone who has a free spirit. You moved to San Francisco on a whim, without a job or a place to live. Athletic. You could run a marathon if you wanted to, Devon. It's all in the mind."

Indignant, I cocked my head and continued to glare up at him.

"Are you quite done?" I was ready to smack him over the head with the surfboard, arrogant ass that he was.

"No, not quite." His smile was amiable and deadly as he shrugged into the top of his suit and fastened the zipper over his broad chest. "In control. I don't know how a woman who leaves her cheating boyfriend, moves to a new city, and starts a new life that she loves is anything *but* in control."

I was stuttering, trying to think of a counterargument,

when Zach moved suddenly, dropping the board on the sand. Clasping me around the waist, he lifted me off of my feet and strode toward the water.

"Zach!" Knowing what was coming, I kicked and thrashed. He didn't even seem to notice, or so I thought. But when he unceremoniously dropped me into the waist-high water that he had strode into, sliding me down the length of his hard body, I felt the unmistakable ridge of his erection, pressing against the thick fabric of his wetsuit.

I opened my mouth to call him a jerk; the expression on his face warned me against it. I drew my eyebrows together in a scowl, and he smiled in return, turning to walk back up on the beach to retrieve the board.

"Dunk yourself and get used to the water." I considered telling him where to shove it—the water was freezing.

But if I didn't dunk myself, he would do it for me. No way. I ducked beneath the water, gasping when I came back up, then crouched so that the water covered me up to my neck.

Dammit, he was right. I could already feel myself getting used to the water's temperature. Not that I was going to tell him that.

"Put your hands on my shoulders." Returning with the board, he held up something that looked like a leash with a loop at the end of it.

It reminded me of some of the restraints that he had used on me. I flushed at the memory.

Catching Zach's eye, and the smirk that played over his lips, I knew that he was fully aware of where my mind had gone.

"This is the leash. It attaches you to your surfboard so that you don't lose it if you fall off." I eyed the long cord dubiously. I wasn't at all sure that I *wanted* to be attached to the thing.

"Give me your ankle." Zach knelt in front of me in the waist-high water, and opened the Velcro of the loop. When I balked, he clasped it anyway, fastening it snugly, the touch of his fingers on my skin giving me shivers that had nothing to do with the cold.

"There." Leaning forward, he pressed a damp kiss to the skin just below where the short wetsuit ended.

I hummed with pleasure.

"This not only prevents the board from getting away from you, but it also keeps it from hitting other surfers. Some don't like to wear it, but I think that the safety of others comes before the freedom of movement that you get without the leash." I wasn't about to argue.

"Okay. Up onto the board you go." I blinked at him, nerves making my stomach churn.

"What do you mean, up?" I eyed the sleek, slippery-looking white board with trepidation. "That's it? Just . . . go?"

Zach laughed, and I was distracted by the lack of reservation in the sound. Somehow he seemed different here, away from Phyrefly and all of his responsibilities. He took advantage of my diverted attention to clasp me around my waist and hoist me up onto the board.

"Dammit, Zach!" I hissed as my butt made contact with the hard board. He rearranged my legs so that one was dangling over each long side as I sat up straight.

It felt incredibly awkward.

"Now what?" The board wobbled as I moved. I sucked in a breath and slapped my hands down on the thing, as if that would steady it.

"Devon." Zach placed one hand on the board by mine, and the other at the curve of my waist. I turned to find him looking down at me, his face intent.

"It's just a surf lesson. What's the worst that can happen?"

Soon I realized that he expected an answer.

"Um . . . I fall off?" As I thought about it, I realized how silly

I was being. Yes, I could fall off, into the water, and get soaked. In fact, I probably would.

I could handle it.

Zach smiled the moment he saw me relax. He squeezed my waist, then began to push the board out into slightly deeper water.

"Normally you would paddle out with your arms. But since I'm here, and I want you to have some energy left for other things later, I'll help you out." The space between my legs heated, but I ignored it.

Zach wanted me to do this. It would be good for me to embrace a new experience. I was going to do it.

He tugged the board a little farther in the water, then guided it to an area with few waves. I was still nervous, but with the nerves came determination.

"Okay." At his prompt, I lay down flat on my stomach on the board. "Now what?"

"Now you get yourself into position." Zach looked out across the froth of clear blue water, the sun adding warmth to his skin. My breath caught at the sight of him, wet and disheveled and happy.

"You want to make sure to paddle out in unbroken water if you can. It's exhausting otherwise. Then you position yourself just outside the breaking wave." He gestured to where the small waves were moving from the depths of the ocean to the shore.

The board rocked in the water. Despite myself, I relaxed into its rhythm.

"Once you've got your position, you pop up." He smacked me lightly on the ass and I scowled at him. "It would be easier for me to show you, but I've only got the one board here. So you'll have to do what I say."

"Like that's a surprise," I muttered, and earned another spank, one hard enough to make me yip. Whipping my head around, I found him grinning at me.

"Keep it up, Devon. Makes it all the more fun for me."

With a mock sigh, I pressed my lips together tightly. Truthfully, I wouldn't have minded another spank or two. It woke the nerves in my clit, making me rub my thighs together with need.

"Next is the pop-up." He took my hands and adjusted them so that they were flat on the board on either side of my chest. "As quickly as you can, push yourself up with your arms and bring your legs under your body. Make sure to turn while you do it, so that you face the shore."

This, I knew, was what was going to tip me over into the water. And it did, over and over again. But as I sputtered to the surface for the fourth time, I realized something.

I was having fun. Even if I never managed to do it, I was having fun trying.

On my fifth try I managed to get my weight on my feet without tipping the board. I whooped with joy, holding my arms to the sides to get my balance.

"Perfect!" I looked down and caught Zach's stare. Elation whipped through me, hard and fast. "Try to keep your balance. I'm going to nudge you into position this time."

"Okay!" I didn't even want to argue anymore. The waves that he steered me toward were tiny and close to shore, but I didn't care.

"Have you ever been skiing, Devon?" Every muscle in my abdomen and thighs screamed as I tried to keep myself steady while the board slid through the water.

"A few times." My parents had given me lessons as a teenager, but I had felt pressure to excel and as such had never shown an aptitude.

"Riding the wave isn't that different. Position your weight so that you move down the wave, or downhill. Try to stay in front of the white water. Then have fun."

Before I could reply, he shoved the board forward, into the

path of the oncoming wave. My eyes told me it was hardly more than a foot high, but beneath my feet it felt enormous.

"Aah!" I screamed as the water propelled me forward. I squeezed my eyes shut, expecting to tumble into the water at any moment.

Instead, I found the wind whipping my hair and droplets of salt water spraying my skin. Stunned, I opened my eyes wide.

I was on the board, and the board was on the wave. The wave was moving, carrying me closer to shore.

"Fuck!" Exhilaration and adrenaline slammed through my system. I grinned until my cheeks hurt, reveling in the sensation until the wave died and I tumbled into the water.

When I surfaced, Zach was there, and he looked concerned and proud.

"Well?" With a hand on each of my shoulders, he checked me over, looking for scrapes or bruises.

There were none. I felt fantastic.

"That was incredible!" He took the board, then knelt in the shallow water and removed the leash from my ankle. "Oh, can't we do it again?"

He looked up at me, and his eyes blazed with heat.

"I told you, you need to save some energy." With a hand on my butt, he nudged me forward and out of the water. "We can go again tomorrow."

"Hmpf." Once on the sand, I turned and watched him pull the board in. The desire to try riding the wave again melted away as I drank him in.

He looked like a water god. As he dropped the board and tugged his wetsuit off, I nearly swallowed my tongue.

I hadn't seen him get ready before my surf lesson. Beneath the wetsuit he wore a snug black bathing suit that cut off at the top of his thighs, leaving every other part of his glorious body open to my avid stare.

Need washed over me like the wave I had just ridden.

Looking up, he caught me looking.

"Take off your wetsuit, Devon." His eyes followed the movements of my fingers when I did as he said, peeling the thick, clinging fabric down the length of my body.

The soaking-wet scraps that made up my bathing suit did nothing to hide my sudden arousal. My nipples were hard peaks, and the midday sun cast shadows on my skin.

"Take off your bikini." I decided to see how he would react to being teased.

"I want to surf some more." I pouted deliberately, and caught the hint of amusement on his face. "I liked it. It's even better than sex."

He pounced, knocking me off balance. Before I knew it he had lowered me gently to the ground. My back to his chest, my cheek was pressed into the sand, my ass in the air.

"I think you're confused. The board must have hit you in the head when I wasn't looking." With steady fingers he undid the strings at the sides of my bikini bottoms, then removed the fabric and threw it across the sand.

"Look at your gorgeous ass." There was the sound of fabric pulling against wet skin, and then his naked pelvis pressed against me from behind. His flesh was cool from the ocean, but his cock was hard and warming rapidly.

"Oh." Pressing back against him, I rotated my hips. He pulled back, breaking contact, and I groaned with disappointment.

"I thought surfing was better than sex." One hand clasped me at my hip, and the other worked its way between my thighs, teasing the soft skin there. "Maybe you shouldn't get any more sex, since you don't appreciate it."

"No!" I panted when he removed his fingers, as well. He laughed, then returned them, this time sliding two right into my slick, waiting heat.

"Say sex is better than surfing."

Half laughing, half moaning, I pushed back against his fingers. My pussy clenched around his fingers, and he began to work them in and out.

"I'm waiting." Zach fucked me with his fingers until I felt my nerves begin to sizzle, then withdrew until only the tips remained inside of me. I cried out, trying to draw him back inside, but he held me steady with his hip.

"Say it, Devon." His hand squeezed my hip, coaxing me to do as he asked. "You know it's the truth."

"Fine, you bastard!" A strangled cry escaped my lips as he pushed those talented fingers back inside of me. "Sex with you is better than surfing!"

He stilled for a moment, and I whimpered. I was so close.

Then a hum of satisfaction left his lips, and the hand on my hip slid forward and down, coming to rest on my clit.

"Come for me, Devon." Clasping my clit between his thumb and forefinger, he began to roll the engorged flesh in a steady rhythm that made my knees buckle. He moved with me as I lowered closer to the sand, the press of his fingers relentless on that sensitive nub.

I came soundlessly, riding a wave of desire that was both hard and sweet. When the tension in my muscles eased, he pulled his hands from my flesh.

I wanted to collapse in a boneless heap on the sand, with Zach pulling me close. In the post-orgasmic haze, though, I found that I couldn't even murmur a protest when he stood and hefted me into his arms. "What now?"

I liked the sensation of being cradled against his chest. I liked the way his muscles rippled as he carried me across the strip of private sand, to the winding stone staircase that led us back up to the house. "My bikini bottoms. And the surfboard!"

"I'll get them later." I might have dreamt it, but I thought I felt him nuzzle my wet hair with his lips.

"I can walk." I shifted against him, but didn't put up much of a fight. I was too comfortable in his arms.

"Devon." Zach's voice was stern, but when I looked up into his face, his eyes held nothing but warmth.

"Let me take care of you."

My brain chafed at the idea of needing to be cared for. My body, however, had other ideas. I found myself snuggling into his embrace, warmed by the idea of someone looking out for me.

The past few years, I had had no one but myself watching over me. If this was life with Zach, then I knew, with a sinking certainty, that I wanted more than just sex.

CHAPTER FIFTEEN

"Wait here." Zach's voice was firm as I snuggled into the towel that he had wrapped around me. His eyes were full of need as he brushed his knuckles over my cheekbone. The tenderness of the gesture made my breath catch as I watched him stride into the bungalow, unabashed in his nakedness.

I supposed that he didn't have any neighbors up here to gawk at him, but still, I had grabbed for the towel he brought to me, feeling incredibly exposed in my skimpy bikini top and nothing else.

I sniffed at the towel, hoping for a whiff of his scent. Instead, I found that the cotton smelled a bit musty. Zach hadn't been kidding when he'd said that he had never brought anyone up here. A man with as much wealth as he had would, I assumed, have someone stop by now and then to look after the house.

This towel told me that that wasn't the case. For some strange reason, that made me happy.

"Warming up a bit?" Zach exited the sliding glass patio doors of the bungalow, carrying a stack of more towels and a large men's shaving kit.

"Yes. Thank you." I eyed the kit warily. His rigid cock told me exactly where his mind was.

I watched as he set the towels and the case down by a large wooden post. I hadn't noticed before, but the top of the post had a showerhead attachment, and the tiled stone flooring at its base dipped into a drain with a grate.

He turned the handles and water rushed from the shower-head. I shivered when I saw the steam rising into the air, recognizing quickly that the muscles in my body that had been abused while surfing were craving the heat.

"Come here." I followed his beckoning finger and moved underneath the outdoor shower. A sigh of pure, hedonistic pleasure escaped my lips as the water flowed over my body in a torrid rush. The contrast of the water with the chill in the air woke every nerve in my body and set it to singing.

Strong fingers toyed with the strings at the neck of my bikini, peeling the fabric away from my breasts. It fell in a sodden heap at my feet moments before those hands began to massage something that smelled of strawberries and champagne into my hair.

"Never had an outdoor shower before?" I groaned in pleasure, answering his question without words, as Zach rubbed the shampoo through my hair, kneading my scalp in the process. He took his time, rinsing and rinsing again before moving to my shoulders.

"Have to get rid of all of the sand." He lathered soap over my shoulders, my breasts, my torso and farther down, washing me thoroughly. His touch was firm enough to make me very aware of his hands on me, but still so light that it was nothing more than a tease.

I relaxed as I realized that his shaving kit had held shampoo and soap, rather than the toys I had imagined.

His hands between my legs made me inhale sharply. I panted through the sudden surge of arousal, pushing against his firm strength at my back.

His cock was thick and hot where it rubbed against my

backside. I wanted him to slide inside me and take me as we showered.

"Put your hands on the post." *Finally*, I thought, and did as he asked. The eyes that I had closed with anticipation flew open when I heard a metal snick and felt something snap around my wrist.

"Zach!" He secured the second bracelet. I could move my arms up and down, but wrapped as they were around the post, now secured with handcuffs, I couldn't do anything else.

Panic flared as I realized that I was bound there, helpless.

Zach looked down at me, his expression serious. He held up a tiny silver key.

"This is the key to those cuffs, Devon. I have it, and can unlock you in seconds." He placed the key on the bench that ran the perimeter of the patio area, where the late-afternoon sun teased out a metallic glint. "Tell me. What is your safe word?"

It was hard to breathe, but I knew that he was expecting an answer.

Yes, I knew my safe word. And yes, I trusted that if I used it, Zach would stop immediately.

I may not have been able to trust him with my heart, but with my body I had no doubts.

"Good girl." Bending to the shaving kit, he rummaged through before pulling out two objects, a white tube and an object that I couldn't identify.

It looked like a small, elongated light bulb, with a flat circle on one end. I cocked my head, studying the thing, when a realization hit me.

A tube of lubricant. And something that was about to go where nothing ever had before.

"I'm going to fuck your ass tonight, Devon." Zach's expression was dark, smoldering, and dangerous. I knew that I could use my safe word, but feared that Zach would shut down on me completely if I used it.

Oh God.

"This is to warm you up so that I don't hurt you." Opening the tube, he squirted a clear gel up and down the length of the plug. Pressing one hand to my waist, he pulled me until I was out of the direct stream of water, though still close enough to be warmed by its steam.

"Are you nuts? That thing isn't going to help. You're huge." Somewhat frantic, I pulled at the handcuffs, which held tight. I noticed then that they were lined with fleece, probably to keep me from marking my skin, but it still hurt, and I sucked in a pained breath.

"Do not do that." Zach's voice was flat. He wasn't at all pleased with my attempt at freedom. "If you want out, then use your safe word. Otherwise I expect willing participation."

A whimper escaped my lips. I knew what anal sex was, of course, but I had never considered it. Ever. The idea of Zach's huge cock pressing through the tight flesh was nerve-racking—and, if I were honest with myself, incredibly arousing.

No matter what he did first, it would hurt like hell.

"Zach. I . . . I don't think I can." I didn't want to use my safe word, didn't want this to be over, but as I stared up at him beseechingly his face seemed as if carved in stone. As if no warmth or emotion had ever warmed his features. "Please, no."

"You have your out, Devon." His words were softer than the look he gave me, and I had momentary hope, but it was quickly squashed. "Part of this relationship means that you will trust me to push your limits, but to take you no farther than you can go. In return, you'll receive more pleasure than you've ever dreamt of."

A snort escaped me—I couldn't help it. Even as he glowered at me, I couldn't stop the sarcastic comment from leaving my mouth.

"Don't you mean that *you* will receive pleasure?" I cried out when, in the blink of an eye, he had moved behind me and spread my cheeks.

I tensed, waiting for the invasion. But even in my nervous state, I realized that not once did I truly consider using my safe word.

"Trust me." I felt the tip of the plug press against my tight opening, and I objected with a cry. The plug was cold and hard and just felt wrong.

But when Zach's free hand slid from the cheek of my ass to splay flat over my stomach, arousal twined with the wrongness of it all, and my emotions became horribly tangled and confused.

"Push back against me." Biting my lip and hesitating for a moment, I did as he asked. I cried out when the unyielding plastic pushed the virgin muscles open. Pain blinded me for a moment, and then it eased, the plug pushing through the tight ring of muscles and settling inside of me.

"Oh, God." I froze. I had no idea what to do. It felt so foreign, so strange, and not at all like the sensation of Zach's cock inside of me.

"Hands on the post, Devon." I bit my lip. Well, this might not be any fun for me, but the barely suppressed excitement in Zach's voice told me that he was aroused to the point of pain.

Swallowing a groan, I did as he ordered.

"Now. Push back against me again." Taking a deep breath, my stomach rolling with nerves, I did. My eyes widened and I cried out as the plug slid farther inside of me.

It burned. The heat spread until my entire ass was on fire. It was uncomfortable. It was painful. It awakened nerve endings that I hadn't even known existed.

"One more time." I couldn't. I swallowed a moan. I couldn't have that thing any farther inside of me. It wouldn't fit.

I wasn't going to use my safe word.

"Now." I pushed back again and gasped at the burn. When Zach lowered the hand that was on my belly to my clit, I jumped at the startling stimulation.

"There is pleasure in this for you, Devon. You just have to decide if you're going to let it in or not." A sarcastic laugh escaped me, even as I wondered if he could possibly be right. I still felt stretched too far, uncomfortable, my flesh on fire. But his fingers circling over my clit added pleasure to the mix, and I cursed as the onslaught of sensations threatened to take me under. It seemed I would get no relief from the intensity of Zach's sexual urges.

It would have been so much easier to fall for someone whose taste in sex had less earth-shattering results for me.

When Zach pinched my clit lightly, a whisper of pain merging with pleasure, the thought was wiped from my mind.

"Stop fighting it." Zach murmured in my ear, and I tensed as I felt movement from the plug. He was pulling it back, easing it out of my flesh, and I gulped in air as I worshipped him in blessed relief.

"No." I growled when he pushed it back in, still so very slowly. He didn't respond, and I felt something cold pour through the division of my ass, followed by his fingers massaging it, swirling around the entrance filled by the plug.

"Yes." The plug moved back out again, until only the very tip was in. When he pressed it forward yet again I paused in my protests. The extra lubricant helped ease the passage of the object into my body. It was still uncomfortable, but the cool gel banked some of the fire.

Zach's fingers slicked into my wet pussy, gathering my liquid heat, then back to continue working my clit. The pleasure of his touch there and the new, unexplored sensations elsewhere made me begin to tremble, unsure of what was happening to me.

"Hang on tight." My fingers curled into the damp wood of the post as Zach's fingers began to move faster on my clit, rolling it in that expert way he had. Despite all of my protests, I felt tension begin to build in my very core.

"Come now." As if he had commanded it, pleasure exploded through me. As I gasped my way through my climax, I was dimly aware of the plug beginning to move inside of me, harder and faster and deeper than it had before.

"Zach." I moaned my protest, but was surprised to find that I didn't truly mean it. My climax had sweetened the edge of pain, and now it had all turned into pure sensation.

"That's my little minx." My voice echoed into the air as he used the plug to fuck in and out of my ass, the sensation still strange but something I found myself thrilling to.

I groaned softly when he pulled the object out of me entirely. Though my muscles eased, I felt strangely empty.

Then I thought of what was coming, and I tensed all over again.

"Easy." I wished I could see his face, but all I could do was hold on. Something warm and wet was poured over the entirety of my bottom. I arched into the touch when Zach began to massage the flesh there, rubbing the liquid over my cheeks and into the crevice. When he worked a finger inside of the place where the plug had been I found that it actually felt good, and I squirmed, wanting that sensation of fullness again.

"Open your legs farther." Something hard slid between my legs. I shifted, confused and aroused, as Zach's finger followed, sliding into the heat. He pressed his finger against the slick, bullet-shaped thing inside of my pussy, and a moment later my knees buckled when vibrations burst to life in my womb. "Don't you dare let that fall."

"Zach!" His hands returned to my ass, again spreading my

cheeks. I had a mental image of what I must look like to him, bound, open to his stare, pink from arousal.

Then he pressed the head of his cock to the pucker between my cheeks, and I found myself retreating to a place where all that existed was sensation, and I couldn't think at all.

Incomprehensible sounds fell from my lips as he slowly, slowly pushed inside of me. His erection was far bigger than the plug had been, and my flesh protested as it was stretched to its fullest extent.

It hurt. But as he eased in, then out a fraction, then in a bit more, I found that the hurt felt good.

"All right?" he asked me. I didn't need to stop to take stock; I nodded frantically, suddenly afraid that the sensations would stop. My breaths came shorter and shorter as he continued to ease in, pull back, and push farther into me.

Finally he came to rest with his pelvis cupping my bottom. I could feel the heavy weight of his testicles pressing against the tender flesh of my labia. Though he didn't move, the fullness of his cock inside of me created pressure on the vibrator that worked in my pussy.

It was too much. It wasn't enough.

"More." I barely recognized the voice that spoke, though it was my own. "Please. I want more." I thought that I heard Zach murmur my name with pleasure before he wrapped my wet hair in his fist, pulling my head back toward him.

"Mine." I wasn't sure who spoke the word, and then I didn't care. Zach slid almost all the way out of me, and then all the way back in. My moans became pleas as he set a steady rhythm, never rough yet always moving at that unrelenting pace.

"I can't hold back much longer." Zach's voice was grim as he slid his hands between my legs. One parted my lower lips with sure fingers, and the other slid inside of me, catching the vibrator between thumb and forefinger and driving it up inside of me farther.

He thrust inside of me again, and though there couldn't possibly have been room, he pressed the vibrator up inside of me as far as it would go. It pulsed against the thin membrane that parted my two most intimate places, and the sensation was so intense that I tried to pull away.

Zach's strong body held me in place.

"I—I can't. Zach . . . it's too much!" My words were fragmented. His breathing was becoming ragged himself as he ignored my feeble protests and helped me to accept the sensations.

He thrust inside of me, deeper than he had yet. I felt him begin to tense, a sign that I now knew meant he was approaching climax. Knowing that I had brought him the pleasure made me want to give him even more. I pushed back against him, taking him in another fraction of an inch. When his cock began to pulse inside of me, filling me with liquid heat, the added pressure sent me hurtling over the edge into a violent climax that slapped me in the face with its intensity. I screamed into the steamy air, shuddering brutally as we each rode our pleasure to the end.

His arms wrapped around my waist tightly, supporting me so I didn't hang limply from my bound wrists. Though the tsunami of my orgasm had receded, I trembled, my muscles refusing to hold me up.

I hissed when, after a long moment in which he cradled me against his chest, Zach eased out of me. His sure fingers slid between my legs and extracted the vibrator, switching it off before tossing it aside.

My body felt abused and wonderfully lax. My emotions felt as though they had been pounded by the waves of the ocean that I could hear below us.

What had just happened?

To my mortification, tears sprang to my eyes. I turned my face away, desperate to hide them from Zach. He didn't comment, instead stroking a finger down my back reassuringly before retrieving the key and unlocking my cuffs.

"Ssh, Devon, my little minx." He massaged my fingers and palms, working blood through them. "It's normal to feel a lot after something like that."

I shook my head but kept my lips pressed tightly together as he nudged me back under the spray of the showerhead. He poured the delicious-smelling liquid soap over my backside, letting the suds and the water clean me and ease the sting.

I was afraid to part my lips to speak. I knew what I wanted to say, but I didn't think it was anything he wanted to hear. So I allowed him to wrap me in another towel, to dry my skin and my hair. And as I did, I wondered what to do with myself now that I knew, for me at least, that the mutual sexual pleasure had blossomed into something that felt an awful lot like love.

Zach and I had both remained somewhat subdued as we gathered our toys from the patio and beach below and made our way into the house. He had ordered dinner to be delivered, and as I explored the house, he had dressed in faded jeans and a ripped T-shirt.

But his next statement jolted me out of my relaxed state. "You will remain naked."

The demand brought the banked fire inside of me to life again.

"You're dressed," I pointed out as I slowly backed toward the bedroom, where the bag that had been packed for us both still sat on the bed. I had an idea, and his order put a definite kink into it.

"I'm the one who gets to make the rules." He looked so

pleased with himself that it made up my mind. I might be punished later, but I had a feeling that it would be worth it.

"Please, Zach." I continued to back toward the bedroom, and he continued to move forward, stalking me. "Just give me a minute. You'll like it, I swear."

He paused for a moment, and I grasped the opportunity. Whirling and running into the bedroom, I slammed the door shut behind me before diving across the room for the nightgown that I had retrieved from the car while Zach was getting dressed.

Inhaling deeply, I shook the tissue paper covering from the scrap of blue silk, then pulled it over my head.

I heard the door open as I smoothed the lingerie around my hips. Turning, I clenched my fists at my sides and faced Zach, who looked for all the world like he had just caught his prey and was about to feast.

He stopped in his tracks when he saw what I had done.

"Do you like it?" The impetus for buying the nightgown may have been to spice up a dull sex life, and I may have convinced myself that the exorbitant price was a present to myself. But as Zach's eyes traveled over me, absorbing the sight of me in the slip, I knew that it had been for him all along.

"You're beautiful." He spoke softly as he crossed the room toward me. My mouth went dry when he wrapped his arms around me and pulled me in for a deep, drugging kiss.

My heart began to do funny things inside of my chest. When he slid his hands down my back, cupping my bottom and lifting me into his embrace, I wrapped my legs around his waist and opened myself to him entirely.

"Amazing." I was laid on the bed with exquisite gentleness. I watched through half-lidded eyes, shivering slightly, as he stripped off the clothing that he had just put on, then lowered himself onto the bed until his heat ran along my entire length.

"So soft." A single finger ran over my breast, tracing the line of fabric where skin and satin met, as he parted my legs with his other hand and slid a finger into my heat. It seemed that I was always ready with him, and when he positioned his cock at my entrance and pressed inside of me, he glided in with ease.

Our stares were locked as he balanced his weight on his elbows, his pelvis pressing down as mine thrust up. We moved with an easy rhythm, one that started slow and sped up only a fraction before pressure began to build.

"Sweet Devon." Lowering his head to my breast, he suckled my nipple into his mouth through the thin silk of the slip. The fabric pulled tight over the engorged flesh, forcing a pleased cry from my lips. At the same time, he began to circle my clit with his hand, bringing me shuddering to the peak with sure fingers.

"I want us to come together." He pressed the fingers at my clit together tightly, trapping the bud in their grasp as I surged upward. Stars danced in the air before me as, following in the aftermath of my shudders, he pressed as deeply inside of me as he could, groaning my name hoarsely as he spent himself between my thighs.

He nuzzled his face into the side of my neck as we tried to catch our breath, and I rubbed circles over the taut skin of his back with my palm.

The words slipped from my lips without my meaning to speak.

"I love you." Caught in the moment, I voiced what I felt for him. The loving he had just shown me had been so tender, so sweet, that it was a full minute before I realized that his body had gone rigid as stone on top of me.

"Devon . . ." Zach withdrew from me and slid off the bed, running his fingers through his hair with agitated movements. He said nothing, but the shock and discomfort on his face told me all that I needed to know.

"I see." Tears threatened, but with them was anger. I froze for a long moment, the slip clinging damply to my skin and leaving me feeling more exposed than if I had been naked.

I could have told him that it didn't matter that he clearly didn't return the feeling, just to put him at ease, but it would have been a lie. He watched, dumbfounded, as I drew in a shaky breath, then pushed myself off the bed and toward the duffel bag.

"What are you doing?" Shielding myself from his eyes as best as I could, I pulled out a T-shirt that must have belonged to him, since it was far too large for me. I didn't care, tugging the slip over my head and the T-shirt on, thankful for the coverage. A bit more digging yielded a pair of leggings.

Swallowing against my outrage and hurt so hard that my throat burned, I ignored his question and marched out of the bedroom. I couldn't stay in his presence a moment longer, not when the words I had spoken hung in the air between us, unwanted by him and so important to me.

"Devon. Stop right now." I continued to ignore him, slipping my feet into my flats and grabbing my purse. Moments later I was out the door, my chin held high.

That chin trembled as I reached the long, winding driveway, Zach's angry shouts echoing behind me.

First things first. I tried to push the pain away as I attempted to form a logical plan. It was what I did best, after all.

I would walk into town. I would find a motel to stay in for the night while I gathered my wits. In the morning I would rent a car and drive back to San Francisco, where I would think about what I wanted to do next.

I liked my job, but I wasn't sure that I could be around Zach now. I couldn't be with someone who insisted on denying the spark that flashed between us, who wouldn't share his past with me so that we could move on and have a future.

"No." The word was a pained cry that broke the dam holding back my tears. It would have been better if he truly hadn't felt anything for me back. What was killing me was that I knew, *knew* that we had enough between us to be happy.

But Zach was dominant to the core. He had given himself orders, and he would never break them.

I couldn't stop the tears. I reached the end of the driveway and turned onto the shoulder of the road, wiping blindly at my eyes. My entire body shook, and I felt as though I might be sick.

The scream of tires punctured my consciousness in a deafening roar. Voices, the bass of a loud song, laughter, then screams.

I whirled and found a blur of bright red coming straight toward me.

My scream was soundless as my body froze. My rigid frame was yanked out of the way, right off the shoulder of the road to the grass, as a car packed with teenagers, two surfboards strapped to the top, swerved over the area where I had just stood.

I fell to the ground with an impact that knocked the wind out of me. In my panic, as I wheezed, trying to catch my breath, I realized that the arms around my waist belonged to Zach. He was trembling with rage as he watched the car drive away, the obnoxious, bass-heavy music fading into the distance.

My heart leapt, making its presence known through the surge of adrenaline that made my limbs shake and my teeth chatter. But when I turned to look up at Zach, to thank him for what he had done, I found myself faced with a wall of ice.

My mouth opened and then closed soundlessly. I had no idea what to do with the anger, the pure rage that was undulating from him in waves.

"Thank you." I had to say it, though my voice was quiet and small when I did. The words had the effect of his turning his eyes to look at me, but the frost in them told me that nothing had changed on his end.

"Get back to the house." His words were clipped and raw. My heart wept even as my tears dried and my hands balled into fists.

"We're going back to San Francisco."

PART VI

TEMPTED TO POSSESS

CHAPTER SIXTEEN

W aiting on my desk for me the next morning when I
arrived at the office was a small package wrapped
with exquisite attention to detail. I knew it was
from Zach before I opened the card.

My inner voice told me to hurl the small gold-wrapped
box down the building's garbage chute. Miserable as I was to
be apart from him, I had had enough of Zach's games.

The night before had left me a mess. It was Friday, but I
had an entire day to get through before I could be finally,
blessedly alone. And after the way in which Zach had col-
lected me from the office the previous morning, I knew that I
was about to be the subject of gossip everywhere I went, some
benign, most malicious.

"Fuck." Slumping down at my desk, I poked a finger into
the curled ribbon that adorned the box. If I wasn't going to
throw it away, then I should probably open it before my coworkers arrived for the day, before the office was filled with
eyes eager for more details in the saga of Devon and Zach.

My hands trembled as I pulled the ribbon off the parcel,
then slit the tape with my nail. Inside the paper was a velvet
jeweler's box—and even though I knew better by now, hope
ran through me in a torrid rush. What was this?

Holding my breath, I opened the box. A handful of silver
and blue fell into my palm, catching the light of the room and
shining brightly.

It was a bracelet, made of delicately etched platinum holding a stream of small blue stones. Each stone was opaque, and when the light caught it at the right angle, I could see a white star trapped inside the sapphire blue.

Clutching the bracelet tightly in my fist, as if I couldn't bear to let it go, I opened the card. The pen had bitten into the paper under Zach's heavy hand.

> The blue of these star sapphires reminded me of the beautiful slip that you wore for me last night. The bracelet is a thank-you for the time that we have had together, which I will never forget. I'm more sorry than you know that I can't give you what you need.
>
> Always,
> Zach

Sitting back in my chair, I closed my eyes tight and tried to compose myself. I didn't even want to think about the strings that he must have pulled to procure this bracelet sometime between when we had gotten back to the city and my arrival at work.

I couldn't keep it. I wanted to, not only because it was beautiful, but also because it seemed like it just might be the only reminder I might ever have of our time together. Now that we were over, he had finally surprised me and revealed a sentimental side that I'd always suspected lurked beneath his dominance when we were together.

Yet if I held on to the thoughtful gift, I knew that I would never fully be able to let him go.

My fingers felt thick and clumsy as I carefully tucked the bracelet back into its small box. A shudder racked my body as I opened the top drawer to my desk and slipped the box inside.

"Morning, Devon." Looking up with a start, I found Tony

on the other side of the desk. I felt myself tense, uncertain of my welcome here in the office, after the scene that Zach had made the day before.

"Morning." My voice was tentative, soft. Tony seemed pleased when I managed to work up a smile, though he couldn't have known that I didn't feel up to it at all.

"I brought coffee." My eyes flicked down to his hands, each of which held a paper cup. He held one out for me, and I could have wept with relief at the normalcy of the gesture.

"Thanks, Tony." A hint of genuine warmth crept into me as I accepted the steaming cup. He smiled back, a bit sheepishly, then turned toward his own desk, and I felt my feelings toward him change, just a bit, as I realized that he wasn't going to mention yesterday's scene.

Being in the same department meant that I couldn't date Tony. Moreover, I didn't want to. I didn't have feelings for him in that way. But it was definitely nice to have a friend.

"My office please, Miss Devon Reid."

Mrs. Gallagher's voice broke the clatter of midday business in the office. Startled, I backtracked to the glass door to her lair, which I had just passed.

"Yes, Mrs. Gallagher?" I eyed her warily as I entered her office. Her reading glasses were perched down on the end of her nose, and her expression was stern.

Whatever she was about to talk to me about, I didn't want to hear it. It had been a pisser of a day.

"Close the door." Her voice was firm, and I groaned inwardly but did as she asked, resentment burning through my veins.

I was sick of being told what to do. When I left Sacramento, I had decided to explore parts of myself that I had never known before. Now it seemed that I was back in the same rut I used to live in—Devon the biddable, Devon the sweet.

Devon the good girl.

"Sit down."

I couldn't quite mask my scowl as I flopped into one of the seats across the desk from where Mrs. Gallagher sat. I raised my eyebrows, gesturing for her to start.

The look she gave me in return was pointed, but she didn't comment on my rudeness. Instead, when she spoke her voice was gentle, a far cry from how she normally spoke to her employees.

"Devon, what is going on with you?" I huffed out a laugh that held no mirth, my mind whirling over the vastness that that question encompassed.

The night before, Zach had ignored my insistence that I call Charles to come get him, and that I drive back by myself. His fury had been so overwhelming that I hadn't been able to make even a dent in it, though I wanted to scream at him that love was a gift, even when it wasn't returned.

His anger went far beyond what I thought was reasonable for what had happened between us. His reaction hurt me beyond compare. Add to that the stress of almost being run over, and the never-ending ride home with Zach, who tensed every time another car came anywhere close to us, and my nerves were about to snap.

"Devon." The unexpected kindness in the older woman's voice snapped the frayed thread of my control. Tears began to well up in my eyes, and I stared at Mrs. Gallagher, openmouthed and mortified to be losing my composure in front of her.

"Oh, honey." Picking up a remote, she pressed the button that frosted the windows to her office, then handed me a box of Kleenex. I accepted one gratefully and used it to blot my eyes. I had no idea how to respond to the woman our entire department feared. She was acting so out of character.

It was tempting to spill the entire story, just to share the burden with someone. I bit my tongue because I knew how much trouble I could get into. Even if there wasn't an official rule about it, I knew that confirmation of how far my affair with Zach had gone would make my life here at Phyrefly miserable.

Despite Tony's kind gesture that morning, I hadn't yet decided if I wanted to stay here. I did, however, know that I wanted the choice to be my own.

"I understand what you're going through better than you think." Leaning back in her chair, Mrs. Gallagher took off her glasses and rubbed her temples before leveling me with her stare. I was struck again by what an attractive woman she was, once she dropped the stern demeanor.

"I also understand why you don't want to talk about it. So let me lay out what I think has happened." That penetrating gaze pinned me in my seat, and I squirmed uncomfortably.

"You and Mr. St. Brenton became involved before you became employed here. He secured the job for you."

Shame welled up in me once more, and I bit my lip, the tears threatening to fall over.

I sounded like a harlot.

"I— It's not what you—" She shushed me, and I stared at the floor.

"Now before you go getting all upset again, know that he would never have given you a position here if you weren't fully capable of benefitting his company. He didn't become a billionaire by being stupid." I looked up at the sound of a desk drawer opening. To my utter shock, Mrs. Gallagher set a bottle of amber-colored liquid and two plastic cups on her desk.

It was early afternoon. At the office. This was Mrs. Gallagher, the woman who disapproved of everything.

"Drink this." She poured two fingers of scotch into the cheap tumbler and pushed it across the desk toward me. Stunned, I picked up the cup, sniffed, then coughed over the fumes.

Since she seemed to be expecting it, I sipped. The liquor burned a scorching path down my throat and into my gut, heating me where I had been chilled since the night before.

"Now. I don't know the man beyond the monthly department-head meeting. But I know from my own experiences, that a man with as much power as he has can play some wicked games with a woman's heart." Slamming back the rest of my scotch in a great gulp, I found my interest piqued.

"Your experiences?" I didn't feel bad about asking, because the woman had opened herself up by calling me into her office for this discussion.

Mrs. Gallagher nodded, and her eyes went flat and cold. "I used to work for another big company. I had—well, the owner was nearly as enigmatic as Mr. St. Brenton. Rich, worldly, handsome, and he paid attention to me. I was young. It didn't end well."

I felt a surge of pity at the bitterness in the other woman's voice, and at the same time my heart sank.

If her affair hadn't ended well, why would mine?

"So. You've gotten involved with one of the most eligible bachelors in the world." I nodded miserably.

She pinned me with her gaze. "Not the brightest idea."

"I'm sorry. Really." Suddenly I wanted to leave. I wanted to go home. And yet, I had no idea where home was. "I— Please don't fire me. I like it here." At least her words had cleared up one dilemma for me.

I didn't want to leave this job, this city. It might not have felt like home without Zach, but I wasn't done here yet.

"Don't be ridiculous." Mrs. Gallagher snapped the words, then stood. Awkwardly, I followed suit, uncertainty shadowing my every move.

"The way that Mr. St. Brenton behaves around you is worlds different than the way my lover once treated me. Initially, I intended to warn you off of him, but it's easy to see that he cares about you. Deeply. More than that, you're a bright, determined woman. You can change his mind."

I stared, dumbfounded. This conversation was incredibly one-sided, and I wasn't sure I could keep up.

"Now, you have a decision to make. It might be easier to walk away now. And you're strong enough that you can. But do you want to, Devon?"

I found I couldn't answer. My mouth was dry, my head swimming as I shook it slowly. "No. No, I . . . I don't need him. But I *want him.*" I wanted him with every fiber in my being, even if he didn't want me the same way.

"Well, then. Show him what he's missing." Standing, Mrs. Gallagher gathered her purse from beneath her desk and hoisted it onto her shoulder.

"I'm going for a late lunch. You may stay here for a few minutes if you need to make a private call."

The woman was halfway out the door of her office when I found my voice again.

"Thank you." I couldn't think of anything else to say. I was still reeling at the unexpected turn of events. The last thing I had expected was for my cold boss to show me such uncharacteristic concern.

Without any further conversation, just a half turn and a nod in my direction, she left her office and sailed on to the bank of elevators, leaving me alone to think.

My fingers were cold and clammy as I shut the office door behind her, then moved to the other side of her desk.

Then, slowly, I picked up the phone.

"St. Brenton."

I nearly dropped the phone in a surge of anxiety when I heard the sexy rasp of Zach's voice on the other end of the line.

I ached at the sound, wishing I were there next to him so that I could reach out and run my hands over his skin.

"Hello?" His voice was irritable, and though it made me shiver with nerves, I also felt a tendril of hope curl through me. He sounded every bit as miserable as I felt.

"Bini, what is it? I have someone in my office." My world came back into focus. He'd answered the phone because he thought it was one of his department heads.

I could only hope that he wouldn't hang up when he learned that it was me.

"It's not Bini." The silence on the other end of the phone was weighted . . . I felt certain that he recognized my voice, but he didn't hang up.

Show him what he's missing.

This might be my last chance.

"I wish your cock was inside of me right now." I breathed out the words before I could lose the nerve, then reeled, shocked with myself.

The silence on Zach's end of the line stretched out, deepened, and I cringed.

"I have someone in my office." Finally he spoke, and his words were carefully measured. Still . . . he didn't tell me to go.

I was terrified, for so many unspeakable reasons. I had no idea what I was doing. Yet what did I have to lose?

"Do you remember the first time you had me in your office? You flipped up my skirt and used the martinet on my bottom." I heard his sharp intake of breath, and worried that I had gone too far.

"I do." He was playing along. Joy surged through me, followed quickly by arousal. I felt as though his eyes were on me at that moment, intent, gauging my body's response.

Before he could think better of it, or tell me to stop, I continued.

"If I was in your office right now, I would take off my skirt, my sweater, my panties and bra. You would be seated at your desk, like I imagine you are now. I would walk over to you, unzip your pants and pull your cock into my hand. It would feel so good for you, your erection so hard that it needed to be free from restraint." I sucked in a great mouthful of air, my face flushing with both arousal and embarrassment. It felt so wrong to say these things aloud. I had never done anything like this before.

"Continue."

I tried to stand, to ease the sudden ache between my own legs, but the sound of his caressing voice had me dropping back into the chair.

"I want to sit on the edge of your desk, then bend over to take you into my mouth. I would be able to taste you as I sucked on your cock, deep in my throat. You would groan. Then you would pull my hair with one hand and spank my bare ass with the other, just to show me how much you want me."

"And how do you feel about that?" To the other person in his office, Zach likely sounded as though he were discussing nothing more than the details of a client meeting. I had heard the sounds his voice made when he was driven beyond control, however, and so I was able to detect the very slight hitch in his breath that told me he wasn't nearly as calm as he was pretending to be.

It gave me confidence. Sliding a hand up to fondle my own breast, I rubbed lightly, and when the nipple pebbled beneath my fingers it was because, in my mind's eye, it was Zach's hand on my skin.

"The touch of your hand on my skin would make me want you as much as I always do." My voice came softer now; the words that I spoke had no pretense. "I would be wet, just from your touch, your taste."

I heard him inhale, just the slightest bit. I had no idea how he was remaining so composed. My skin had heated to the point of fever, and I ached all over.

"This is true." His words were an admission. He knew exactly how much he affected me. Dammit, he knew that I loved him.

I wished he could open up and tell me how he felt in return.

"I wouldn't be able to take it anymore. I'd have to slide from the desk into your lap. Taking your cock in your own hand, you would push into me until I cried out because you had filled me completely. Then I would move. I would ride you in your desk chair, completely bare to you, until I felt your hips arch beneath me and your heat spill inside of me." My hands shook on the phone. I wanted this so badly to be reality that I could almost taste the salt of his musk on my tongue.

"And you?" His tone was still light, still matter-of-fact, but I could hear the seriousness that belied the question.

If it were real, I knew that he would make me come.

It wasn't real. I didn't know if it would ever be real again.

"I would slide off of you once you were done. I would get dressed and leave, because this was a gift for you." The heat inside of me cooled rapidly as my emotions began to overtake me again. My tease had become much more metaphorical than I had intended. "I just want for you to be happy."

Dammit, I could *feel* his hunger, his need for me, permeating his silence. Attraction wasn't the problem.

He didn't love me back, and he couldn't simply accept what I wanted to give him.

"Good-bye, Zach." Not waiting for him to reply, I replaced the phone in its cradle. Finally overwhelmed by the events of the past twenty-four hours, I gave in. Laying my arms on Mrs. Gallagher's desk, I buried my face in them and cried.

The tsunami of tears had done me good. As I entered the parking garage that evening after work, I felt . . . well, I still felt as though I had been hit by a semitruck. But the hopelessness had abated somewhat. I would get on with my life.

Regardless of what he said, after that phone call, I knew once and for all that I had the power to affect Zach. He cared for me, and whatever his reasons were for rejecting me, it didn't have anything to do with me.

And I had given it one last shot. Now I could try to move on without regret—*try* being the operative word.

I still craved him with every fiber of my being. I hoped that would pass.

Opening my car door, I had just decided that I deserved ice cream and wine for supper, and that I would dine in a steaming-hot bubble bath, when I caught a shadow from the corner of my eye. I shrieked and jolted, my ankle folding in my high heel and sending me pitching forward.

The next thing I knew there were arms wrapping around me tightly. Then I was lifted into a strong embrace. I screamed again, looking across the lot to where the parking attendant should have been.

The small, gray-haired old man was gone. In his place was Charles, and though the man's face held a hint of sympathy, he didn't look as though he would be coming to my aid anytime in the near future.

"What the fuck do you think you're doing?" I shouted the words at the hard planes of Zach's back, since I was draped over his shoulder unceremoniously. I relaxed immensely as soon as I realized it was him, but frustration and fury quickly replaced the fear. "I can walk, damn you."

"You're coming to my house." Then he didn't say anything more.

I upped the intensity of my kicks when we passed Charles, who held open the door to Zach's private garage to let us pass.

I scowled at the older man. He looked away.

"Did you consider asking me whether or not I *wanted* to come to your house?" I tried not to enjoy the sensation of Zach's rock-solid body pressed against mine. It was even more pleasurable when he slid me along the length of him until my feet touched the floor. I tried to break away, but he tightened his grasp and pinned me to the side of the car with his hips.

He was fully erect, and the heat of his rigid cock pressed into my belly.

"I considered it. Then I decided that I wasn't in the mood to care one way or the other." I gasped with outrage. As I sputtered, Zach opened the door to the backseat of the car, then lifted me from the waist and nudged me inside. I didn't cooperate, and wound up on my knees on the hard floor, my hair tangled around my face, my cheeks flushed.

Zach climbed in after me, and after he calmly—gracefully—settled himself on one of the bench seats, he surveyed me as I glared up at him.

"You started this." His reminder was calm, but didn't take much fight out of me. I had so many things that I wanted to say to him, but I couldn't even find a place to start.

"It's like that, then, is it?" Bending, he grasped the neckline of my cardigan and pulled. Bits of the plastic buttons went flying, skittering into the corners of the car, and then the sweater hung open, baring my breasts.

"You have a choice. We can talk, or if you're not in the mood for conversation, you can suck my cock. The decision is yours." Those long hands of his loosened the dark purple silk of his tie, and then with another lightning-quick move he pulled me against him, tugged my arms behind my back, and looped the length of silk around my wrists securely.

I was stunned, and also aroused.

"I thought you said I had a choice!" My mouth was dry as I

spoke. I knew, deep down I knew, that if I really wanted to I could refuse both choices and demand that the car be stopped, that I be let out.

I also knew, and Zach knew, that that wasn't was I truly wanted.

"The choice is yours." He smirked a bit, looking down at me seductively, though his eyes were deadly serious. "But even if we're going to talk, I like looking at you like this, arms bound, breasts thrust forward."

I moaned softly, not able to hold the sound back, given my extreme arousal. Pressing my lips together in a tight line, I nodded toward his lap. "Open your pants."

His expression darkened as I spoke, and my pulse skittered.

"You don't get to make the rules here, little minx." The warring emotions and arousal in his eyes, the clenching of his jaw, told me that I was moments away from being pulled over his knee and spanked until I couldn't move.

Wetness surged through my pussy at the very idea.

"Fine. Open your pants . . . sir." I thrust my chin forward defiantly. Zach raised an eyebrow, his face shadowed.

"Keep it up, little brat." Lifting his hips off the seat, he undid the buckle of his belt and then released the zipper. The metallic rasp grated on the air.

The sight of his hand on his cock as he pulled it free of his pants sent heat crashing through me in a tidal wave. As usual, he wore nothing beneath his pants, and so there was nothing to hinder my mouth when he leaned back on the leather bench seat, splaying his legs so that I could crawl between them.

I shivered as I looked up at him. Now, more than ever, I was struck by his dark beauty. His face, his body—everything about him appealed to me on a level so basic that it felt stamped into my very DNA.

"Take me in your mouth." Zach kept his hand wrapped

around the base of his erection, holding it out for me. With the other, he guided me across the floor of the car on my knees, keeping me from losing my balance when Charles, safely secured behind the privacy panel, started the car. Zach caught my shoulders with his hands, then helped me to settle between his legs.

When I closed my lips around the head of his cock I shut my eyes in surrender. The taste of him flooded my mouth and soothed the emotions that had been scraped raw.

"Yes." As if our feelings were connected, I looked up to find satisfaction and relief emblazoned on Zach's features. He laced his fingers together at the back of my head, his touch light but enough to hold me in place.

Our eyes met and a surge of emotion jolted through me. I had thought never to see him like this again, yet he sought me out after I placed that teasing phone call to him.

I began to suck, hollowing my cheeks out. Though his breath quickly turned from shallow to raspy, he held still, apart from the occasional upward flex of his hips when I lightly scraped my teeth below the head.

I was at his feet, my sweater torn open, my hands behind my back, Zach's cock in my mouth. Still, I had never felt more powerful. Determined, I continued my ministrations, though my jaw was beginning to ache and my throat burned.

"Devon, stop." I could tell that he was nearing climax when the muscles of his thighs tensed. It was what I wanted, so I ignored him and continued to work his cock with my mouth.

The hands on the back of my head tangled in my hair and pulled me back. I had no choice but to let his erection slip from my mouth. I hissed, feeling the sting from the threads of hair he tugged on.

"You're adding to your punishment, minx." He was slightly

out of breath, but still managed to make me shiver with the heavy promise in his words.

The shivering turned to a full-on shudder when he spoke again, and I realized that, by teasing him with my phone call, I had awakened the beast.

"I'm not going to come until I'm deep inside of you. Until then, your body is mine."

CHAPTER SEVENTEEN

"What the hell is that?" Zach had refused to remove his tie from my wrists. After helping me from the car, he had lifted me into his arms, my head cradled against his chest, and carried me through the garage and into the house. I was thankful that Charles had disappeared beforehand, because though I was sure he knew what Zach and I had been up to in the back of the vehicle, confronting him with my smeared makeup and torn sweater was far beyond my comfort zone.

So was the wooden contraption that Zach had placed me down on my feet in front of. Resembling a picnic table without the wide, flat top, it came to just below my waist and was padded and covered in dark red leather.

He didn't reply, and I looked over to find him staring at me with displeasure. Immediately I understood that I was in trouble. When he channeled the dominant side of himself—well, the *more* dominant side—he became larger, darker, relentless.

This was the Zach that I saw now. My ass was still tender from the night before, so I was quick to drop my eyes to the floor.

"I'm sorry." Still, I couldn't stop myself from glancing back up at the table with wary eyes.

"I'm sorry. *What*?" Zach had shed his suit jacket and now undid the top few buttons of his shirt. The result was that while he still seemed dangerous, he looked slightly more relaxed.

Relaxed and ready to play.

"I'm sorry, sir." The faintest hint of pleasure curved his lips as he stalked toward me. My nipples bunched into tight peaks before he even touched me. He saw and inhaled with satisfaction.

"What is your safe word, Devon?" I knew him so well that the intense stare he directed my way felt like his hands on my body—so much that when his actual fingers touched me it was as if two men caressed my skin. He pulled my damaged sweater off of my shoulders, then flicked open the front clasp of my bra and did the same.

"Dark." As I spoke he slid my sweater down to join the silk tie, adding an extra layer of restraint, my torso left bare.

"Very good." Tracing a hand up my inner thigh, Zach cupped my moist heat through my thin panties, then slid one finger in and out quickly, testing my dampness.

"Where is the bracelet?"

I blinked, trying to make sense of the question, and clear the fog of lust that had fallen over me. Zach repeated the question impatiently. "The bracelet that I sent to you this morning. Where is it?"

"Um. In my purse." Turning on his heel, Zach moved to the leather satchel that he had carried into the house with me. I grumbled to myself as he delved into its contents—a woman's purse was supposed to be private.

I watched as he found the small gold box, then pulled the bright link of sapphires from it.

Returning to me, he fastened it around my left wrist, above where the silk of his tie still bound me.

"You didn't answer." As he fastened the bracelet that I still hadn't decided I was going to keep to my wrist, I pushed at him. Dangerous, but I had to know. "Zach, what is that ... that *thing*?"

"You are permitted to ask questions about the toys I am

going to use on you, so long as you use a respectful tone." A minor chastisement. I was far too distracted by his fingers, which ran along beneath my hip, where my legs met my pelvis. He hooked his fingers in the slim elastics at the sides of my bikini briefs, and I cried out when he yanked down hard, tearing them off of my body.

"That is a spanking bench." The scraps that had been my panties fell to the floor, followed by my skirt, which he unzipped in one sure motion. Completely bared to him, I felt his eyes caress me when he looked the length of my body.

"You are going to be punished for your impertinence in making that phone call today, followed by the minor infractions of your resistance in the car and your rudeness right now." My mouth fell open, stunned as I always was when he spoke to me as if he were preparing to spank a toddler. "This bench makes it easier, and more enjoyable, for me."

"I—" I started to protest, but snapped my lips shut when I remembered that he would just add to the punishment. Pressing my lips together tightly, I swallowed my grievance.

"Very good. You're learning."

Then I forgot what I had been upset about when he stepped closer and claimed my mouth with his own. His tongue teased the seam of my lips, making me moan, as his hands ran a heated trail up and down the sides of my body.

"Now. Onto the bench." A sound of disappointment escaped me when he broke the embrace, turning me and, with a hand pressed flat against my bottom, positioning me over the thing that he called a spanking bench.

My entire body tensed.

"You have your safe word, Devon." His words were reassuring, but his hand pressed me forward until my torso lay vertically down the bench. "You have the power to stop this at any time. If that is truly what you want."

I inhaled deeply, willing myself to calm down. His words weren't a magic wand—they didn't make all of my fears disappear. The things that he had used on me before—the cuffs, the martinet, even the paddle—had seemed small compared to this. He was asking me to give up every shred of power that I had, to be bound and restrained and more vulnerable than I ever had before.

I was terrified, and I was aroused. I also understood that this may be the opportunity I had been waiting for.

If I could be vulnerable to Zach, then maybe he would see that he could be vulnerable to me.

"Okay." I heard the slight tremor in my voice, and scolded myself for it. I could do this.

I trusted him. That was the entire point.

"Good, little minx." Zach stroked his hand down my back softly, tracing my spine, as I finally stopped fighting it. I arched into the touch like a kitten being stroked. "You can trust me. You know you can trust me."

Right, said my mind. *So said the wolf to Little Red Riding Hood.*

And I was right. Soon after he had me warm and all but purring beneath his hands, I felt something cool placed at the width of my waist. I stiffened, placing my hands on the narrow expanse of the bench, and tried to look back at what he was doing.

The cool object was a leather restraint of some kind. Within moments he had me bound to the bench at the waist.

"I don't think I like this." My nerves sped up again, as did my breath.

"Slow, deep breaths, Devon." I wanted to curse at him. He wasn't the one being strapped to the bench. "You can do this. The whole point of being bound is to force you to give up control."

Another strap went around me, at the top of my rib cage. I balked to find myself bound, immobile from the waist up. I was strapped firmly to the heavy wooden bench, not so tightly that it was uncomfortable, but it was still strange. Unfamiliar.

The cool leather pressed into my breasts and cheek; the restraints were a heavy presence on my back. I could touch the ground on the balls of my feet with my legs spread, and flat-footed if they were together.

I jumped when I felt his warm hand close around my ankle, urging my legs to spread again.

"No!" My voice was sharp, but Zach kept on, strapping my left ankle to the leg of the bench, then moving across to do the right. "Didn't you hear me? I said no!"

I heard him stand, his steps moving to the side of the bench to which my cheek was turned. He crouched, coming down to eye level with me.

"Are you using your safe word?" His face showed no expression, as if he didn't care one way or the other.

But I knew he did.

"No." My voice was curt. I trusted him, but I wasn't comfortable, nor was I enjoying myself.

"All right, then." Encouragement flickered over his face before he stood, moving back to the end of the bench. I heard the loud smack reverberating throughout his bedroom moments before I felt the palm of his hand on my left buttock.

"Ow!" I tried to move away from the sting.

I couldn't. I was bound, and at his mercy.

"If you're staying, then no more complaints. You will give yourself to me entirely, mind, body, and soul." I swallowed hard, a delicious thrill finally beginning to work itself throughout my body.

I didn't know why, but I loved it when Zach took control.

"Do you remember this, little one?" He moved to where I

could see that he held the small leather tool that he had had me deliver to his office the day he first gave me a taste of his life-style. That day seemed like a lifetime ago—so much had happened since then.

"Yes."

Before I finished speaking, he was growling at me, and I cleared my throat and hastened to say the rest. "Yes, sir."

"Good." He returned to the end of the bench, and I knew that he was studying the bare curves of my behind. I tried to squirm, frustrated when I couldn't move.

"I am going to use this on you, Devon, as punishment for that phone call today." A noise of protest left my throat before I could stop it, and I bit my lower lip quickly, cutting off the sound as quickly as I could.

"Do you have any idea what it was like for me, sitting there in a meeting with Glen, while you said those things in my ear?" I had a quick mental flash of the expression that would have crossed the face of the man who had hired me if he had known what was going on in that phone call. "From the moment you said hello, I was harder than I've ever been in my life. I wanted to come and bend you over your desk, wanted to fuck you right then and there, no matter who watched us."

Flames begin to lick along my skin.

"I had half a mind to put you on speaker phone, just to shock that nervous expression right off of Glen's face." Zach's voice held a trace of amusement, and a giggle broke out of me, despite my nerves and arousal. I couldn't help it.

"Think that's funny, do you?" Zach's voice was a growl. The martinet brushed softly over my bottom, teasing me with the soft tendrils of leather, only a moment before those tendrils were flicked over my flesh with medium force.

I tried to move away from the sensation, though of course I couldn't. It didn't quite hurt, but it had crossed the line past a sting. When the slinky tails of the martinet whisked over my buttocks for a second time, I inhaled sharply, trying to breathe through the sensation.

"That's it. Breathe past the discomfort." Zach's voice had grown husky; I knew that he liked this, liked flicking the martinet over my exposed flesh and watching it grow red.

"I'm going to give you ten more blows, Devon, and each one will be a little bit harder than the last one. You're going to count out loud. Do you understand?"

I flinched. Ten? Surely that was excessive.

The martinet flicked over me again. "Every time I have to use this to get you to answer my question is a free turn." He chuckled when I growled.

"Yes. I understand." He didn't give me even a moment to catch my breath. The martinet came down on my bottom again almost before I had finished speaking.

"One!" The lash made my bottom burn. It wasn't as painful as being spanked, yet the sensation was more intense.

My eyes widened at the thought of another nine blows. Even through the pain, I burned with arousal.

I counted my way through, my discomfort growing with each blow. By the tenth, my voice wavered and wetness hazed my vision. I wasn't sure how much more I could take.

At the same time, my pussy grew ever wetter, and my clit burned with need. I was shaking with want. It was the strangest combination of sensations, one that Zach had sparked in me before, but never with this intensity.

"Ten!" I sobbed out the word, every nerve in my body sizzling. I was aware of my body in a way that I had never been before, and it wasn't entirely comfortable.

"Wonderful." Zach ran his hands over the heated expanse of my backside, and I shied away from the touch, not because it hurt, but because I wasn't entirely sure I could handle any further stimulation. "Look at that ass. So pretty, so pink. You did so well. You're ready for what I have planned next."

"Next?" I began to tremble. "Zach—I don't think—"

"You've had the pain portion of the evening, Devon." Breath whooshed out of my lungs, an exhalation of relief. It was short-lived, because I heard Zach opening something, followed by another noise.

"Now it's time for the pleasure." Some sort of liquid, warmed by Zach's hand, was drizzled over the expanse of my behind. I sighed with pleasure as the sultry sensation began to ease the ache of my abused bottom.

"This is going to feel intense," Zach warned me.

I felt myself frowning, not understanding what he might mean. Intense? All I felt was delicious warmth, soothing the skin that had been struck by the martinet.

Then . . .

"Aah!" The heat hazed over with a thin sheen of ice, the dual sensations overwhelming in their intensity. My body was tense as I tried to squirm, to move, to obtain just a moment's relief.

Zach sighed with pleasure from somewhere behind me.

"Japanese mint oil. This has a few purposes for us tonight." I cursed as I wiggled, and he chuckled quietly. His hands came to my bottom to massage the oil into my skin, and the added layer of heat nearly made me weep.

My hips tried to buck, to gain friction of some sort. He hadn't even touched me erotically yet, and I was ready to explode.

"The mint, of course, has a cooling effect. Very stimulating when massaged into the heat of a tender ass. And I want to show you it can be stimulating elsewhere, as well." His hands moved from where they massaged my cheeks down to my inner thighs, then to my lower lips. One finger moved to rub over my clit in a firm, insistent circle.

Even without the bite of the oil, his touch was practiced, designed to bring me quickly to the edge. A strangled cry exploded from me as I climaxed in a great shuddering wave.

Zach chuckled again when I moaned weakly, the waves loosening the tension in my muscles.

"Thank you." I wasn't trying to be funny, and couldn't understand when Zach broke into a great roar of laughter. The sound was infectious, and I found myself giggling in unison with him, though I had no idea why. It had been such a strange and intense evening so far, but Zach managed to give me pleasure in so many ways.

"Well, hopefully that took the edge off, little one." He smacked me lightly on the butt as his mirth died down. "But you needn't thank me for it."

"Took the edge off?" I heard myself echoing his words suspiciously. I had been expecting him to untie me now. I was slightly panicked to discover that there was more.

"We're not even close to being done." Zach's voice was full of sultry promise. I gasped sharply when his finger dipped into the crevice between my cheeks, spreading oil there. "You can go much deeper."

"Zach!" I tried to shy away when he slipped one oiled finger inside the tight channel of my ass. Though it was infinitely smaller than the cock that he'd had there the night before, the muscles were sore, unused to the activity.

"I'm not going to fuck you here tonight." A shudder of relief worked through me, as well as a trickle of disappointment. "Though it's very tempting, with your ass such a tantalizing red from my attentions."

"Ah . . ." If he wanted to, I would do it for him. But it would hurt. I hoped to avoid it.

"Relax, Devon. When you give up control to me, part of my job is to take care of you. I wouldn't be doing that if I tried to force myself inside of you before you've had a chance to recover." He worked his finger back and forth a few times, massaging the oil into my entrance. I moaned at the unexpected ache of pleasure, then at the loss as he removed his finger from me entirely.

Before I could even catch my breath, something hard and unyielding replaced Zach's finger. Startled, I pushed back before I could even think about what I was doing, and the small plug that Zach had also lubricated with the mint oil seated itself inside me, stretching me just enough to wake up the flesh.

"No." The sensation was uncomfortable. I was still too sore. "Zach, I can't."

"Devon." Tugging on the plug once, just enough to set off a chain reaction in my nerves, Zach moved to crouch beside the bench again. "Don't you trust by now that I'm not going to take you further than you can go?"

I didn't speak, just regarded him with wide eyes. I had too many thoughts whirling through my mind to formulate them into words. All I knew for sure was that this felt right with Zach.

Squeezing my eyes shut as tightly as I could, I heard the rustle of Zach's clothing falling to the floor. Tucking my hands beneath my hips, I waited for him to remove the plug and to enter me.

Instead, I felt the head of his erection nudge at the opening to my pussy. My eyes flew open when he pushed inside an inch, gave me a moment to adjust, then thrust the rest of the way.

"Unh." I couldn't speak. I couldn't think. Zach's cock fit tightly inside of me even without a plug, and with the additional intrusion to my body, I felt full, tight.

I sucked in air, and felt the separate points of hardness rubbing against one another, separated only by a thin membrane. It was uncomfortable, and a bit painful.

It was also one of the most erotic, arousing sensations that I had ever felt.

"Stop thinking so much." Zach's hands strayed from where they rested at my hips up to plump the mounds of my breasts. Easing his fingers between my flesh and the leather of the bench, he took each nipple between a thumb and forefinger and began to roll the tight buds.

Liquid heat shot through my center. When I moaned loudly and tried to push my breasts more fully into his hands, to show him how much I wanted this, he pulled his pelvis back, withdrawing his cock to the very tip, then pushing forward again, slow and steady.

I cried out, trying to free myself. It was too much. I couldn't enjoy any one sensation, when I was bombarded with them all.

"Ssh." Zach pushed all the way in, rotated his hips in a way that made my eyes roll back in my head. "Devon. Stop fighting it. Stop trying to control it. Empty yourself of everything, and then let sensation fill you back up."

I opened my mouth to protest that I couldn't possibly, and closed it once I'd thought for a moment. Zach was right, I knew he was right. I was uncomfortable because I was trying to control the moment.

Biting my lip, I breathed in, then out, slow and full, trying to let my mind go blank as I did. I wanted the pleasure that Zach could bring me. I wanted to share this with him, whatever this was.

Zach slid back into me, seating himself fully, then back out, until only the head of his erection remained inside. In, then out. His paced quickened. I timed my breaths to his thrusts, and finally my body relaxed into the rhythm, broken only by the occasional small tug that he gave to the plug.

My ass was still on fire, and though the tingles from the icy mint oil had faded, they were still there, humming over my skin. I was aroused to the point of pain, filled in every way imaginable, and to top it off my breasts were on the receiving end of the most delicious kind of torture.

The combination of sensual touches became too much for me. I heard the slap of Zach's flesh on my own as he began to increase his pace. I felt the bite of the leather bonds, all that was keeping me tethered to reality. My entire body hummed with the promise of a pleasure that I hadn't even known was possible.

"Come for me, Devon." Zach's words sounded like they were spoken through water. I tried to lift my cheek from the bench, but it was like moving through quicksand.

"Now!" Freeing my breasts, Zach's hands moved between my legs. One held my lower lips open, and the other pinched over my clit, in a series of short, sharp squeezes that sent all of the sensations I felt curling into a small, atomic ball low in my belly.

The ball burst, the release detonating inside of me and melting everything in its path. My mind went blank, able to comprehend only one thing.

Bliss.

I shuddered, over and over and again, and when I finally started to come down, Zach rubbed his hands through my heat again and another wave crashed over me. As I shook, having lost all conscious control, I felt him thrust inside of me, as deep as he could possibly go, and then felt the heat of his shouted release warm me from the inside out.

I lay there, unable to move for long moments before a thread of consciousness came back to me. I knew when Zach pulled out of me, and flinched a bit when he pulled the plug from my tight passage. In the intense pleasure, I had forgotten about my bondage until I felt his touch as the straps around my ankles were released, and my feet massaged to get the blood flowing again.

Then the straps over my waist and my back were removed, and I was wrapped in a thick, warm blanket, and nestled into Zach's arms, which lifted me easily and carried me to the bathroom.

I knew that he whispered endearments to me as he carried me, but I was too far gone to understand what he said. I had never experienced anything like this before. I was empty, and yet I was full; floating on something that, if I had believed in such things, I would have said felt like pure energy.

"Drink this." Zach seated me on a cushion on the heated floor tiles by his massive bathtub, the blanket still wrapped around me. He pressed an open bottle of water into my palm, staring at me until I lifted the bottle to my lips and mechanically took a sip.

Satisfied, he nodded, then moved to turn on the giant streams of water. He added a liberal splash of an oil that smelled like tangerines, and the sharp citrus scent brought me one step closer to coming back to myself.

I thought, absentmindedly, that an artist would be thrilled to see Zach as I saw him now, knee-deep in water, the shadows of the undulating ocean sky outside throwing his muscles into sharp relief. Placing one knee on the edge of the marble tub, he pulled me to him, gathering me into his arms and into the water, blanket and all. The water sucked at the dense wool, then licked at my tender flesh, and only after I hissed with contentment at the heat of the bath did Zach pull the sodden cloth away from my skin.

He tossed it to the side of the tub. I cocked my head after it curiously, wondering why he hadn't removed it before he pulled me into the bath, but not having the energy to ask.

"I didn't want you to get a chill." Wrapping an arm around my waist, Zach pulled my back to his chest, seating me in his lap as he positioned himself on the ledge inside the bath. He grabbed the water bottle that I hadn't finished and held it to my lips, ensuring that I drank the rest.

"Oh." I struggled to make myself finish the beverage, though I knew that he was right and I needed it, after the intensity of what had just happened. He hadn't wanted me to get a chill—the small detail made my heart do a shaky flip before it filled so full I felt it could burst.

I had already known that I was in love with this man, but now . . . I didn't think I could ever walk away from him again. I was head over heels, crazy in love. He brought me an intensity of pleasure that I had never dreamed of, and he was the only man who had ever cared for me so deeply.

The realization helped me to shake the lethargic bliss away, to snap back into control of myself. As soon as I did, I felt my muscles begin to tense, felt my mind begin to try to fence off my heart, warding it against certain pain.

"And she's back." Zach's hands moved from my waist to my hair, toying with the sweat-dampened strands. He ran cupped handfuls of water over it, then squirted shampoo and began to rub.

I closed my eyes, leaned back, and sighed with ecstasy as his thumbs worked at a knot at the base of my skull.

"Why are you doing this?" My voice was quiet as he again poured water over my head, rinsing away the strawberry-scented shampoo, careful that none ran down over my face. "Not the sex. I understand that, because no matter how much either of us tries to deny it, we connect there on a level that I didn't even know was possible."

Beneath me Zach stilled, his body tensing. I felt him deliberately relax as he reached for a bar of sweet-smelling soap.

I wasn't sure that he was going to answer, but as he massaged the suds into my skin, he did.

"A dominant is responsible for the care of his submissive

after . . . after." A tendril of anger took hold, even though I had thought that I had nothing left inside of me. My hands clenched into fists, and I felt frustration build.

Here we went again, the same pattern. We wanted each other. I was willing to give everything. Zach felt that he couldn't.

I decided to try a different tack.

"Since you're the king of finding out things about me that I haven't told you, I suppose you know that my parents died in a car accident?" Zach's fingers bit into my skin painfully at my surprising pronouncement, and I felt him deliberately relax them, one by one.

"I did." The barriers had slammed closed, I could hear it in his voice. Though I trembled, I pressed on.

"They were on a trip when it happened. A romantic little weekend getaway. I wasn't even there." Zach's hands had been soaping my breasts, and his fingers closed over my nipples sharply, a warning.

I ignored it.

"Even though I wasn't anywhere close, I still had night-mares, dreams that felt so real that I couldn't get into a car for months afterward. I might never have, except I knew that being able to drive, to be in a moving vehicle equaled freedom."

I clenched my teeth tightly together, partly from the memories that I had done my best to forget, and partly because I was waiting for him to yell, or to order me out.

"Drop it, Devon." His words were devoid of emotion, but that, I knew, was the way he coped.

"Make me." I knew from experience that sometimes a person needed an uncomfortable push to face facts and start to heal.

I gasped when he spun me on his lap, spreading my legs so that I straddled his lap. He shoved his cock into me without warning, and I gasped as he began to thrust up, over and over and with brutal force. I knew he was deflecting, changing the subject, but my body was so conditioned to arousal at his touch that I found myself unable to do more than hold on as he lost himself in my body.

My breasts floated on top of the water. Slipping his mouth beneath the surface as he continued to move inside of me, he sucked first one nipple, then the other between his lips, sucking hard, then laving with the rough surface of his tongue, driving me mad.

I wanted him to slow down, to let me gather my wits, to continue to push the conversation, but he drove us on, taking us both relentlessly towards climax.

Reaching between my legs, I circled his cock with my thumb and forefinger. As he continued to thrust, I added a small twist of my wrist, wanting him to remember who it was that he was inside of.

"Fuck. Devon!" His movements faltered for a moment, and I took advantage of his momentary uncertainty to pull off of him.

"Sit on the edge of the tub." My voice sounded far more firm than I felt, but if he was going to use my body as a diversionary tactic, then he was damn well going to enjoy the experience.

His eyes shadowed with something dangerous, and I gestured again.

"Now." Casting me a look that said I would hear about it later, Zach pulled himself from the warm bath, bracing his weight on the edge of the tub.

I moved in quickly. Palming the heavy weight of his testicles in one hand, I sucked his cock between my lips with the other. He groaned, his hips shoving his cock farther into my mouth, his hands fisting in my hair as I sucked, swirling my tongue over the head and continuing to twirl my free hand around the base.

The first taste of salt trickled over my tongue, and I felt satisfaction wash through me. I continued my assault on his erection, and moments later, when I felt his sac begin to tighten, I knew that he was about to explode.

"No." Pulling my head back by the hair, he slipped back into the water. I was ready for him when he turned me, my back to his front, and again seated himself inside of me.

He could control me completely from this position. All I could do was curl my legs underneath his thighs and go along for the ride.

My breasts bobbed above the water with each hard thrust. His hand moved unerringly between my legs, playing over my clit in the exact way that he had discovered I liked.

"I haven't tasted you enough." His arousing words made me shudder. "One day soon, I'm going to tie you open and drink your sweet pussy for hours." The words, combined with his fingers on my clit, sent me hurtling over the edge. Another thrust and he followed me, his heat burning low in my belly.

When he had finished, and I delighted in yet another impossible climax, we stayed in place, cocooned together until the water in the bath began to cool. As I pressed my damp cheek into his shoulder and felt the pulse of the bond between us, I wondered whether this could be enough for us.

Could I live this way, knowing he hadn't been able to break through that final barrier for me? My mind told me that the idea was an invitation to heartache and disaster.

My heart, however . . . my heart told me I just might be happier with the pieces of Zach that I could have than with no Zach at all.

CHAPTER EIGHTEEN

came out of the bath, damp and seeking the warmth of Zach's arms, only to find the bedroom empty. Cocking my head, I padded out of the room, my feet leaving damp imprints on the plush carpet.

The smell of spices tickled the insides of my nose as I followed the scent. I found Zach in the kitchen, a room I hadn't yet been in.

It was warm, and bright, the overhead lights illuminating cream walls and a charcoal slate backsplash. Bright copper pots dangled overhead, and a massive flat-screen television was mounted on the wall above the table.

I might have wondered further about the need for such a thing in a kitchen, but my attention was drawn to Zach.

His back to me, he stood at the stove, browning what appeared to be ground beef. As I watched silently from the doorway, I found that though he seemed less sure of himself here than he did in the boardroom—or the bedroom—he still commanded the space, filled it, as he added handfuls of chopped red peppers to the pan.

I tugged at the hem of his T-shirt, which I had pulled on after the bath. I didn't keep nightclothes here, and I wasn't secure enough in my body to go running around naked. I knew it was silly, since he had seen every bit of me, but I couldn't get rid of the feeling.

Standing there, wearing his shirt, watching him cook something that was obviously for me, brought all my feelings bubbling to the surface. This man, this beautiful, complex man, made me weak in the knees.

Unless he could give me everything, though, it wasn't going to work.

Enjoy it while it lasts. Squeezing my eyes shut tightly, then opening them wide, I went on instinct. Before I could over-think it, I moved behind him quietly, then wrapped my arms around his waist and squeezed.

"Hey." Leaning around his torso, I sniffed at the pan. The scent made my mouth water. I hadn't realized that I was hungry, but that was Zach. Always anticipating my needs. "Whatcha making?"

He always seemed to know what I needed before I did.

He stiffened in my embrace, then slowly relaxed. I didn't comment, instead stepping back and hitching myself up to sit on the counter.

"Taco skillet." There was something in the depths of his eyes when he turned that I couldn't quite read, but his expression was warm as he ran a hand easily up my thigh and pressed a quick kiss to my lips. "Want some wine?"

I murmured my assent as he moved to the fridge to remove a bottle of wine, then to the cupboard. The first one that he opened held plates. The second had coffee mugs. Growling with frustration, he flung open the door to the third, removing the two wineglasses that he had been searching for.

I couldn't quite stifle a giggle as he poured a glass of the straw-colored wine and handed it to me.

"Something amuse you, minx?" His smirk was self-depre-cating as he pulled a package of tortillas from the freezer and tore the bag open. I watched, mesmerized, as he cut the tortillas into strips.

He clearly didn't cook very often. That he was doing so for me made my heart beat a little too fast in my chest.

"Don't spend much time in here, huh?" The wine was both tart and sweet as it slid over my tongue. When Zach turned, insinuated himself between my legs, I wasn't prepared for the firm, playful pinch on my bottom and I squealed, only half in protest.

"I don't have much cause to." Dipping a finger into my wine, he painted it over my lips, then leaned in for a taste. He was bare chested, and his black lounge pants slung low on his hips. I expected his hands to move to the usual places, to tease the heat from me.

Instead, the kiss held warmth, and familiarity, and comfort.

When he turned back to the stove, I found my whole world had shifted off balance.

"I can make this easy enough. Ground beef, peppers and tomatoes, tortillas, cheese." Pulling a plate from the counter to the pan, he portioned out several large spoonfuls. "I can also make scrambled eggs and toast, and spaghetti. And I'm the king of anything from a box."

Setting the plate beside me on the counter, he opened one drawer, then another, until he found a fork. I could feel the heat emanating from the dish, warming my skin, and even as my stomach growled I eyed it dubiously.

"Zach, I love that you cooked for me, but I can't eat all of that." He grinned as he settled himself between my legs again, standing far enough away that he could hold the plate between us. Scooping up a forkful, he held it to my lips.

"It's not all for you. We're sharing. Less dishes that way." My mouth fell open, and he used the opportunity to place the bite in my mouth.

He had cooked for me. He was *feeding* me.

If I didn't know that something big still stood in our way, I could almost have believed that we were a couple, one like any other.

"Well?" Zach watched as I chewed and swallowed. It was

good—not fancy, but the fact that he had cooked it for me made it the best meal I had ever had.

I couldn't tell him that, not without him shutting down completely. So I made a show of shrugging nonchalantly, then picked up my wineglass for a sip.

"Well, it's not scrambled eggs and toast, but I suppose it will do." I yelped when he reached for my hair, winding the damp tail through his fingers. He tugged gently until my head fell my back, my neck exposed.

He pressed a kiss to the base of my neck, then looked down at me intently. I squirmed under the stare, but didn't wriggle out of his grip.

"I don't cook for just anyone, you know." Though his words were light, his expression was not. I felt my heart stutter in my chest as we stared into each other's eyes, the air between us thick.

"Have you ever cooked for anyone before?" I had time to stop before I spoke, but I wanted to know.

"No."

I flinched inwardly, waiting for him to shut down. Instead, after a long, long pause, he leaned forward and pressed the lightest whisper of a kiss over my lips.

I blinked as he scooped up another forkful of food and held it to my mouth.

"Now eat up. You're going to need your strength. I'm not done with you yet."

The last barriers that I had been able to keep in place, the ones protecting my heart, dissolved as the fork met my lips.

I was done for.

I was hovering on the edge of sleep when Zach's hand sought mine in the darkness. He twined his fingers around mine, and I smiled sleepily, moving closer to the warmth of his body.

When he spoke, his voice was tight. Sensing what was about to happen, I propped myself up on my elbow, suddenly alert.

"You have no idea what I've come from." In the dark, I saw that his face was turned toward the ceiling, the shadows from outside dancing over it. "My mother left my dad and me when I was just a kid. My dad never raised a hand to me, but after she left, every word that he said to me, every time he looked at me, I saw that he wished it had been me who'd gone, not her."

The self-loathing in his voice shocked me to the core. I'd known he had issues, but this, the full extent of *this* had been hidden very, very well.

"It was pretty clear that there was no love for anyone in that house. A shrink that I had . . . later . . . showed me that I made sure there was none for me anywhere else, either. I was a violent kid, angry, always starting fights at school. I smoked a lot of pot, drank whenever I felt like it, and kept to myself, to make sure that no one got close enough to hurt me again."

Apart from the drinking and the drugs, he could have been talking about himself now. I kept that thought to myself, not wanting to break the spell that had allowed him to say even this much.

"Marie . . . was someone who slipped past all of that. She was exactly the kind of girl that I resented. She was a cheerleader, an honors student, on student council. She came from a loving, unbroken family. She had everything that I didn't." He laughed, and the sound wasn't bitter as I'd expected. I tamped down hard on the surge of jealousy that I felt for this girl who had been in Zach's life long ago.

"We were partnered up in a biology class. I knew that she was flirting with me, but at first I thought she was just trying to piss off her parents, or was attracted to bad boys. Something, there had to be something, because I couldn't understand why she would be interested in me." The awe was clear in his voice. I felt myself shift uneasily, not comfortable with the story.

What did you expect, Devon? That whatever was haunting him would turn out to be made of sunshine, puppy dogs, and rainbows? Of course there was someone else before you.

"She wasn't like that, didn't have a pretentious bone in her body. She actually liked me. I liked her back. And that was it. Marie broke down my barriers with a smile and her sweet personality, and for the first time in my life, I knew what it was like to love, and even more, to be loved in return."

I hated her. I hated this long-ago girl, whom I knew almost nothing about. I hated her because once Zach had loved her, and unlike with me, he had accepted her love in return.

My fingernails bit into my palms until the sharp pain forced me to relax them.

As though attuned to my distress, Zach rolled to his side, then placed my palm flat and open before him. He traced patterns on it with his finger, staring down at it in the dark, so that he didn't have to look up.

Didn't have to look at me.

"We dated for nearly two years. She straightened me out, set me on a better path. I pulled up my grades enough to start at a community college after graduation. She went to a much bigger school, but we still saw each other whenever we could." I swallowed thickly, encouraging him with my silence to continue speaking.

His tone had darkened, and I tensed. I knew that what came next would be the crux of his issues. I just wondered if he would be able to tell me.

His breath hitched, and after a long pause he resumed his story. I exhaled in a rush that made me dizzy, relieved that he hadn't stopped.

"She was back home for a visit at Christmas, the first year we had both been away at school." Zach's voice went flat, tense.

The finger tracing designs into my palm stabbed harder, and I winced but didn't pull away.

"We went to a party. Neither of us drank. She just didn't like it, and I had drunk enough in my early teens for a lifetime." Oh, no. I saw where the story was going, and my heart started to break.

"We were on our way home from the party. My dad was away for the weekend, and we were excited to spend the night together." I knew what was coming, and yet I couldn't stop that frisson of jealousy.

I was a horrible person. Even knowing that, I couldn't help it.

"You can guess the rest, I'm sure. It's not a unique story. A drunk driver hit us head-on. I walked away with a few scratches. Marie was killed." My heart felt as though it was being squeezed in a giant fist. Any feelings of jealousy and anger I had felt disappeared in an instant.

That poor, poor boy—that boy who had grown up to be Zach. Powerful, distant, billionaire business mogul Zachariah St. Brenton.

"You were driving." It wasn't a question. So many things made sense now, including his need for control.

"Yes." His voice was terse as he bit out the word. I felt a jolt when, after avoiding my eyes for the entire conversation, he looked straight at me, his expression defiant even in the dim light.

"In Cambria, when you left. I was coming after you to tell you that I just needed some time to wrap my head around . . . around what you had said." Propping himself up on one elbow, Zach ran a hand through his hair, something that I had come to learn meant that he was agitated. "When that car almost hit you . . . that fury, that wasn't because you had said you loved me.

It was because I was so scared that it had very nearly happened again."

I held my breath. My heart began to beat triple time. He was so close, so close to saying what I so badly wanted to hear him say.

"It made me realize something."

Yes. Yes. Please. Tell me that you love me, too.

The three little words that I was waiting for didn't come. Instead Zach reached for the remote that sat on his bedside table and hit a button. The overhead lights came on, dim, but overwhelming to eyes that had adjusted to the dark.

He pulled my arm out from my side. I followed his gaze as he ran his hands over a series of small pink bruises. Made by his fingers as he had thrust inside of me, they were barely noticeable to the naked eye, and they certainly didn't hurt.

Guilt was painted over his face as he studied each and every one.

"These were completely consensual, Zach." I tried to keep the edge of panic from my voice. He had finally broken down and shared with me. I couldn't let him withdraw now.

He stared into my face, and a hint of dominant Zach peered through the dark depths of his eyes.

"I saw a shrink for years after the accident." He looked so ferocious that I was afraid to interrupt. "My need for control, the dominant side of my personality, was birthed during that car accident. The doc thought that it went a step further, though. He was certain that my . . . lifestyle . . . stemmed from guilt from Marie's death. He thought that when I indulged in BDSM practices, I was doing my best to drive away a potential partner, since deep down, I didn't feel that I deserved one."

I froze, pinned beneath his stare. Poor Zach. No wonder he ran so hot and cold. He had been put through the ringer.

"I don't agree." His expression dared me to argue with him.

"My dominance came from the accident. Yes, I think that's true. But I know that I live the lifestyle that I do because I need something that the vanilla world doesn't offer."

I had no idea what to say, though his eyes raked over my face, searching for clues to my thoughts.

"No matter where it came from, that ... need ... it's a part of me now. It's how I live my life. And while there are lots of women who like some kink while they're getting fucked, when it spills into other areas of their lives, they're gone." I knew that he used coarse language deliberately to shock me, but still, the statement hit me like a slap in the face.

I was one of those women he was referring to, at least in his eyes. I was here for a good time, for some kink in the sex we shared together.

Why couldn't he understand that I loved him, loved all of him?

Maybe I was competing with the ghost of sweet Marie, after all.

Even though he had shared his story with me, I could see clearly that he wouldn't—no, couldn't—give me that last piece of the puzzle.

"I see." I felt my inner barriers rising, walling off my heart as I shoved the covers off and slid out of bed. I fumbled with the clasp of the bracelet that he had secured around my wrist earlier. When the heavy weight fell into my hand, I clenched my palm around it, then threw it at him.

"You know what, Zach? This time I'm going to go before you throw me out. Hear this, and hear it loud and clear. I'm done."

It was getting to be a bad habit, sitting at my desk at work, trying to hold it together after an emotional showdown with Zach.

This time, there was one big difference, however. I was strong enough to know that this mess, this entire clusterfuck—this had nothing to do with me. I had tried. I had given everything, had given things that I hadn't even known were mine to give.

Though I was in a lot of pain, I found some comfort in that.

"You look great today, Devon." I looked up to find Tony giving me the once-over, stark admiration in his eyes. I raised my eyebrows at him, and he shrugged sheepishly. "We're not allowed to date, but that doesn't mean I can't look."

I rolled my eyes and laughed, though I felt somewhat buoyed by the comment, a lifesaver in a dark-water kind of day.

"I brought you a coffee. It's on your desk." Tony looked over to where the paper cup sat in front of his computer, then smiled back at me at the gesture. A tendril of pleasure wove its way through my misery.

I had deliberately done my best to look good that morning. The new Devon, the one who had stepped all the way out of her shell and would never go back in, refused to hide in black clothing and shyness anymore.

Today, I wore a turquoise blouse that actually fit, rather than hanging loosely over my frame in an attempt to hide my figure. My slacks were the color of a mocha latte, and my shoes matched, with a heel significantly higher than I was normally comfortable in.

I was dying inside, but no one needed to know that but me.

As I waited for my computer to boot up, I reached down for the purse that I had secured under my desk. My mouth was sore from Zach's assault on it the night before, and I was desperate for a good dose of medicated lip balm.

When I again straightened, he was there, his expensive black suit fitted to him in ways that made my body jealous.

"You're here." His voice was full of surprise. I narrowed my eyes, taking no little satisfaction in the fact that the normally unflappable Zachariah St. Brenton looked like a mess, apart from the suit.

His skin was pale, and dark shadows bruised the skin beneath his eyes. He didn't look as though he had slept for even a minute, and his hair stood on end.

"Of course I'm here." I fought hard to keep the waspish tone out of my voice. I had already given this man everything. I wasn't going to let him know that he had my grief, as well. "I work here. Why are *you* here? And by 'here' I mean at my desk, keeping me from doing my work."

His eyes widened, and he actually looked taken aback. I didn't care if he was about to get mad from my lack of respect, or whatever else he could come up with to get his panties in a twist about.

His emotions were no longer my problem. I had learned that much.

"I can't believe you stayed." He cocked his head, studying me intently. I stared right back. I thought I detected a hint of astonishment in his eyes, but it was gone as fast as it had appeared.

"Am I not supposed to be here?" If he was about to try to fire me because I'd been screwing the boss, then I wasn't going to go down easy. "I like it here. I'm staying. With or without you."

"No, no. Of course you're supposed to be here. I just . . . I'm surprised." In my peripheral vision I could see that we were beginning to attract nearly as much attention as we had the other day. I shifted uncomfortably at the realization.

I truly did like my job. If we weren't together, then these little visits from Zach were going to have to stop.

Otherwise, my life at work was going to become a living hell. I would forever be the woman who had had an affair with the CEO, and nothing else.

"Miss Reid. Can we talk?" I felt myself wavering at the entreaty in Zach's voice, but I steeled myself against it. "Let's go for breakfast."

"I think everything was said last night, Zach." I kept my words to a whisper, aware that the entire department was trying to eavesdrop. "Please. Leave me alone."

My words seemed to trigger something in him. Before my eyes he transformed, dominant Zach coming to the fore. Even through all of my anguish, I felt heat rush to parts that I shouldn't have been thinking of.

Cut it out! I lectured myself to no avail. I was so deeply attuned to this man that it was going to take me years to get over him.

He looked down at me intently, and I understood that in that moment I had all the power. I sputtered, unable to come up with the right words.

"Unless you use your safe word, I am going to continue." He fixed me with the look that told me if I argued, I would be punished later.

I felt my world, and my self-control, spinning out of my grasp.

"Now I must insist. Come with me." I opened my mouth to say no, and he countered. "I don't want to scoop you over my shoulder and carry you away, but I will if I have to, so you might as well come."

He turned and walked away, and I saw that his steps weren't as sure as they normally were.

The uncharacteristic uncertainty boxed me into a corner, and I had no choice but to do as he said. Fuming, I followed him into the conference room, where I grabbed the remote and began to randomly hit buttons, trying to frost over the windows.

Instead I made a projection screen drop down out of the ceiling, and turned the lights out.

Zach calmly took the remote from my hand as I exclaimed

with frustration, the sound echoing off the walls of the closed room. Pressing the correct buttons—of course—he turned on the lights, frosted over the windows, and sent the screen back into the ceiling.

"Please hold still and listen." His tone told me that he expected to be listened to, but there was a nervousness to the way he held himself before me. To put my own stamp on his instructions, I planted my feet shoulder width apart and stood with arms akimbo.

As I faced him, I realized anew just how angry I was. I loved this man—really, truly loved him, a feeling that was worlds apart from what I thought I had felt for my ex. I was so hurt, and so angered, at his treatment of it.

"I know I've handled this poorly." His voice was somber, a break from the commanding tones that usually sounded when he spoke. It had the desired effect, I thought, because he halted my inner tirade in midstride.

"Just . . . listen for a moment, all right?" Running his hand through his hair, showing me his agitation, he began to pace. It was something that I had never seen the cool, calm and in control Zach do before. Ever.

"I am sexually dominant. You know this. You are sexually submissive. You may not want to admit it, but you know that that's true, too." My heart gave a giant throb, remembering the state of nirvana that his dominant nature had brought me to the night before.

"I don't know what that has to do with anything, Zach—" I started to protest, but he held up a hand, palm out, and silenced me with one look.

"With you—God, Devon, with you I don't have to control everything. It's the first time in years that I've been able to breathe." His eyes sought for and caught my own, and I inhaled sharply when I saw the raw honesty reflected there.

"You could have fooled me." I raised my eyebrows at him. I was sure that he believed what he was saying, but part of it didn't ring true for me. "You seem to be quite in control when it comes to me."

The barest hint of a grin curled Zach's lips, and he looked so damn sexy that my stomach clenched.

"Needing control and enjoying it are two separate things." The faint smirk faded, and he moved forward, catching my stiff fingers in his own. "The second you walked out the door last night, I wanted you back. I didn't expect this to go so far, and I don't know if I'm any good for you in the long run, but I don't know if I can live without you, either."

His words took the wind right out of my sails. I stared at him, mouth agape, my brain furiously trying to comprehend what he had just said.

"I—I don't understand." My voice shook. I wasn't sure that my heart could hold to another of Zach's come here–go away changes in mood.

But . . . oh, how I wanted him. Wanted him forever.

"What's changed?" Though I was still wary, I felt my heart thaw, just a fraction, when he released my hands, then curled his fingers around to the back of my waist. The possessive gesture, his fingers at the small of my back, made need unfurl inside of me like a flower reaching up for the sun.

"Up until the moment you walked out the door last night, I was convinced that I had to be strong enough for both of us, that it wasn't right to inflict my demons on your life." I huffed in frustration—this was what I had been running from when I landed in San Francisco, a life that followed the expectations of others. "But when I told you my story . . . you didn't flinch. You didn't turn away. You weren't disgusted with me."

Irritation washed through me.

"Of course I wasn't disgusted with you. Why on earth

would I be?" Exasperated, I shoved at his chest, staring up at him like he had grown a second head when he threw his head back and started to laugh.

"Zach, are you feeling all right? I know you couldn't have gotten much sleep last night." I moved restlessly in his arms, trying to free myself, but he only drew me closer, nuzzling his face into my hair.

"You don't even see it, do you? Most people would have been turned away by my never-ending issues. But you see only the good. You're a gift." His lips grazed over the tender skin that covered the pulse in my neck, and my knees went weak.

"Zach, I can't do this again. I need all of you, or nothing at all." He let me push him away this time, and I stepped back until I was out of his aura, where I could *breathe*.

When I looked back up, he had the bracelet in one hand, and a small box in another. I felt my blood begin to fizz through my veins in decadent anticipation, even as my mind rapidly ran through a list of every bad thing that could possibly happen in the next five minutes, trying to prepare me.

"You are the first woman that I have met since losing Marie who is worth the risk."

I began to tremble when he took my hand in his and fastened the bracelet on my wrist again. The circlet of star sapphires winked up at me, warm and stunningly beautiful.

"I would rather take whatever I can have with you and risk the notion that I might lose you someday, than never have you at all." Once the bracelet had been secured on my wrist, Zach held out the other small box. I felt as though I was trying to push through a heavy fog in the air as I closed my fingers around it.

Chills shimmied up and down my spine as I opened the box and found a ring inside. A solitary star sapphire winked out of its white gold setting at me, making me promises that I couldn't quite believe.

"What—what is this, Zach?" I stared up at him, wide-eyed. This couldn't possibly be happening. I was dreaming; I had to be dreaming.

"It's whatever you want it to be, Devon." A small, choked sound escaped my throat as Zach took the ring from the box, and slipped it on my finger—my left ring finger. Feeling a little bit wild, I began to tremble.

His hand, stroking the tender skin on the inside of my wrist, brought me back down to earth.

"I mean it. I will do whatever makes you happiest. Devon, you've taught me that I can be dominant and still take risks with someone. I want to be with you, whatever that means for us. I will marry you tomorrow if you'll have me. Or we could get engaged. Or it can be a token from someone who loves you." His voice shook over the one word that I had been so longing to hear. "I'll even accept that it's a friendship ring, so long as that friendship comes with undying devotion . . . and sexual benefits."

I barked out a laugh, reaching out to bury my fingers into the fabric of his suit jacket.

"Say it again." Light began to fill me, and I still felt as though I were dreaming.

"Say what?" He shot me a sexy grin, all innocence and light now that he saw my response clearly in my eyes. "Sexual benefits?"

"Don't tease me! Say it!" Zach extinguished all traces of humor. Taking both of my hands in his own, he looked down into my eyes, and I saw what I needed to know before he said it.

"I love you." My heart stuttered in my chest. "I love you, Devon, and this ring can mean anything you want it to, anything at all, as long as it includes love."

"I love you, too." I closed my eyes for a long moment as I let the bone-deep bliss wash over me. I had no idea how we had arrived at this point—the last two months had been a wild ride.

But now my life was on track, and I had everything that I could possibly want.

"How about this? The ring means that I am yours. It means that you are mine." I found myself crushed against Zach's chest, my lips devoured the instant I was done speaking. Heat poured through me as he pinned me to the long, hard length of his body.

One hand slid up to palm my breast through my blouse. I gasped as my nipple pebbled beneath his touch.

"You look amazing today." Releasing my lips only long enough to whisper in my ear, Zach closed his teeth over my pulse, marking me, before he returned to kissing me senseless. "You need to wear color more often. I'll buy you some."

"What are you doing, Zach?" I moaned into his mouth as he released my breast, clasped me around the waist, and lifted me up. My legs twined tightly around his waist, my heated core blazing against the firmness of his erection.

"I'm going to take you on the conference room table, Devon." He placed my bottom against the edge of the table, my legs still entwined around him, and busied himself with undoing the buttons on the front of my blouse.

I blinked with surprise, even as I arched into his touch.

"Here?" Reaching for the waistband of his slacks, I slipped my hand inside and ran my thumb over the hot velvet of his erection. "Now?"

"Here," he confirmed as he groaned and thrust into my hand. Not bothering with the clasp of my bra, he simply pulled the wire and lace down beneath my breasts, pushing them up to him like an offering. "Now. And you're going to let me. You know why?"

"Why?" I arched my back, giving him better access to my erect nipples. Nerves skittered along my skin, knowing that all of my coworkers were just on the other side of the conference room door. The nerves added to the potency of my arousal, and I knew that I would have a hard time being quiet.

Zach slid his hand down the front of my pants, into my panties, and found my clit. As he began to stroke with sure movements, he slid another finger inside of my liquid heat, grinning at the way I responded, pushing myself against him, all reservation gone.

I would do anything for this man.

I would do everything for him.

He possessed me, body and soul.

"You'll let me because I love you."

Zachariah St. Brenton was rarely wrong.

Now that you've enjoyed Devon and Zach's

passionate romance, don't miss out on

Elijah and Samantha in

BREATHE

Available now from Signet Eclipse.

Keep reading for a special preview. . . .

The sculpture stood on a small marble table in the center of the spacious resort lobby. A perfect, slender column of emerald green glass rose in a straight line nearly three feet high before overflowing into streams of glass that sparkled like crystals. Some were as thin as a pinkie finger, looking delicate enough to snap off at the slightest breath, and some of the tendrils were as thick as a pillar candle. All varied in tones from the merest whisper of mint to the green of a dense forest.

This piece had been the manifestation of a desire that had been haunting Samantha Collins's dreams lately. Dreams that she wasn't entirely sure what to do with.

It had been a long time since she'd had sex, true enough, and her stress levels had been through the roof lately. But these needs that had been tugging at her had been growing stronger . . .

She'd half hoped that putting these urges into her sculpture would exorcise them.

It hadn't.

"Wine, señorita?" An impeccably dressed waiter in a black suit made an appearance at Samantha's elbow. On his hand he balanced a tray of crimson wine in sparkling glasses.

"Thanks." Gratefully she accepted a glass. The flavors hit her tongue as she sipped eagerly, and she recognized it was much finer than any of the wines she was accustomed to drinking.

"Quilceda Creek Cabernet, 2005." The waiter beamed as if he had produced the wine himself.

Samantha pasted a smile onto her face and nodded enthusiastically. "Yes. Very nice."

Samantha liked wine, but the ones she tended to purchase came in a box or, if she was feeling fancy, in a bottle with a screw cap. She'd never heard of Quilceda Creek, though it tasted nice enough.

"Ten-dollar bottle, hundred-dollar bottle, the end result's the same," she spoke quietly to herself before lifting her glass in a silent toast. As she sipped, she looked down at her sculpture, still hit by a sense of disbelief that it had been chosen for exhibition.

Indulgencia was a luxurious resort located in the tourist-saturated town of Cabo San Lucas. It was infamous both for its wealthy patrons and for Devorar, the small BDSM club that catered to the varied sexual predilections of its clientele.

Once a year Indulgencia held an art exhibit with an erotic theme. The owner of the resort, some wealthy tycoon from the States, flew in artwork from around the world to showcase for the event, and when Samantha had submitted her piece, she hadn't been hopeful about her chances.

Though the twists of glass had been created with one of her most erotic dreams in mind, the result was a million miles away from the human-sized copper penis, which was the next sculpture over in the exhibit.

Samantha hadn't been sure that the wealthy mogul, who'd organized the show and selected all of the pieces himself, would see what she did, even though it was the most erotic sculpture she'd ever produced. She had put all the sexual frustration she had been feeling in the last few months into the work.

Being at this show wasn't helping that frustration. Not at all.

"Lovely piece, isn't it?" The voice came from just behind her shoulder, startling her. Samantha whirled around to face the speaker, her wine sloshing in her glass.

When she saw him, she nearly swallowed her tongue.

The man was tall, at least six feet, and though he wore expensive-looking black slacks and a dress shirt, she could see enough of his physique to appreciate the muscular body beneath the clothing. Combined with his dark blue eyes, flaxen hair, and sexy-as-hell smile, his sudden appearance made it seem as if all of Samantha's heated dreams had just come to life.

That sexy dream man cocked an eyebrow at her, and she belatedly realized that he'd asked her a question.

"Do you like this particular sculpture?" he repeated helpfully.

"It's . . . oh, yes, it's very nice." She wasn't about to tell anyone here that she was the artist. She wasn't ready for anyone to ask what had inspired it, especially this man, who discomforted her with his focused attention.

Deliberately she shrugged, and tried to catch one thin strap of her sundress as it slid down her shoulder. She tugged it back up and caught the man's eyes following the movement. "It's such a pretty, saturated color."

She almost bit her tongue as she said it. She knew, of course, the painstaking effort that had gone into creating the gradation of color in the sculpture, the hours she had spent gathering the molten material on her blowpipe, rolling it into finely ground glass of different shades, then setting the colors in by sweating over the smaller of her two glass furnaces—but she wanted to take care not to tip her hand that she was more than a casual admirer of the artwork.

She assumed the man would simply nod in agreement. Instead, he reached out and ran one slender finger over a curling tendril of glass, much as she had done. The care and attention of his touch over the smooth surface made Samantha think of those dreams she'd been having lately, the ones that had produced a constant ache.

In fact, last night's had featured a man running his hands over her body exactly the same way this man was doing to the sculpture. The memory made her shiver.

"Would you like to know what I see?" His blue eyes pinned her with their intensity, and Samantha lifted her glass to her lips to give herself something to do with her hands.

"Yes, I'm curious." She nodded, her breath catching in her throat as his fingers closed around hers where they rested on the stem of her wineglass.

The man captured the glass from her fingers and handed it off to a passing waiter. He secured a fresh one and had it in her hand without ever once taking his eyes from her.

"I see a meeting of male and female." She felt herself getting lost in the deep, husky tones of his voice as he continued. "But more than that, I see a balance of two opposites, each feeding a need in the other."

Samantha's lips parted in surprise, and her heart began to pound.

That was exactly what she'd intended. How on earth had he known? No one else ever saw what she'd intended in her art.

"That's what I— I mean, yes. Yes, I see that as well." She worried her lower lip with her teeth as she spoke, afraid he would ask her about what she had started to say.

With her heart still beating double time against her rib cage, she turned from the sculpture to look up into the man's face. He looked vaguely familiar, as if she'd met him once a long time ago.

More than the familiarity, though, there was a sense of connection. He'd understood the meaning behind her art, and with that came a tug on an invisible rope that seemed to stretch between them, pulling them ever closer.

And God, he was sexy. There was something in his demeanor that attracted her, made her want something she couldn't quite articulate.

Liquid heat pooled between her legs and she held herself back from reaching out to touch him.

"What are you thinking?" The man's voice was low, but Samantha could hear him as if he were the only other person in the crowded room. His sharp gaze made her feel like the only woman in the world, and she had the insane urge to spill all her secrets to him.

If she did, would he understand that—more than anything—she yearned for a man who would be strong enough to take control for her?

Samantha started to speak, then shut her mouth tight as the rational part of her brain took over. She couldn't even admit these desires out loud to herself . . . she certainly wasn't about to tell them to a stranger.

No matter that the stranger was the most gorgeous man she'd ever seen.

"I'm Samantha." Swallowing back everything she wanted to say, she gave him the big smile that she used on the rare occasions when she poked her head outside her studio. Her name seemed to break the heavy tension between them, but the slight cock of his eyebrow hinted that he knew there was something else she wanted to say.

Then he took her hand in his, encasing her fingers in the heat of his palm, and she forgot all about trying to keep her thoughts to herself. The simple touch, the way he rubbed his thumb over the curves of her own palm, sent sizzles shooting through her arm.

If he wanted her, he could have her. It wouldn't even occur to her to say no. *Wait—where did that come from?*

"Elijah Masterson," he said, continuing to stroke his fingers over her hand, his eyes telling her that he wanted exactly the same thing she did. Overwhelmed by his sensual touch, she didn't register the name right away. After a beat, the light went on in her mind.

Elijah Masterson. His gorgeous face, with that devil-may-care grin, had been on the front page of the local paper several weeks earlier, for an interview about the erotic art show he'd been putting together for his resort.

His resort. Indulgencia.

Good Lord, this man owned the entire place.

"Oh, ah, I mean . . ." Samantha tried to tug her hand free. She should escape this encounter while she could. But she felt she should thank Elijah for accepting her piece into his show, although that would mean admitting it was hers.

"What brought you here tonight, Samantha?" Elijah gave her fingers a firm squeeze that spread through her body before he let her tug her hand away. Those bright blue eyes stayed focused on her as if she were the most interesting woman he'd ever come across.

"I . . . I don't know." The lie left her feeling uneasy. The sculpture had just been the first piece to the puzzle. Once her piece had been accepted into the resort's exhibit, she'd longed to know more about the erotic art scene. From there she had made some subtle inquiries, asking around to see if anyone knew what exactly went on at Devorar, the club inside the upscale hotel. She'd looked online to educate herself, entering every search term imaginable, since she wasn't entirely certain what it was she was looking for.

Yes, she'd been curious to see what her sculpture looked like on display, wanted to see if its sensuality still shone when surrounded by the more overtly sexual pieces that made up this showing. But more than that, she'd thought she might get a glimpse into the lifestyle that had started to fascinate her so much.

Apart from the wildly suggestive art, however, there was nothing there that suggested anything other than opulence and luxury. She wasn't sure what she'd been hoping for—waiters in leather chaps? some whips and chains?—but none of Devorar's secrets were revealed in the posh lobby of Indulgencia.

"Don't lie." Elijah's tone was stern. Startled, Samantha looked up into his eyes. He didn't appear angry, but the look on his face made her feel guiltier than if he had been. "Tell me why you're here."

Samantha couldn't quite work up the courage to speak. She began to tremble with nerves, thinking about what to say, and was exasperated with herself for the anxiety.

With it came an unbidden memory, a face from her past. The man in her mind's eye was old enough to be her grandfather, with salt-and-pepper hair and cold, dark eyes. But he too had been rich, and commanding.

She was her own woman, and wanted to think she was strong enough to live her life the way she wanted, without painful memories overshadowing things. But the truth was, she just didn't know if she'd wind up hating herself for what she wanted.

"You won't find any judgment from me, kitten."

Samantha gaped for a moment. *Kitten*? He'd called her *kitten*?

She'd just been insulted. She should have felt insulted.

She didn't.

"I . . . I'm curious," she finally admitted, feeling her cheeks flush the same color as the wine she was drinking. "I've heard about Devorar and I . . . I thought someone here might have some answers for me."

"Answers to what questions, Samantha?" As he'd promised, there was no censure in Elijah's tone. Instead there was heat—enough that Samantha felt herself start to burn as the flush spread from her cheeks through the rest of her body.

But she froze as thoughts of her mother came wending their way into her mind. Another reason she had held herself back from going after what she wanted.

Her mother's . . . vices . . . had nearly ruined her daughters' lives. If Samantha weakened, gave up control, was she any better?

"I . . . I think I'd better go." Closing her eyes against Elijah's penetrating stare, Samantha pressed her hands to her temples and turned away. It was tempting, so tempting, to give in to what she was quite certain she wanted.

But the memory of her mother's mistakes was a reminder that giving in to temptation could lead to disastrous results. No matter how much she felt this need, deep in her very core, she shouldn't have come here.

"Samantha." Elijah's voice was firm as Samantha began to walk away. She turned back halfway, not enough to see the gorgeous man again, but enough that she was confronted with her own work of art.

The sensual visual overwhelmed her senses and made her ache.

"Come back anytime." There was a note of concern in Elijah's voice that made Samantha hesitate. Not all men were like the ones who'd flitted in and out of her mother's life. Rationally she knew that.

But this man was gorgeous, wealthy as sin, and likely into some very kinky things, given that he had opened a BDSM club in his resort. That was enough danger to send Samantha running, even as she nodded, acknowledging his offer.

Even though, rather than walk away, she found herself

wanting to tangle her fingers in that messy golden hair. Wanting to tilt her head up to receive his kiss.

She said nothing, though she felt his penetrating stare on her back as he watched her. It caused heat to simmer low in her belly, a sensation she'd never felt before.

The sensation didn't abate, not even as she exited the resort and walked to her car, a ramshackle bucket of bolts she'd purchased two years earlier, when she'd first moved to Mexico. She sighed as she slid into the driver's seat, the image of Elijah's sexy-as-sin face and his interest in her warring in her mind with the memories of that other man.

Samantha twisted her lips together as she put the key into the ignition and turned.

It was going to be a long night.

Elijah was puzzled and horny as hell.

He had been part of the BDSM lifestyle for a long time, and over the years had become incredibly adept at reading people, especially women. The slender goddess of a redhead walking away from him had looked him directly in the eyes, then had steeled herself and walked away.

Elijah wasn't overly caught up in himself, but he had never lacked for a woman when he wanted one. That woman, Samantha, had clearly come here looking for something. Yet the fact that she had walked away from him was not suggestive of someone with a naturally submissive personality.

And yet something about her pulled at him, made him yearn. He'd learned the hard way that he needed someone who was truly submissive to make him happy, and in the years since his divorce he had trained himself not to even look twice at a woman who didn't meet that one particular criterion.

But the combination of sass and fragility in this particular woman—Samantha—very nearly had him running after her.

When the application for the stunning green sculpture currently showcased in his exhibit had come in, he'd been immediately entranced. It was innately sexual, the artistic expression colored with a dark need. When he'd seen it in person he'd become nearly obsessed. It painted a perfect portrait, to his eye at least, of dominance and submission, and he'd known at once that the artist behind it must have had a perfect understanding of the lifestyle.

Now, after meeting Samantha Jane Collins—he'd done some research, for the biography that had accompanied the application had been woefully incomplete—he wasn't so sure. She'd been interested, had responded to his dominance, he was sure of it.

But though she had come to the exhibit, though she'd admitted that she had questions, he'd bet one of his properties that she was a neophyte.

It had been on the tip of his tongue to offer to teach her—he knew he hadn't imagined the heat that had sparked between them. But then she'd reached within herself for something, what he had no idea, and had walked away.

"Damn it." Bad marriage or not, Elijah was a man accustomed to getting what he wanted—in the bedroom, at least.

Suddenly he wanted Samantha.

In his younger years he would have been arrogant enough to be certain that she would submit to him regardless of her sexual preferences. He'd since learned that it took a very strong woman to fully submit care of herself to another.

He'd yet to find that woman, and so he remained alone, limiting himself to sexual encounters here and at a few other clubs that he had part ownership in, particularly In Vino Veritas, the combined wine bar and club that he owned with two friends back home in Vegas.

He'd been with enough women that he'd learned a hard truth. Unless he could find a woman who would submit herself to him entirely, he would be miserable. But that didn't necessarily mean that he couldn't enjoy a diversion with the woman whose skin flushed so deliciously when he looked at her.

Elijah slid his hands into the pockets of his suit pants as he watched Samantha hurry through one of the open stucco archways in the lobby. The hem of her little sundress slid up her thigh as she got into the ugliest car he'd ever seen.

It was an affront to his senses—a woman that beautiful belonged behind the wheel of something sleek and sexy. Yet his eyes moved past the hideous vehicle and greedily took in the lithe curve of her leg, which ended in a strappy, high-heeled red sandal that made his mouth water.

Need pooled low in his belly. He was a sucker for sexy shoes on a gorgeous woman.

Hell. He wanted her, whether she was submissive or not. Maybe he was playing with fire—he had no desire to be proven wrong again, and something about their instant connection told him that Samantha had the potential to be more than a quick fuck. But the more he thought about further exploring his interest in her, the more he decided he had to have her.

Snagging a glass of wine from a passing waiter, he sipped as he contemplated. Mouton Rothschild. His friend Alex had introduced him to this one, and it was now one of his favorites. It added to the heat in his gut.

Damn it. He was going to pursue Samantha Collins. He knew it.

He just hoped he wouldn't be consumed in the fire that was sure to come with it.

Lauren Jameson is a writer, yoga newbie, knitting aficionado, and animal lover who lives in the shadows of the great Rocky Mountains of Alberta, Canada. She's older than she looks—really—and younger than she feels—most of the time. She has published with Avon and Harlequin as Lauren Hawkeye and writes contemporary erotic romance for New American Library.

CONNECT ONLINE

www.laurenjameson.com
www.laurenhawkeye.com
www.twitter.com/LaurenHJameson